I0700896

ON WINGS OF STONE AND LIGHT

Copyright ©2025 by Jill K. Sayre
All rights reserved

This is a work of fiction. Names, characters, businesses, places, events, locales, and incidents are either the products of the author's imagination or used in a fictitious manner. Any resemblance to actual persons, living or dead, or actual events is purely coincidental.

Library of Congress Control Number: 2025941028

Cover Design by: Alexios Saskalidis
www.facebook.com/187designz

No part of this book may be reproduced or transmitted in any form or by any means without written permission from the publisher.

For information please contact:
Brother Mockingbird, LLC
www.brothermockingbird.net
ISBN: 978-1-960226-29-7 Paperback
ISBN: 978-1-960226-30-3 EBook

This book is dedicated to my father, Yaya, whose love of monster stories ignited my own fascination; to my husband, John, whose unwavering love and support allows me to do what I love: write; and to my son, Alden, who inspires me to embrace creativity as a vital source of life's fulfillment.

The Moon

The Moon orbits the Earth, and the Earth orbits the Sun, causing the Moon to change how we see it in the night sky. The Moon takes about 27 days to orbit the Earth.

The Moon has eight phases: Full, Waning Gibbous, Third Quarter, Waning Crescent, New, Waxing Crescent, First Quarter, and Waxing Gibbous.

During the Waxing phase, the Moon becomes increasingly illuminated by the Sun and moves toward becoming Full. Once it reaches Full Moon, it begins its Waning phase, gradually progressing to the New Moon, which appears completely dark.

The Moon is described as "Crescent" when less than half its surface is lit by the Sun, and "Gibbous" when more than half is lit.

Every phase reminds us that nature and life are constantly changing, but it's never too late to start over again—and no matter the phase we are in, we are always whole.

PART ONE
This is where it all began.

CHAPTER ONE

May 29th, Memorial Day, 2023

Madeleine

Our perception of life is based on personal experiences, what our parents teach us, and the influence of society. So, it's not surprising most outgrow their ability to see angels. Yes, what I'm saying is true. All humans are born seeing their celestial guardians, but the propensity gets stripped away once babies learn that only solid objects are real. Well before a person reaches their first birthday, those glowing spirits that hover and protect become invisible, even though they remain nearby for the rest of their human lives.

But I'm an anomaly. I never stopped seeing my archangels, "The Arcs," as I call them, and that has made me a bit of an outcast.

I remember being four years old, sitting on a cold metal examination table in a white-walled room.

The pediatrician's brows met in the middle of his forehead as he asked, "Did she have a normal birth?"

"Yes, everything was fine," my mother answered, frowning from a nearby chair.

"Did she have a bad fall or experience any seizures?"

"Not that I'm aware of."

"Her eyes don't track as they should, and she keeps staring into space." He took a penlight from the chest pocket of his lab coat, shined it in each of my eyes, then clicked it off as a hum came from his lips.

"I know some adults who are preoccupied…" Mom cleared her throat. "But that doesn't mean…" She shook her head.

"I'm sorry, but I believe your child is autistic or has a sensory processing disorder. I'll refer you," the doctor said, leaving the room brusquely.

As a toddler, I was content to lie in bed for hours, watching the colorful people-shaped lights with diaphanous wings float around me. They were beautiful and comforting, and they soothed me in the exam room that day.

As a child, I thought *everyone* saw angels, and I wondered why adults ignored me when I talked about them. But, at age five, it clicked that only I could see them. That's when The Arcs asked me to keep them a secret, so I never mentioned them to anyone again. Once I started school, I watched my classmates' guardian angels linger near them, either in human form or as stunning swirls of light. I learned the lessons taught by my classroom teacher, but I was also tutored by my celestial team, who whispered the ways of the angelic realm to me.

My angels also escorted me home each day. We'd talk and play hide-n-seek, and they'd point out nature's miracles along the way: the intricate weave of a robin's nest, clumps of white wild violets poking through dead leaves after the last snow, diminutive heads of ground squirrels popping out of earthen holes… Anyone who saw me thought I was crazy, speaking to no one, laughing with and chasing what they perceived as nothing.

"Why won't the kids in my class play with me?" I asked The Arcs.

"They don't understand your gift," the angels replied. "And remember, you can never tell them about us. They will not understand."

"I always follow your advice, Arcs."

"You do, except for calling us "Arcs." Not all of us are archangels," they'd say. "Archangels are messengers of higher status than some."

"I don't care," I'd reply sternly. "You're all of the grandest rank to me."

But people can be cruel to those deemed "different," especially in a tiny, remote town. Born in Hartstown, Pennsylvania, 100 miles north of Pittsburgh, with a population barely over 200, adults and children whispered their theories about me— "odd" was their favorite word. My teachers labeled me as slow, and the specialists added "extreme ADHD" to my diagnosis. It hurt at first, but I found self-acceptance and joked to myself that my actual affliction was an excess of celestial whimsey, which I called "angel-itis."

At the end of eighth grade, my father announced we were moving east to Gascony, Pennsylvania, 70 miles from everything I knew. I had meticulously crafted a life of staying under the radar, along with Sierra, my sole companion in invisibility. Her Tourette's makes her blink her eyes a lot, so kids call her "Morse Code." However, her tic went away when we were together. I never told her about me seeing angels, but we held each other up in times of tribulation.

However, a new school did mean a fresh start in a larger community. With a population of over 1,700, there were higher odds of more open-minded people. I'd have a clean slate to earn the teachers' respect. And I secretly hoped maybe I'd even find a boyfriend.

So, our belongings were packed into large cardboard boxes and loaded on a truck. My teary goodbye to Sierra left me feeling as empty as the acres of open fields we passed driving to Gascony. I dressed in a musty hotel along Route 80 in my usual t-shirt and shorts that Monday morning, eating a small box of Frosted Flakes with a plastic spoon after pouring milk from the mini fridge directly into the lining. Outside, the asphalt parking lot smelled like rubber tires, and my stomach was in a knot. I was surrounded by farmland—perhaps my new town was as provincial as Hartstown.

"Let's check out Main Street while your father runs errands," my mother declared, appearing with keys jingling in her hand. "I hear Gascony is quite quaint—it was founded in 1796."

"Quaint? I was hoping for metropolitan." I sighed.

Mom smiled assuringly as we got into the car. "Everything will be fine. Don't worry."

I clicked my seatbelt into the buckle, then rested my head on the passenger window, trying not to cry.

After driving a few minutes on 80, we turned into a treed neighborhood with deteriorating wooden houses barely held together by rusted nails.

"It looks like it hasn't changed much from 1796," I groaned.

The crossroad ahead, Main Street, flanked by old brick

buildings, was blocked by police cars and barricades for the parade.

"So far, I think the town is charming," my mother said cheerily as she parked the car in front of a pale blue house with a yard full of knee-high weeds. "It's way bigger than Hartstown."

I got out and closed the door. We walked past an orange and white-striped barrier and joined the crowd, which consisted of a dozen soldiers and around two hundred people gathered on a green iron bridge with large rivets that stretched across the Dunburgy River. It was Memorial Day.

I looked left and then right. "I wouldn't say Gascony is *way* bigger. It only has two stoplights."

"That doubles the number in Hartstown." Mom winked.

I rolled my eyes as she pulled me into her side with a quick "it's-gonna-be-alright" squeeze.

The air smelled of gunpowder and popcorn. Up close, the buildings were a bit nicer than the ones in Hartstown, and there was something "Mayberry" about how everyone said hello with a kind smile as they moved to make room for us to watch the ceremony. A sliver of hope rose in me like a crescent moon.

We stood by a brick building with ornate trim and unmistakable mystique. Above the marquee was its name in gold: The Gascony Theater. Dozens of glowing angels hovered around it, mesmerizing me. They usually hung around churches, not movie theaters, looking for people to help. Seven carved beasts with reptilian, human, and animal parts were high on the pediment. They watched over us like vigilant, sinister soldiers. They were awesome!

I was especially taken by one gargoyle on the right near the top with a man's muscular chest and arms, a bird head, and dragon legs. His stone eyes enthralled me—they were full of anguish. And a spectacular pink light rippled around him, making my heart beat quickly.

CHAPTER TWO

Ryon

Military veterans in crisp white shirts and wedge-shaped caps stood on the iron bridge. These men fought for what humans cherished, and I envied them. For nearly a century, I witnessed their salutes before they sent honorary wreaths down the fast-moving creek; shiny red, white, and blue ribbons bobbed in the water as they floated away, vanishing from sight. People gathered solemnly on the bridge, men clutching hats over hearts as a bugler played "Taps," the saddest music ever created. The first twenty-three notes were eloquent and haunting, but the final one lingered in the silence that followed, with only the American flags on the light posts snapping proudly in the breeze.

Why can't I be one of them? I moaned. The world was a living movie for me, and I was destined to be in the audience forever. *I want to walk, talk, go to school with a backpack slung over my shoulder, sip Mountain Dew out of a bright green bottle, go to the movies with a pretty girl…*

Your 16-year-old humanness is flaring up again, said Anee, my gargoyle friend mounted below me for 138 years. She knew how I dreamed and prayed—all my stone companions did since we communicated through a thought flow called "threading" using words, colors, and images. Anee cared about my feelings, but most of the others reacted to my outbursts with a red-tinged mental light of annoyance.

It's cruel to be able to think and feel while being frozen in granite! I ranted. *I want freedom! Grrowr!*

Do we have to listen to this AGAIN? grumbled Geidhuce, a grotesque directly to my right. *You're pining over lowly humans who would be better off in our stomachs. They do smell so delicious, don't they? And need I remind you, they put us here. You should hate them as I do.*

Geidhuce's reprimands were chiseling blows that made my stone body feel insufferably heavy. I swore if my granite eyes could cry, frequent rainstorms would have puddled on the sidewalk below. But no one, stoney or otherwise, felt a drop of my pain. I was stuck in eternal paralysis.

Geidhuce continued, threading in scarlet, *Ever since the church changed to a movie theater decades ago, you've become highly dramatic, and we're stuck listening to your over-the-top soliloquies. Knock it off!*

I tried to stop my emotions, but they spilled out. *Listening to the movies about how humans live, love, travel, laugh, cry, fight wars, and celebrate victories makes me hate my life in stone.*

You'd be doomed either way. Geidhuce laughed. *I can see your profile from here, and it's nothing but beak. You'd terrify those delicious snacks if you walked among them.*

I was seething. *Humans aren't snacks…*

Enough, you two! roared our commander, Cletas, from the top of the pediment above us.

I immediately turned my threading black, so no one knew I was boiling over. I tried to calm myself by watching the wind carry a single leaf high into the air. It danced and bobbed, circled my face, and then plummeted down until it landed on the shoulder of a girl below.

That girl stood on the curb, looking up. Her long auburn hair flowed in soft waves around an angelic face, and the morning light caressed her cheek, making me envious of the sun. She studied us, the rigid beasts looming above, her eyes falling upon me last. A smile bloomed upon her rosy lips, and Cupid's arrow struck me through the rough cement of my body, piercing my concrete heart.

"Madeleine, let's go," called a woman who was older but the girl's mirror image. She paused to dab patriotic tears from her eyes with a crumpled white tissue. "Dad just texted. The moving truck comes tomorrow at 9 a.m. sharp, and we need to finish cleaning the new house."

Madeleine, I repeated.

"Coming, Mom." The girl's voice was soft, but my condor ears easily heard. She walked slowly down the sidewalk, her eyes still affixed on me.

See that? I asked, switching from black to a pink thread of adoration.

She's staring at you because she finds you hideous, threaded Geidhuce. He laughed, and others joined in, but I was too enamored to care.

The girl wore ripped jean shorts and a white t-shirt while taking graceful steps, her upturned face radiating a mesmerizing golden light. I surmised she must have been about 15 years old, a year younger than my human parts. She moved like I'd imagined a princess would… but then stumbled on the uneven pavement, scuffing the toes of her black Converse high-tops. Her cheeks blushed as she broke eye contact with me and looked around, whispering something over her right shoulder that even my sensitive condor ears couldn't hear.

She's quirky, I thought. I'd heard that word several times before and never understood it until that moment. *Quirky is captivating.*

Then, she rounded the corner, out of view, but the imprint of her enchanting face was seared into my memory, and her name played like a song in my head: *Madeleine!*

After that day, I constantly watched for her. Sometimes, she visited the shops on Main Street and always passed by on Sundays just before the church bells clanged a few blocks away. Madeleine nodded to townspeople as she strolled down the street, her smile reverberating through me like thunder. I grew fonder of her every time she appeared.

For over a year, I anxiously waited to see Madeleine, my shining human star, dreaming of her when she was not in front of me. I tried suppressing the crushing truth that I was a mere granite slab.

The building we gargoyles and grotesques ("gars and gros" for short) were mounted to began as The Church of Gascony, and sermons were preached about "God is love" and "Love one another without judgment." Then, 59 years later, when converted to the Gascony Theater, love echoed again through the mortar walls in movies like *Romeo and Juliet, The Way We Were, The Notebook,* and my favorite of all time, *Casablanca.* We could hear every word as the dialogue, music, and sound effects vibrated into our granite bodies. Those stories and sermons taught me about human autonomy and how it led them to their heart's desires.

Is Madeleine searching for love? Will it happen in front of my eyes? A sharp twisting ache bolted through my chest. *Grrowr!* Heartache was so great that whenever a storm blew through, I prayed lightning would strike me into a million pieces and put me out of my misery…

But then, one day, everything changed.

THE COUNTDOWN FROM ONE FULL MOON TO THE NEXT BEGINS...

FULL MOON

"Your life has reached a turning point, but emotions run high,
so keep your cool as you honor what has already come to fruition."

CHAPTER THREE

April 23rd, 2024 (Nearly One Year Later)

Ryon - Day 30

100% Full

I woke to the earthy smell of paper and could hear the familiar town clock striking several times in the distance. Fraying shreds surrounded me and tickled my body, a sickeningly weird sensation I'd never felt before. Last I remembered, it was an ordinary day perched in stone atop the theater, watching the world. Then, I heard men's voices on the roof above me, and in what felt like seconds later, I awoke in a dark abyss of irritating fibrous strips.

Even stranger…my chest was moving! I felt air pass into my throat through my nose and mouth.

Am I BREATHING?

And something was thumping inside my chest! A dizzying energy flowed through me—I could hardly believe it… *I'm ALIVE!*

The beating in my chest became quicker. *I HAVE to get out!*

Without much thought, I moved my arms and dug a channel through the shreds with my hands until I hit what I guessed was wood. My legs moved, too, so I kicked and punched the planks repeatedly. The walls were strong, but I was stronger, and eventually, they cracked from my blows. Amber ribbons of light appeared.

An explosion of energy spread through my limbs, and invigorated by my strength, I banged harder and harder, smashing the planks, the streams of light opening into large beams. The more I thrashed, the more power I felt until, finally, the box fell away. Bits of paper floated on the air like confetti in the parades I'd watched from above.

I'm FREE!

I immediately thought about Madeleine, and that tickling feeling from the shreds went straight to my belly.

Should I go to her now? Or is this just a dream?

Pain in my extremities proved it was real. Small trickles of red liquid oozed from cuts, and wood splinters were embedded in what I realized was human skin upon my hands.

Blood!

I froze, attempting to control my heaving breath while a new reality sank in.

How did this happen? Did I pray hard enough to make it come true, and heaven listened?

As the pulsating sensation in my body slowed, I took a joyous deep breath, marveling at the miracle of life I'd been given. As my surroundings came into focus, I was overcome by a strange mixture of newness and familiarity. I stood upright, alone in a large interior space with cement block walls, dimly lit by orangish bulbs dangling from the ceiling. Several huge pine crates were near me, each marked: "GARGOYLE."

Through some kind of alchemy, I had been chiseled into a stone beast with the ability to think and read, which came from the boy who modeled for my human parts. I innately knew that, somehow, I'd retained his knowledge, building off it by listening and observing the world all those years on high. Of course, I also had traits of a condor and dragon, my other carved parts. My keen condor ears listened to what people said on the street, the sermons during church services, and later, the plays and movies inside the theater. My sharp, condor eyes watched everything and everyone on the sidewalk below. Due to my dragon senses, I also took in smells, from the flowers blooming and food cooking to stinking garbage. But I had no sense of touch, even when the pesky pigeons landed on me or when icicles formed off my nose.

But now, I'm REAL!

And, I hadn't been able to utter a word from my stiff, mortar lips during the century on that building. So, I took in a bunch of air through my mouth and then pushed it out hard while clenching my throat. A startling sound came out of me, deep and squawky, like those annoying birds that like to sit on my head.

I tried again, this time controlling the airflow, reading the crate I faced: "*Gar-goy-le.*"

The word, written boldly in red, triggered a prickly sensation on my neck. Technically, I was a 'grotesque' and not a gargoyle since I had no drainage pipes running through me for spouting water on rainy days. Yet, I came to resent the name 'grotesque' once I realized it meant 'vulgar' or 'offensive' to humans, although my enormous bird beak and serpentine scales left much to be desired. I always knew I was no Humphrey Bogart, whom I'd seen on the movie posters reflected in the storefronts I faced.

But what do I look like now?

My new heart pounded with worry as I stretched out my arms, forcing myself to take a good look at them. Human skin covered my hands, elbows, and shoulders. *Phew!* I flashed back to when that 16-year-old farm boy sat on a stool, posing for the sculptor. The sun had beamed on him from an upper window like a spotlight, emphasizing the toned muscles of his body. I looked down at my new fleshy chest—it looked just like his. My heart fluttered with happiness. Perhaps I was "hot" now, a term I'd heard girls use.

However, my enormous feet caught my eye. They were covered with overlapping green scales. My midsection flip-flop as the word 'vulgar' returned to mind. The dragon part of me had also become real. Twisting at the waist, I looked behind me, and sure enough, a monstrous scaly tail whipped from side to side. And there was something else… brown, feathered wings. I willed the huge things to unfurl, and they did so easily, reaching far beyond my body. Then, I flapped them vigorously, creating gusts that carried those paper snippets back into the air as if I were inside a snow globe.

I took a deep breath, then gently touched my forehead and eyes. They felt human, and hope bubbled inside me. But when I got to my neck, I felt thick rolls of bumpy, hanging skin. Fluffy down lined my collarbone, and although I had soft human lips, my nose was a large, hard, pointy beak. I'd dreamed about having voluminous hair like Clark Gable on the *Gone with the Wind* poster but found more bumpy skin on my head.

With trepidation, I searched that dingy room for something

reflective amongst the cinderblock walls and crates. But then I looked up. High above was a transom window, slightly open and angled downward. I took my first steps, legs twitching like a newborn calf, reaching the space below a muted light shining downward directly across from the window. I stared at the floor, my heart a wild drum.

You must look to know.

I closed my eyes, tilted my head upward, and forced myself to open them. Looking back was a giant, hideous man-monster.

The room started to spin, and I sensed the shrinking of my heart…

…then, loud sounds erupted around me.

Several crates were rocking and rumbling. *The others!*

I grabbed the closest gyrating box, prying a loose board off it with all my strength. My hand slipped, and a terrible, sharp sensation shot through one finger.

Grrowr!

A large splinter of wood lodged into my new skin, so I quickly plucked it out with my needle-sharp beak, and a drop of red blood domed in its place.

Pain is a horrid sensation!

Anger flared and rattled through my body, reaching my feet where spiky claws extended involuntarily. An even greater power overtook me, and I lashed out, kicking the box, muscles flexing in my now sturdy legs. Armored with scales, they had no sensitivity to splinters and cracked the crate open like an egg.

I bounded to each agitating box, breaking open those timber prisons. Adrenaline pulsed through me as my breath filled and emptied my chest, and it felt good. Soon, the crates were shattered planks on the floor.

Blurs of creatures with colorful feathers, scales, and manes emitted squawks, growls, and roars as they paced, the mayhem settling while another snowstorm of confetti fell. Their eyes were filled with fear, and they threaded in an anxious blue, accented by a strange array of animal sounds vocalized like a nightmarish zoo.

I threaded as forcefully as I could, *Everyone, STOP! It's me, Ryon!*

They paused briefly but returned to their chaos, adding my name to the clamor.

Please, everyone! I smacked my tail on the cement floor with a loud *thud!* startling them. They quieted once more. *This is all strange and scary, and I'm not sure what's happening either, but please calm down.*

They stopped and stared. Through the hazy darkness, I saw that they were no longer stone. All human-sized like me, each was an amalgamation of real animal, dragon, and human parts.

Vervalt, I threaded, pointing first at the silver, scaled fish-man. *There's Isel, that's Telber, who is next to Anee.*

Where are we? threaded Anee in cobalt. Her new gold lioness fur matched her eyes.

I don't know, I replied.

H-h-how are we alive? threaded Telber, now with a brown donkey head accented with a bristly mane.

I shrugged.

Bloop, bloop. Let's get out of here! Vervalt announced, causing an azure barrage of threads:

Yes, yes, let's go!

Maybe this way!

I need to get out!

What are we going to do?

Pandemonium again.

"Everyone, calm down!" I yelled in my new voice, surprising myself as much as the others who stopped in their tracks, mouths open. I lowered my voice. "We need to find the other two."

Copying me, they tried to speak too, all at the same time. I had lost control again, and the tumult grew louder, but then a bone-chilling sound came from above: "Hoooos!"

Everyone became still and silent, gaping at a massive object on the ceiling above us. We shared an emotional cerulean thread of terror.

"Hoooos!" it hissed again, the giant mass swaying.

Then, it plummeted to the floor!

Simultaneously, we all lurched backward, teeth-gnashing and claws extracted, ready to fight.

A grand, hideous creature crouched before us, poised on reptilian dragon legs with an incredible wingspan of brown leather wings. He had black furry forearms with giant canine paws, a human chest, and a snarling wolf's head.

Geidhuce!

He began to laugh as if mock-pitying his prey. "You're acting like fools." His voice boomed. "And it's no wonder since Ryonac is trying to be in charge." He looked at me and smirked. "I've been observing from above, and it's pathetic, like human toddlers who can't find their mommies. Wah, wah!" He began to pace. *I'll switch to threading since we don't know who could hear us but look at us. We're strong, powerful, and awesome! So, stop your sniveling. Our general will take command and tell us what to do. Where's Cletas?*

Isel ran to Geidhuce's side and tilted her dappled grey horsey head to the side, batting her dark lashes. *We haven't seen him.*

Isel, your new look excites and intrigues me, Geidhuce crooned, threading in pink. He placed his dark, furry paw beneath her chin. *As second in command— and for you, my pretty pony— I'll take over for now.*

Isel whinnied approvingly as she stepped backward, her smile revealing large, buck teeth. She turned and winked at me. I grimaced.

Geidhuce tucked his wings along his back. *We'll split up, leaving one here to keep watch. Isel and Vervalt, go left. Aneeguaru and Telber, go right. And remember to keep those animal screeches in control. Now, all of you, go!*

Everyone scattered.

Wishing I were following the others, I asked, *So, I guess I'm the one keeping watch?*

I want to talk with you, Ryonac. Geidhuce began to circle me, his eyes studying my new body slowly. *Now that you are alive, I know who you want to see...*

I blocked my threading of her name.

...but your transformation wasn't quite...to your advantage now, was it? he continued, still walking, shaking his head.

The feathers on my neck stood on end.

He stopped when we were face-to-face. *Horses, lions, large prehistoric fish, and wolves are powerful, but you're merely a bird.* He flapped his large wolf arms in the air as he added, *Tweet, tweet.*

Fury simmered in my gut.

The other gars and gros are made up of formidable creatures with a touch of humanness, Geidhuce continued. *You may be dragon from the waist down, with silly feathered things instead of hefty dragon wings like the rest of us, but you're more than half human! That makes you half nothing. That makes you weak.* He grinned wickedly. *And you truly are grotesque, with beady bird eyes and a lumpy head, not to mention that gigantic beak…your Madeleine will see nothing but a monster.*

Grrowr! I threaded in bright red, flicking my dragon tail and spreading my wings.

But I was speechless. He was right.

Look, Geidhuce! Isel interjected in sorrowful purple, visibly shaken. She held a large piece of cement in her horse-hoofed arms. *We found pieces of what we think is…* She gulped. *What was…*

Set it down and gather the others! Geidhuce commanded, kneeling beside the chunk of stone placed at his feet. His threading was black, and I swore I saw him leer.

A somber mood washed over everyone as the others returned with more pieces. Shattered mortar antlers, hooves, and scaly dragon parts were what remained of our leader, Cletas Luxajo, who had been at the very top of the theater's pediment. We encircled the shards of his fractured body, and a brief ceremony was held for our great general—buck, dragon, and human—who had been tough but fair. He'd been our "man on high" for 138 years. I had to blacken my mental thread to hide how worried I was about navigating the future without Cletas.

Anee threaded a doleful lavender prayer, and then we bowed our heads in silence, which was quickly interrupted by Geidhuce.

As next in line, I humbly accept the position of your new leader, he announced with a disparaging grin.

I continued to block my mental thread, concealing my true feelings. The others praised him for being so valiant.

Come, let's leave this place, Geidhuce threaded, standing akimbo. *We must find somewhere to roost.* He looked directly at me, his yellow wolf eyes flashing fire, adding, *And I'm starving.* Then, he shoved me aside with one of his paws as he passed.

The others raucously agreed as they followed—they needed food. But I struggled to decipher what I felt. Did hunger or anger roil in my belly?

We could escape through the large windows up high, said Isel, pointing with her front horsey hoof. *Someone could climb up and shatter them.*

Good idea, dearest Isel. Geidhuce bowed his head to her. *Ryonac, since you have those fabulous human arms, take care of it, will you?*

I swallowed my vexation once more, sliding an unbroken crate below the window, and after picking up a long piece of broken wood, I climbed onto the box. The ugly monster I'd become stared back at me from the glass. Exasperation flaring, I smashed my horrific image into a thousand shards, exposing a dark sky dotted with twinkling stars.

I scaled the wall and exited through the opening, and the fresh air sobered me. The others came behind me, and we arrived on a large, thick lawn, keeping to the shadows and ensuring no humans were around. It was the first time cool grass was between my toes, and it felt wonderful. I wanted to roll around on that herbaceous carpet, reminding me of children's laughter and revving lawnmowers, then run across it and far away to find

Madeleine. But I knew I couldn't. Not yet.

Instead, I huddled with the others where a bank of trees ended at the edge of Main Street. The chaotic threads of fear and confusion returned, sizzling in my head. Geidhuce's thread remained black. I knew he could still hear everyone, but he gave no direction, probably busy plotting evil things in his head.

That old bank building has a flat roof with a tall ledge around it, I said, trying to quell the mental mayhem.

I pointed to the abandoned structure with the year "1886" carved in stone, top and center, the same year our building first opened as a church. Our old place was directly across the street and surrounded by scaffolding. It looked plain and desolate without gargoyles and grotesques affixed to its façade. The marquee still said *The Wizard of Oz* in black letters, and the movie poster beside the box office, which I remembered seeing reflected in the bank building's front window before coming to life. Revival movie theaters like ours only showed something for four days, so our removal and enlivening was recent.

It'll be a good place to hide when the sun comes up, Anee seconded.

The others looked at Geidhuce for approval, their waiting eyes mirroring the moon's light.

Familiar surroundings and sounds will give us comfort, Geidhuce replied, attempting compassion. *The bank rooftop is our new hideout.* He stepped forward to lead the way. *Avoid the streetlights as much as possible as we quickly cross the road.*

We followed him single file, our freakish shapes casting bizarre shadows on the ground in the moonlight. The street was empty, and we quickly reached the other side, assembling behind the decrepit building.

And that was when dinner appeared—poor man, innocently walking the alley, probably heading home after working late or drinking with friends. The second I saw him, my fingers went cold. I knew what was about to happen, and I couldn't stop it.

The conglomeration of beasts outweighed the humanness. Driven by a blind, ravenous frenzy, those creatures made of scales, skin, fins, and fur encircled and devoured that man with grisly clamor. He only yelled out once. I'd heard similar unearthly sounds in movies like Stephen King's *Cujo* or Hitchcock's *The Birds*—but this bird could not participate. A lump formed in my throat, and what I figured were tears burned my eyes as I stood, immobilized by the gruesome mania.

Before I knew it, metallic-smelling blood pooled around my dragon feet. Splatters of red sparkled like stolen rubies on my scaly legs. Human juice.

I admit I wanted to eat him, too. My mouth drooled from the warm, salty scent of his body, and my stomach beckoned with a potent hunger. But willpower prevailed—this innocent man didn't deserve to be ambushed and eaten alive, poor thing! But I couldn't help but watch, his innards vibrant red, skin and bones pale white, jeans in shreds—the colors of American freedom: crimson, ivory, and blue. What a hideous way to exercise our liberty.

As a grotesque on a building, I wanted to be alive so badly that my stone chest ached. I imagined I'd be overjoyed if it ever happened, dancing upon the solid earth and running to meet the girl I admired. But reality had many unexpected twists, like my hideous posse's uncontrollable force of hunger for human flesh.

The smell of death mingled with rotting garbage in the

nearby cans, and rough gravel poked the bottom of my scaly feet as the sanguine puddle grew. I realized that the same fluid probably ran through me, and I stared into that dark liquid like quicksand, pulling me downward to hell. The moon reflected upon the surface like a bright staring eye. Watching me. Seeing the ugly truth. Regret jabbed my innards, even though I was the only one who didn't partake.

The insanity subsided, and dark silhouettes of monsters loomed over the remains of their kill. The town clock struck one just as sirens screamed in the distance.

A fearful blue thread pierced my conscience. It was Geidhuce. *We must hide!*

He pointed toward the top of the crumbling brick building beside us.

But first, Ryonac, turn on that hose over there, Geidhuce commanded, nodding to his right.

But…the sirens! I pleaded.

Rinse the ground, he commanded, his wolf tail wagging wildly. *No drop of blood can be left behind.* Then he thrust his fiendish face inches from mine. *And don't you dare disobey me!*

I slouched and gritted my teeth, feeling their sharpness press against the inside of my mouth. *Why does it matter if there's blood…?*

Do it! he threaded in vibrant red.

I leaped to the spigot on the building, swiftly turned the handle, and grasped the end of the gushing hose. Warm, algae-smelling water spewed forth, rattling the gravel on the ground. I quickly rinsed the blood as each beast flew to the roof with their leather dragon wings, disappearing into the dark sky.

The sirens were louder; red and blue lights flashed within sight.

Dash away, dash away, dash away all! Geidhuce threaded in bright blue as he flew past the others. *I feel like Santa with only five little reindeer.*

Every muscle in my body tensed as I finally finished, dropped the hose, and shut off the water. I stretched my new feathery condor wings and caught the wind easily, my feet leaving the ground just as the emergency vehicle's lights bounced in the alley. I prayed they didn't see me. I flew up over the building's edge and landed on the rough rooftop.

All six of us lay flat.

Turn off your threading so we can listen to the police officers, Geidhuce commanded.

I heard the car pull up across the gravel, the engine turn off, and two car doors open and slam shut.

"Someone reported loud animal noises and a human scream…" said one officer.

"Holy crap!" said another. "Those look like human-sized bones."

"Here's a wallet," the first officer announced. "It still has money, credit cards, a license…it's Nate Green!"

The men gasped in unison.

"What kind of deranged being could do this?"

"Looks like the work of animals to me, torn up like he is."

"Must've been a pack of 'em."

The investigation continued with firefighters, paramedics, the town coroner, and radio calls adding to the ruckus. We had to keep still for quite a while, which was so much more difficult as living beasts.

Tears rushed to my eyes when Mrs. Green entered the scene. "My baby! My boy! Oh, Lord, You have taken his soul!" Anguish rattled her voice and my insides. I saw Geidhuce grin, and heat flushed through my body.

Her speaking to God took me back to when our old building was a church. Preachers had spoken about humans being made of flesh and soul. Now that I was of flesh, did that mean I had a soul?

Anee rolled over on her side, her lioness eyes dark and regretful. Then she curled into a furry ball.

Several hours passed, announced by the town clock, and the humans wouldn't leave. The sensation of being tired was new and strange, so some dozed off, abstractly threading in their sleep.

When the officials finally left, the sun was rising. Anyone asleep woke up, and everyone turned on their threading again. Telber and Anee were genuinely remorseful for eating that man, but the other three demonstrated horrific green threads of pride.

Bloop! Can we stretch our new dragon legs now? threaded Vervalt, who had started to smell like a Friday fish fry.

No, Geidhuce directed. *Humans might see us when the sun shines on reality. We must wait until midnight when dark figments are more accepted.*

We all shared blue threads of fear-laced confusion as we waited even longer on that rooftop, wondering why we were alive and what that meant for our future—except Geidhuce, who proudly threaded only emerald green contentment.

WANING GIBBOUS

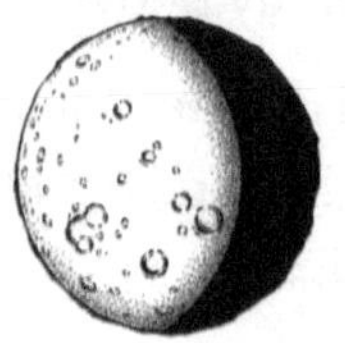

"Reflect on what you have learned so that you can release what no longer serves you and move ahead with wisdom."

CHAPTER FOUR

Ryon - Day 29

99% Waning Gibbous

When I was a stone grotesque, I used the chiming of the town clock as a marker of human activities below me. I lay there anxiously listening to it count to midnight that night, dying to stretch my crumpled new muscles.

The second the first chime of twelve clanked, my best friends Anee and Telber joined me at the rooftop's edge. I marveled at their new appearance, both with greenish dragon scales on their legs and human torsos. Telber's human skin was pale like mine, and Anee's was a rich chocolate brown. The rest of their bodies were furry, and Telber had a donkey head and arms, whereas Anee's were those of a lioness.

Look at us, Anee threaded. *We're new and improved-ish.* She spun herself around.

Telber grinned, showing gums above his long, yellowy teeth. Then, we peered out over the town we knew so well, the moon lighting up the scene.

Ta-da! threaded Anee. *I see Dunburgy Pharmacy, and it looks bigger-ish from here.*

Y-y-you and your "ish" words, said Telber, shaking his black donkey mane.

Well, it does look bigger-ish, she retorted. *And I love the red check-ered tablecloths in the ice cream shop.* Her golden eyes got large and round. *I can't wait to taste…*

Ice cream, ice cream, the tastiest treat!

Domes of deliciousness we love to eat,

And when the bright sun gives off some heat

Ice cream drip-drips on your feet!

Telber and I laughed. Anee and I loved writing silly poems to pass the time, and that was one of our favorites.

Th-th-there's Hal's Bar. I didn't know they had a deck over the creek, announced Telber. *I-I-I just want to lie on it in the sun all day.*

I strained to look far down the street along the theatre's side, the direction Madeleine always walked to and from on Sundays.

You have your threading off, Ryon, Anee said, twitching her lioness whiskers. *What are you surprised about?*

I flipped my threading back on. *The green metal bridge extends farther than I thought, and its rivets are massive. It's incredible humans can build such a thing.*

Then, we all stared directly across the street at our old roost, The Gascony Theater. The new vantage point made my heart swell with joy. *The theater looks way better without us,* I added smugly.

B-b-but it's covered with boards, and the stone is crumbling… and there's so much dust, Telber remarked, his thread purple-tinged with sadness.

Anee smiled at me with her feline face, white canines showing. *He's kidding, sweet Telber. Ryon's just happy to be alive and no longer a stone grotesque.*

I-I-I wonder if we'll ever be statues again, Telber replied, his thread white with hope.

The three of you need to stop your nonsense! Geidhuce reprimanded. *I need quiet to figure out our next steps.*

The three of us blackened our threading, and he walked away with a snort.

"Let's whisper our real voices so the others can't hear our threads," I whispered. "We must be conscious about sharing our thoughts."

"Look," Anee said while rolling her almond-shaped eyes toward Isel and Vervalt, who hovered close to us. "We have spies."

"Split up," Isel demanded as she ran her horse hooves across my back.

"Who are you to…" Anee began, looking Isel up and down.

I put my hand on Anee's furry shoulder. "Let's spread out on the roof." The last thing we needed was conflict in such an uncertain time.

Isel and Vervalt scowled, telling their own secrets to each other as I moved to the side facing the alley, and Anee and Telber took two of the other corners. The rough shingles were abrasive on the skin of my hands, making me aware of my new self, and with my threading still blocked, I racked my brain to explain our transformation. What had happened between the time we were perched on the side of that old building and becoming alive inside a crate? And now that we were living, could we get sick? Grow old? What would a human do if they saw us? Capture us? Kill us?

Then, my stomach made a monstrous grumbling sound— I was starving. I hadn't eaten anything, unlike the others. I instinctively listened for a rustle or a chirp, finally hearing a squeak a few feet away. Crawling slowly toward the sound, I discovered a crevice in the roof where I spotted a tail. I grabbed it with my hands and pulled out a fat rat. It squirmed as I opened my mouth and dropped the animal in. I swallowed it with one gulp.

Then, I lay down on my back, tucking my wings and closing my eyes, gazing at the twinkling stars. The odor of musty rat fur remained on my hands, and a satisfying aftertaste lingered in my mouth. I was hungry for more, but all I had to nourish my living body was fresh air. I took a deep breath and expanded my chest, concentrating on the rhythm of my breathing. I could do it fast or slow, but it also happened independently. But I had no control over the beating of my heart…or did I? I thought about Madeleine, and my heartbeat raced.

Being nearly half human made me sad, but not because of weakness, as Geidhuce had often rudely said. The problem was I wasn't human enough. If I were, I'd be free to explore the world, ride a bike, eat a hamburger, or go to the movies. How wonderful to see the picture shows I'd listened to for decades.

Hours passed with me wide awake and wondering about so many things. By the time the town clock struck 5:00 a.m., all five of my comrades had fallen asleep, threading wildly in their sleep. My hunger was replaced with an ache, and I had to do something besides wait for Geidhuce to decide our fate.

I crept over to Telber. "Wake up," I whispered.

He jolted awake, fearful at first, but then his lips curled backward into a grin.

I tiptoed over and gently yanked on one of Anee's fuzzy ears. "Let's go explore before the sun rises." She chuffed a bit before rolling over and opening her golden eyes.

Telber stretched his scaly hind legs. *Hee-…*

"Shhh!" I put a finger across my mouth as I'd seen humans do before. "We've got a little over an hour before the sun rises," I whispered. "And I'm starving."

"I'm game!" Anee quietly replied, bounding to her fuzzy lioness feet and mouthing her catchphrase, *Ta-da!*

I walked toward the back of the building and hung my dragon legs over the side, the patina of the scales on them shimmering in the nearby streetlight. I scaled down the ruddy bricks, and my friends followed. A giddiness filled me—I really felt free. We gently flapped our wings, lowering ourselves to the ground in the alley where it was quieter than the monsters we had left threading noisily in their sleep. The air smelled like stagnant water and bleach, no longer of flesh and bone. We tucked our wings, and Telber and Anee bowed their heads.

"I don't know what came over me, Ryon," Anee said, casting an orange glow of regret, her pupils large. "I know how disappointed you must be in me, eating a human."

"I-I-I couldn't stop either. I-I-I was so hungry. . ." Telber added with the same sunset color.

I set a hand on each of their furry shoulders. "Just promise it won't happen again. We can't give in to our beastly sides because, well, it's murder to kill a person. But also, a string of deaths will send humans looking for us, and no telling what they would do if they found. . ."

"D-D-Doesn't that make them our enemy in a way then?" Telber asked, lifting his head.

"We look like monsters to humans, and they may react in fear, especially if we kill some of them."

"We didn't think," Anee said.

I removed my hands from them and nodded. "Anyway… it's a beautiful morning, and we are alive, so let's go!" I started walking toward the street, and Anee followed, but Telber didn't move.

"What's wrong?" Anee turned and asked.

"I-I-If Geidhuce catches us…" Telber said softly.

"He's asleep. You heard them all dreaming," I assured. "Besides, they can't even hear our threading once we're out of range."

"W-w-we only think that's true. We've never tried it," Telber replied, giving off a bluish, fearful glow, referring to our innate knowledge that threading could only be heard within a half mile.

"There's only one way to find out…" Anee said, grinning and flicking her gold tail. "Come on, Telber."

He reluctantly followed us across the asphalt road and down the narrow street alongside our old theater. It was strange to be the ones moving while everything else stood still—it felt like the world had flipped on us.

We came to a line of trees behind the theater. I flew up into the thick leaves, and the others followed, each landing on a sturdy branch.

"Let's thread now so we can hear each other better, and so humans can't hear us," I suggested.

Hee-haw! Telber threaded, nearly slipping off. *C-C-Climbing isn't so easy when you have hooves!*

You'll get the hang of it, Anee retorted. *Don't donkeys climb steep hills?*

Y-y-yes, but not trees. How far are we going, anyway? Telber asked, straddling a branch.

I think her house is pretty close… I stopped myself.

Anee sighed loudly. I turned and saw her whole body droop.

Don't worry, Anee. I'll make sure we won't be seen, I threaded, knowing full well that's not what bothered her. *I just want to see her house. I think we'll be there if we follow that tree line for about two blocks.*

I'd once heard Madeleine tell a shopkeeper she lived near the grocery store. People with grocery bags had come from the direction we were going. Sure enough, I spied Quality Market through the branches on our left. Madeleine, or Maddy as her friends called her, had also described her home as "a simple yellow house with white shutters" where she "planted flowers in a front yard wheelbarrow."

We continued along the tops of the maples, picking our way through woven branches, staying hidden by clusters of bright green leaves. The sky was black, and the moon was a glowing orb lighting our way. And then, there was the quaint little house just as she'd described. Like a busted fire hydrant, I gushed with excitement. I stopped and parted the foliage blocking my view of the small, lemon-colored house with white shutters and a charming wooden bench swing on the porch.

There's the wheelbarrow, I said, admiring the bright pink and purple petunias that trailed out of it. *Her flowers are pretty, but not as lovely as she.* I sighed.

Telber and Anee shook their large heads. Then, Anee ad-libbed a rhyme:

Dramatic and lovesick,

My friend does not see

That falling so quick

Is only in mov-ieeees!

Very funny, I threaded, and the other two chuckled.

You know where she lives now, Anee grunted, her thread un-abashedly jealous-yellow. *Don't be a creeper, Ryon. Let's go back to the others.* Then, she turned around and disappeared into the boughs.

Telber looked at me sternly, then threaded in purple sad-ness, *Y-y-you're not coming back with us, are you?*

I took a deep breath before answering, *No. My dream of living has come true. I need to be free.*

Wh-wh-what are we supposed to tell him when he realizes you're gone?

You and Anee should stay with me. Geidhuce is evil! You owe him noth-ing. Knowing she could still hear me, I pleaded, *Anee, please don't go. Stay. Together, we'll be stronger.*

Telber wrinkled his mule brow. *Y-y-you risk all our safety…you were just saying what humans would do if they caught us.*

I could hear Anee continuing into the depths of foliage, get-ting farther away. My stomach twisted, the knot growing tighter until I lost my appetite.

Well, how about you? We've been together for 138 years, I threaded as pink as possible to show how much I cared.

He paused, but only blue, fearful threads came. *I-I-I can't.* He shook his head rapidly. *Th-th-the roof is much safer, and there's safety in numbers. I-I-I think you should come back with me.*

I can't do that. My heart won't let me. I pressed my lips tightly together. *We'll find someplace even more sheltered than the roof.*

Telber's large black eyes turned glassy.

Don't worry, dear friend, I continued. *I'll make sure we're not seen.*

Please stay.

Telber just shook his head.

Water unwillingly flourished in my eyes. One drop fell, trickled down my large beak nose, and lingered on the tip. I swiped it away.

Telber's long donkey ears lay flat against his head. *J-J-Just be careful.* Then he gave me a half-smile and headed back into the trees.

Emotion clogged my throat. I was all alone for the first time, in stone or flesh. I couldn't move as a suffocating fog settled over me. I considered following my friends back, but then a grassy area with an arched sign over the opening that said "Dunburgy Park" caught my eye. Madeleine's house was on one side, and the wide, rapid creek was on the other. Its banks were lined with trees, making it perfect for finding critters to eat.

That's when I smelled something delicious that made hunger pangs churn my belly again.

I climbed through the treetops to near the creek and spied a young deer that had succumbed to death. I used my wings to glide down beside it. Flies buzzed like crazy as I took in the decaying food's aroma—a gourmet feast. I picked chunks of raw flesh with my beak and ate as much as possible. The texture and taste were exactly what my new body needed, and I was euphoric when my hunger was satiated.

But then the town clock struck six, and I needed a place to hide before the sun fully rose. I flew back into the trees, scanning the area and seeing a shed next to the park entrance, across the street from Madeleine's house.

I climbed back through the branches until I was above the

rickety wooden structure, then soared down to land beside it. The early morning light cast a shadow that exaggerated my beak, wings, and bumpy skin on the wooden siding painted white, a reminder to be careful as I circled the shack.

The main door faced the park with a padlock looping through a latch. I could have easily smashed it, but someone walking by might have noticed it was broken. A dirty window faced Madeleine's house and the road, but I could be easily seen entering and exiting from there. The third side was all wood, so I crept to the back and found another filthy window facing the creek. *Perfect!* However, it was stuck shut. I firmly pounded the white, flaking outer edges to loosen the old paint. I hoped the sound of the rushing creek behind me drowned out the thumps. I tried to lift the sash, but it still wouldn't open. A couple of cars passed, and I ducked, making sure my wings were tucked in close, then worked again, panic growing. Finally, I yanked on the window sash, and it slid up and down easily.

A lightness came over my body. It was a blessing to have human hands instead of paws, fins, or hooves like the other gars and gros. *See, Geidhuce, human parts rock!* I thought as I climbed inside and slid the window shut.

Inside, it was dark, cobwebbed, and about twenty degrees cooler. The heady smell of mold and damp earth filled the air. An old gas lawnmower and an assortment of dirt-encrusted gardening tools leaned against the walls. My condor hearing discerned grocery clerks unpacking boxes, someone snoring, an alarm clock dinging, and a rooster crowing in the distance. I listened to the world wake up as the sun rose and brightened the dirty windows.

I'm really here, out in the world, away from the theater. I could hardly believe it.

Shortly after the town clock chimed 7 a.m., the auricular feathers around my ears tensed. A familiar voice made my soul dance. I leaped to the window facing the street, and through the dirt-encrusted glass was a hazy, moving figure. Quickly, I spat on my palm and wiped away the grime, clearing a three-inch circle like a captain's spyglass.

There, just across the road, was Madeleine.

I froze, mesmerized by her every move. She smiled radiantly from her porch like a queen. Brilliant sunlight glistened on her hair as she hoisted a bulging backpack onto one shoulder. I knew she was sixteen—she'd been driving her red Toyota past my old building for a few months. She gracefully held up keys adorned with a black remote. *Click!* went the locks in her car as she descended the front steps of her house. She stopped at the bottom when her mother came out of the door.

"Bye, Mom," she said, turning to face her, her voice like a flute in a symphony. "See you tomorrow. Sleepover at Julie's, remember?"

"I'm only allowing it on a school night because you'll be working on your science project," her mother said, hand on hip. "Don't stay up late."

"It's the last project of my sophomore year." Madeleine let out a big sigh. "Summer feels like it'll never get here."

"You only have, what, less than three weeks left? I think you'll make it."

Madeleine posed with both hands over her heart as she recited, "Don't abide in borrowed certainty. There is no real certainty until you burn; if you wish for this, sit down in the fire."

She's a poet! The corners of my human mouth involuntarily turned upward.

"Rumi?" her mother asked.

"How did you guess?" Madeleine put her arms down.

"Honestly, you quote Rumi so much, I swear he IS your *roomie*." Her mother chuckled softly. "And what does it mean?"

"Simply put, ideas are just ideas until they're experienced. So, summer break doesn't exist until it actually begins."

"How on earth did I end up raising a guru?" Her mother shook her head.

"I can't help if I'm enlightened," Madeleine remarked with an exaggerated hair flip. "But Rumi wasn't a guru. He practiced Sufism, not Buddhism or Hinduism."

"Seriously, the things you know…"

Madeleine turned back toward me and glided to her car in the driveway, opening the door. "Love ya, Mom!" Then, she slammed it shut, and my object of admiration was gone in a puff of dust.

The moment passed too quickly—I wished I were one of her classmates.

But I knew monsters couldn't be any part of Madeleine's world, and a cauldron of angst bubbled inside me, giving rise to a spontaneous growl that made Madeleine's mother stop and look around before heading back inside the house.

I pounded the dirt of the shed floor with my fists, dust billowing into the air. The animal in me had taken over. My wings involuntarily unfurled, scraping against the walls and knocking down rakes and shovels.

Damn these infernal things! I yanked on my feathery wings until shocks of pain made me stop. Anger blanketed my body, so heavy and potent that I had no choice but to lie down on the earthen floor and wait for calm. My heartbeat competed against my breath in a race, but after a while, both slowed down.

I needed a plan. Living in a shed, forever watching and listening, wouldn't work for long. Besides, as Anee had remarked earlier, it was already creepy that I was camped outside her house. So, I stayed on the grungy floor and thought of options while watching a fly frantically bang against the hole of light I had created on the window, trying to emancipate itself beyond the shack's walls. I related. I was freed from being solid stone, but I still wasn't liberated. My heart sped up again, mimicking the frantic zigzagging of the fly, so I took several deep breaths and closed my eyes.

CHAPTER FIVE

Ryon - Day 28

97% Waning Gibbous

Bam! I jumped awake. The day had turned to night, so I scampered in the dark to my spy hole but saw nothing. Then, *Bam!* I heard it again, clearly from above. I dashed to the back window and quietly slid it open. I climbed through the opening and spotted a dark, sinister shape on the shed roof, and I instantly knew it was Geidhuce. He radiated a red light of displeasure.

Hoooos! I found you, fool! He loomed over me, his wolf arms crossed as he snarled and whisked his furry tail. The moonlight illuminated the edges of his giant body.

I left the pack, I threaded, trying to sound firm, pushing myself to confront him even though I wanted to run and hide.

We're a brigade of gars and gros! You can't defect! Geidhuce put his paws on his dragon hips.

After over a hundred years, I'm finally free, I recounted. *You know this is what I've always wanted, to be living.* My hands tightened into fists. I couldn't believe I was standing up to Geidhuce in this way.

"Impossible!" he growled out loud, leaning over the roof's edge. The anger in Geidhuce's yellow eyes glowed in the dark.

Shhh! I nodded toward Madeleine's house. *Our transformation proves that nothing's impossible.*

Geidhuce exhaled irately, his breath spiked with fire. Surprised, I jumped backward to escape the heat.

I'm in charge and command you to return at once! he threaded.

My body was shaking, so I took air into my lungs and put my shoulders back, channeling Wallace from the movie *Braveheart.* I spread my wings and flew up to the roof, landing near him. *I heard your threading for decades, and all you want is power. You'd pray that our honorable leader, Cletas, would somehow come loose and shatter on the sidewalk below so you could step into his role.* Then it hit me. *Did you smash him to pieces before he came to life?* I'd argued with Geidhuce hundreds of times, but his live form was even more intimidating.

What are you accusing me of, ingrate? The hair on his neck stood up in spikes.

My mouth was bone dry, but I continued. *You want power and to murder humans!*

Do you think living here and watching this girl makes you free? Geidhuce growled. *She's a human, and you're a beast.*

I can do what I choose. Then, borrowing Wallace's words, I added, *You'll never take my freedom!*

So, you'll stay here, watch her fall for some man, and bear offspring while you die alone. Your new gift of life would be wasted! His eyes grew wide, showing the whites. *We won't have to hide in the shadows if you follow my plan. Humans will respect us. And if we must eat a few to gain reverence, well, you'll see how delicious their flesh tastes…*

Plan? I asked, but then, a group of male teenagers was coming down the road on skateboards. I quickly jumped off the roof, landing behind the shack. *Come down here! Quickly!* I threaded.

Not unless you agree to come back with me, he replied, stepping more into the moonlight.

They'll see you! You're putting all of us in danger! I hissed.

I stayed in the dark shadow of Geidhuce's large body cast by the moonlight, and the boarders whooshed past without noticing him.

I let out a sigh of relief. *This is precisely why I don't trust you.*

His glare still burned through the dark. *You'd better watch your back, and so should she!* He sent a visionary thread of Madeleine, weary, battered, and bruised. Then, he disappeared into the canopy of shadowy green just as the town clock struck two.

It took all my strength to stop my inner beast from chasing and fighting him, but I needed to stay to ensure her safety. So, I dragged a green garden hose rolled up in one corner to the middle of the dusty cement floor and sat in it like a nesting bird, watchful and listening. A rhyme formed on my tongue:

"Not my old roost—

More like a nest—

But being near Madeleine

Makes it the best!

Now, all I can do

Is wait and rest."

CHAPTER SIX

Madeleine - Day 27

94% Waning Gibbous

The best birthday present I could have ever imagined was my Toyota, which I named Clio after one of The Nine Muses, the Goddess of History. I peek out the window at her all the time. Sure, she's used and has some miles on her, but she's my pride and joy. Four-doored and fire engine red, I love how the outer corners of her headlights point upward like cat eyes.

I'd just come home from school the day after I'd slept over at Julie's, and spring teased with summer-like weather. I was happy it was nearly the end of my sophomore year. I was admiring how the afternoon sunlight made Clio's chrome sparkle when I noticed something.

A magenta light was coming from the old gardener's shack across the street. My intuitive messages were always accurate, but I never knew how they'd show up—seeing angels all the time made me ready for anything. I'd sensed something malign nearby the day before, and The Arcs often use flashes of color that go hand-in-hand with a feeling. However, the fuchsia glow felt sweet and loving, reminding me of the days when I used to play with my brother, Gerard, or Gerry, as we called him.

As early as I remember, he and I would play outside together, singing as we circled the trees in the tiny yard of our old house in Hartstown. Hide-and-seek was his favorite, and he insisted on always having a chalk hopscotch on the sidewalk. He loved crayons and only colored the pages with an animal in my coloring books. But the best thing about him was that he knew when I needed a friend, like when teachers overlooked my raised hand or the other children called me names like "weirdo" or "*Mad*-eleine." Gerry's light was always a happy, brilliant purple, and I forgot my worries when he was with me, and hope blossomed in my heart.

My brother died of pneumonia when he had just turned five. I was born a year after he passed, but his spirit was as real as any earthly person to me. My parents had a few photos of him around the house, and sometimes, I'd catch my mother staring at his sweet face in the frame, tears welling in her eyes. We always had root beer floats after dinner on his birthday— my mom and dad didn't know that Gerry attended those celebrations or that he usually stayed close to my mother, stroking her hand. She didn't cry on those days, probably because she could feel his soothing nature.

Then, one day, when I was ten, I felt something had changed. I ran to the yard and peered behind every tree.

"Angels, where's my brother?" I asked.

"He is gone," said an Arc who appeared to me with wings that glowed like two blue flames.

"How can he be gone? He's a spirit," I replied.

The angel hovered beside the trunk of a tall oak. "Your family's consistent love has freed him, and he has crossed over to heaven," she replied. The Arc had starry eyes, and her dainty feet dangled just above the ground. "He stayed until he knew you would all be okay."

I dropped to my knees and sobbed because I knew how terribly I'd miss him. But, eventually, warmth filled me, knowing he was where he should be.

So, when the magenta light showed up across the street, I wondered if my brother had come to visit us in Gascony. Or was it another spirit or an angel with a message?

The following day, Saturday, a noise came from that shed.

"Go to the sound, Madeleine," Arc Ariel whispered. "Your assistance is needed."

So, I followed the tiny cry and discovered a fluffy little kitten all alone. Its fur was matted with dirt, and the poor thing was skin and bones. It looked up at the magenta glow swirling above its head, so I figured it saw an angel or maybe my brother's spirit, since animals can see them readily. Thank goodness, not all angels are revealed to me. It would be overwhelming.

Still confused by the pink light emanating from the garden shack's wall, I peeked inside a small circle cleared in the dirt-hazed glass but only saw gardening tools. I took a deep breath and trusted that The Arcs would show me anything I needed to see. I bent over and scooped up that little white ragamuffin, holding it snugly against my body, assuring it was safe.

CHAPTER SEVEN

Ryon - Day 27 and 26

94% and 88% Waning Gibbous

I'd spent two days in the shack alone. After 138 years with six others who threaded raucously, I wasn't used to the silence or solitude. But at least I had the excitement of seeing Madeleine. She returned from her sleepover, hair billowing across her shoulders and earrings glinting in the sun. Every Madeleine sighting was like a drink of cool, refreshing water, and I was a sponge soaking it up, saving it, hoping it wouldn't evaporate too quickly.

I took only one piece of advice from Geidhuce: the safest time to be outside my hiding place was after midnight. So, that was when I hunted for delicious rodents and birds or garter snakes that slithered down my throat. I drank from the nearby river, cupping my fleshy hands and sipping the cool liquid. My hunger and thirst were easily satisfied, but my heart ached like a gaping wound for more liberty.

However, something strange and wonderful happened on the third day in that dingy shack. A few hours after the day's light began, I heard a tiny cry in the distance that came closer and closer. Then, a tiny pink nose surrounded by wisps of white whiskers poked through a low knothole, and soon I heard rocks crunching beneath feet.

"Kitty, kitty?"

Madeleine!

She was nearing the shed, her lush scent growing more intense with every step. Fear and awe locked my muscles. "Oh, kitty…there you are! Arc Ariel told me you needed help. Now, don't be afraid." Her voice was as soothing as the ocean waves in the movie *Cast Away*.

The outline of Madeleine's hair in the sun glowed against the dirt-encrusted windows.

She's so close!

I sat on the dirt floor, pressed my body against the rough wood, and closed my eyes, focusing on the duet of rhythms performed by Madeleine's steady heartbeat and the rapidity of the kitten's.

"Come, little one," she said softly. "I won't hurt you, you poor thing. Who would be so cruel to leave you all alone?" I heard her stroking the kitten's fur, and a gentle rumbling ensued. "Aw, you're purring. I promise I'll take good care of you."

I gasped at her tenderness, but the beast side of me also found the smell of them mouthwatering, and my stomach growled loudly.

Madeleine stopped moving. "Hello? Is somebody there?" she asked.

I held my breath.

"Kitten, I feel another presence—kind but very lonely."

Yes, that's me! I wanted to yell.

My pulse throbbed as her footsteps paraded around the

entire wooden building. "I don't see anyone, but that magenta light is still illuminating from this shed," she narrated.

Magenta? Can she see my emotional thread?

I quickly shut it off and slunk into the darkest corner just as her eye peeped in through the hole I'd cleared in the window. I froze.

"Nothing but a bunch of tools and a garden hose. Hmm."

There was silence at first, but then I heard footsteps going away. I ran to my window peephole and watched wistfully as Madeleine and the wriggling ball of white fur disappeared inside the house.

○   ○   ○

That night, I slept upon my bed of coiled garden hose, replaying Madeleine's sweet voice hypnotically in my head, stirring up the lucid dreams that haunted me my entire 138 years in stone…

Hazy memories loomed of being chiseled and chipped by artists' tools of blades, hammers, rasps, and grinders, then sanded and smoothed by water and rough paper. The steady pulse of thwacks and the smell of burning metal were touchstones of my existence. My sculptor, Monsieur Salles-Bris of France, was a stout man with long, jet-black hair and a large mustache waxed into a curly cue on each end. In two years, he had made all seven of us with the help of his young Croatian apprentice, Ruza Prekrasna. She was fifteen, and her tanned, creased face had already signified a rough life. She compulsively brushed her curly brown hair from her forehead with an olive-colored hand, revealing high cheekbones and subtle beauty.

I listened to the sculptor and his apprentice when my feathery ears were chipped out. Monsieur spoke to Ruza in English, which I understood from the inherent knowledge I received from the carved human part of me. Both also mumbled to themselves in their native tongues, French and Croatian. I struggled to understand the meaning of any of those words.

We'd been made in a large, old wooden barn converted to a studio in a field near the town. Great drapes were drawn open to let morning light spill into the space, and every day, at six o'clock, Ruza closed up shop after Monsieur left to find a sip of wine, *une gorgée de vin.*

This is where my memories get foggy…Ruza did something strange before shutting the drapes. She whispered indistinct words while gently rubbing scented oil upon all our monstrously carved heads. I recall the smell of incense as Ruza held dried bundles of plants tied with string. Using a white feather to fan the pungent smoke that plumed, she made it swirl around our sculpted curves.

Real or a dream? I wasn't sure.

Then, the pictures in my head jumped to the grand celebration in 1886—a copy of the flyer had been posted to the wall of the studio:

Come to the Unveiling of The Gascony Church!

100 E. Main Street

April 19th

4 p.m.

Ice cream will be served afterward in Rostand Park.

Workers labored to attach each gargoyle and grotesque, mounted with steel rods and giant bolts high upon the façade of the church building. Once secured, we were covered with large sheets of white fabric that rippled in the wind and tied with rope.

When first mounted, I was shrouded and could see nothing. I had a peculiar feeling of floating in the air. All I could do was listen to the construction workers and their tools. I missed the comfort of the studio, the sounds and smells, and being able to watch Monsieur and Ruza work. But once the sun no longer illuminated the drape over me, it grew very quiet… until a strong voice boomed inside my head: *Who's there?*

Although I tried, my stone lips didn't move like Monsieur and Ruza's. Instead, I answered using my mind, *I am Ryonac, a grotesque. Please call me Ryon.*

Well, hello, Ryon. I am Cletas-Luxajo, a grotesque as well. But you can call me Cletas. His voice was like having a speaker up against my ear.

We can communicate by thinking?

It's called threading, he replied. *We've been given a gift to pass the time.*

How do you know about this?

Well, I was created to be the leader, so I intrinsically know things. We've all taken on characteristics of the animals and humans from which we were carved.

Cletas didn't thread anymore the rest of that night, and as soon as the sun rose, I heard drills and jackhammers again. But, on that second evening, he threaded the same question as the night before: *Who's here?*

I answered, *Me, Ryon, the other grotesque.*

And then another voice answered, gruff and stern, threaded, *I'm Geidhuce, and a grotesque as well.*

Welcome, Geidhuce. I'm Cletas-Luxajo, your leader, and I'm also a grotesque.

I was supposed to be mounted second! Geidhuce exclaimed. *I'm second in charge!* And for a long while, Geidhuce threaded red-angry thoughts about me being mounted before him.

I know we are new to this, Cletas eventually threaded. *But if you fill your mind with the color black, like spilling a bottle of ink over your thoughts, you can shut your thinking off from others. It does take some conscious effort and practice. Then, think of the color white to turn it back on.*

Why is Geidhuce's threading red? I asked.

Our thoughts are tied to emotional auras, each with a different color, Cletas explained. *For example, green is happiness, blue is fear, and red is anger.*

I'm not angry! Geidhuce threaded in blazing red, making Cletas and me laugh.

Let's all practice shutting down our threading, shall we? remarked Cletas. *Remember, think ink.*

Then, soon, Geidhuce's threading went black.

Over the next four days, the roll call happened again after dusk, and a new voice would state their name and type: Telber, Isel, Aneeguaru, who wanted to be called "Anee," and Vervalt were all gargoyles instead of grotesques. The word "gargoyle" comes from the French word for throat, *gargouille*, from which the English word "gargle" comes. Their job was to spew water from the gutters through their mouths when it rained.

With seven of us, the nights and days were filled with a

prism of colored emotional thoughts, confused memories, won-derings, and feelings. Cletas often reminded us to try to "think in ink."

Although white cloth blocked our sight for several days, we finally heard people gathering on the road far below, buzzing like flies on abandoned food. Music and excitement were surging in the air.

Just after the town clock chimed four, the crowd began to quiet.

"Welcome, ladies and gentlemen! From architectural plans to today, we have waited three long years for The Gascony Church to be built and officially open for worship in our wonderful town of Gascony, Pennsylvania." Applause laced with approving vocalizations lasted several seconds. "We won't make you wait a minute longer to reveal its stone guardians. Help me count to three, everyone!"

A mass of voices chanted from below, "One, two, three!"

Our white veils *whooshed* and fell away like angels descending to earth. The sun lit our view of the crowd, gasping in amazement. Then, clamorous applause exploded, accentuated by whistles and cheers. The townspeople of Gascony, young and old, stood on the cobblestone streets and gazed up at us, gaping, pointing, and smiling. Some wore overalls and boots, while others were well-dressed in suits and delicate lace gowns, topped with crisp hats in black and brown, the rage in 1886. Others wore uniforms: police officers, cooks, nurses, doctors, and servers.

In a long, black robe and white collar, Father Marguerite stood beside a podium on a bunting-edged stage with a white megaphone. Lifting the giant cone to his mouth, he pointed skyward. "Folks, please take a moment to notice the grand cross at the top. It came from the Meneely Foundry in New York State, forged in bronze. Below the cross, the seven stone carvings on the pediment are gargoyles and grotesques. These are "apotropaic," which means "to have the power to repel harm or evil." Their job is to keep our new church safe from the wicked and depraved."

Cheers erupted from the crowd yet again.

"Now, let me introduce you to the talented sculptor, Monsieur Salles-Bris, who carved these marvelous creatures," the priest announced, nodding toward the front row.

Our creator stepped onto the platform, dressed in a black suit and a white shirt with a thin black bow at the neck. The crowd clapped even louder, with a few *bravos* mixed in.

Monsieur took the megaphone as he waved a single white feather over his head. "'Panache' is a word with two meanings," he began in his French accent. "It is a confident style or…"

Suddenly, he struggled to speak, his face turning red as the audience whispered concerns to one another.

Then, the air quickly filled with a white mist, and the boisterous crowd and the priest went silent and still. Everyone was as motionless as those of us in granite.

That's when Ruza appeared. She made her way to the stage with the stealth of a cat, carrying a giant, old book. She flung it open to a crisp yellowed page and began reading in the language she used every night before leaving the studio. The wind picked up as she read. Dust and leaves swirled around the people frozen on the streets, and funnels of debris drifted up and up until they surrounded those of us on high. A twisted crackle of lightning shot across the sky, accompanied by an enormous clash of thunder.

Ruza repeated a phrase seven times, emphasizing it each time: "Postanite čudovišta kakve ste trebali biti." Then, she slammed the book shut, tucked it under her arm, and looked up at us with a mischievous smile. Turning quickly, she ducked behind the church and disappeared.

Ruza was never seen again.

The weather returned to calm and sunny as quickly as the disturbance had begun. The people moved again while Monsieur finished his speech as if nothing had happened. Afterward, the crowd went inside to tour their new church and then down the street for a scoop of ice cream…

Those old memories stopped when the clock struck 11, waking me. Blue, worried threading came from the dark night outside: *Ryon!*

I slid the sash up just enough to see out. There beside my little shack were Telber and Anee, hunched over, their eyes cautiously scanning the area.

Come in! I threaded, pushing the window all the way open. They took turns climbing inside, and I slid it closed.

Three six-foot monsters with giant wings barely fit in the small space, and Telber kept knocking over the rakes and watering can, but we made it work by huddling up shoulder-to-shoulder, our wings pulled in tightly.

My friends, I have missed you so! My loneliness gushed. "Let's speak quietly in case a gar or gro is nearby. Does Geidhuce know you're here?"

"No," they said in unison.

"How are you?" Anee asked with concern. Her lioness voice sounded similar to her threaded one, but I enjoyed seeing the vibration in her throat and her tongue moving.

"I'm quite well. I have plenty to eat and a place to hide… but I just had a crazy flashback about Monsieur and Ruza. What do you remember. . .?"

"Heehaw!" Telber interrupted, his aura exuding blue. "Y-y-you need to find somewhere else to go. R-R-Right away!" His scaly dragon legs were shaking.

"I plan to find someplace else soon," I replied. "But…"

"Y-y-you're in danger!" Telber blurted out.

Anee's pupils grew large, and she tried to hold back a sad, purple light, but I saw it. She wrapped her golden lioness tail around the front of her body and dipped her head downward.

"I am?" I asked.

Anee raised her head. "Yesterday's paper… the front page headline read: "Gargoyles Masterfully Stolen."" She watched me intensely.

"Well, that doesn't mean anything. They'll look for us in all the wrong places." I grinned. "And we'll be right under their noses."

Anee went on, "Some professor at the University of Pennsylvania who specializes in Antiquities and Ancient Historiography claims there's a curse on us. And remember Father Marguerite? He passed away long ago, but he had documented evidence that we are enchanted. Some people believe the theory. Apparently, other statues have disappeared as well."

I shook my head. "It's the twenty-first century. No one believes in curses anymore." We'd seen the world progress considerably in over 100 years. "For humans, fantasy only exists in movies."

Anee stared at me. "You want to take that chance?"

"Th-th-that is the least of your worries, Ryon." Telber pressed his front donkey hooves against my manly shoulders. "G-G-Geidhuce is gonna send someone to capture and kill M-M-Madeleine." He let go of me, his eyes still pleading.

"He threatened that when he came to see me, but he's just a big talker," I argued.

"Oh, he's different now that he's living." Anee snorted. "He angers easily, and you pissed him off by separating from us. He thinks you'll return to us if she's no longer a distraction." She emanated a glow that fluctuated between jealous yellow and regretful orange. "He means it."

As wrath burned inside me, I dug my clawed feet hard into the earth.

"You need to go," I growled.

"Not without you," Anee argued.

"I'm not coming. Please go!" I flung out both elbows and smacked them against the wooden wall behind me. The whole shack shook.

Telber's eyes grew wide. "M-M-Maybe the three of us can take Geidhuce, Isel, or Vervalt… whoever comes." Telber's donkey arms began to quiver in unison with his legs. "W-W-We can scare whoever comes into leaving Madeleine alone. Right, Anee?"

She hesitated but then grabbed a nearby hoe and held it up.

Incensed by Geidhuce's plan, I yelled, "No, you must leave! Grrowr!"

"Wh-Wh-What if we refuse?" Telber's donkey arms crossed over his furry, gray chest.

"We are The Three Musketeers!" Anee added. "All for one and one for all!"

"I can't endanger you. Geidhuce will never forgive you for helping me. You need to go! Now!" I went over to the window and flung up the sash. "Sneak back before Geidhuce knows you're gone. GO!" I roared with the screech of a condor about to snare its prey.

"B-B-But…" Telber recoiled, his eyes dark and sorrowful.

"GO!"

Finally, they left, the blue haze of their fear lingering for several moments.

I began vigil over Madeleine, repeating a little rhyme I made up on the spot:

"Geidhuce says he will attack,

Unless I leave here and go back.

The way he leads is so unjust,

He isn't one that I would trust.

Who's to say if I do leave

The plan he has up his sleeve

Is to hurt her anyway,

So that is why I choose to stay."

CHAPTER EIGHT

Madeleine - Day 25

80% Waning Gibbous

Although changing to a new school my sophomore year was tough, life in Gascony was much better than in Hartstown. No one judged me on my past, and I kept my angel sightings to myself. Teachers and students alike were intrigued by the novelty of a "new student," and everyone went out of their way to help me acclimate. I swore that one day I'd pay the kindness forward.

I loved putting on pajamas, climbing into bed, and Face-Timing with my bestie from Hartstown. The angels had told me her P.M.T. (Persistent Motor Tic) would eventually subside, but her eyes were blinking more rapidly than I'd ever seen.

"Are you okay, Sierra?" I asked.

"Everyone is so mean in high school," she said, her fluttering eyes filling with tears. "Today, some jerk left a beat-up copy of the book *Blink* on my seat during class. Then I heard snickers behind my back."

"I'm so sorry," I said, indignation nipping at my heart.

"High school is supposed to be fun, but I have no social life." She took a shuddering breath.

My throat tightened. "I wish I weren't so far away."

"I miss us," Sierra said, tears dripping with every blink.

"I miss us, too. Do you think you could come to visit me sometime?"

She grinned, red-faced. "I'd love that. I'll talk to my parents."

"If it makes you feel any better, I have very few friends here as well."

"Oh, but your life is so much better now. No name-calling or petty jokes at your expense."

"Hold on a minute." I set my phone down and spoke to the angels in my mind, something I had mastered since I was ten, no longer needing to talk out loud for them to hear me. *What advice can I give Sierra? I want to help her feel better.*

The handsome Angel Raguel appeared, and though some angels don't have faces, he did and was movie-star handsome with pale blond hair, bright blue eyes, and a chiseled jawline. His white feathered wings framed his large body, draped in a cobalt gown adorned with metallic gold ropes that crossed his chest. He rested his hand on my shoulder, and a calming warmth filled my body. His mellifluous voice was as soft as his downy feathers: *Sierra's strength is being challenged right now, but we constantly protect her. She will discover true happiness by doing what she is passionate about.*

The angels were never wrong, but they were often not very specific. *Thank you!*

I picked up the phone. "Sorry about that. The kitten was scratching at the door," I lied.

"Oh, let me see her. She's so cute."

"Ah, she already ran away, Silly Genevieve." Lie number two. I hated not being honest with Sierra, but I made a solemn promise not to tell a soul about my relationship with The Arcs. "Listen, I want you to do me a favor."

"What is it? You know I'd do anything for you." Her rapid blinking had slowed, and she looked pretty with her dark eyes and shiny black hair.

"'Let the beauty of what you love be what you do,'" I recited.

"Rumi?"

"You guessed it." I smiled. "Figure out what you're truly passionate about. Maybe it's art or music or… I don't know but focusing your efforts on that will help you forget those short-sighted meanies at school."

"I'll try," Sierra said with little enthusiasm. Then, she broke into the rhyme we used to say as kids: "I wish I could ride in your pocket."

"I wish I could live in your hair," I answered.

We recited the last part in unison:

"And oh, what things, what wonderful things,

We'd see as a miniature pair!"

"Talk to you soon, Bestie," she said.

"Goodnight, Bestie," I replied, then ended the call.

I fell asleep that night thinking about Sierra, wishing people could see her gracious heart. If she worried less, it would help her with her affliction. But we were both trying to live in a normal world with abnormal conditions. The only difference was that she couldn't hide hers, and I could. I knew our particular challenges were given to us for a purpose, but sometimes that was hard to see. I snuggled beneath my blankets and drifted off to sleep.

At around 5:30 a.m., I was jolted out of bed by a loud noise, like metal crunching outside. Then, my kitten leaped from the foot of my bed when my car alarm started honking.

"Clio!" I peeked out my bedroom curtains, hands shaking, and it was still dark out. Two large figures fled from beside my car, one with a halo of pink light around its head, the other surrounded in a harsh red. "Angels, I'm afraid," I said out loud.

"One is harmful, but the other is kind and protecting you," whispered an angel I could hear but could not see. "You are safe."

I threw on my robe, grabbed my car keys, and rushed to the front door where both my parents stood, also in their night-clothes. I clicked off the car alarm and slipped the keys into my pocket.

"Stay inside," my dad said firmly. Then, he opened the front door and investigated, so my mom flipped on the porch light.

"I called the police," she said as she put her arm around me.

"I saw two figures out the window. I think they damaged Clio," I said, realizing my palms were sweaty. I wiped them on my robe.

Mom and I stood in the open doorway, the cool morning air on our faces. Light beams from my father's flashlight bobbed around the yard. I strained to look for the magenta and red auras, but they had vanished.

A few minutes later, a cop car pulled up, and two policemen emerged.

One took our statements indoors while the other searched around the yard. The sun had begun to rise as we all met outside to see the damage, and it shook me to see my treasured car looking like a sasquatch used her hood as a springboard. Tears welled up in my eyes. Then, the other officer showed us a knife he found beneath Clio. They figured a couple of guys fought in our yard, and Clio got beaten up in the struggle.

Suddenly, a loud slapping sounded across the street, like a rubber mat landing on wet concrete. My parents and I looked in that direction, and the police, who had started to leave, stopped in their tracks. And there, above the old gardening shack, was the magenta-red glow I'd seen earlier. It fell like a shooting star behind the shed.

Had the same person been near the shack when I found the kitten? This should have scared me, but The Arcs assured me that the flow of magenta light stemmed from genuine benevolence.

Did I have a secret admirer?

CHAPTER NINE

Ryon - Day 25

80% Waning Gibbous

Madeleine's safety was a nagging worry.

She'd be unharmed during daylight hours because my evil comrades would not risk being seen when the sun was out, but I'd have to be vigilant the minute night fell, especially when the clock struck midnight. Perched on the shed roof, I crouched low, praying my giant form blended with the darkness. As one, two, three, and four a.m. passed, I listened and watched with my condor senses, but the world was still.

I tried to guess who Geidhuce would send if he followed up on his threat. I didn't think Anee and Telber would hurt Madeleine—and if forced, they'd probably side with me instead. Geidhuce could come back and do the job, but something told me he preferred bossing others around. So, it would be Vervalt, the slimy fish-man-dragon, or Isel, the wicked horse-woman-dragon. They were more than willing to do Geidhuce's bidding.

When the clock struck five, the slightest hint of daylight emerged on the horizon. I used my wings to glide quietly to the ground, surprising a nearby mouse that dashed over my dragon feet, skittering across the road and under Madeleine's car. I hadn't eaten for hours, and the fuzzy creature smelled appetizing, so I chased it, diving with extended arms beneath the running board and snatching it by a leg.

And just as I gulped the furry body down, I heard a wet *bloop! bloop!* and smelled old fish. Then, dragon feet scuffed along the opposite side of the car… *Vervalt!*

We'd been compatriots, and though we were far from best friends, we were cordial to each other. Although he sided with Geidhuce during most arguments, sharing deep-seated hatred for humans and a longing to taste their flesh, he never picked a fight with me. He was intimidated by Geidhuce and not confident enough to think for himself.

I got to my feet and leaped over the trunk of the car, tackling the giant fish-beast. I pinned his fins to the gravel driveway, slippery and wet in my grasp. *Get away from here!* I threaded in fire red, glaring into his glassy fish eyes. *Leave or else!* The beast inside me instinctively took over, and I lifted my fist, ready to punch him.

Don't kill me! he threaded with blue fear.

I should! I replied, secretly relieved he didn't want a fight.

He squirmed like a fish on a hook. Then, his enormous fish-tail slapped me hard across the flesh of my back and tucked wings, fueling my anger. I pinned his tail to the ground with my knees, fist still aimed at his slimy head.

Don't be Geidhuce's puppet. He's evil! I threaded, the fire in me returning.

Geidhuce is our leader, he threaded back, shifting between red and prideful green like a Christmas tree.

A true leader can be trusted, but he's selfish and power-hungry! He sent you here because he doesn't care if you get killed or captured. And if you got caught, we'd all be in danger.

Vervalt threaded in apologetic orange, *Geidhuce only sent me to see if you're okay.*

I lowered my fist. *I don't want to hurt you. I thought you came to harm Madeleine.*

I'm here for <u>you.</u> Please, believe me! Vervalt gasped, his mouth opening and closing, gills flaring.

Why should I? I used both hands to shove him harder into the ground to show my seriousness.

I promise, if you let me go, I'll leave, bloop! bloop!

Do you promise never to come near Madeleine or me again? I pushed down on his fins, my dragon legs heavy on his, and my hind claws jabbed into his caudal tailfin.

Yes, I promise, bloop! bloop!

I climbed off his clammy body, and we both scrambled to our feet. Vervalt looked shaken, and I felt sorry for him, being forced by Geidhuce to harm.

I held out my right hand. *Let's part as gentlemen...*

His elastic lips grinned, and a long, sharp dagger popped out of his toothless mouth.

He hurled his pointy face at me, swiping the blade near my body, but I pushed him away. The knife, still in his mouth, scraped the side of Madeleine's Toyota with a *screech* as he fell, then popped out as he hit the cement driveway and slid beneath the car. Vervalt lunged after it, but I whisked him away with my dragon tail. He swept my reptilian legs with his fish tail, and I landed on my back as he slithered beneath the Toyota again, trying to suck the blade like a vacuum cleaner. I yanked him backward by his dragon legs just before it reached his mouth.

We wrestled on the rough asphalt, hitting, scratching, and pulling on any body part we could grab. Vervalt rolled on top of me, but I managed to get both of my hind legs between us, catapulting him six feet. He landed on the car hood with a *thunk!* setting off incessant honking and flashing lights.

In a rush of adrenaline, I grabbed Vervalt by the slimy barbels that hung below his nose, remembering it was a sturgeon's most sensitive part, and dragged him quickly across the street behind my shack.

Up! I threaded still in red but tinged with blue fear. His barbels were still in my grip, and we unfurled our wings and flew past the small building, into the tree above, out of sight.

Don't you dare move! I twisted his barbels. He grimaced and obeyed, huffing and puffing to catch his breath, blue light streaming from his primitive fish body. My heart beat loudly against the inside of my chest.

We watched as the great din and flashing stopped. The porch light turned on, and a man I assumed was Madeleine's father came outside in pajama bottoms and a T-shirt. He walked the yard with a flashlight and illuminated the giant dent in the hood.

"Darn it all!" he said, feeling the massive depression.

A police car pulled up, and two officers got out. One went inside the house while the other walked the perimeter, aimed his flashlight under the car, got on the ground for a closer look, and stood.

Then, Madeleine and her mother came outside in robes, the police officers meeting them in the front yard.

"Seems like a couple of burly guys fought on your car." The policeman pointed his flashlight at the hood. "I found this underneath it." He held up a clear bag.

"A knife!" Madeleine's mother gasped.

"Well, we'll keep it as evidence," said the officer.

The mother put her arm around Madeleine. "What if they're still around?"

"I think I heard them run off toward the creek," said the father. "Probably running along the banks to Buffalo by now."

"Call us if you hear or see anything suspicious," said the other officer.

As soon as they leave, your girl is mine! threaded Vervalt, vengeful and green.

I slugged his human chest with my elbow. He slapped me loudly with one of his fins just as the two policemen reached their patrol car.

"Did you hear that?" asked one.

Vervalt and I froze like we were stone again.

"Yep. I think it came from the river's edge. Let's check it out." The officers got in and drove away slowly, scanning the trees.

We waited, watching the sunrise in the sky, until Madeleine and her parents went inside.

Let go! Vervalt commanded, wet drops of saliva dripping from his mouth and gills, landing on the leafy branches beneath our dragon feet.

If I let you go, you'll return without her, and Geidhuce will be very angry. He'll send someone else to make sure your terrible deed is done. My stomach crumpled at the thought. *No, you're my prisoner now.*

Prisoner?

Yes, I want to send Geidhuce a message. I held his barbels so tightly that they began to bleed, and he was still rendered helpless. *I'm taking you to my shack.*

Madeleine loves me, not you, sneered Vervalt, bright pink love illuminating his thread.

What was that, fish boy?

Madeleine doesn't love you. She loves me. Geidhuce said I could have her.

Maybe she'd love to have you filleted for dinner with a squeeze of lemon! The redness of my thread glowed and pulsated. *And she's not Geidhuce's to give!*

Remember? She said I was her favorite, bloop, bloop! Then, Vervalt threaded a memory of what had happened six months prior:

Madeleine had stood below us with her friend.

"Aren't those gargoyles creepy?" the girl had asked. "They give me nightmares!"

"I like them," Madeleine had replied. "That one, right there, with the bird head and half dragon, half human, has kind eyes." She had picked me out first, and my admiration for her doubled that day.

"But which one's your favorite?" The friend arched her palm across her brow to block the sun.

"The fishy one. He's a sturgeon, and they're one of the oldest species on Earth, dating back over 200 million years. He's the most unique," Madeleine had said as they continued down Main Street.

I'm her favorite! Vervalt threaded in pink. *Not you, Ryonac! You're wasting your time.*

Grrowr! And what were you going to do with that knife in your mouth, kiss her while you slit her throat? I let go of Vervalt's fin and shoved him hard against the tree trunk. *You're horrid!*

Like you're any better, he threaded back, thumping my chest with his front fins for emphasis. *At least sturgeons make caviar. She'd never love you, with your warty head and ginormous beaked nose!*

A flash of crimson lightning struck in my head. Fire literally flamed from my mouth, like when Geidhuce had come and breathed fire at me.

Vervalt reeled, then climbed the branches back toward the rooftop lair. I quickly caught up to him, hooked my fingers in his gill plate, and dragged him back through the treetops toward the park. He struggled, secreting so much fish slime that he slipped out of my hands and fell to the ground. I jumped, landing on top of him. We punched, rolled, and twisted, a blur of bodies traveling down the river embankment, over rocks, roots, and brush, splashing into the river. I feared Vervalt's fishy tendencies would kick in and give him an advantage, but he was a fish who never knew water. At first, he sputtered as much as I did, and we were equal in strength. But soon, he discovered he could breathe underwater, dragging me down with him. I fought to keep my head above the surface, gagging and choking.

We raged on, the morning light stretching across the water, walloping each other and drifting downstream. I prayed no humans would spot us. We traveled to deeper, swirling water beneath the bridge, and Vervalt got leverage on an underwater boulder. He held me by my submerged head. I tried hard to get away, but he wouldn't budge.

Growing dizzy, I gave up the struggle.

I die for the glory of love.

As my body became more weightless, and my head woozier, I pictured Madeleine's lovely face so clearly that I could almost touch it.

I hope God will take a beast like me so that I may watch you from heaven.

Just then, my legs drifted into something sharp, and my eyes flew open. Sunbeams shone on a giant tree limb in the shadowy depths, jutting like a longsword from the rocks below, as I'd pictured in the movie *Excalibur*. I mustered every ounce of strength I had left to stretch down to grasp it, but I failed.

I fought hard against Vervalt's grip, and he pushed me further into the depths, enabling me to snatch the branch with my clawed foot. In one swooping motion, I plunged the wooden point into his scale-edged human chest. Blood and scales floated on the water.

He let go of me, and I surfaced, gasping for air.

I held onto that branch for a bit, gulping oxygen, floating in the river's current, with Vervalt's lifeless body impaled on the other end.

The sun had moved higher in the sky, its rays warm on my wet skin, but I feared someone would see me. So, I swam toward a part of the bank covered with shrubs, dragging my weapon and victim behind me when, suddenly, my load went light. I watched Vervalt's body get swept up in rapids and quickly disappear.

Did I kill him? I didn't mean to…

My body went numb with dread. I let the branch slip from my hand.

I barely remember how I got back to my shack. I just knew I was careful not to be seen, and once safely inside, I shook, anxiety making my belly churn. I sat within those splintery walls, crumpled in the corner, reliving the horror of what happened repeatedly, and grateful that Madeleine was kept safe.

CHAPTER TEN

Madeleine - Day 24

71% Waning Gibbous

Although life in Gascony was better than in Hartstown, I still felt unsure. At my old school, teachers had labeled me an under-achiever, and my classmates thought I was crazy, but that wasn't the case at Gascony High. However, most students had grown up together and formed cliques that were difficult to break into.

But there was one boy who caught my eye: Chris Newtown. His brown hair flopped over his face like a sheepdog, and he spoke like the surfers in the movie *Point Break*. His guardian angel was more interesting than most I saw hovering around students at school. A faceless, androgynous shape that glowed gold, he had cloud-like wings and a body that sparkled like dazzling diamonds. Chris's eyes had the same golden glint.

Chris always said, "Hey," as we passed in the halls.

"Hey," I murmured back, my eyes darting away from his handsome face as heat seeped across my face.

Then, during the second semester of sophomore science, we were assigned as lab partners. My heart flipped like a fish out of water. Was it serendipity or the angels helping me out?

He flashed a smile, and I had to sit on my hands to hide the trembling.

The teacher hushed the class and then passed out our first lab assignment. When she got to us, she whispered near my ear, "This one may need a little extra help," nodding toward Chris before walking away. He winced, so I knew he heard her, too.

I put my hand on his arm and said, "We got this."

I couldn't tell if my heart flip-flopped because I was near him or how the teacher treated him. I related to the bias he was facing. True, he was a senior in sophomore chemistry, but people learn at different rates. I detected his kindness, and my angels assured me I was not mistaken. He was good-hearted.

During lab, we talked about everything from what was new on Netflix to our favorite TikToks. I learned he was really into *Star Wars* movies, didn't like strawberries, and loved ice cream. He wasn't sure what he'd do after graduation that coming May and had a lot of pressure to figure it out. I shared how I loved philosophy, chocolate chip cookies, and my kitten, Genevieve, who gave me so much comfort, and I told him how I'd found her near the garden shed. Besides my spirit brother, he was the first boy I'd ever made friends with.

Chris and I spent four months messing with test tubes, formulas, and chemicals. We got all A's on our assignments and shared high-fives to celebrate. Our giggling caused the other girls in the class to sneer at me.

"Don't mind them," Chris told me. "They're jealous of our awesome teamwork."

And when we took the midterm, we both got A's again.

"I hope you'll never underestimate yourself," I told him as we smacked palms.

His goofy smile was so cute, it gave me instant butterflies.

Then, the teacher called me to her desk, and we chatted quietly for a few minutes.

When I returned to my seat, Chris whispered out of the side of his mouth, "What was that all about?"

"She asked me if you cheated."

"What did you say?"

"I told her that you're the best lab partner I've ever had, and you earned every point on that test," I quietly replied, pretending to listen to the lecture.

"Thanks for sticking up for me," he said.

"I meant it."

So, he was my natural choice when the end-of-the-year dance rolled around. I dropped hints, letting him know I was free that weekend, but Chris didn't ask me. I told myself it was fine—he just saw me as a friend. But when I FaceTimed with Sierra in Hartstown and talked about our sad love lives, those feelings of being left out came rushing back. At least my Gascony bestie, Julie, and I had planned a fun night at home watching movies the night of the dance… but she canceled via text three days before. A tall boy with a locker beside hers had asked her to go, and she accepted. Julie felt terrible, but I texted back that I understood. My breathing was stunted by the realization that I would spend another dance at home alone. I needed fresh air. Pent-up feelings of insecurity and disappointment came out in tears the second I stepped onto the porch, and I begged The Arcs to help me understand why I was always excluded.

Usually, they would whisper a suggestion or give some esoteric advice I'd understand weeks later, but The Arcs were silent. Even though everyone's guardian angels constantly murmur suggestions into human ears, angels respect a person's free will and would never force anyone to do anything. So, I knew they couldn't make Chris ask me to the dance.

Then, minutes after my plea, Chris and his friend, Neil, arrived at my house.

Wiping tears, I remembered Rumi's words: 'Put your thoughts to sleep; do not let them cast a shadow over the moon of your heart. Let go of thinking.'

I needed to quit overanalyzing and let life lead the way.

CHAPTER ELEVEN

Ryon - Day 24

71% Waning Gibbous

My leathery condor head was fog-filled, and I could still feel Vervalt's saline breath on my neck.

Did I really kill him? Or maybe Vervalt survived.

The things he said about Madeleine had ignited my beastly impulses, making me lose control. Maybe I really *was* a monster. And whether Vervalt did or didn't return to the rooftop lair, it was just a matter of time before Geidhuce sent someone else after Madeleine. Exhausted with worry, I soon fell asleep, snoozing past midnight. I woke in my splintery hovel just as the town clock struck four and had a hollow pit in my stomach.

When I stood, discomfort rattled my body. In the dim streetlamp light coming in through the dirty windows, I saw several oozing gashes on my scaly legs, and my human arms and chest were covered in throbbing bruises that kept rhythm with my new beating heart. Physical pain was still new to me, and I wallowed in self-pity, feeling broken, afraid, and alone. I wanted out of that isolating shed, but I had to stay to protect her. Everything was silent, and my keen ears hadn't heard any disruptions, so I prayed Madeleine was safely sleeping in her bed.

I knew living in isolation was bad for my mental state, especially after watching and listening to the world from on high for so long. I forced my aching body to go outside, despite my pain. Blood had clotted on my skin, feathers, and scales, and every movement was an agonizing chore. The first task was to eat something to keep up my strength, but my reflexes were slow, so I decided to try the tangy blackberries that grew along the road beside the park. My mouth rejoiced at those delicious, tiny clusters of juice, but I had to pick them carefully—they bit back with prickly branches. After my finger got poked for the tenth time, *Grrowr!* I stopped.

The town clock bonged five times, so I limped back to my hovel, well before sunrise. And just as I slid the window open to climb in, I heard the clattering of a bike chain and a *thump!* Madeleine's newspaper had been delivered.

I'll return it after a quick peek.

I fought my aches again, quickly limped across the road, grabbed the newspaper, and returned to the shack. Then, I held the front page beneath a beam of morning light that began to stream through the peephole. A headline sprang off the front page: MALE TORSO FOUND ON RIVERBED. My breathing became labored as I continued to read:

GASCONY, PA—The torso of an unknown man was recovered from the Dunburgy River near the Sarra County line late Sunday evening, according to the Gascony Forensic Center. Forensic anthropologist Monty Fleur is working to identify the body, Gascony coroner's investigator Rosey Bill announced today. No other parts of the victim's remains have been found, and how the limbs and head were removed is unknown. "We believe he was in the water only a few hours," Bill said. "Strangely, the muscles and arteries look to have been dissolved, not cut." Toxicology and DNA tests are pending, he said. This is the second murder victim found in Gascony within a week. Last Tuesday, the remains of Gascony citizen Mike Green were found in an alley off Main Street.

It was confirmed... I'd killed him. That thought banged around in my mind for hours, and I could think of nothing else. Even though the spring day was filled with twittering birds and bright sunshine, I remained overwhelmed by an incredible sadness.

Small sobs filled my ears, but they weren't coming from me.

Madeleine?

I dropped the newspaper and pressed my eye to the peephole, forgetting my pain as I moved. There she was, sitting on her porch swing, her face buried in her dainty hands.

My heart raced. *Is she hurt? Did another heinous gar or gro harm her?*

Then, she spoke out loud with upward eyes. "Arcs, you say that someone who cares is nearby, and I feel it. But there's no one when I look toward the glowing pink light." She took in several choppy breaths. "If someone likes me, why didn't they ask me to the dance?" Her sobbing continued.

It's me! I'm your adorer! I yelled in my head.

I waited and watched, wishing I *could* take her to the dance. Instead, helplessly, I listened to her weep, and each despondent whimper made my heart ache.

Suddenly, a metallic powder-blue Mustang rumbled up to the front of her house and stopped. Two young men emerged, walking with a swagger of trying to impress. One boy was tall with brown hair that bobbed as he walked, and the other was six inches shorter with a blond buzzcut. Both were "too cool" in their baggy jeans and oversized t-shirts.

"Hey, Maddy. What's up?" said a low voice.

"Chris, man, I think she's crying," said a higher but still masculine voice.

The boys stopped about six feet away from Madeleine, and I could hear her sniffling.

"What's the matter?" asked the one called Chris.

"I appreciate your concern, but I don't want to discuss it," she answered softly, turning her body away from them.

The two boys stood and stared.

Madeleine turned back toward them. "Why are you guys here?" She used the sleeve of her jacket to dry each eye.

"Well, say something else," said the high-voiced one in a loud whisper, shoving his friend in the lower back.

"I don't know what to say, Neil!" Chris replied, also in a hushed tone, but my sharp ears heard every word.

"Uhhh," Chris mumbled.

"If you two don't mind, I'd like to be left alone." Her voice was thin.

That's right, Madeleine, get rid of them.

"Chris wants to ask you something," said Neil.

"Never mind," Chris said sharply. "Let's just go. Bye, Maddy."

Both boys headed toward the car.

I grinned.

"Wait!" Madeleine shot to her feet. "What did you want to ask me, Chris?"

Chris tapped Neil on the shoulder, thumbed briefly toward the car, and shoved his hands into the front pockets of his jeans. Neil dawdled back to the passenger side door, looking at the ground. Chris walked to the bottom of the porch steps. Madeleine stood at the top, looking like a princess who needed rescuing.

Chris froze, cleared his throat, then said, "She's so pretty," under his breath.

For a second, I hated how well I could hear. I leaned closer to my peephole, tensing my jaw.

"Would you like to go…" he cleared his throat again. "Sorry."

"Christopher Newtown, have you been hanging out around my house lately?"

"Well, not really."

"It's okay if you were." She smiled warmly.

Grrowr! It's me. I'm the one! I sighed.

Chris looked at his feet, each hand in a back pant pocket. "Any chance you'd like to go…" Then, he mumbled to himself, "You got this…"

"Chris, are you trying to ask me to the end-of-the-year dance?"

"Yep. I am." He looked up at her, his demeanor more like

a golden retriever than Cary Grant.

Her expression became serious and distant. "Well, I had planned to binge-watch *Dawson's Creek* that night…"

"You're busy then? Okay…" He spun around, head drooping, and walked back toward his car.

Whew! She had me fooled for a minute… adieu, Chris!

But suddenly, happiness swept across her eyes, enhancing the sparkles that twinkled in them.

"Silly, I'm just kidding. Of course, I'll go to the dance with you!" She smiled as brightly as the glowing sun, her lovely face burning an afterimage in my mind. Then, she pranced lightly down two steps, stood on her tippy toes near the tall dope, and kissed him lightly on the cheek.

I turned quickly from the sight, a furnace of fury igniting inside my belly. Gulping deep breaths, I was torn between watching them and burying my terrible face into the ground. I crumpled to the dirt floor, unable to watch anymore.

Then, Chris asked, "Could we hang out tomorrow night? Maybe grab a burger?"

"Sure," Madeleine said, giggling just before I heard her front door close.

I had to peek again and saw a huge grin plastered on that boy's face as he walked down the sidewalk, right past his car.

"Hey, Chris! Where you goin'? You *drove* here!" called Neil from the passenger side.

"Oh, right!" Chris ran to his Mustang, red-faced but still smiling, and the two boys got in. After hollering and high-fiving inside the car, they drove away.

I muffled a growl and extended my condor wings inside

those prison-like walls surrounding me. Or was my body the prison, covered in hideous leathery skin, scales, and feathers? Either way, it was too much to bear. She and Chris had shared the movie-like romantic moment I'd always wanted.

Grrowr!

I used my clawed dragon feet to shred the newspaper I'd been reading into a thousand pieces. The bits flew around like ash as fire burned in my chest. On the verge of losing control, I forced myself to plop in the middle of the floor. I buried my leathery bird head in my human hands.

I need to control my animal rage. It caused me to take a life!

So, I closed my eyes and breathed deeply, repeatedly, feeling the inferno in my body slowly reduce to embers.

When I opened my eyes, a torn piece of newspaper shaped like a crescent moon had landed on my scaly haunch. I moved to flick it away, but two words on it caught my eye: *assist* and *conscience.* It gave me an idea.

CHAPTER TWELVE

Madeleine - Day 23

61% Waning Gibbous

Sure, Chris was super cute with his flouncy hair and blue eyes, but I liked him because he made me laugh when we were lab partners. However, something changed when he asked me out on a date. He became utterly tongue-tied.

He pulled up in his Mustang for our first official date and honked. I saw disapproval on my mom's face as she sat at the kitchen table sipping her tea. She stood and headed toward the front door, but I touched her shoulder.

"These days, guys don't meet the parents the first time they go out," I explained. Then, I kissed her on the cheek. "I promise, he's a good guy. I'll be home by curfew."

"It's a school night, so ten," she declared.

I gave her a thumbs-up as I left the house. Chris was standing in the street, his head peering at me over the top of his car. Magenta light streamed out from behind him.

I knew the pink light was coming from him! My heart cartwheeled inside my chest.

I walked to the car's passenger door, opened it, and climbed in as he plopped into the driver's seat.

"Hope you're hungry. We're going to Dairy Queen for some Signature Stackburgers," he announced.

"Sounds delicious," I replied, feeling giddy about sitting beside the cutest boy at school.

But then, he didn't say another word.

We drove down Main Street until we reached the highway, the air thick with tension and the piney scent of the tree-shaped air freshener dangling from the rearview mirror.

"Been to the movies lately?" I asked, trying to start conversation.

"Nope," was all he said without glancing my way. The butterflies in my middle were acrobatic.

I nervously filled the silence: "I hardly ever go either, now that the town theater is under construction, and we can stream almost anything at home. But I do love eating buttered popcorn at the theater. It just tastes different when you're there. And I always get Red Vines if they have them. Once, I pulled a part of my tooth out while eating one. The tooth must have been cracked, and I didn't know it…"

He smiled, and all he said was, "Yeah," his eyes fixed on the road.

Stop rambling, Maddy, I told myself, settling into the seat and looking out the window.

We drove past several farms, and then he exited, only the rumble of the engine in our ears. I used the silence to detect his magenta aura, but strangely enough, it wasn't there. His guardian angel quietly hovered over his shoulder, as lovely as ever, but even my own spirit guides were mute. I figured they wanted to allow us to get to know each other naturally and not interfere, so I rolled with it.

Once we reached the restaurant, Chris pulled the car into a parking space and turned off the engine. There, standing outside the entrance, was Neil.

How is this a date? I thought.

The Arcs finally spoke: *He's uneasy, Madeleine. It'll be fine.*

I swallowed my disappointment and got out of the car, catching up to Chris, who hadn't thought to open my door and was already standing beside his friend.

"Hey," said Neil, seeing me approach.

"Hi, Neil," I replied, trying to sound happy to see him.

We went inside, ordered, and Chris paid, which was nice. We found a table near the large plate glass window and sat with Chris and me next to each other on one side, with Neil across from us. We watched the cows graze in a field across the street. The days were growing longer as summer approached, so light was still in the sky. A server brought a tray to us covered in burgers, fries, and shakes. Neil passed out the food.

We ate while the boys talked about all the dumb things they did, like jumping off a roof into the bed of a truck, crashing through a trampoline, and falling off ski lifts. Their antics often led to a broken bone or some other injury. I wondered if I was the third wheel.

"Well, that was fun," Neil said, carrying our wrappers on the plastic tray to a nearby trash can. "What's next?"

"Over in DuBois, they're showing *Demolition Man* at seven, starring the very cool Sly Stallone," said Chris.

He pronounced DuBois "Doo-Boys." I didn't have the heart

to correct him.

"Sounds awesome," said Neil. "That movie has lots of rad explosions."

Chris looked at me for the first time that night. "Since the Gascony Theater is closed, except for special events…" He turned bright red, remembering that the dance would be held there. "… and you like buttered popcorn and Red Vines…." Chris smiled. "Wanna go?"

The fact that he paid attention to me earlier made me feel better. "Sure."

So, we piled into Chris's car, leaving Neil's Ford truck in the Dairy Queen parking lot. Neil gave me shotgun, and we headed to the movie. Chris blasted rock music on the speakers the whole way there, so talking was impossible.

It was getting dark outside when we pulled up to the old art deco theater. Its name, The Boucheron, was lit in bright yellow, and its marquee had a scalloped edge of neon green. The smell of butter and Clorox hit my nose when we stepped inside. We ordered Cokes and a giant tub of popcorn to share, Chris paying for mine, further confirming this was actually a date in his mind. We found seats in the middle of the theater, sitting in blue, velvet-covered chairs, Chris between me and Neil. There were only a dozen other people there, and I would have liked to have sat toward the back where it was more private for snuggling, but not with Neil there.

I felt all tingly sitting next to Chris in the dark, elbow to elbow, our hands sharing the armrest between us, but he didn't even try to touch me. Once the movie ended and the credits were rolling, we stood up and walked platonically back to Chris's car. Once inside and seat-belted, the rock music resumed, blocking any chance of conversation again.

Just as we headed to the Dairy Queen, where Neil's truck awaited him on the other side of Gascony, Chris's engine began to sputter and die. Luckily, he was able to coast to the side of the road where gravel met tall grass.

Neil leaned in between the front seats. "Dude, you ran out of gas!" He laughed, pointing at the gauge.

Chris's face was red even in the dim light. "I guess we'll have to walk the rest of the way. Or we could call someone to come get us."

"It's getting near my curfew, and we're just outside Gascony. Mind walking me home first?" I asked.

"Sure. I'm sorry," Chris said, Neil still chuckling in the backseat.

So, the three of us crossed the dark highway and walked twenty minutes to my house. We arrived five minutes before ten, and the light came on inside the kitchen. Mom was waiting up.

Chris walked me to the front door, but I sighed to myself. With Neil and my mom around, there would be no goodnight kiss.

"Thanks for everything. See you tomorrow at school," I said, smiling at him before going inside.

My mother stood in her bedroom doorway, yawning.

"Chris's car ran out of gas on the highway, and we had to walk," I explained.

"You could have called. I would have picked you up."

"We were only a mile away," I said, yawning.

"You have fun?" she asked.

I nodded. "Goodnight, Mom."

I went into my room, closed the door, flopped down on my bed, and stared at the ceiling, trying to understand why Chris would bring Neil on our date. The Arcs had told me he was nervous. At least we had the dance in two days. "Angels, please help Chris find the confidence to show that he likes me."

CHAPTER THIRTEEN

Ryon - Day 23

61% Waning Gibbous

The injuries Vervalt had inflicted were incredibly tender, with white pus oozing from several of them. So, I just lay in my garden hose bed that day, hoping to feel better.

I watched Chris arrive around six to pick Madeleine up for their burger date. He parked, honked, and Madeleine ran out of her house and jumped into his car. According to many movies and faint memories, a gentleman should always walk to the house, chat with the parents, and hold the car door open for his girl before driving away. Chris needed to learn chivalry.

Jealousy simmered as I anticipated their return, eager to conduct my plan. No matter how I felt about her, I knew she'd never have romantic feelings for a monster—*Beauty and the Beast* was far-fetched. But maybe I could help Madeleine. I just wanted her to be happy.

I need to talk to Chris, though. I thought about climbing through the trees and following him home but realized he could live on a farm outside town. Trees abundantly lined the dusty streets, but they didn't connect to the rural pastures peppered with silos and cows. I knew this because the model I was sculpted from lived on a nearby farm.

Besides, I couldn't stray too far from Madeleine's house. Geidhuce could come or send another one of his thugs. I just needed to get Chris alone, without him seeing me.

The nine o'clock hour came with no sign of Madeleine or Chris. Usually, I was starving at this time, but I had no appetite, and my mouth was dry like a dirt road in the summer. And just before ten, the couple and Chris' cohort, Neil, appeared on foot. My jealousy let up a little, seeing it hadn't been just Chris and Madeleine all night. As they approached the house, a light clicked on inside. Neil stopped on the sidewalk, allowing Chris to walk Madeleine to the bottom of the porch.

"Looks like Mom's been waiting up," Madeleine announced.

Chris flipped his hair to the side, staying uncomfortably silent.

"Thanks for everything. See you tomorrow at school," she added, but her tentative tone made me think she was just being kind.

She flashed a smile and disappeared inside. Chris just stood there gawking, the epitome of awkwardness. Finally, he ambled to Neil, and the two boys walked back the way they'd come, towards Dunburgy Park. I quietly left my shed to follow. I forced my aching body to travel along the branched pathway above them, hidden in leaves that glistened in the streetlights, listening to Chris and Neil talk.

"Do you think she had fun?" Chris asked.

"Yeah, dude, of course she did," replied Neil. "Whenever you're around girls you like, you get a little goofy, but you were trying, man."

"She's so smart and pretty…it's intimidating, you know?"

I smiled to myself.

"Next time, just follow the advice on how to stay calm when giving a speech. Picture her in her underwear," Neil teased.

"Thanks for that suggestion! That's the one thing I was trying *not* to do," Chris joked, giving Neil a gentle arm punch.

"Just kidding. You're getting to know each other. Give it time."

I followed them near the park entrance, and I had to think quickly to keep them from going too far. So, I balanced on a low branch full of leaves, and the second Chris was directly below me, I bounced to make the limb I was on dip, and whispered gently like the wind, aiming for his ears only, "Chris!"

He stopped, and Neil kept walking. "Who…what…was that?" Chris asked, looking around. I scrambled high up in the tree so he couldn't spot me.

"Chris, I need to talk to you… alone," I murmured softly.

His eyes grew large. "I'm getting out of here," he announced, about to bolt.

"It's about Madeleine," I moaned, ghost-like.

"Huh?" Chris, visibly confused, stopped and scratched his head. "What about Maddy?"

"Hey, where'd you go?" Neil asked, many yards away. "Hurry up, slowpoke!" he hollered once he spotted his friend.

"Who are you?" Chris asked, squinting at the trees.

"You have nothing to fear. I'm your divine guardian. I've come to help you."

Neil called from a distance: "You comin'?"

"Ah…" Chris hesitated.

"Let him go so I may assist you."

"Assist me with what?" He looked in my direction, then toward Neil, and back toward me.

"Hurry up!" Neil called back.

"I can help you get the girl."

Chris thought for a moment. "Hey, Neil, go on without me," he yelled.

"You sure?" Neil called back.

"I may try to see Maddy again. You go on, okay?" Chris replied.

Neil answered, "Oh, okay! See ya tomorrow, buddy." His footsteps faded into the distance.

Chris shined the light from his cell phone into the trees above him. "Now, show yourself to me." I ducked deeper into the foliage and held my breath. "Are you still there?"

"Yes, but you can't see me."

"Why not?"

"I don't physically exist. I'm in your mind. You conjured me up from your deepest thoughts," I replied. "I'm your conscience."

"My conscience?" With a puzzled look, Chris put his hands on his hips. "Do you grant wishes?"

"Well, not magically speaking, but practically speaking, yes."

"Huh?"

"I know all about your desires, worries, and fears."

"So, you know that I'm going to college in the fall, that I

got into electronics school at the community college, but I don't know if I'm smart enough."

"Yes, of course, I know that," I lied. "However, you *are* ready for college."

"I am?"

"Yes, you just haven't come to terms with leaving home yet," I surmised.

Chris thought long and hard. "I guess you're right. What else do you know about me?"

"Someone special has captured your heart."

"Maddy."

"Yes."

"Then you know she's by far the prettiest and smartest girl in school, and that she's a freshman, so a few years younger, and that she said 'yes' when I asked her to the dance?"

"Yep, I know all that too." *He sure is making this easy.* "She'd only accept your invitation if she liked you." I choked a little on those words.

"I'm not sure about that. Whenever I'm around her, I can't talk straight, my palms sweat, I'm clumsy, so she probably thinks I'm a dufus." Chris dropped his head and stared at the ground. "She's just so awesome."

"Well, my friend, I can help you with that."

"How?"

"Baby steps. Meet me here tomorrow night at midnight for step one. Be sure to come alone and don't tell anyone about me, or else I won't appear to you."

Chris's brows protruded, casting deep shadows over his

eyes. "Is this for real?"

"It's as real as you make it," I said, holding my breath, hoping he wouldn't question my ambiguity.

He scratched his head in deep thought, and for a second, I thought he would tell me I was full of it and walk away. But instead, his face relaxed, and he said, "Okay…I'm in."

Phew!

"See you tomorrow at midnight." Chris slowly walked past the park, looking back several times to search the treetops. Finally, he shrugged and vanished into the dark.

I waited on my branch until I was certain he was gone and climbed back through the trees to my shed, gently landing on the grass beside it, trying not to aggravate my injuries. I smelled a juicy opossum nearby, and my stomach gurgled with hunger. Sneaking from bush to bush, I followed the delectable scent to the nearby parking lot behind Quality Market. It darted around a cinderblock wall, leading me to a metal dumpster beside a small loading dock. The aroma of rotting food made my mouth water. I'd hit the jackpot!

"Well, little fellow, since you led me to this goldmine, I'll spare you tonight," I announced.

I grabbed a plastic container filled with six smooshed chocolate cupcakes with vanilla frosting. As they crumbled on my tongue, I thought of how Anee had dreamed about tasting chocolate while we were stone, and I wished she were there to share the sweet, creamy, roasted sensation. I also chowed down two raw sirloin steaks that were slightly green and three bruised red apples—a feast of flavors. But then, sleep called to me.

As I turned to go, I spied a pad of yellow paper with light blue lines and a dark blue ink stain the size of a quarter in the middle of it, nestled amongst a wad of bubble wrap. I fished it out and tore off the top pages until I got to the unmarked ones. The top of the page said "RECEIPT" and "Manny's Tires," with some other printed writing on the bottom of each sheet. I tucked it inside my neck skin.

Looking around, I spied a cylinder of writing implements on a desk inside the small loading dock office window. Before I knew it, I was smashing my fist through the glass. The horrible screech of an alarm went off as I grabbed the whole container and scrambled up the closest tree.

I quickly moved through the canopy toward the shed, sharp pain radiating through my right hand where blood seeped from fragments of glass stuck in my human skin. I spent the next hour with the window open, using the moonlight to reflect the pieces to pull them out. I counted twelve shards and then took an old rag I found in the shed to tie around my hand to stop the bleeding.

Despite my pain, I dozed off with a full belly and a feeling of happiness that my plan was in motion.

○　○　○

Curled up on my hose nest, I vaguely remembered hearing Madeleine's front door slamming and her car revving at around 7 a.m. when she left for school. I had no energy, not even to lift my head.

I woke up when Madeleine returned that afternoon. She belted the song on her car radio, "Endless Love." It was a sign of what I planned to do next.

She exited her car, backpack in one hand and a tall Styrofoam cup in the other that permeated the air with the scent of peaches and strawberries. *Ambrosia for my goddess.* She entered the house.

I was rested and ready to write my prose. Words of romance gushed in my mind like a broken fire hydrant, but I needed to capture the right ones.

I'd never physically written anything before, at least not as a beast. My human part had seen words and learned to read them, but the act of putting pen to paper was a distant memory. My hands were strong but clumsy with the pen. I tried writing with both my left and right hands, and my right hand had more success, though it pulsated from hitting the glass the night before, still tied with a bloody rag. The words were rough and wobbly, but finally began to take form:

Dearest Madeleine—

You are the radiant sunshine that illuminates my day. You grace the earth with similar light, bringing joy to all who see you, and I melt into a blissful puddle of happiness in your presence, yearning to drink from the wellspring of our love and gently touch your rosy lips. I am the moon reflected in that pool, vigilantly watching over you at night when you sleep. I will gather stars and bring them to you by the pocketful, for you deserve their wondrous magic that can make all your wishes come true.

Yours, as faithfully as the moon loves the night,

Tears dropped onto the page. I slowly signed the name "Chris." How lucky he was to hand her this letter, watch her beautiful eyes skim the words, and see happiness grow within her.

Then, I got an idea.

I wiped my tears and wrote a second version of the same letter on another piece of paper, making it as neat as possible, a piece of art, and signing it "Ryonac."

I folded the note for Chris in thirds and slipped it beneath the can of pens for later. Then, I stuck my copy on a protruding nail so I could read it all the time. My handwriting needed improvement, but the sentiment was genuine. I pictured myself reciting those words while holding her hand, then kissing it, her skin soft against mine. She'd smile and blush, maybe even titter, as I handed her the note to keep. Then she'd hold it to her breast, beaming with adoration.

I replayed that scene countless times and well into the night.

LAST 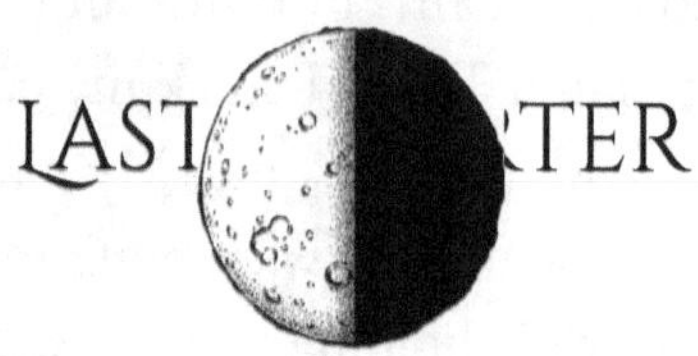 RTER

"Reflect on the past to make adjustments, while forgiving yourself and others with love, as you prepare for new beginnings."

CHAPTER FOURTEEN

Ryon - Day 22

50% Last Quarter

Midnight arrived at a turtle's pace, and my body was scabby and sore but healing. My hand still wrapped in the rag that was brown with dried blood. With the letter for Chris in the leathery folds of my neck, I left the shack wishing I could give it to Madeleine myself.

I got there ahead of time and waited, questioning why I was doing this. Was it the human boy part of me that understood his need to "get the girl?" It would no doubt hurt to watch her fall for someone else, but given my circumstances, living vicariously was all I could do. I rested on the tree branch just outside the park where I last spoke with Chris, contemplating.

"Hello?" he called. He was wearing jeans and a plaid flannel shirt. He took his phone out and pointed its flashlight my way.

"Turn that thing OFF!" I roared.

Chris jumped backward and clicked it off, slipping it back into his pocket. "Sorry, man, you sound like you're right above me…"

"I told you, I'm in your mind," I firmly reminded, my claws protruding and spearing the branch I stood on'as anger simmered. "Don't get tricky with me. If you do, I'll go away."

"Okay, okay." Chris held up both hands in surrender.

I took a deep breath. "You conjured me up in your mind, so you must look inward, not outward, and trust."

"Trust in something I can't see?"

"Yes, there are plenty of things in life that cannot be seen, but we have faith it's there, like gravity, the air we breathe…and love."

Chris scratched his forehead. "I guess so."

"Our relationship will not work without trust. Understand?"

"Yeah, sure." He nodded. "If you can get Maddy to like me, I'm in."

"That's our goal."

"Thanks, man." He grinned widely and pretended to shake hands with an invisible person.

Although this boy was simple, something was charming about him. I also missed Anee and Telber, so it was nice to have a friend.

"Here, I brought you something." Chris reached into the back pocket of his jeans and pulled out a shiny, silver package with the word "Pop-Tarts" on the side. "But I'm wondering, how does a conscience eat?"

"Consider it an offering, like you'd put on an altar." I hoped he'd buy my logic. "So, just set it down in front of you, and I'll get it later."

Chris walked to the tree trunk, set down the metallic pack, put his hands together as if praying, bowed at the waist, and walked backward to where he'd stood. "I'm ready to get started." He looked up in my direction, eyebrows raised.

"Step one will be to write the girl a letter."

"A letter?" Chris looked down at his feet. "I'm not good at that." I opened my mouth to reassure him, but then he cleared his throat, "Eh-hem," and began to recite in a singsong voice: "Hey, Maddy! You're cool. And you smell. . . Um, smell *nice*." He paused, then asked, "Or is it fancier to say she smells *nicely*?"

"No. "Nicely" is the *action* of her smelling something."

"Oh, that's not what I mean." Chris put his hands over his heart and began reciting again. "Hey, Maddy! You smell *nice*, and I don't mean how you sniff something with your nose…"

"Chris," I interrupted, "you don't have to worry about what to say. I've already written a letter for you. Now, close your eyes."

He did as I said, so I retrieved the letter from my droopy neck skin and dropped it between the boughs. The yellow paper rocked from side to side as it drifted to the ground.

"You can look near your feet now," I announced.

Chris opened his eyes, spotted the letter, and picked it up. "Thanks!" Then, he unfolded it and read aloud: "Get a free tire rotation with the purchase of…"

Oh, boy. "No, my friend. The other side."

"Oh!" He flipped it over and read silently for a moment. "Girls want a letter like *this*? It's so… mushy."

"I promise she'll love it."

"But…" Sadness overtook Chris's eyes. "She'll never believe I wrote this. It's too…good."

"Most artists are regular people who express themselves creatively through their chosen medium. Monet didn't only paint, and Edgar Allan Poe didn't only write. They lived ordinary lives while creating extraordinary art."

"I don't know who Moe and Ed are, but I think I understand—I may talk dumb, but Maddy will think I am creative when I write."

"Exactly!"

"But I'm embarrassed to tell her these things… *gently touch your rosy lips…*"

"Wouldn't you like to kiss her?" I asked, a lump of jealousy rising in my throat.

"Well, yes…"

"That's a romantic way to say it."

"And she'll get what this means?"

"She won't only understand it, she'll love it. Trust me. Just take the letter to her."

"Alright, I'll give it a try." Chris let out a big sigh. "But it's late now. I'll give it to her tomorrow before school."

"Good luck. Let me know how it goes."

"Won't you already know, being my conscience?"

"Yes, but it's important to reflect," I backpedaled. "Let's meet after the dance, at our usual time of midnight."

"Sounds good." He refolded the note and put it in his shirt pocket.

"Also, hold doors open for her, including a car door. She'll appreciate the chivalry," I added.

"Seems a little hokey, but okay. If you think she'll like that." He hesitated. "Are we done here?"

"Yes."

"Then bye," he said, waving, then sauntering away.

I made sure Chris was long gone before swooping down to get the Pop-Tarts and flying back into the tree. I climbed through the branches, the cellophane-covered treat in hand, to the river to rinse my wounds before returning to my shack. Once inside with the window secured, I sat on my hose nest and ripped open the silver packaging. Those crumbly pastries, with frosting on the outside and sweet jelly inside, were scrumptious.

I slept deeply that night, dreaming I was lying in a field of Queen Ann's Lace that stretched out like a white filigree sea beneath a bright blue sky. My winsome Madeleine appeared, not speaking as she lay beside me, my body cupping her from behind. Her hair smelled of honey and jasmine, and the nape of her neck was as creamy as whipped butter.

○ ○ ○

I awoke and didn't want to open my eyes, holding onto my beautiful dream, swearing I could feel Madeleine next to me. I took a deep breath, and a familiar scent drifted into my beaked nose—but of someone else I knew. My eyes flew open.

"Anee!" I exclaimed, sitting up.

Her scaled legs, furry lioness paws, arms, and golden head rolled over to face me. She purred with half-opened sleepy eyes.

I gave her a soft nudge. "Anee, wake up. What are you doing here?"

She yawned, her sharp, white teeth glinting in the subdued

glow of morning. "Hey, Ryon," she whispered. Her lioness voice was low and soft.

I sat up. "Why are you here?"

"I came to speak to you," she announced with a huge, toothy grin.

"Are you crazy? The others will notice you're gone." I stood and began to pace. The orange light of dawn streamed through my peephole. "They'll look for you here first. You need to go back!"

Anee sat up, unfazed, pulling her dragon legs beneath her fuzzy body. She studied my wounds. "Those look bad." She reached out and touched my wrapped hand. I winced, pulling it away. "And don't worry. Isel's covering for me."

"Isel? You can't trust that mare-faced fiend." I shook my head.

"It's alright, Ryon. We made a pact."

I stopped pacing, folded my human arms across my chest, and glared at her.

"Well, since Vervalt disappeared, we've been lying low," Anee said calmly, half yawning. "The police are extra nosy right now. And Geidhuce is using this time to plan something awful." She stretched her back.

"Geidhuce *is* awful."

"Trust me, I know. And it's tough for Telber and me to keep ourselves from thinking badly about him. We "think ink" a lot-ish."

I couldn't help but smile at Anee's unique expression. "How is Telber?"

"As good as can be expected." She took my unhurt hand in her furry paw. "Isel hangs all over Geidhuce, and they plot together for hours. Their hate for humans is growing by the day."

I pulled away and paced again. "Then, how can you have a pact with Isel?"

"I caught her mental thread accidentally running full force." Anee gazed at the ground. "She pulsated purple sorrow, and her heart was breaking. She's in love, and her love isn't returned." She gulped.

"But Geidhuce dotes on her." I sat in my coiled-up nest, dust specs drifting in the beams of bright morning light coming through tiny cracks in the shed walls.

"Well, that's not who she loves." Anee looked up. "She loves you."

My jaw dropped. "Me? She's tricking you."

"It felt real, and she's no Greta Garbo." I could tell Anee was struggling against her own mental thread, keeping it black as night.

"What else?"

"Well…" Anee stretched her wings, and the green lizard skin opened like army parachutes and then closed again. "We agreed that if Geidhuce was gone, you could become our new leader."

"So, you and Isel want me to take out Geidhuce?"

"Please, Ryon." My beloved friend's eyes were two dark saucers of hope.

"I still don't trust Isel." I tapped my beak with my fist.

"Don't you want to help me and Telber at least?" Anee's

lion tail flicked rapidly across the dirt floor. "And, besides that, I believe Isel."

"How?"

Anee's breath shuddered as she locked eyes with me. "I know what it's like to long for someone so much that it makes you willing to do anything to be with them. *Anything*." Tears welled up in her golden eyes.

I stood up and wrapped my arms around her, thinking about Madeleine. "Me too. Sometimes, a heart takes its own path no matter how hard we try to steer it elsewhere," I whispered, rubbing her soft back.

But then, Anee's bubblegum pink thread of emotion broke through her blacked-out thoughts. *For me, it's you, Ryon. I love you so much! I have for decades. How could you not know?*

I let go of her and backed away. "I…" I almost said I had no idea, but that was a lie. I knew how she felt and always avoided it, but hearing it told sent my head spinning.

Anee got up, shaking, and walked to the corner of the shed. Besides making sure my threads were blocked, I didn't know what to do or say. I loved Anee, but as my dearest friend, I didn't want to hurt her, but my heart belonged to Madeleine.

Silence became an invisible barrier between us.

Finally, Anee spoke. "I tried to hide my feelings all our years on that building. Sometimes, I had to concentrate really hard to keep my mental threads concealed." Tears dripped down her feline cheeks. "And I listened to your thoughts for the tiniest glimmer of love for me."

I opened my arms to her. "Please, sweet friend, come here." She came over to me, and I held her tight again. "You're wonderful, beautiful, and loving. I cherish you."

Her body trembled as she lifted her face to me, her chin quivering. "I miss you so much it hurts, Ryon. Please kill Geidhuce and become our new leader. You'll be fair and honest, the town will be safe…" …*and we can be in each other's lives again.* This thread was green with contentment.

I let go of her, wiping the wetness from her golden, furry cheek. She closed her eyes and chuffed.

"How much time do we have before Isel can no longer cover for you?" I asked.

"I told her I'd be back before midnight, hopefully with you. We thought you could pretend you changed your mind about living with us and then kill Geidhuce in his sleep."

"But Geidhuce is clever. He doesn't trust me and would sleep with one eye open."

"For a while, but just when he lets his guard down… What's that?" She pointed to the piece of yellow paper on a nail.

"Oh, something I wrote." I snatched it from the wooden wall.

"Really? May I read it? You have such a way with words." She took it from my hand.

"No, Anee, please. . ." I slumped my large head.

Her eyes darted back and forth across the page and then were fixed upon my face. A faint growl vibrated her throat.

"Anee, I can explain..."

"A love letter? To that *human?*" Her lips curled above her teeth, exposing their sharpness. "Are you crazy? She belongs with her kind, and you belong with yours!" Rage flashed across her furry face.

"But, I have this ingenious plan to make her fall in love with..."

"With who? YOU? Have you seen yourself? To me, a gargoyle, you're so handsome, but to her, you are…"

Every word stabbed like a dagger. I finished her sentence with a sad, purple thread: *Grotesque!*

Anee held up the letter, her face softening. "Sorry, but life's not like the movies we heard all those years in the theater. You'll never have a romantic relationship with a human."

I stared at her, trying to become immune to the poison she was making me taste. But I knew she was right.

She moved close to me, and we were nearly nose-to-nose. Tears welled up in her deep yellow eyes once more. "Ryon, I forgive you for this. Suddenly coming to life is very confusing, and I can see you got lost-ish."

I turned my attention to a trail of ants on the dirt floor carrying Pop-Tart crumbs away on their backs.

"My sweet Ryon, everything's gonna be okay," she muttered, nuzzling her smooth, vinyl nose against my bumpy, leathery neck. "Come back with me and be our leader. We need you. We love you."

I closed my eyes and pictured killing Geidhuce in his sleep, but the regret of Vervalt's death, even though he was demonic, made bitter bile rise into my throat. But Telber and Anee deserved the freedom I'd come to love, and they'd never have it with the wolf-jerk around. Maybe there was another way besides murder, and if I went back with Anee, at least I'd know where Geidhuce was at all times, keeping Madeleine safe.

Lifting my head, I nodded acceptance.

Joy spread across Anee's face as she held out the letter. I snagged it from her paw and tore it into pieces.

Anee grinned, threading in happy green, *Let's go!*

It's light out now.

We'll be careful. And I found a tree path that gets us directly to the alley.

Anee pushed the window open. I looked around the shack. I wouldn't miss the rusty tools, dirt floor, and spider webs.

Then, a sweet tone filled my ears.

Dancing upon the wind was a melody I can only describe as "nectar-sound." It whirled around me, and I was lightheaded from its beauty. I dashed to my peephole, and Madeleine was singing:

"The moon in the sky

fills my heart with love and song—

I can't deny

that with you, dear, I belong…"

She moved forward and back on the porch swing, the rhythm of the creaking chain keeping time. Her angelic voice glided across the blades of grass and swirled upon the petals of flowers on its way to me.

Anee glowered, then quickly climbed out.

Stop! She might see you… I pleaded.

But Anee kept going, and though it was imperceptible to the human ear, I heard her sob as she traveled through the trees, off into the distance.

My heart was torn. *Madeleine's outside, a moment I live for… but Anee's been my best friend for over a decade, and she needs my help….* I climbed out the window to catch up to Anee, but then a car whizzing along the pavement grew louder until it stopped in front of Madeleine's house—Chris's Mustang.

He was about to give her the letter.

I quietly climbed into the trees to a better vantage point and saw a treetop path to a thick branch near Madeleine's porch. Careful not to rustle a single clump of leaves beyond what a gust of wind might do, I snuck above the two lovebirds. I was so close to Chris on the stairs that I could see his chest expand and contract with each nervous breath he took. I couldn't see Madeleine.

He was dressed nicer than usual, wearing a short-sleeved, button-down shirt and khaki shorts. He even smelled like cologne, a mix of frankincense and campfire.

"You look dapper today," Madeleine said.

"Thanks," he replied.

"What's going on?" Even when speaking, her sweet voice was songlike. "I was just about to leave for school."

"I… I… I just wanted . . ." His voice shook.

"Yes?" she twittered.

"I…"

Then, there was maddening silence.

You can do it, Chris.

As if he felt my nudging, he confessed, "I brought you something…ah, made you something."

Yes!

"Actually," he continued, "I *wrote* you something." He quickly pulled a yellow wad from his back pocket, and his hands shook as he uncrumpled the page, smoothing it against his chest, clumsily trying to get out the wrinkles.

"Wanna sit for a minute?" the girl asked sympathetically. "Will you read it to me?"

"Read it?" Chris resembled a statue, blanched and still.

"Or, I can read it to myself. Either way, come sit." I heard her hand tap wood.

Then, he disappeared under the roof. I scrambled to the far side of the tree, where I could watch them from behind through a screen of leaves.

Creak, creak, creak went the porch swing chains as Chris and Madeleine gently pushed against the cement floor with their feet, their seated bodies side-by-side, hypnotically moving forward and back.

"What did you write?" Madeleine asked coquettishly as she pulled her feet up onto the edge of the swing, hugging her knees with delicate arms. "A slogan about whitewalls?" she asked, looking at the back of the note in his hand.

"No, no." He used the back of his hand to wipe his forehead. "I wrote you a poem, I think. Or a letter. Maybe it's just a letter."

"Well, is it a poem or a letter?"

"You... you decide." He handed over that atrociously crinkled paper, and she smiled. My heart fluttered anxiously in my chest.

Chris sat nervously on the edge of his seat.

Madeleine read silently, her head popping up when she'd

finished. "*You* wrote this?"

"I know I don't talk so good, but yep, I wrote it. It came from my conscience, so it was all me."

"That's really sweet," she crooned, holding up the letter. "May I keep it?"

"Of course. It's for you."

"Chris, you surprise me. Other boys text or DM, but you come in person with a romantic note."

She thought it was romantic. I was delirious with happiness.

"I have this… gift—a sixth sense about people, you could call it," she continued. "And right now, I feel a celestial warmth, and behind you in the tree, I see a pink light that…" Madeleine stopped, her body twisted to point toward me, then put her dainty hands in her lap. "Sorry. That sounded pretty silly…"

"I like to hear you talk," Chris replied, leaning against the swing as if something heavy had been lifted from his back. "What were you saying about 'sill-est-you-all'?"

"Oh, nothing." She sighed. "I'm looking forward to tomorrow night."

"Really? What are you doing?"

"Going to the dance with you, silly." She laughed, then looked at her phone, next to her on the swing. "We need to leave." She sprang to her feet and folded the wrinkled page in half. "Thanks for the sweet letter."

"Ya, sure. Can I drive you?"

"I have a meeting after school, so I'd better drive myself. But I'll see you there," she said before going into the house.

Chris got up and headed toward his car, muttering, "Dang,

of course, tomorrow's the dance!" He smacked his forehead with the palm of his hand. "Why am I always such a knucklehead? Why can't I talk or think around her?"

After Chris pulled away, I was about to head back to my shack but halted because the lovely Madeleine had returned to the porch swing and was talking to the air like I'd seen her do.

"Oh, Archs," she said softly. "Chris has true feelings for me, doesn't he? I felt his tenderness, and the bright pink light returned." She paused. "But I don't understand why the glow came from the tree over the porch and not around Chris's head like auras usually do."

It was me! I shouted in my head. *And those words that melted your heart came from mine.*

Tears ran down my grotesque face. As Anee had reminded me, I was half human, half monster, and this was the closest I would get to speaking to her. Blind rage boiled inside me, and I quickly clambered to my shed, shutting off any pink glow. Once inside, I flung my body against those constraining walls, crashing the rusty watering can with a large *clang!*

"Who's there?" Madeleine called out. "Archs, is that you? Hello?"

Then, I heard quick footsteps, the door to her car opened and shut, and she drove away.

I fell to the ground, tormented by my grief, my ugliness. I lay there as fever swept my body, unable to move. I didn't chase after Anee like I knew I should. Instead, I shivered, sweated, and hallucinated about *me* reciting the letter, my heart laid out for Madeleine's taking. And she surrendered hers to me.

WANIN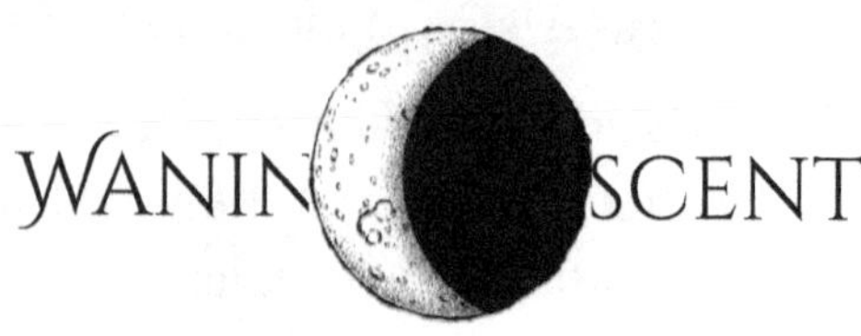SCENT

*"Rest and prepare for a new cycle by surrender-
ing to the flow of life while releasing bad feelings and
emotional pain."*

CHAPTER FIFTEEN

Madeleine - Day 21

39% Waning Crescent

Just when I'd convinced myself that Chris didn't care about me romantically, the day before the dance, he stopped by on the way to school with a letter. With words like: "*I melt into a blissful puddle of happiness in your presence,*" all dressed up and smelling of cologne, I was, as they say, over the moon.

We saw each other in the hall at school that day, and he said, "Hey, Maddy," followed by a cute wink that made my knees turn to jelly.

His tongue got tied up when Chris spoke to me, yet he wrote such a beautiful letter. I hoped he'd become more comfortable and talk like that to me in person over time.

I'd never told anyone, not even my closest girlfriends, that I can hear and see angels. Not even my parents. And The Arcs discouraged revealing my secret. Never having had a boyfriend, I wondered if someone was that close to me, could I hide it? Would they catch me speaking to what they would perceive as nothing and think I was crazy? Was it fair to keep such a big secret from my loved one? I knew I'd have to tell the man I married, but that was far down the road.

As a little girl, I could only speak aloud to them. But since I was ten, I learned to talk to them in my mind. "Arcs, please send me a guide," and with a bit of patience, one will appear. Sometimes, I ask for a certain one, like Michael or Ariel, but they send the one they feel I need at that particular time. Their messages come through to me like a stream of consciousness.

Every person on Earth has angels who constantly whisper guidance into their ears, but most people don't listen. Instead, they get tangled up in the negative influences of the human world and judge others based on looks, popularity, fortune, etc. These are the snags of humanity, not of nature's spirit. Religions may be different, but we are all humans with souls. I'm convinced there would be more peace and love between each other if humans slowed down and paid attention to what their angels are saying to them.

So, after Chris brought me the letter, I reread it several times and then posted it on my bulletin board over my desk, where I could always see it. An electric energy pulsed through me every time it caught my eye, like a force drawing me to its author.

Before falling asleep that night, I asked The Arcs, "Can I have a relationship with Chris while keeping you a secret?"

Archangel Uriel appeared, large and masculine, with a golden cloak that sparked sapphire blue with electricity along its edges. "You are pure of heart, Madeleine," he replied. "Your goodness will shine, and that is what is important."

It was true. I could never bring myself to lie, cheat, or steal. And besides, the Great Ones would know if I did.

"Arc Uriel, please tell me the truth. Are Chris's feelings genuine, or will he break my heart?"

"All I can say is you will encounter true passion at the dance tomorrow night. The magenta light will be your guide to find it." Then Uriel disappeared.

I closed my eyes and smiled, placing both hands over my heart. It seemed my dream of finding love was coming true.

CHAPTER SIXTEEN

Ryon: Day 20

28% Waning Crescent

In between deep fits of feverish sleep, I watched Madeleine's car pull out of the driveway in the morning and into the driveway after school. My hose bed was a tangle from tossing and turning, so I got up, straightened it, and then recoiled it, my muscles and sores aching. I kept busy organizing the shack while waiting for Chris to pick Madeleine up for the dance.

At around 6 p.m., the Mustang roared out front, and Chris belted, "Pour some sugar on me!" with an ear-shattering lack of melody. The car's engine stopped with a sputter, and I watched him walk to the house, spinning twice on the way to the door as though he were Fred Astaire. Wearing a black suit, red tie, and shiny brown shoes, his hair was molded with gel, and he held a clear plastic box, the sweet scent of freesias traveling to my nose.

Madeleine's mother answered the door, and Chris slipped inside. I heard compliments on what a good-looking couple they made, searing my heart. The minute the front door opened, everything moved in slow motion: Chris led Madeleine by one hand as she waved goodbye with the other, her shiny hair billowed as she glided like royalty in her purple dress, with bare shoulders smooth as alabaster, and a cluster of flowers swayed upon her wrist. Chris let go of her hand and headed toward the driver's side of his car, but his face registered a recollection, and he quickly went around to open the passenger door for her.

Both pride and envy swelled in me.

As he flitted back around to the driver's side, a red rose boutonniere on his lapel, Chris's cell phone rang. "Hello? Yes, we're leaving now." Then, he whispered, "She looks amazing, dude!" and hung up.

And before they pulled away in a puff of dust, he gave her a quick peck on the cheek. That image bore into my mind, making me ill.

What else did I expect? I encouraged this. But it ate me up inside.

I went mad, picturing Chris and Madeleine embracing, laughing, and kissing at the dance. I paced the dirt floor of my shed, growling and fretting, until around 8 p.m., when I couldn't take it anymore. I scrambled out the window and up to the treetops, breaking my rule of not going out until midnight. Luckily, the moon was a sliver, barely giving off light. I heard a raucous in the distance—the chatter of teenagers and loud music. As I climbed further into the boughs, the strong scent of fresh flowers, clove cigarettes, alcohol, and hairspray assaulted my nose.

There it was, my old roost, the Gascony Theatre.

Scaffolding and dangling ropes still covered the outside, but alongside them were limos and small buses carrying noisy teenagers.

I went as close as possible through a row of large maple trees, and then I leaped onto an itchy cedar, where I huddled and imperceptibly watched. The parade of swishing chiffon dresses, clicking high heels, and loud, fist-bumping young men carried on for quite a while before most were inside. I didn't spot Madeleine but saw the Mustang parked around the back.

The tall building was extremely familiar, yet I'd never seen the inside. All I knew was it had a stage from which actors' voices echoed while performing plays and a screen for showing movies. I considered returning to my shed—I could easily get caught with so many people around. But, as screenwriters and playwrights had taught me so many things as a stone grotesque, the best plots happened when someone took a risk.

So, once most of the teens were inside, I took a giant leap from that cedar, flying part of the way across the wide street to a deck of scaffold planks set up on metal braces. Then, I scaled the outer bricks of the theater, searching for a way in. At the very top was a row of windows, so I climbed up and tested each one, constantly looking over my shoulder to make sure no human saw me. Finally, I found one that opened and stuck my condor head inside.

Thick, burgundy velvet drapes cascaded down on either side of the stage below. Beyond them, the students and chaperones twinkled with sequins and shiny cufflinks. Ten feet away was a wooden bridge that stretched high above the stage, so I folded my wings down tight, squeezed my body through the window frame, sprang, and landed on it. The music was so loud that no one heard the thud of my feet.

It reminded me of being made of granite as I watched the young people laugh, cheer, and dance. I saw couples hide in dark corners, whispering with faces nearly touching, and teachers shooing them out when caught. I looked all over for Madeleine and Chris.

My heart was beating rapidly. *I wish I were a boy with my girl down there.*

Then there they were, Madeleine and Chris, on the dance floor, bopping around to the booming music. I tried to extract her laugh from the din and watched as she threw her lovely head back, a joyful, glowing smile on her beautiful face.

I wished I were close enough to smell her perfume, be near her. Chris was a good guy, but my jealousy was not easily controlled, especially being part beast. All I could do was stay on that catwalk, full of anxiety and gritting my teeth, watching.

Suddenly, the music stopped, and a matronly chaperone in a light blue dress stepped up to the microphone center stage. "Now, for the crowning of your Spring King and Queen!" she announced.

The crowd cheered wildly.

"Drum roll, please."

Two young men in blue suits appeared from the wings, each with a large bass drum at waist level and strapped over their shoulders, drumming so rapidly their hands were blurs.

"Gascony High School's Spring King is. . . Antoine Thomas!"

Cheers ensued as a dapper bloke arrived on stage. He bent over at his waist, and the woman placed a metallic gold crown on his curly blond head.

"And the new Gascony High School's Spring Queen is..." the drummers' fast cadence began again, "... Maddy Robin!"

The world stood still as Madeleine approached the stage— of course, she was their queen! I didn't hear the cheering, see the crowd mash together in a frenzy, nor see Chris's smile, which undoubtedly happened. All I saw was a glowing angel of light drifting across the lacquered floor to accept her crown. A large bouquet of red roses was placed in her arms, and she waved to her subjects, more divine than any movie star I'd imagined.

Without thinking, I dashed to the end of the catwalk and slid down a rope, landing gently on the floor backstage. Then, I crept behind a stage curtain and quickly wrapped myself inside its lush velvet, with an opening just enough to see out. There she was, less than 20 feet away.

"Madeleine!" I called. The applause was ending, and the music was starting again. "Madeleine!"

She turned toward me, her head cocked to the side. "Chris?" The crown glistened in the lights as she came closer.

"Yes, it's me," I lied, turning on my pink emotional thread.

She smiled and walked more quickly. "Where are you?" Her eyes searched the area. "It's so dark back here. I can't…"

I gently pulled her into me with one arm, carefully keeping all but my hand covered in the ruby drape. She screamed in surprise.

"Congratulations, my queen," I whispered, holding her closer to my body. The sweet smell of her hair made me light-headed.

"You scared me to death, silly," she giggled. "And you're crushing my roses." She adjusted the bouquet that was still in her arms.

"You looked so beautiful on that stage, I can't help myself… You know I get all tongue-tied when I see you in the light. I want to whisper words to you in the dark."

I felt her body relax. "Okay…I'm game."

I freed my other hand from the fabric and wrapped my arms around her waist, keeping covered. "I love holding you. Your beauty awes me more than the aurora borealis, and your kindness and intelligence sparkle like a many-faceted diamond." I nuzzled her a little on her neck, my face wrapped in fabric, and I felt her lean in. "You mesmerize me."

I was sure she could feel my heart throbbing through the velvet.

She dropped the roses at her feet and stroked the soft curtain. "You're so sweet…" Then, she reached both arms around my waist on the outside of the curtains. I feared she might feel my wings, so I tucked them in tight, but I knew I was good when she moaned softly.

"The things you're saying are so sweet," she whispered. "You radiate adoration for me. I can see it, feel it."

I didn't move or speak for a bit, trying to make the moment last.

Then, she asked, "Chris, will you kiss me?"

I compulsively drew back enough curtain to poke the bottom of my face through, drawing her deeper into the darkness by the waist, tilting my head back to make sure my large beak didn't interfere. I kissed her mouth with my human lips, long and tenderly, passion building so quickly that the nails upon my dragon feet sprang into daggers and pierced the tops of her delicate feet.

"Ow!" She jumped back, and I let go. I could smell her blood.

I pulled the curtains in tight around me and shut off my pink light. *I've hurt her! I'm a monster!*

I scrambled up the thick fabric until I reached a wall, slipped behind some scenery, and moved quickly back to the dark catwalk. I was horrified seeing her staring at the tops of her bloody feet.

"I must have cut myself on some nails or something," she said, flinging back the curtains. "Let's get out of…Chris? Where did you go? Chris?" she called while picking up her roses, searching left and right. "Chris?"

"Right here," the real Chris said, coming up from behind her. "I've been looking all over for you."

"Yeah, right!" she said. "You were right here…"

"I don't know what you're talking about."

"But you…the curtain…" She bit her bottom lip.

"I want to dance with the Spring Queen, so what do you say?" he said, flashing her a goofy smile that reminded me of a cartoon character.

Her eyebrows were knitted together as she asked, "How did this happen? I'm new here. No one knows who I am, really. How did I get voted Spring Queen?"

"I may have campaigned a little for you," he replied. "I wanted tonight to be special."

"You are the sweetest, aren't you?" She touched one delicate hand to his cheek. "I definitely want that dance, but mind if I wash up first?" She nodded toward her feet, which were trickling blood.

"OMG, what happened?"

"I scratched them on some scenery or something…" She rubbed her chin with one hand, still contemplating what had happened. "I'm fine."

"Oh, this is my favorite song!" He offered her his arm. "What's a little blood?"

Madeleine tilted her head and was about to speak, but Chris grabbed her hand and dragged her away. She glanced upward at my exact location, and I leaned even more into the shadows. Then, they melded into the crowd as I realized what had just happened—I had kissed Madeleine!

I sailed up the wall and out the window, floating from limb to limb back to my shed as if love had relinquished gravity's hold on me. I felt I might drift up to the sliver of moon that grinned its sideways smile in the sky. Her scintillating scent, glorious hair, how she felt in my arms, how her hands held me, the alluring quality of her lyrical voice, and every nuance of our kiss were embedded in my memory.

I'd only been inside my shed a short time before the Mustang returned. Chris and Madeleine got out and walked to the door in silence, the engine idling in the background. The energy between them had changed.

"Thanks again," she said quietly, her eyes shimmering in the porch light. "Goodnight." She went inside with her crown and flowers, closing the door behind her.

Chris returned to his car, sitting there with his window rolled down as it idled. Then, Madeleine's porch light went out, and he shook his head.

The town clock struck one, and then I heard him call out into the night, "Please show up tomorrow at midnight, Conscience. I need your help." Then he peeled out into the night.

CHAPTER SEVENTEEN

Ryon - Day 19

18% Waning Crescent

Guilt rattled me for not returning to the rooftop lair as Anee wanted, but it was clear I had to help Chris. It was pleasantly warm outside as I gobbled six squashed apple pies from the market trash, still giddy about kissing the girl of my dreams. I was blissful when I reached the tree outside the park.

Chris was not.

"Conscience, where are you?" He paced, looking up into the trees. "You're making me look like a total jerk out here in the dark," he whispered harshly. "I'm trying to conjure you up, but I can't." He contorted his face and grunted, looking more like a monster than I did.

I watched for a minute, laughing, then took pity on him. "Hello, Chris. Sorry to keep you waiting."

He scowled. "Why can I only conjure you around midnight? I've tried other times, like during the day at school or in the morning, and you don't come."

I took a beat to gather my reply. "Midnight marks a magic moment. It's the limbo time between yesterday and today, like when you're not quite awake and not quite asleep, and a liminal consciousness takes over. That's when your deepest thoughts surface," I said. I'd become good at making up stuff. "Remember what time it was the first time we met?"

"Hmm." He furrowed his brows. "Around midnight?"

"Exactly. Now, tell me why you're so upset."

Chris closed his eyes and held his breath.

"What are you doing?" I asked.

"I'm showing you everything that went wrong at the dance. Since you're my conscience, you can see in my mind, right?"

"Right…well, in a nutshell, you struggled to talk to Madel… ah, Maddy, and the night didn't quite go how you planned."

Chris opened his eyes and grinned slightly. "So, you also saw how she said I was different after some kiss," he continued, "but I didn't kiss her. I wanted to…" He flushed red. "She also said I didn't have a glowing "oh-rah" anymore, whatever that means…"

"Right. I saw that, too," I fabricated. "And, by the way, it's called an aura."

"What's that?"

"Let's just call it the light of love."

He tilted his head and pursed his lips. "So, what should I do next? I need to get that light back." He closed his eyes again. "Don't tell me." He touched an index finger to each of his temples in deep concentration. "I've got it! We sing her a song this time." He opened one eye and waited for my reply.

"Can you sing?" I asked.

"I'm terrible at singing."

"Then, no."

Chris closed his eyes again, fingers still pressing either side of his head. "Okay, let me think." It was silent momentarily, except for the sound of the nearby creek gurgling in the distance. "I know! How about I go to McDonald's and get her a large order of fries, hand them to her, and say, "Fry like you, a supersized amount." He opened both eyes and smiled at the sky, dropping his hands. "Get it? "Fry" sounds like "I"… supersized…"

"Although that's an excellent idea," I cleared my throat, "we have an even better one."

"We do?"

"Yes, you're going to tell her how you feel."

"I can't *talk* around her. My mind gets all goopy, and my tongue starts spazzing out." He shook his head with gusto. "No way."

"But what if I go with you? I'll tell you what to say. You just repeat after me."

Chris grinned and nodded. "I think I could do that. But does that mean I have to say all kinds of mushy stuff?"

"You do if you want to win the girl."

Chris sighed. "I do. I really do."

"Then, let's go now."

"Now? Seriously?" Chris rubbed his hands down both pant legs. "It's kinda late."

"No time like the present." My head was filled with words I wanted to say to her ever since the kiss. "Waking her to share your feelings is romantic."

"Okay, if you say so," Chris replied, then pressed his lips together.

Chris traveled along the sidewalk, and I followed in the trees above, the chirping of crickets and cicadas cheering us on.

Halfway there, Chris checked in. "You still there?"

"Yes," I called back.

Once we arrived at our destination, Chris stopped behind Madeleine's dented car and spoke to the sky. "Now what?"

"We must sneak around to her bedroom window," I called from a tree ten feet away.

"Ah, gotcha!" he said way too loudly.

"*Shhh!* We don't want to wake her parents up."

Chris nodded and tiptoed along one side of the wooden house until he was just below Madeleine's window. Although it was a one-story house, the window was two feet above Chris' head. I moved to a large, leafy limb several feet behind his head.

"Now, gently toss a few pebbles at the glass to get her attention," I whispered.

Chris gathered a few small stones from the ground and tossed each one, *tap, tap, tap!*

A light inside the room turned on, the sheer curtains opened, and a sleepy-faced Madeleine appeared on the other side of the glass. Her mussed hair looked like a shimmering veil. She took my breath away.

Chris jumped up and down, waving his arms overhead like a fool. She threw open the sash.

"What are you doing here, Chris?" Madeleine asked in hushed tones.

Chris whispered, "What do I say?"

"Huh?" asked Madeleine, the sweetness of her voice like spun sugar.

"Tell her, "I'm trying to find the right words to express how I feel!"" I muttered back.

"I'm trying to blind the night birds to express how I feel!" Chris announced. "Blind the night birds?" he mumbled.

"Okay..." Madeleine replied slowly.

A fiery spark of frustration ignited in me. "No, no!" I hissed. "Say, "I've come to express my feelings!""

"I've come to press some ceilings," he exclaimed. "No, that's not what I mean..."

"I think you're a little nervous," she said with a small laugh. "But I find it sweet."

I tried again. "No, you're the sweet one—as sweet as honey," I said quietly to Chris.

"No, you're sweeter than a bunch of money," he announced proudly.

I shook my head.

"Have you been drinking, Chris?" she asked.

"If I'm drunk, it's only from love," I whispered.

Then, Chris said, "If I'm drunk, it's 'cause you're above."

"Well, why don't I come down there then?" she asked. "Then, we can talk."

"No, please stay there, and let me woo you like *Romeo and Juliet*," I roared.

"Hey, I'm the one talking," Chris grumbled.

"Well, I'm taking over," I snarled.

"Who are you talking to?" Madeleine queried. "Is someone else out there?" She stuck her head out the window, looked around, and I dipped into the shadows.

Then, I took the stage. "Allow my voice to travel upon the air to your ears on this lovely evening."

"Aw, your lovely words have returned, Chris." She giggled. "But you sound different."

"Yes, protected by the night, my romantic side can speak."

"Okay," she said with a happy exhale, leaning her elbows upon the sill. "I'll just listen."

"I knew you were special the moment I first saw you. The heavens obviously celebrate you from how the light dances in your eyes. I dream about you all the time. When a bell chimes, it echoes your name, and every love song is about you. I fear my heart may burst with so much joy."

"Chris, you're kind to say such things. I care about you, too," Madeleine purred, making my heart leap. "And your aura has returned, but…"

"A kiss!" Chris blurted.

"What?" I whispered gruffly.

"I want to kiss her now," he said between his teeth.

Madeleine replied, "It's funny to ask for a kiss like that."

"I got carried away," I said. "I'm so sorry."

"No, I'm not," Chris said, hands on hips.

"Are you arguing with… yourself now?" she asked, her lovely eyes wide.

"Yes, I guess I am," Chris replied.

Then, a knock came from an outlying door. "Maddy, who are you on the phone with at this late hour?" a voice from inside said.

Madeleine glanced over her shoulder. "Oh, I have to go." Then, she called out, "Sorry, Mom. I'm going to bed now." She whispered, "Chris, thanks for coming by. Let's talk at school, okay?" Quickly, she eased her window shut and pulled the curtains closed.

I was ecstatic. I got to speak my heart to the loveliest girl on Earth. This was something I'd always wanted and the closest I'd felt to being human.

"That went pretty well, aside from not getting my kiss," Chris said. "Pretty amazing how I talked to her with my conscience like that." He grinned from ear to ear. "Hey, Conscience, are you still there?"

"Yes, I'm here."

"I'll let you know when I need you again."

"It's best to stand in front of Madeleine's house to do your conjuring, okay?" I replied. "It's where you have the most mojo."

"That makes sense." He nodded a few times. "And can I just call you "C." for short?"

"I'm *your* conscience, so, of course. Bye, for now," I replied, heading back through the trees toward my shack, exhilarated.

I heard Chris walk toward the park entrance, letting out a "Yahoo!" that started several dogs barking.

Once settled on my hose nest in my shed, I recited:

"Euphoric fervor in me began

The moment I first kissed Madeleine.

Even a monster can make a plan,

With the help of a gullible gentleman,

To woo the girl like an artisan,

And not be seen as a bogeyman!"

I laughed at my silly rhyme as elation engulfed my heart.

CHAPTER EIGHTEEN

Madeleine - Day 19

18% Waning Crescent

Nature calms my soul. I love planting seeds and growing flowers for bees, bugs, birds, and fairies. Yes, fairies are as real as angels and are fierce protectors of the natural world. They love gifts like candy and shiny objects, and if you leave them goodies and respect nature, they'll help your garden grow. Sometimes, I call on the fairies when I need grounding.

So, after Chris came to my window, I sat beside the giant lilac bush blooming in my backyard that afternoon after school and asked the wee ones for guidance. A bright red cardinal flitted overhead on a branch covered with purple flowers, and its throaty song sounded like, "Seeee-air-ah!" I knew I needed to call my best friend in Hartstown. I took out my phone from my pocket and dialed.

"Hey, Maddy, how was the dance?" she asked immediately.

"That's why I'm calling. It didn't exactly go… well, you be the judge," I said. Then I told her about the pretty corsage he gave me, how we danced, and being crowned Spring Queen.

"Sounds like a magical night."

"It was, but right after I received my crown, Chris called me over to him before I walked off the stage. He was wrapped up in one of the stage curtains, then… he kissed me."

"Why was he in the curtain?"

"He said he could only show his true feelings if hidden." I sighed. "He gets nervous and can't talk to me otherwise."

"Honestly, I don't know if that's weird or romantic."

"The sweet words he said to me, and then the kiss, were extremely hot."

"So, what's the problem?"

"He clammed up again the second we left the dance. He didn't talk, hold my hand, or even try to kiss me goodnight." *And the magenta light was gone*, I added in my head.

"Seems to me your relationship with Chris is up and down. You were good friends as lab partners, but then he acted weird the second he had romantic feelings. One minute, he brings his best friend on your date, and the next, he's kissing you in the curtains."

"Yes, I go between really liking him and feeling awkward and confused."

"Maybe you need to take a paper grocery bag with you on your next date. He can wear it so he can't see you and maybe act normal," she snickered.

I laughed. "I can draw two eyes and a nose on it."

"And cut a big hole in the mouth for kissing."

We giggled like when we were ten.

"But there's more. He showed up last night, after midnight, throwing rocks at my bedroom window, and said weird stuff at first." I sighed. "It's strange, but it didn't sound like his voice when he finally got his words together."

"And boys say *girls* are hard to figure out," she grumbled.

My heart was lighter when we hung up—the fairies steered me right. I realized that girlfriends were everything when it came to life's journey. I just needed to ride out the relationship a little longer and see if he could relax around me. And if not, I'd know it was time to end things. Besides, summer vacation was less than two weeks away, which was time for fun before he went to college in the fall.

But is it better to end it before we get attached?

The wind picked up wickedly as I pondered, blowing dark, foreboding clouds overhead. Thunder rumbled angrily in the distance, and I heard a spirit guide's voice: "Take shelter, for something ominous comes. We will shield you but stay inside until morning."

I'd never been warned about a thunderstorm before, but something told me it was more than that. Maybe those thugs who hurt my car were returning? What did they want? Was I in danger?

CHAPTER NINETEEN

Ryon - Day 18

10% Waning Crescent

A storm came out of nowhere, and the thunder and pounding rain kept me from falling asleep. Late into the night, I was jolted by a large thud upon the shack roof.

I opened the window and climbed outside. Above me was the familiar dark silhouette of a giant beast. My extremities tingled—Geidhuce was back. I always backed down when we were in stone, but after becoming a living monster born of a scaly dragon and a feathered bird of prey, I'd become inexplicably bold. I flew up to the roof's edge as he stepped out of the shadows, eyes glinting with rage through the sheets of falling rain.

I made my thread calm and steady. *Let's talk, like gentlemen.*

He lunged, stopping inches in front of me. *Hooooooos!*

I stood my ground and took a deep breath, determined to keep my head this time, unlike Vervalt's visit. *Please, Geidhuce. There's no need to fight.*

Flecks of burning ember blazed in his canine eyes. *You left the pack, defied my orders, and I'm sure you killed Vervalt!* Fire sparked from his wolf nostrils, his giant chest heaving in and out.

I retracted from his hot breath. *Come inside and out of the rain.* I pointed toward the shack below us.

I decide what happens from here on out, not you! he roared, his threads fiery red.

My heart pounded in my ears, and my beastly anger took over. *I don't take orders from you. Cletas was our leader.*

I'm your leader now! The pack has chosen me! The claws on his giant wolf paws extended into daggers.

You inserted yourself, and now that we're alive, our rules when we were stone no longer apply. Adrenaline pulsed through my body. *And as for Vervalt, I tried to reason with him, but he came to kill Madeleine.*

Geidhuce smiled wickedly. *Well then, Ryon, you have two choices.*

Choices? I stayed poised for an attack.

Geidhuce lowered his wings, tucking them along his back. *If you come with me now, the girl lives to continue her pathetically human life. Or, stay here, and you can have total freedom. However, she'll be dead before the light of day.*

Neither choice is an option.

Face it, I'm stronger than you and certainly stronger than the girl. With my lupine hunting skills and dragon power, a bird-man will never beat me.

Grrowr!

Geidhuce continued mockingly: *Telber and Anee are gravely concerned about you here alone. Don't you want to be back with your dear friends?* Then, Geidhuce showed me a visionary thread of Telber and Anee huddling in the corner of the building rooftop, Isel bucking them with her horsey hindlegs.

Fury rumbling through my muscles, I rocked forward and back, ready to pounce.

Face it, he continued calmly. *Even Telber and Anee think you're an idiot for being away from us. There's safety in numbers, not solitude. It's what's best for everyone.* He nodded toward Madeleine's house.

I made sure my threading was black so he wouldn't know how I'd shared my emotions with her and shared a kiss. I'd risked so much to stay near and protect her. But I knew Geidhuce meant what he said. The world would be *unbearable* without her gracing it. He was her only threat, and if I returned to the rooftop with him, I could keep her safe.

I relaxed my stance in surrender. *Yes, Geidhuce, I see what you're saying.*

You made the right choice.

I nodded, my heart heavy with the idea of being unable to see her anymore or that silly boy, Chris. I knew I'd be letting him down, too.

The rain suddenly stopped, and Geidhuce shook his coat as wet dogs do. His thread turned to a contented green. *Looks like we can talk like gentlemen, after all.* He walked to the roof's edge. *Let's go.*

Just one thing. May I go inside the shed to get a letter I wrote to Madeleine? I want something to remember her by. My threads were purple with sadness.

Ah, this letter. I'm aware of it. Anee was heartbroken when she saw it but said it had been destroyed.

Yes, it hurt dear Anee to see it, but I rewrote it, and it's all I have left of my time here near Madeleine. A tear fell from my eye, tickling as it ran down my leathery face.

Being a magnanimous leader, I'll allow you to get it, but I'll go with you.

Geidhuce followed me down the siding to the shack window. He watched from outside as I grabbed a blank piece of yellow paper while threading to myself: *I hope he doesn't see that rope in the corner.*

Thanks for the idea. He grinned devilishly. *Get it.*

No! I dropped my head and sighed. *You were clear about what's at stake. Don't you trust me?*

I don't, so hand it over.

I blacked out my threading as I handed the scratchy coil to him, secretly slipping a pair of pruning shears into the folds of my leathery condor neck. Then, I climbed out the window and snugly closed it behind me.

He wrapped the rope around my waist, knotted it, and tied the other end around his middle. *We'll be able to climb, but anywhere I go, you'll go too.* He glanced at the folded yellow paper in my right hand and scoffed.

The night was dark with flares of light where the streetlights dimly glowed. He scaled the shack and leaped into the tree, leaving enough slack in the rope for me to do the same. We bounded at an even pace through the shadowy branches. Geidhuce looked over his shoulder every so often to make sure I was keeping up.

When we got to a giant maple tree close to Main Street, we could see the building where the gargoyle lair was across the way. Geidhuce stopped, studying the surroundings. *We must proceed with caution here. Once we leave this tree, there's a chance of being spotted. Those damn humans keep trimming the branches.*

And while he ranted and checked for humans, I quickly and quietly climbed up to a broad branch as high above him as I could go without yanking on the rope.

Okay, the coast is clear, but we must go swiftly. He turned around. *Ryon, where are you?* Geidhuce yanked on the rope, which was now taut, his eyes following it into the dense canopy. *Ryon, I command you to come back down!* He yanked again, but I held firm.

Then, like a wrecking ball, I swung toward Geidhuce, the rope draped over the large branch I'd been standing on. Slightly above him, I had the shears in hand and slashed his furred face, blood gushing from the gashes.

He held up his giant wolf paws and shrieked.

Momentum allowed me to swing back into the foliage, straight into pointy branches that scratched my tender human skin. Then down I went again, like a pendulum, toward that evil beast, the weight of my body lifting Geidhuce in the air. Dangling, he growled and writhed savagely. But I lost my velocity when I smacked into the tree trunk, landing next to him—two hideous monsters, dangling from each end of the rope.

Geidhuce beat me with his wings and scraped my fleshy chest with his canine paws. I fought back, pushing him away with my dragon feet as I used the pruning shears to cut the rope. Violent chaos ensued—whacking, jabbing, pounding—but after a few minutes, the rope finally snapped. I landed on a branch about four feet below me, clinging to it, trying to catch my breath.

But Geidhuce fell downward until I heard the thump of his body hit the ground.

My heart moved to my throat. I climbed through the branches to view Geidhuce's body on the grass, and a pool of blood was forming around his head.

Have I killed him, too? I studied his chest with my condor eyes—there was movement in his chest. I listened with my keen ears and heard the faintest thump of a heartbeat.

Dead or alive, I needed to move him so no humans would find his body.

Every inch of me ached as I climbed down and stood beside where Geidhuce lay. The blood continued to ooze from his head as I dragged him with the rope that was still around his waist toward some nearby hedges…

… and he suddenly bounded to his feet!

I held the shears high above my head, ready to strike. He stood there, malevolent as ever, uttering a most vicious version of, *"Hoooooos!"* Then, he quickly limped away behind the hedges.

I went after him but only saw a trail of blood leading to an abandoned gas station. I followed it, but it ended, and he was nowhere. I couldn't hear or smell him.

I'd brewed even more trouble by standing up to Geidhuce and wondered if I had made the wrong choice.

○　○　○

I was restless back in the dusty realm of my shack. Even the slightest sound made me jump. I tried to distract myself from the pain in my body from being beaten up by thinking about the feeling of Madeleine's sweet lips upon mine.

I needed a new plan. Whether Geidhuce was dead or alive, I was no longer safe in my shack, and Madeleine was in even more danger. So, I tossed around different scenarios, watching the sun come up through the hazy, dirty window. Then, I was struck by the truth: I was the only one who could stop him. Isel supported him, Anee and Telber were too afraid, and we were the only ones who even knew the danger lurking in the town of Gascony.

Well, I'd rather die trying than die giving up, so if I have to, I'll defeat one hundred men!

A distant rooster sang its version of Reveille, and I heard footsteps and scrambled to my peephole. Madeleine was walking slowly and plaintively across her front lawn, coming closer and closer, making a beeline for my shed.

I frantically looked around for a place to hide, darting beneath a dirty, blue tarp, covering myself and tucking in my tail. Then, I turned off my threading color. *Think ink, not pink.*

I held my breath as she spoke out loud, her voice incredibly close by. "Hey, Arcs. I didn't sleep very well last night, so I came to talk to you, away from the house, near where I often see the pink light. Archangel Uriel, since you're so good with decisions, I need help. I have a last-minute opportunity as an intern at *The Dallas Morning News*, which is exciting since I love words, but it's partly remote, partly in-person. I'd be leaving early tomorrow morning to stay with my sweet Grandy and Grampy for the whole summer, who live about an hour outside Dallas."

Dallas sounded far away, and my heart felt ripped from my chest.

"I'd book the 6 a.m. flight, and my teachers said they'd let me finish the year remotely." She sighed loudly. "But what about Chris? Should I leave just as things are starting?" She paused. "The new moon is the day after tomorrow, a time for fresh starts, but is the job or this relationship what I should focus on? Please help, Arc Uriel. Any sign will do."

Then, I heard nothing but her breath.

I peeked from beneath the corner of the tarp. Her hands were pressed against the dirty window's glass. I could tell her head was down.

I crawled out from beneath my cover, hoping she couldn't hear the crinkly sound it made, and slithered along the ground, crouching below the window.

It's me you feel and my glow you see! I threaded, turning back on the bright pink. *Please don't leave! How will I make it without you?*

Then, risky as it was, I kept my body low and reached up, pressing my hands to hers on the other side of the glass. I could feel energy crackle through my fingers and palms.

A mystical voice whispered, "The road ahead may be long and winding, but it'll bring you safely back to love."

"Oh!" she said.

Oh! I threaded at the same time.

It was a message for us both.

CHAPTER TWENTY

Madeleine - Day 17

4% Waning Crescent

Touching an angel's hand feels different than a human's. Sparks ignite, but they aren't electrical or painful—they're soothing and full of magic. I felt that *zing!* the day I went out to the shed, where I often saw the magenta light. Sometimes, I saw it when Chris was around, but other times, it was there like a beacon of its own. Perhaps a spirit was trying to guide me toward love, and I wasn't understanding how.

That comforting "angel spark" radiated as I spoke to Arc Uriel, my hands against the windowpane, filling me with a tingling adoration that warmed me from head to toe. Then the words, "The road ahead may be long and winding, but it'll bring you safely back to love," echoed in my head. Was the message from Arc Uriel or another divine being? I wasn't sure. All I knew was that no matter what, I should trust that my heart would find its way. So, I needed to take the internship. Staying for love made no sense—it would find me when the time was right.

"Mom!" I called once I got back to the house. "I decided to go."

She entered the front room from the kitchen, a spatula covered with frosting in her hand. "And I just baked your favorite… angel food cake with lemon buttercream. Thought it might ease your mind as you decided, but…"

"That's so nice. Can I take some with me on the plane tomorrow?"

"Absolutely." She handed me the spatula to lick. "I'll go pay for that plane ticket on hold." She disappeared into the small office to the right of the front door.

The frosting was tangy and sweet, and I licked the spatula clean on my way to the kitchen, setting it in the sink. To my right, the glorious cake sat on a crystal, footed cake stand and smelled of sugar and sunny days. I had about 20 minutes before I needed to leave for school, realizing it would be the last day of my sophomore year. I dug my suitcase out from the back of the closet and laid it open on the bed, filling it with some folded clothes from my dresser.

My cell phone sat on the bedside table and caught my eye. The angels were prodding me to do the right thing. I sighed and picked it up, plopping down on the edge of my bed. Then I dialed.

Chris answered. "Hey, Maddy! What's up?"

"I've got some news." My heart ached a little. I knew he'd be disappointed.

"Okay."

"I got chosen for a summer internship."

"That's cool. Congrats. Where?"

"*The Dallas Morning News.*"

"It's remote, right?"

"That's the thing. It's 50-50. So, I'll stay with my grandparents who live just outside the city."

There was a long silence, then Chris finally said, "Well, we have a week before school is out, so at least…"

"I'm leaving right away. I got permission to finish school online… I'm sorry."

"Oh."

I could feel his dismay like a weight on my chest. "I'll be at school today, though. I don't leave until tomorrow morning, so if you want to stop by after school…"

"Yeah, uh, I'll come by."

"See you soon," I said, attempting to sound cheery.

After hanging up, I grabbed my backpack near the door and headed out without saying goodbye to my mom. As I descended the porch steps toward my car, I looked at the giant oak tree to my right. I ran over to it with arms outstretched, wrapping them around its enormous trunk.

Usually, angels console me when my soul aches. But sometimes the power that comes from a tree, its roots connected to the earth's energy, with limbs reaching high up to Heaven, gives me instant calmness. I let myself sink into its rough bark, listening to its leaves rustle a soothing "*Shhhhhhhhhhh!*"

CHAPTER TWENTY-ONE

Ryon - Day 17

4% Waning Crescent

The dark sky matched the asphalt street, and at midnight, there was the tiniest slice of moon, like the white of a fingernail. My moment with Madeleine, hands nearly touching, had renewed my spirit. Though I didn't want her to go, I realized that with her safely far away, I could finally leave my shack and take care of a few things before she returned at the end of summer.

I needed to know if Geidhuce was dead or alive, so I planned to go out that night. If he were living, I'd do as Anee requested, join the other gars to keep an eye on him. Madeleine, Telber, Anee, and the town of Gascony deserved that, even if I had to pretend to want to be there. And if he weren't alive, that would be much easier—we'd all live freely.

"Safe travels, Madeleine! I'll dream of you always and see you when you return," I said as I shut the shed window behind me and blew a kiss toward her house.

Then, I traveled through the branches until I reached the last tree across the street from the rooftop lair. Although my body was injured again, I was focused on my mission. I scrambled down the tree's trunk, bolted across the empty street, and slipped into the alley. I heard no threading nearby, figuring the gars were somewhere hunting. Feeling hungry, I sniffed out a large opossum, trapped it inside a nearby trash can, and enjoyed a delicious meal. I licked the blood on my hands clean behind an old, rusty car parked in the alley and waited.

After about half an hour, Telber arrived.

"Psst! Telber! Come here!" I whispered, careful to black out my threading so the others wouldn't hear.

He looked around quickly, finally spotting me, and cautiously approached, his equine eyes wide. "R-R-Ryon, is that you?" He let out a low bray, "Heehaw!"

"Yes." I smiled. "It's great to see you, dear friend."

He sprang over, patted me on the shoulder with his hoof, and grimaced. "G-G-Geidhuce will be back soon. H-h-he moves slowly right now, so he's way behind the rest of us."

"So, he's alive," I grumbled, not sure I was happy or disappointed. "Well, I'm here to rejoin the group."

"Y-Y-You wounded him pretty badly. I-I-I'm not so sure he'll let you."

"I'm gonna try to make amends."

"W-W-Why the sudden change of heart?"

I hated lying to Telber but knew it was in his best interest, so I sighed and dropped my shoulders. "Madeleine loves a human boy." I squeezed out a tear, it rolled down my face, and I wiped it with the back of my hand. "It's just too hard, seeing them together, knowing Madeleine will never love me. . ."

"Tah-dah, it's Ryon!" Anee ran up and thumped my chest with her long lioness tail. "What are you doing here?"

"I've come to ask for forgiveness." I bowed my head. "I've hurt all of you because of my stupidity."

"A-A-And Madeleine loves a human boy," Telber added, sending Anee a knowing, buck-toothed grin.

Anee swished her tail back and forth. "It's not going to be easy. Geidhuce is very angry with you…"

"Well, well, well." Geidhuce limped from the shadows, Isel holding him up, his face gashed in several places, scabs of dried blood covering both the fur and human skin of his body. One of his wolf eyes was swollen shut, and he stepped towards me with a limp. "You have a lot of nerve coming around here," he snarled.

I bowed at Geidhuce's feet. "I realized you're right. I belong with the pack." Those words tasted sour. "I want to come back."

"The prodigal son has returned, all full of humility and self-pity," Geidhuce said sarcastically. Then, he used his wolf paw to push my head firmly to the ground and held it there.

I didn't fight back. "Please, I realized living near Madeleine is a waste of time." I stayed still, waiting for a reply.

Geidhuce lifted his paw, and I slowly stood up. I caught lava-red glimpses of his threads, including a vision of my body hanging from a tree with a bloody rope around my neck. And between the horrific threads was a loud crackling noise like a radio out of tune.

"I understand," I said, bowing my head.

Then, he threaded what he wanted me to do for me to stay.

Pain shot through my heart like an arrow. "No!" I growled. The others saw it, too, and stepped back, gasping. "Geidhuce, anything but that!" I put my hands together in prayer. "Please!"

"If you cannot do that, there's no deal."

I looked at Anee. She dropped her head and stood perfectly still. *Do it,* she threaded, fighting the sad purpleness that tinged her thought.

"No, Anee, no!" I panicked.

"Do it or die, Ryonac! I have a new army of gargoyles behind me, and they will rip you limb from limb if I command it."

I was puzzled. "An army?"

Anee lifted her head, her lion eyes black and cold. She nodded.

"And I'd like to see Telber hold her so she can't move," Isel added, a hideous grin upon her equine mouth.

"If it pleases you, my lady," Geidhuce cooed. "Telber!"

Telber slinked forward with an emotional thread of fear-blue. His hooves shook as he held Anee's dragon wings and lioness arms back.

It'll be okay, Anee threaded, trying to turn it green to show contentment. *I'm tough.*

I thought about scurrying back into the trees and never returning, but too much was at stake. I double-checked that my threading was black.

I walked up to Anee, and with great force, I punched her in the face. Blood trickled down from her nose, sanguine against her beautiful golden fur. I kicked her in the stomach with my dragon leg, and my claws dug gashes into the scaly part of her body. Anee was silent, emotionless, but though she blacked out her threading, I swore I could feel her pain.

Isel clapped her front horse hooves together. "Ooh! This is fun! More, more!"

Telber continued to hold Anee, the pupils huge in his brown donkey eyes, and she didn't fight him. I struggled not to puke the opossum in my sorrow-twisted stomach.

"My darling wants another hit, it seems. I guess she's not quite convinced," Geidhuce said with a smirk, wrapping a wing around Isel's human torso and pulling her closer.

Taking a deep breath, I leaped onto Telber, shoving him to the side, his scaled body and furry hide skidding along the alley's concrete. I then took his place, pulling Anee's wings across one another with a hard yank.

Hearing Telber whimper, she let out a fierce roar, and I let go. Anee bounded away but then turned to face me, crouched as if ready to pounce, anger burning in her eyes.

"I'll destroy you, Ryon, if you continue!" she threatened through sharp teeth.

"Seems they may no longer be friends. Well, isn't that a pity." Geidhuce clucked his tongue. "What do you say, Isel, my love? Can Ryonac stay?"

"I don't trust that big-nosed monster," Isel replied, looking me up and down. "But he did beat up Anee *and* Telber." She winked at me.

"Ryon, you may stay, but if you do anything I don't like, there will be no warnings. You'll be killed," Geidhuce said matter-of-factly. "Now, all of you, to the roof." Then he slowly climbed up the building, wings barely flapping as Isel pushed him from behind.

Telber, Anee, and I watched them, thinking ink, and they finally reached the roof together and disappeared into the shadows.

"Anee, are you alright?" I asked, running to her side,

blood dripping from her wounds.

"I will be, Ryon." She began to sob. "I'm sorry he made you do that."

"Oh, please don't cry, sweet Anee! *I'm* sorry...I never expected he'd make me hurt you!" I turned to Telber, who was hobbling over to join us, his legs and arms with long bands of bloody, red patches. "And how are you, friend? I'm sorry you had to be part of my demonstration."

"I-I-It burns, but wounds heal. I'm just glad you're back with us," Telber said, flinching as he hovered toward the roof.

Anee and I slowly flew beside him. She began to cry even harder.

"Dearest, Anee! Does it hurt to move? Oh, I can't bear the pain I caused you!" I considered scrapping my plan altogether.

"Oh, Ryon, these are not tears of pain but joy. As Telber said, my aches will disappear, but I'm so happy you're with us again!"

I didn't deserve these two friends. They overlooked what I had inflicted and stayed loyal. Even after I'd chosen Madeleine over them. My heart melted.

○　○　○

It was strange to be back on that familiar rooftop, now cluttered with garbage and blankets. The Gascony Theater had become the desecrated centerpiece of that dingy, grey town. I lay beneath the stars, threading black, listening to the creek in the distance, the random cars that passed by, and an owl ominously hooting in a faraway tree. The sky was so wide it could swallow me whole.

I wished Geidhuce and Isel would sleep, but they were huddled together, whispering for hours. So, I sat with Anee and Telber on the far side of the rooftop, speaking quietly.

"Geidhuce *is* gathering an army," Anee began, worry in her big, gold lioness eyes. "He and Isel met with an underground group of *other* gargoyles and grotesques. Apparently, we aren't the only ones Monsieur made, and several others have come to life after removal."

"Seriously?" A chill ran through my body.

Anee nodded. "Incredible, right? They call themselves The Chimeras. They all plan to come here, take over the theater as their headquarters, and kill anyone who tries to stop them."

She leaned in closer. "But, since you beat him up, he can't control his thoughts fully," Anee added. "Did you notice how his mental thread has become static-ish?"

I nodded.

Then, Telber began to shake uncontrollably.

"What is it?" I asked.

Anee stroked his mule mane with her large paw. "It's alright, Telber." His large donkey head dropped, and she soothed him by chuffing gentle breaths. "Geidhuce has made Telber his note-taker."

"H-h-have you ever tried to write with your mouth?" Telber held out his two front hooves.

"Geidhuce strikes poor Telber if he doesn't write fast enough." I could feel Anee's angst.

"I'm so sorry, Telber." I dug my scaly feet into the rough rooftop, guilt-ridden for leaving them to deal with abuse.

"Telber's appointment as scribe has become more intense as Geidhuce struggles to keep the facts straight…" Anee added, keeping her paw on Telber's back. "He's forcing us to become thieves. He sends us out in the dark of night to grab items he wants: food from the Quality Market delivery trucks, blankets from the Amish carriages parked outside town stores, and even paper and pens from the Five & Dime for creating Geidhuce's notes and maps."

"You could easily get caught."

"We've been lucky so far, but you're right." Anee sighed.

The town clock chimed 4 a.m.

She'll be heading to the airport soon, I thought, still blacking my threading.

Anee leaned back on her fuzzy elbows. "The Chimeras discovered a secret passage that runs beneath the theater to city hall and a cave. It was part of the Underground Railroad used in the 1850s to ferry enslaved people from the South…"

Geidhuce and Isel rose, and we froze. They left the rooftop without a word, stumbling over the side like a geriatric and his keeper.

"I need to follow them," I announced, panicked. "Geidhuce threatened to kill Madeleine. I need to be sure she's okay."

Anee and Telber's eyes got as big as dinner plates, and the scales on my back prickled—

Geidhuce and Isel were standing right behind us.

"Well, aren't we all chummy again?" Geidhuce leaned down toward me, his hot breath on my beak. "Seems we need another reminder of who's in charge."

Isel locked my head in her horsey arms, squeezing tighter.

My body was already in pain, and she was making it worse.

I tried not to struggle. "This is unnecessary," I said, feeling the blood pulse through my veins. "I'll do whatever you say, Geidhuce."

"Liar!" hissed Isel, yanking me by the throat. "We heard your concern for that human girl. You never planned to stay with the pack."

"Telber, come!" Geidhuce commanded. "I want you to gather the chains and restrain him. Be sure they're nice and tight."

Telber shook as he gathered the metal links piled near a vent poking out of the roof. They clattered in his trembling hands, and the blackness of his pupils reached the edges of his eyes.

"Don't make him do this, Geidhuce," I begged. "My place is with all of you."

Geidhuce grabbed me by my shoulders as Isel released her grip, and he dragged me toward the corner. They both shoved me hard against the brick siding where four large, metal eyelets poked out of the cement, two over my head and two near my feet, with open padlocks hanging in each one.

"Anee and Telber, lock him up!" Geidhuce yelled.

I'm sorry, Ryon! So very sorry! Anee threaded in streaks of blue and purple. She fumbled with the heavy metal as Telber wrapped one end firmly around my wrist.

And just then, a voice boomed from the ground below, "What's going on up there?"

A human! I threaded in cobalt.

We dropped to the floor, allowing me to shed the chain. I crawled across the roof toward the alley side of the building.

Isel grabbed my leg, and I dragged her with me as Geidhuce lunged, landing on top of me with a moan. I fought with all I had to deflect the blows Geidhuce rained upon my body. The grit of the roof scraped my tender skin, and Isel dug her nails into my scaly foot. I managed to smack Geidhuce hard between his eyes with my elbow, and he became dazed, letting go. Anee came up behind Isel with a thick piece of wood, hitting hard on her back, and she released my leg.

Again, we heard a human talking beside our building. "I can hear scuffling up there. Maybe some animals." The others froze, but I continued to inch toward the building's edge.

"That building's been empty a while now. No telling what lives in it," replied another human.

"But I would have sworn I heard someone talking…"

"Maybe it was an echo from the bar deck across the street."

"Yeah, you're probably right." The humans started walking away, feet crunching the gravel street.

I finally reached the ledge, stopped, and looked back. Anee was crying, a broken two-by-four at her lioness paws. Telber was gesturing for me to keep on going, and Isel was still reeling in pain in the middle of the roof.

But where is Geidhuce?

And in a flash, I saw him.

He came running, low, like a wolf on the plains, and slammed into me.

I plummeted backward off the building, free-falling. I unfurled my wings but couldn't catch the air. Panic halted my ability to think ink, so memories passed through my head: awakening in the crate full of paper shreds, breaking free from its splintery confines, feeling grass between my toes, making home in the dusty shed, talking to gullible Chris… the last thing I remembered was Madeline's glowing smile before I hit the ground.

CHAPTER TWENTY-TWO

Ryon - Day 16

1% Waning Crescent

It's strange how a living body reacts to trauma. You think every sensation will be amplified, but sometimes it's the opposite. Impact can be silent and peaceful, your body numbed by shock— and it's beautiful in a way, your mind in a space of nothingness. It's afterward, if you survive, when you hurt.

I woke with Anee leaning over me, her beautiful golden fur glinting in the sun, alive and vivid, making me smile. "Oh, Ryon, I'm so happy you're conscious!" she purred, wiping my forehead with a cool, damp cloth.

"Where am I? What happened?" My vision was blurry but coming back into focus.

"It was terrible," was all she said. Then, silence lay heavy in the air, and I felt an ache in my chest with each breath.

I tried to sit up, but my back was stabbed with pain.

"Stay still, Ryon," Anee insisted, helping me lie back down. "What do you last remember?"

"Falling into a perpetual abyss. And then, darkness."

Anee inhaled deeply. "Geidhuce pushed you off the building lair. You fell and . . ." Her pupils replaced nearly all the gold with black. "Well, Geidhuce hasn't been right since you two fought a couple of days ago, and this time, you slammed him in the head and rattled his mind even more. Isel was bleeding, so while they were preoccupied with their issues, I was able to get us away. I brought you to this abandoned house in the hills above Gascony."

My surroundings came more into focus. I was on a hardwood floor, looking at a white plastered ceiling with spiderweb-like cracks. The room smelled of fireplace ash and mildew. Light shone through two windows opaque with dirt, each divided into smaller square panes. The space was dusty and small, but cozy.

"I appreciate your help, Anee, but you must return immediately—they'll be searching for you. How long has it been?"

"A little over 18 hours."

"That's too long."

"I'm just glad that you're…" Anee's voice cracked, and she closed her eyes. "I thought you might never wake up."

"Dearest Anee, you saved me. I'm forever grateful. But you need to save yourself by going back."

"No, I won't go back!" she snapped. "I'm staying here with you." Then she sent a rose-colored thread, *I love you!*

I gulped. "I love you, too. You're a wonderful friend. More wonderful than I deserve . . ." I reached out and weakly touched her soft, furry face.

"No, Ryon. I *love* you. I always have. You're the one I dream of at night. I fight back threads of love to keep you from hearing them, but I'm tired of holding it in. I thought I'd lost you, and while you were unconscious, all I did was regret never telling you how I felt. You're kind, smart, and strong." She stroked my shoulder with a gentle paw, and then she kissed me below my beak nose, her soft lioness mouth upon my human lips. "Humans see you as a monster, but you're the most handsome, perfect creature to me."

I studied her beautiful face, full of light and hope. I should have loved her back. I tried to make myself, but images of Madeleine loomed in my head. I tried to think ink so Anee wouldn't see, but it wasn't easy. I was weak.

"You're truly wonderful, and you mean so much to me," was all I could say. It was true—but the electricity I had kissing Madeleine wasn't there.

Anee smiled as she reached for a mason jar full of water and gently lifted my head, putting it to my lips to drink. Then, she set the jar down and presented me with a white, chipped China bowl overflowing with plump blackberries.

"I'll go and catch you a bird or rodent in a minute, but this will give you something in your stomach," she whispered, popping a juicy berry into my mouth. Then, she dipped her head slightly. "What do you see in... her?"

I gulped. "Anee, I wish I could control my feelings. I wish my heart would love you and not her. I truly do!"

She stood like she was about to leave, the bowl of berries beside me on the floor. "Anee, please understand..."

"I don't care," she announced, akimbo.

"What?"

"I don't care. The uncontrollable love you feel for that human girl is the same as what I have for you, so I get it. The thing is, I'm here, and she's not." A smile returned to her face.

"Besides, you're smart. One day, you'll realize that the one you should be with was here all along."

I was speechless.

"I'm going to hunt for something yummy-ish." Anee walked to the door leading outside, stopped, and turned to face me. "Let's not keep secrets, okay, Ryon? You know mine now, and I stand behind you no matter what. Let's not hide anything from each other anymore."

I smiled at her. She demonstrated unconditional love, more precious than gold.

"And what about Telber?" I asked, changing the subject.

"Oh, we're just friends," she replied, smiling coyly.

I laughed, but pain shot down my legs. "I know. I mean, is he still there with Geidhuce and Isel?"

"I had to leave him there. He's terrified to leave, Ryon. I asked him to come with me, to help you, but he wouldn't … He's not as strong as we are. Geidhuce has really messed with his head. There's no doubt Telber cares deeply for us both, but he chooses safety over friendship. We need a plan for me, Telber, and you to live free from Geidhuce and Isel.".

"Yes," I replied, but I repressed the truth. My heart had a different plan.

Anee left to hunt, and the house was silent aside from crows cawing nearby. With intermittent shots of pain, I managed to pull myself up on my elbows to finish the delicious berries. I took inventory of my injuries: my scaled legs were full of bloody gashes, I had road rash all over my human skin from being dragged along the scratchy roof tile, but my wings hurt the most. They must have caught my fall, and I could barely move them without the feeling of knives piercing my back. I lay flat again.

Madeleine had said tonight's new moon was time for a fresh start. Please, Archangel Uriel, will you help a defenseless, living grotesque driven by love?

CHAPTER TWENTY-THREE

Madeleine: Day 16

1% Waning Crescent

I wondered why relationships were such a big deal. I thought falling in love was as easy as falling asleep. However, after my experience with Chris, I realized how complex and nuanced a romance could be. Being responsible for someone else's happiness, as well as your own, wasn't something to take lightly. I hoped Chris wouldn't be so hurt about me leaving for the summer that he wouldn't talk to me anymore.

I had gone to school on that new moon day, thinking about how I'd be following the moon's cue and starting something new myself. I collected work and instructions from my teachers and was a little jittery about my adventure.

I saw Chris in chemistry class, and the smell of formaldehyde hit my nose. He sat in the chair next to me.

"You doing okay?" he asked just as the bell rang.

"Yes." I sighed, relieved he was still talking to me. "But I'm beginning to wonder why I chose to make my life so complicated."

"It's not too late. You could change your mind…" he said with a hopeful puppy dog look.

"You're sweet," I murmured just as the teacher began the

lesson for the day.

There was no lab, so we took notes for the entire 55-minute class, and my hand ached from all the writing.

When we were finally dismissed and packing up, Chris asked, "Can I still stop by your house tonight?"

I smiled. "How about at eight?"

"I'll be there," he replied, flipping his brown hair to the side before we each went our separate ways.

Making sure I had everything arranged, I stayed extra late at school and didn't get home until close to 5 p.m. Then, I finished packing and ate dinner. Being a checklist-loving girl, I looked over mine several times. It was eight o'clock before I knew it, and Chris was already ringing the doorbell.

"It's for me!" I called, running to ensure I got there first. I opened the door. "Hey, Chris." My heart started doing double-time. He looked so cute, with a tendril of hair over one eye.

"Hey, Maddy."

For a second, I felt lightheaded. *I've made a big mistake. I should stay...* but then I looked for the magenta light over his head. It was gone, and I was missing the warm feeling, like a blanket fresh out of the dryer.

"What's the matter?" Chris asked, shoving his hands into the front pockets of his jeans. "The cat got *your* tongue now?" He chuckled nervously.

"I suppose so," I said, collecting my thoughts. "Porch swing?"

He nodded, and I pulled the door closed behind me. Leading the way, I sat on one end of the bench seat, and Chris sat on the other.

We used our toes to swing forward and back, finding our rhythm and creaking the support chains. It gave me time to check in with The Arcs: *What happened to the light? Where did that tender feeling go?*

But all they kept saying to me was, *The moon says it all.*

Chris spoke first. "I wish…" he began, staring out into the darkness.

I interrupted. "I want you to know it wasn't an easy decision."

"Yeah, I get that." Chris ran a hand through his hair. "You have a good opportunity. It's just that… the timing sucks."

"I know. We were just starting to get to know each other. But soon you'll start college, and I still have two more years of high school…"

Chris dropped his head. "So, it's over?"

I swallowed hard. "You've heard me talk about Rumi, right?"

"That philosopher-dude?"

"Yes. He said, "Life is a balance between holding on and letting go." I think there's something to that."

Chris thought for a second, his face turned upward. "How do you know when to grab something and when to let go?" He looked at me, waiting for my answer. His face was extra handsome in the dim porch light.

"When I'm not sure, I ask the moon."

"But there's barely a moon tonight," he said, leaning forward to see the sky.

"That's because it's almost a new moon."

"That's when it's all black, right?"

"Yes, and it encourages new beginnings. It will be black tomorrow, and then it will get fuller and brighter as days progress."

"New beginnings," he repeated, then hung his head again.

"You know, there's a new moon every 27 days or so. It's a reminder that we always get the chance to have lots of fresh starts."

He nodded slowly.

"This isn't goodbye. I'm coming back, and in the meantime, we can text. Check in with each other."

Chris looked at me and smiled, pretending to hold a glass. "To new beginnings."

I did the same, lifting my invisible drink. "And new moons."

"Clink!" he said, motioning his imaginary glass toward mine.

"Clink!" I repeated, but then I gave him a real hug before going back into the house.

New Moon

*"A fresh start is here, and it is time for reflection.
Plant the seeds of your intentions and move toward
your dreams."*

CHAPTER TWENTY-FOUR

Ryon - Day 15 and 14

New Moon and 3% Waxing Crescent

Two days passed in that abandoned house on the hill. The brown, upholstered furniture reeked of rot, the floorboards squeaked and bounced with each step, and the walls were decorated with blotches of black mold, but it quickly felt like home. We named it "The Hideout." The house was tucked between several large trees, with waist-high grass full of insects and rodents. Spring weather encouraged flowers to pop up everywhere, and we were so isolated that we could go outside and enjoy the glorious sun upon our bodies.

Anee loved caring for me, and her sweet, furry face always smiled. She was excited about "playing house," nourishing me with juicy berries, teacups teeming with fat grubs, and plenty of rats, birds, and ground squirrels. She used an old bedsheet she found to secure my broken dragon wings to my human torso, and I was in a lot less pain. My body quickly grew stronger thanks to her, but I was anxious to be well.

"What's on your mind, Ryon?" Anee asked as we strolled through the meadow filled with bobbing heads of golden black-eyed Susans behind our new abode. We walked upright on our two hind legs and talked using our voices, like humans. Threading was kept to a minimum to make sure no gar or gro could hear us from afar.

"Since we're being honest with each other…" I hesitated, enjoying the smell of fresh grass being crushed beneath our feet. "I'm planning to leave soon. I need to stop Geidhuce and his Chimeras once and for all."

Anee swallowed hard. "What about Isel?"

"She's not genuine and power-hungry, too. She needs Geidhuce for her survival, so I'm sure she's nursing him back to health, especially now that he's the leader of The Chimeras."

I picked a red blanket flower edged in yellow and slipped it behind Anee's furry ear. She smiled. "We need to help Telber before anything else."

Anee stopped and stared me square in the eyes. "I'm really worried about him. He still has nightmares about that first night when we all… you know, we ate that man… he wishes he hadn't given in to his beastliness."

"The monstrous part of me wanted to eat the guy, too. Maybe the fact that I'm more than half human stopped me. I don't know." I stepped forward to walk again, but Anee moved in front of me, her gaze even stronger.

"Look, since we're being honest…" She hesitated, then blurted, "No one cares about that girl except you. She's not a treasure you have to guard all the time. Geidhuce sent Vervalt to kill her only to get to you."

"Vervalt said he loved her too," I added, crossing my arms.

"Yeah, for a human servant. That's how Geidhuce was going to reward him."

"Grrowr!" My heart picked up pace.

She pressed her pelted paws to the front of my shoulders. "As far as any of them know, you're dead. She's safe as long as they think that. Let her go." Anee dropped her arms and started walking again.

Anee's words stirred my pulse, and I took deep breaths to calm myself as I followed her.

"And who knows? Maybe they think I'm dead too, since I've been away for over two days," she remarked.

We turned to go back toward the house. It was nice being with Anee, talking honestly, walking in the open air, her fur blowing in the warm wind. "What you've done for me, well, I'm very grateful," I said. "I want you to be safe and happy. That's one of the reasons I'm leaving."

"I already knew. I hear your threads at night while you sleep."

"I'm sorry."

"But your plan, well, it's jumbled-ish."

"Probably because I don't have it all worked out yet."

"You'll figure out how to make everything right again. I believe in you. But for now…" She gave me a playful swat with her paws, and I purposely fell face-first into a thick bed of bright yellow sour grass flowers.

"Oh, no!" Anee dropped beside me. "Ryon, are you hurt? I don't know my own strength!" Her face was scrunched with worry.

I pulled her to the ground, laughing, feeling how good it was to have power in my muscles again. "Of course, I'm fine," I said, rolling over. "My wings are still sore, but they're healing."

"Just keep them bandaged as long as you can," she said, her body surrounded by clover-shaped leaves.

"Yes, Nurse Anee." I picked a long, flowered stem and chewed on the end.

She began to purr, snuggling next to me. The sound of bugs' wings vibrated in our ears. "I'm sure you hear my threads at night too, don't you?"

"No, I…"

"Be honest, Ryon."

"Well, sometimes."

Then, she threaded a poem, like she used to when we were stone statues:

> *Let's stay like this forever,*
>
> *And never be apart.*
>
> *Soon, Telber will join us,*
>
> *We'll have a brand new start.*

I closed my eyes, enjoying the sweetness of that moment. I snugged my head to hers and whispered, "I think I know how to rescue him." Then, I threaded her my plan.

Anee sat up, her eyes lit up like the sun. "May I go too? Please?"

"Yes, but we'll have to go incognito."

"Leave that up to me," she said.

O O O

I was restless that night, so I took a walk just before dawn. I spotted a little house just off Highway 12 with the shutters closed tight, dead plants in the flower boxes, and about a dozen news-papers piled on the front walk. Either the people were out of town, or the cottage was abandoned, so I picked up the papers, even the soggy ones, and brought them back to The Hideout.

When I returned, Anee was awake, so we put them in order, with the most current on top, and lay in the morning sun be-neath the big maple tree beside the house. We read, grateful to have the ability to do so.

"Here's another article about a murder in the area. That makes four," Anee said. "Do you think…?"

"If it's Geidhuce and Isel, they'll get us all caught."

"It says most of them have canine or equine tooth marks. Wolf and horse…Hopefully, not donkey."

"That's got to be them." I shook my head, setting my pa-per aside. "Did you know they were murdering more innocent humans?"

"Geidhuce and Isel disappeared at night, but I had no idea what they were doing." Then, Anee tapped her paw on the clas-sified section. "Look, here's an ad in today's newspaper that says: CHIMERAS, 1 AM, THURSDAY."

"So, that's how he announces meetings. We need to get everything together today, for tonight we ride," I announced. Then, my stomach dropped to my feet.

"What's wrong?" Anee asked, seeing it on my face.

"I'm scared. I've always feared Geidhuce."

"But you already beat him up-ish."

I dropped my head. "That was the beast in me, not my true self."

She gave me a half-smile. "But this is Operation Rescue Telber."

"Yes, you're right, for Telber I can do this." I took a deep breath. "You've been to a few meetings, right?"

She nodded slowly, chewing on a nail. "They meet in a cave in the hills."

"How many Chimeras are there?"

She dropped her paw to her lap. "Geidhuce said there were ten, five from a Charleston building and five from one in New Orleans. Monsieur and Ruza carved all fifteen of us."

"It's hard to imagine others are walking the earth." I swooshed my dragon tail in the grass.

"The building in Charleston was renovated when the gars and gros disappeared, and the one in New Orleans removed the statues before it got torn down. Geidhuce said the authorities think a notorious antique thief stole all of them, including us."

"Sounds like a movie," I remarked.

Anee nodded. "Very movie-ish. Two other buildings are still intact, in New York and Chicago. Let's hope those gars and gros never get taken down."

"How did Geidhuce find out there were others?"

"This part human, part dragon, part goat guy showed up right after that article about us being missing from the renovation site. He came to town and listened for our threading. He's part of a group that's been living in the New Orleans catacombs for decades, and he knew the other group living in a hydrant tunnel in Charleston," Anee explained, sitting up and stretching her back. "They plan to get together and make Gascony a gar and gro utopia, starting with making the theater their home."

"More likely, the humans will put all of us in circuses, or experiment on us, or worse…"

"The Chimeras need to be stopped. They'll kill any human that gets in their way, forcing the town leaders to accept their demands." She stood on her lioness feet, looking like furry socks pulled up just above the ankles of her scaly dragon legs.

"But what could stop the humans from burning down the theater and killing them all in it?"

"Hostages. The Chimeras will be strategic about who they capture. The details aren't clear to me yet, but they plan to use them for leverage, and, of course, will eat them if necessary, to show their power." She shook her head.

Disgusted and angry, I gathered the newspapers and followed Anee to the house.

"I noticed some clothes in the closets, and many are black," Anee said. "This must be the old home of an Amish family. Everyone wears black cloaks to The Chimera meetings, and we must fit in. Wait here."

As I sat on the couch, a puff of dust exploded into the air. The beds had that "just slept in" look, and a toothbrush rested near a crumpled tube of toothpaste on the bathroom sink, as if the people living there left in a hurry. There were dishes in the kitchen's dish drainer and old food in the refrigerator, mostly beyond recognition. Everything had a layer of dirt, accented with wispy spiderwebs, including the stack of books on the living room shelf.

Anee returned with her furry arms full of black clothing, dropping the pile at her feet.

"None of these will fit either of us," I remarked. "It's too small."

"I know, silly." She plopped her dragon butt down on the floor. "I'll rip the seams with my claws, and we'll lay all the pieces out flat-ish. Then, you'll sew them together with your human hands, and tah-dah, we'll make two big sheets."

"Sew? I don't know how to sew."

"How hard can it be? They need to be big enough to cover two six-foot creatures from head to toe, that's all," she said confidently. "I even found a sewing kit in the closet."

I got up and sniffed the pile of black cloth. "These smell musty."

"Which will help hide our scent," Anee smartly pointed out.

We sifted through jackets, pants, dresses, and skirts to make our disguises. I clumsily threaded the needle, passing it in and out of the cloth, and I felt like Dr. Frankenstein fitting the pieces together like a giant puzzle. But I got into it and even attached a makeshift hood by sewing the bottom of two pant legs together, leaving one side open, and attaching them to the top of each raggedy cloak. I even made two belts to tie around our waists. It took the entire day.

"Soon, it'll be dark, and we won't be able to see," said Anee. The house had no electricity, so we used candlelight at night. "Hurry and finish."

"Just tying off the last knot." I think I knew how to do that due to a distant human memory.

She smiled. "Let's go to opposite sides of the room and try them on, but don't face each other until I say so."

I laughed as we each grabbed our designated items and

scrambled to the corners. I slipped on the hood and let the rest fall around me, tying the belt around my waist.

"On the count of three, we'll reveal ourselves to each other." She snickered. "One, two, three! Tah-dah!"

We swung around simultaneously, pretending to be sinister, crouching low, growling, and hiding our faces deep inside the fabric.

"You look gooood! Let's wear these to catch dinner in!" Anee declared. "I'll bet we can sneak up on all kinds of critters."

"Okay!"

Even though the sun left the sky, the air stayed warm. Fireflies glistened in the dark, and the stars flickered above us between the bushes we hunted in. Anee threaded green happiness as we chowed on several birds and rabbits.

I picked a bouquet of dandelions and Indian paintbrush and handed them to her once we returned to the house.

"Oh, Ryon." She held them to her nose and took a whiff. "You're so sweet."

"The yellow ones are dandy-*lions*," I told her, grinning sideways.

She smiled briefly and gave me a big, furry hug and a kiss on the cheek. "What's up? You've blacked out your thoughts all evening."

I sighed. "I feel like someone's squeezing my heart and won't let go."

"I know the feeling," she mumbled, removing her cloak and curling up on the dusty, old area rug with worn fringe.

I undressed and lay on the couch beside her, turning on my

side. "Anee, I'm sorry. I don't mean to be insensitive." I reached out and stroked her ears. "But I need to stop by Madeleine's house on the way to the Chimera meeting. I know she's not there, but her essence is, and I need to feel it. There's a chance our plan goes wrong, and I never see her again…" I pulled back my hand.

"Dramatic much?" She yawned. "I get it. As my poem said, we're in this together. We'll leave just before midnight," she announced, closing her eyes to take a catnap. "Just wake me up when it's time to go."

She knew my mind wouldn't let me rest, and she was right. I slid a book off the dusty shelf on wildflowers and sat at the kitchen table, lighting the two-inch nub of candle we'd been using in a tarnished brass candleholder. I tried to read, but my mind wandered.

Tonight's checklist: Adieu to Madeleine, spy on The Chimeras, and rescue Telber.

WAXING CRESCENT

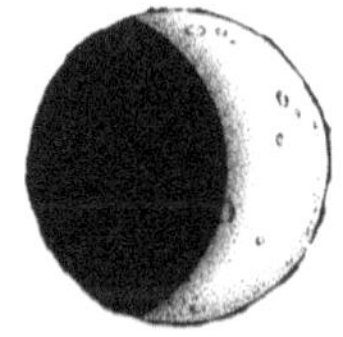

"Have courage and confidence. Initiate steps toward achieving your dreams."

CHAPTER TWENTY-FIVE

Ryon - Day 13

7% Waxing Crescent

I woke Anee from her lioness sleep and got ready in the kitchen. After a few minutes had passed, she stood in the doorway, her eyes catching light like two reflectors from the nearly burned-out candle on the table. We were both wearing our cloaks, with hoods down.

"I'm ready to go, but what's that?" She pointed to the sheathed dagger on the table next to me.

I picked it up. "Say hello to my little friend," I said in my best Al Pacino impression.

Anee shook her head and bit her lip.

"It's just a small knife. I found it earlier in the sewing kit. I think it's smart to have a backup, in case things get…" I shrugged.

"But I don't want you getting all *Scarface*-ish with that thing."

"I won't. I'll keep it here, under my cloak." I slipped one end of a rope I'd also found through the loop of the sheath and tied it to my waist. I pulled my cape closed. "No one will even know I have it."

She rolled her golden eyes. "Let's go." Then, she blew out the small flame.

Blending into the night, we slinked down the hill, across the weeds where crickets chirped and moths took flight when we stepped, toward Gascony. The warm wind blew gently like nature's breath against my leathery face. The distant buildings, which started as small as flickering candles, grew into large shapes of light as we got closer.

We followed the shadows, Anee leading the way, until we could travel by treetop. I struggled to get up to the branches since my wings were tied down but managed to dig my claws into the bark for leverage. Soon, we were descending upon the roof of my old shed like two dark superheroes, climbed down the wooden side, and I slid the window open. The inside was as I had left it.

There, through the peephole I had wiped clean, sat Madeleine's home, hazy in the dim streetlights. A couple of windows were illuminated, but there was no movement inside. The scene was peaceful, but I had the jitters.

I stood peering through that cleared circle of dirty glass for a long time, remembering.

Anee started tapping her large, furry foot. "Can we go now?" she asked, crossing her fuzzy arms.

"Yes, I'm ready…"

The roar of a V-8 engine broke the peacefulness, tires screeching the Mustang to a halt. Chris was cruising Madeleine's house and had parked right beside the shed.

"Again?" Anee sighed. "The last time he showed up, you stayed here and didn't come with me."

"That won't happen tonight," I assured.

Chris rolled his window down and sat there in the night.

"Don't hate me, but he smells…" Anee sniffed the air. "…delicious-ish. He's only the second human that's been this close."

"Be careful. It's the beast in you coming out," I warned.

"I'm not gonna eat him," she remarked sarcastically, quickly wiping drool from her mouth.

Then, Chris stuck his head out and called, "Hey, Conscience, I haven't heard back from you. I've called and called." He sat back in his seat for a minute. "I give up." Then, he rolled up the window and drove off.

Anee's eyes grew narrow. "Ryon, what aren't you telling me about this boy?"

I plunked my dragon rear on the hose coil, pain jolting through my wings on the landing. "Well…"

"Mmhmm…" Her face was full of skepticism.

"Chris likes Madeleine, so I wanted to help him woo her. I tricked him into thinking I was his…conscience."

The muscles in her crossed arms flexed. "So, you talked to him, and he was talking to you?"

"Yes, but I hid in the trees. He never saw me."

Her front paws moved to her scaled hips. "You know how recklessly dangerous that is?"

"I know, but we actually helped each other connect with her." I stopped myself before giving away the entire truth about also kissing and speaking directly to Madeleine.

"I've heard enough," she said, jerking her cape across the front of her body with one large paw. "We still have a lot to accomplish tonight. Let's go." Anee turned and climbed out the window. Her threading was as black as the night sky.

I sheepishly followed her, closing the window behind us. "Off to join the hooded brigade," I joked, hoping to lighten the mood.

We moved silently through the dark branches to the creek below the town's elevation. It would unobtrusively lead us to the foothills below The Chimeras' cave. Going via the Underground Railroad tunnels was too confined and dangerous.

Worry clung to me as we climbed over rocks and tree roots. "Anee, if there's a God, would he listen to the requests of a monster?" I asked.

"He would if He had a hand in making us come to life," she answered, pointing at the bridge, our landmark for where to start climbing toward the cave.

"Maybe we came from the hand of the Devil," I said, a lump in my throat. I followed her, climbing up boulders and grasping onto vines for leverage.

"Look at us, combatting evil, just like dozens of movies we listened to. We're Caped Crusaders. We're the good guys," she argued.

"Do you think Geidhuce has been mistreating Telber since you left?"

The sliver of moon caught immediate tears filling Anee's amber eyes. "Yeah, probably."

We walked up the steep dirt hill covered in shrubs and large rocks for about ten minutes when Anee pointed to an indentation in the hillside.

"Over there," she whispered.

Jumbles of colored threads came from within, creating a kaleidoscope in my mind. So, we cautiously approached, and Anee slid a large boulder backward, revealing a tunnel. Anee and I gave each other a nod, a reminder to turn off our threading and not speak. Beasts are known for their sharp senses, and we didn't want to be detected.

We stepped into the shaft of dirt and rocks, like an earthen tube, which was narrow and dark. The animal sounds and threading were louder, swirling like smoke from a candle. I strained to put the rock back in place behind us, and then we walked in pitch black through the stone tunnel, tripping on rocks and feeling the way with our bodies. After traveling for about five minutes, we saw light in the distance. We continued until the tapered passageway opened to a large, lighted arena. Kerosene lamps hung from giant hooks all over the stone ceiling. I counted thirteen veiled creatures on hind legs or all fours, and glimpses of their monstrous faces flashed in the flickering light, freakish and strange. My heart twisted inside my chest to think I was one of them.

Anee and I observed the crowd in a dimly lit adjacent corridor. The largest of the robed figures, upright but hobbling, ascended stairs to a large stage made from planks of wood laid upon wooden crates, where there was a microphone on a stand and two large speakers at either end. The second I heard the beast speak, I knew it was Geidhuce.

"Please turn off your threading." He waited until it was quiet in our heads. "Welcome to tonight's…" He paused dramatically, leaning the microphone toward his wolf mouth before emphasizing, "…meeting of The Chimeras!"

The group roared, squeaked, and howled in excitement.

"We wear these cloaks not to cover our features but to show our unity. They also symbolize our oppression, forced to hide and stay in the shadows. However, the shedding of our dark robes will happen soon! I see a world where gargoyles and grotesques can walk freely on the streets. Humans will recognize our greatness and show us the respect we deserve."

Again, the audience broke into a raucous, exposing paws, hooves, and human flesh as they excitedly pumped the air.

I searched for Telber and noticed a hunched-over figure near the stage with a donkey tail poking out. I gestured toward him, showing Anee. She spotted him, and her smile glistened under the shadow of her hood. She slowly walked out to meld into the group, and I followed.

Geidhuce continued: "The time has come to take over The Gascony Theater and make it a gargoyle and grotesque sanctuary. In thirteen days, on the next full moon, our kind will become respected and accepted as a new population!"

Again, the crowd cheered, and as the beasts continued their ghastly clamor, chilling threads of death and destruction echoed in our heads.

Then, an earsplitting noise caused everyone to cover their ears, which did not help since it was a thread. It was so sharp and horrible that it made a screeching microphone sound like a symphony.

The piercing noise was coming from Geidhuce. His body lurched forward, and he stumbled, falling to his scaly knees. His twisted wolf face caught the light from a lamp above the stage. The crowd gasped as he fell to the floor, then grew silent with random threads of concern. An Isel-shaped figure ran up the stairs and was quickly at his side, but he pushed her away, motioning for her to address the crowd.

She timidly walked up to the microphone, her horse nose poking out from beneath her hood, nostrils flaring. "The great Geidhuce is just overwhelmed by your support," announced Isel, stepping into the limelight. "He's still our venerable leader, but the truth is that a condor-headed traitor, a grotesque who doesn't believe in our vision, attacked him."

The crowd jeered and wailed. Threads of worry, fierce anger, and contempt for the one who did this to Geidhuce roiled through the crowd.

Geidhuce tottered back to his hind legs and shoved Isel aside again. "I will overcome this attempt on my life, and we will prevail." His voice was hoarse and weak. "We've come up with a masterful plan to take over Gascony, and we can't do it without every one of you." He took a deep breath. "We will show the humans we are not to be messed with," he proclaimed, growing louder and more robust. "Blood will be shed, but in what revolution did no one bleed? The humans will surrender to us. We are mighty! We are The Chimeras!"

The creatures clamored.

I looked over at Telber. His head was down, and he barely moved.

A giant, black form came up to me, sharp horns poking through the top of his mantle. He growled and gave me a rough tap. "Why don't you cheer?" he asked gruffly.

"I have been, but..." I had to think fast. "I want to hear every word our fearless leader says!" I added, mustering enthusiasm.

Then, he approached Anee, and she gave a fervent snarl and exclaimed, "Long live Geidhuce!"

The stranger grunted twice and went back into the crowd.

Finally, everyone calmed, and Geidhuce grasped the microphone between his two wolf paws and removed it from the stand. He walked to the edge of the stage, leaned over those brutes pressed together like honeybees in a hive, and lowered his voice. "On the night of the next full moon, we will meet here at midnight. Then, we'll organize units within these underground tunnels, just as the enslaved people did over a hundred years ago, and seal our freedom."

The crowd rumbled with approval.

"We'll take over the theater first and negotiate after. We won't let anything get in our way!" He gnashed his teeth at the crowd. "The Chimeras will prevail!"

Everyone joined in the chant: "The Chimeras will prevail! The Chimeras will prevail!"

Anee nudged me, nodded, and made her way to Telber. She dragged him out of the cavern through the crowd of shouting dark figures. I said a silent prayer of hope to the angels in case they did help monsters who were the good guys.

I also took the eruption as an opportunity to scurry closer to the stage and hide inside a small chasm in the rock. I didn't let Isel and Geidhuce out of my sight.

The crowd continued to chant, bounding recklessly around the cavern. Several lights swung like pendulums from beastly horns, heads, or wings knocking into them. I felt like a fly inside a strobe light, the room bending and dancing with the moving beams.

I watched as Isel aided Geidhuce, gingerly walking offstage and slipping through an opening in the back of the cavern. I darted after them, staying many paces behind. One of the cloaked monsters showed up and moved a large chunk of rock so they could pass. I scrunched my body down as much as possible, following them.

"Who are you?" the strange creature asked.

"Telber," I replied meekly.

He reluctantly let me pass as well, and I hobbled slowly into a small chamber. A single light was hanging from the center of the ceiling, and just below were Isel and Geidhuce. They sat on a bed of hay on the dirt floor, speaking with their threading turned off.

I crouched in the shadows.

"Did you hear them, Isel? They sound unbeatable!" Geidhuce said feebly, with genuine excitement, nonetheless. "Those humans don't know what's coming." He laughed.

"That's why you should rest," Isel replied, pulling back her hood to expose her horsey face. "Oh, Telber, there you are."

I bobbed my head up and down and sat where I was, several feet away from them.

Isel pulled back Geidhuce's hood and stroked his wolf ears tenderly with her hooves. Geidhuce slowly curled up into a ball. "I can't wait to taste all that human flesh," he mumbled.

Isel lay down next to him. "Don't worry," she neighed. "Soon, you'll have all the human meat you can eat." Then she lifted her head toward me. "Telber, wake us up in an hour."

I nodded.

"Not a minute more, or else," she chided, then closed her

dark, vile eyes.

I let them get nice and comfortable while I stayed tuned to the dispersing crowd outside the cavern, but Isel's words, "Or else," and their tone echoed in my mind. Anger smoldered inside of me as they both began to snore repulsively.

"I could end this all right now," I thought, reaching beneath my robe for the handle of the dagger. I crept up to their bodies, prone and vulnerable in the straw…

…*but I'm not a killer.* I froze, my heart beating in my ears.

Suddenly, Isel's dreadful horse eyes opened and looked right into my face.

"You!" She lunged at me, smacking me hard in the abdomen with her long head. I flew backward, landing on my already injured wings and yelling in pain.

I saw red.

"You tortured Telber! Frightened Anee! Eat innocent humans! Sent Vervalt to get Madeleine!" I shrieked.

Then, it was hard to say what happened next.

All I know is when the blind rage finally abated, Isel's atrocious, severed head was at my feet and covered in blood, with one black abominable eye looking squarely at me, the dagger was in my hand, and the rest of her horse-human-dragon body lay ten feet away in the straw.

And Geidhuce was nowhere in sight.

Every inch of my body shook, and I couldn't think clearly. *I am a killer,* repeated in my mind.

A loud growl from one of the Chimeras outside the chamber snapped me out of my haze. Getting out of the cave was not going to be easy. I only knew one way in, so it was the safest way out. I wiped the bloody knife on my blood-splattered cape and then slipped it back into the sheath tied to my waist. But something caught my eye…

…all but Isel's human torso began to fade away. Like the sun on snow, I watched it melt as distant voices went silent. It was time for my escape.

I pushed the large doorway rock outward, leaving just enough space to slip out, half expecting a guard to be there, but I was alone. Even the main room was empty, but I kept close to the walls, staying in the darkest parts, looking for the exit corridor. I finally found the narrow, pitch-black tunnel I knew led outside and entered, feeling around to avoid tripping over any rocks and sniffing the air to detect others.

Suddenly, I saw light flickering behind me and the red-hot glow of emotional threading. Did they know Isel was dead? Were they searching for her murderer?

I saw something move up ahead, one of the oncomers threaded.

Isel said the traitor is part bird, and I smell feathers, growled another, followed by a horrific cackle.

I hope we get to tear him limb from limb! the first one threaded in an exuberant green.

Their shadows stretched across the walls like grand, moving giants. I heard the rasping of teeth and the evil laughter of a hyena. I kept blocking my threads, but my panic made focusing difficult. Their torchlight glinted upon a puddle of mud to my right. I swiftly rubbed the brown sludge on the light-colored parts of me: my face, arms, and hands, and made sure my cloak was secured tightly around my body, and then I leaped upward onto a narrow protrusion of rock above, clinging for dear life with my hands and feet, my back toward the ground.

The two monsters paused below me, and my human hands burned from the roughness of the rocks.

I smell him… threaded one.

My hands were slipping… I was going to fall!

I used one hand to quickly untie my cloak as I plummeted, crushing them to the ground, the torch still burning beside them. I ran as fast as I could toward the cave opening.

I glanced back, and they were still struggling beneath my muddy cape.

I wish I could use my wings! I thought.

Stealing another look behind me, I saw flashes of jagged teeth, chomping mouths, and tufts of unruly hair in the glow of their torch. Both ran on all fours with razor-like claws and were catching up! So, I tore away the bandages that braced my wings, stretching and beating them to stir up a giant dust cloud. Adrenaline took over, helping me escape even faster, pushing off the cave walls and gaining momentum, propelling myself to the opening, and knocking down the barrier boulder like a cardboard box.

They were still in the passageway when the fresh evening air hit my face. I rolled the giant rock back to cover the door and flew as quickly as possible down the mountain, along the creek, and back to the thick trees leading toward The Hideout. I couldn't catch my breath until I was sure I wasn't being followed, but after waiting a while in the branches beneath the fragmented moon, I listened intently until I knew it was safe to head home. I hoped Anee and Telber were already there, waiting for me.

CHAPTER TWENTY-SIX

Madeleine - Day 12

14% Waxing Crescent

It was the day before Mother's Day, I was over 1,300 miles away from home, and I woke with a nagging feeling that something was wrong. My grandparents were welcoming, ensuring I was well-fed and comfortable that first week, so I figured the ominous sense simmering in my gut meant I missed home. I missed my car, Clio, too. Grampy had lent me his old, brown pickup truck, and it got me the hour-and-a-half drive to and from my internship at the paper in downtown Dallas a couple of times a week. But "Old Brown," as I call it, had nothing on Clio's verve and style. At least I'd brought my kitten, Genevieve, with me. She was the one thing that gave me peace when I was anxious.

I'd always pictured Texas as a desert with oilrigs and longhorn cows, but where my Grampy and Grandy lived, there were ancient pine trees, flowering pears with snowy white blossoms, and their humble grey house was one hundred and twenty steps away from a lake with a dock. It was barely 8 a.m., but I threw on some shoes and headed down to the water to receive energy from the winds that passed through the cattails and reeds growing along the shore. It was so peaceful, the croaking frogs serenading me as I sat in the dockside rocking chair, moving to and fro. Yet I still had worry in my heart.

Thank goodness for FaceTime. I called home from the dock and saw my mom's smiling face, which settled my anxiety for the moment. She was getting ready for church, so the call was brief, but we planned to chat later that evening. I got a little teary once we hung up—she was so happy to hear from me.

I'd been keeping up with Sierra in Hartstown and Julie in Gascony on alternating days, and both made sure I got the latest "tea." But then there were my FaceTimes with Chris. His twinkling eyes and flouncy hair made me lightheaded, yet he struggled to tell me much.

"How's your internship?" he asked.

"It's great. I'm learning a lot and doing a bunch of fact-checking and research. I just wrote my first press release, and my boss said I did an excellent job." Chris's face had glazed over. "What's the latest on college?"

He let out a long breath that made his lips pursed. "I got into Farmington State."

"Congratulations."

"Thanks. I don't want to talk about that."

"Chris, what's wrong?"

"Nothing. It's just… not the same without you here."

"That's sweet of you to say." My face and neck flushed.

"I mean it."

Then, there was a long silence, and I could swear I heard roars and snarls, like a zoo gone wild, off in the distance on his end. "Is something going on there?" I asked, a tightness building in my shoulders. "Go look outside."

"I'm looking out the window, and it's silent here. See?" He

held his phone up so I could see his view. Nothing but fences and farmland. "Must be our connection."

"Don't you hear…?" I stopped, realizing that those tumultuous sounds could be from The Arcs. "Never mind."

"Remind me when you're coming back."

I laughed. "I've only been gone five days, but July 31st. About 77 more days."

"That seems so long."

"Well, remember we said we're going to move forward into our new beginnings?"

"Yep."

"I want both of us to have a great life, and part of that is for you to become a law enforcement tech and for me to be a journalist, like we've always dreamed of, so we should be excited about every step. Let's celebrate you getting into Farmington." I held up an invisible glass. "Clink?"

He smiled and followed my lead. "Clink."

After we hung up, I tried to shake the unrest in my gut.

"Oh, angels, where is this angst coming from?" I asked, but I received no answer. The Arcs had been helping me all week by keeping me motivated and connecting me with new people, but they left me alone with that bad feeling.

The sky was the color of my grandmother's blue hydrangeas, and I was surprised to see the one-eighth of the moon still gleaming in the sky. "Waxing crescent, how can I shake this foreboding?"

Then, a message came through, not from an angel, but from the ethers: "You are prone to emotional fluctuations right now, so don't overthink things. Step toward your dreams with confidence. You're safe where you are." And as I stared at that wafer of moon, it pixilated and turned sparkly, and those sparkles became a brilliant pink, like a million rubies glistening. A soothing feeling came down through the top of my head, traveling my body as the comfort of Mother Nature embraced me.

CHAPTER TWENTY-SEVEN

Ryon - Day 12

14% Waxing Crescent

I was startled by something touching my cheek and jumped to my feet, claws ready to swipe the intruder's flesh. I blinked to shed the blurriness from my eyes. A figure stood before me, lighted from behind like a golden angel... *Is it?*

"Madeleine?" I gasped.

"No, it's me. Anee." Her voice was flat.

I shook my head and looked around. I was beneath our favorite tree beside The Hideout.

She spoke more sweetly. "Ryon, are you alright? You smell like blood."

Then, she came into focus, her amber fur shining in the morning light. "It's you!" I embraced her. "I knocked when I got back last night, you know our code, "thump, thumpity, thump-thump," but no one answered. I was so worried you and Telber didn't make it here, but I didn't want to break in and scare you if you were here... I thought The Chimeras..." I let go of her furry body, the knot in my stomach loosening.

"We got here around 2:30 a.m. and were worried sick about you." Then, she patted my back with one great paw. "Hey, where are your bandages?"

"My wings are better… well, I'm a little sore, and I left my cape in the cave, but… it's a long story." I looked at the sky, and the moon was still visible, a waxing crescent. And then, it broke into glittering facets of pink light that shimmered like countless pink eyes winking at me. For a moment, I was transfixed as a euphoric magnetism pulled me toward it. "Anee, look!" I pointed to the moon, which quickly returned to its regular white light.

"Yes, the moon is still out. It must have been watching over you," she said with a purr.

The sound of someone in a fever-pitch dream threaded in my head. "Is that…?"

She nodded. "Telber. He's threading uncontrollably. Honestly, the night was… rough." Her shoulders slumped.

"I hope he doesn't attract any Chimeras."

Anee's voice cracked as she spoke. "He's in bad shape, Ryon. I'm not sure he's going to…"

I held her again, and she sobbed on my neck feathers. I stroked her back and told her it would be alright, but I wasn't so sure. Anee turned on her threading, sorrowfully purple, and showed me Telber, bloody and puss-ridden, shaken, hunched, and barely able to walk.

"You won't recognize him, Ryon. He's pretty much delirious from infection right now. His threads are full of beatings, torture, Geidhuce's horrible face…it's hard to bear. I don't know if I can help him. He needs bandages, medicine."

"I want to see him," I said, and she led the way.

In the dark bedroom, upon an old mattress, wrapped in a ripped and worn comforter, was Telber, frail, shivering, and covered in sweat. Blood was caked in his mane, and his eyes were closed in sunken bony sockets. His mind ran with uncontrolled threads of electric blue terror.

I dropped to my scaly knees. "Telber, buddy, I'm so glad we got you out of there. We're going to help you. You're going to feel better soon," I whispered.

He did not respond.

I looked at Anee, and her eyes said it all.

"I'll go get supplies."

"How? Steal them? What if you get caught?" Anee began breathing fast, chewing on a claw.

I gently pushed her paw away from her mouth. "Please don't worry. I have a way, but you must promise you won't think badly of me."

"How could I ever think badly of you?" she said.

"Well, it involves Chris, the boy I tricked. He'll get us what we need."

"I don't care, as long as it helps Telber." Hope glinted in her slanted cat eyes.

"However, I need to go to him this time since he's given up on me, and I have no idea where he lives."

"Well, maybe this will help." Anee grabbed my hand and dragged me into the kitchen. She opened a cupboard near the sink. "Tah-dah! The Yellow Pages." She pulled out the stained, dusty book, then pointed at the date on the cover. "It's only five years old. What's Chris's last name?"

I thought hard, knowing Madeleine had said it once or twice. "Newtown. Christopher Newtown."

Anee flipped open the book with her large, furry paw and perused the Ns. "There are two Newtowns in here. One is a Bertram Newtown on Bordeaux Lane, and there's a Jim Newtown on Pasteur Place. Oh, and there's a map you can take with you." She ran a sharp claw along the page near the binding, and the map fell onto the floor.

I picked it up. Then, I grabbed a dusty pen beside the old rotary phone on the counter and marked each name on the corresponding street.

"I should probably scope out both. Who knows—he may not even be listed." I folded up the map and shoved it inside a fold of my neck skin.

"Right." Anee paused, looking dejected. "I wish I could go with you."

I smiled. "I know, but one of us has to stay with Telber."

She nodded.

"And Anee… there's one more thing. Wait here."

I went out the front door and grabbed my dagger, which I had hidden in the bushes. I returned to the kitchen and held it out to her.

"Is that blood?" Anee's large eyes widened.

"Yes. I killed Isel." I shook my head. "I don't even remember doing it. Geidhuce and Isel thought I was Telber, and they threatened me, making me so angry…they fell asleep, everything went black, and… then I saw Isel's head at my feet."

Anee gasped.

"Minutes later, every part of her, except her human torso, dissolved in front of my eyes. I think that happened to Vervalt, too. Only the human parts remain after our…death." I dropped the knife, and it clanked on the floor. I covered my bird eyes with both hands. "I really *am* a killer," I sobbed.

Anee nuzzled my leathery face. "No, you're a hero. You did that to protect me, Telber, yourself. That horrible Isel is not worthy of self-doubt, and neither is Vervalt. You're brave." She purred, then softly added, "You're my hero."

"I'm nothing but an abominable, murderous beast." I stepped away from her and wiped the tears from my cheeks. "I can't control the monster in me. I may have killed Geidhuce, too. He was missing." I gulped. "I don't know if he went off to die somewhere or got out before I could get him. You saw what bad shape he was in to start with…" My body shook uncontrollably. "What if the others figure out that I killed Isel? They'll come after us…"

"Don't worry. We're safe here, and our focus right now is Telber. We need to save him." Her face was dark and sad.

I nodded. "I'll leave as soon as it gets dark." Then I went outside to the tiny creek and washed myself in the cool trickles of clear water. The wind in the trees above spoke softly of peace, and the birds chirped avidly of life. "Please, angels, help Telber so he may enjoy the beauty of living here." I sat in the sun to dry and caught some field mice and a rabbit for nourishment, forcing my knotted stomach to ingest them.

When I returned to the house, Anee was leaving the room where Telber was resting, shaking her head. "I'm worried about getting food in him. He can't chomp down a bird or even a mouse right now. He's drinking a little water, though."

We brainstormed a list of items we might need and then searched the house for supplies, but there were none. We also checked on Telber regularly.

Finally, the sun was setting, so Anee stood up from the couch where she had been resting. "It's time for you to go. Please be safe."

"You, too." I closed the book I was reading and slipped it back on the shelf. "Keep the dagger nearby. For protection."

"Maybe you should keep it."

"No, if someone were to show up, you would need it more."

Then, she handed me a small, rough brown shell with three holes in it, all in a row, with a piece of yarn strung through one aperture, tied in a knot to form a loop. "I found this behind the telephone book. It's like you, rough and bumpy on the outside, but turn it over."

I did, and it was covered in a rainbow of iridescent swirls.

"On the inside, you're a spectrum of shining goodness." She smiled. "Take it with you, for luck." She slipped the yarn over my head, the shell dangling against my chest.

I kissed her on her soft forehead and left.

O   O   O

Trudging down the hill toward town, I kept my eye on the glowing sideways smile in the sky, hoping it would turn pink again. A realization hit me like a wrecking ball: I was no longer responsible for only myself—two other lives counted on me. *I must find Chris.*

The first Newtown home, Bertram's, was on the south side of town, only a couple of blocks away from Quality Market. The other one, Jim's, was on the north side of town in a more rural area.

I climbed through branches whenever I could, resorting to hedges and shadows if the trees were sparse. Bertram Newtown's house was merely a weed-covered lot. At least that was an easy one to check off the list. However, I started to worry.

What if neither of the houses is Chris's? What if I can't find him? My breath grew heavy—I'd have to resort to stealing after all.

It took me a good 30 minutes to navigate my way to the home of Jim Newtown, surrounded by acres of fence, across a massive field, and embedded in a thicket of trees. I crouched and stayed near the fences where the grass grew tallest, cutting across the ground to the modest white, two-story house with grey trim. It looked like an old farmhouse based on its wood slat siding and rippling glass windows, but a Mustang wasn't nearby. The weighted breathing returned as panic set in.

I sat in a giant sycamore tree that grew on the side of the driveway, searching for clues, but nothing could ensure it was Chris's home. My claws extended as I pictured Telber's frail body lying on the bed, barely alive.

He needs me, and I'm failing him! Think!

About to give up, I spotted a row of trash cans against the garage. I carefully climbed down my tree, slid along the wooden fence, and made my way there, sniffing the tall, silver receptacle closest to me, full of potato peels and onions. Flipping open the lid, I saw a pile of opened mail. I turned over the top envelope. It was addressed to Christopher Newtown, 100 E. Fleur de Lis Avenue, Gascony, PA 16371.

Yes!

The envelope had been opened, and the top sheet was an acceptance to Farmingdale State College. The familiar Mustang entered the driveway just then, so I quickly hid in a nearby tree. He parked in the driveway and got out of his car.

"Chris! Chris!" I called in a loud whisper as he approached.

He looked all around. "Who's that?"

"It's me, your Conscience!"

He ambled toward my voice, his head swinging to the side to get his hair out of his eyes. "C.! I haven't heard from you for a week. I tried to conjure you up so many times, but..."

"I was giving you space to think life through for a while without the voice of your conscience."

He paused a moment and sighed. "Maddy left." He dropped his head and kicked a rock with the toe of his shoe. It sputtered across the dirt driveway, leaving a small, squiggly trail. "So, why are you here now? With her away, there's not a lot I can do to "woo" her," he replied, using his fingers to make air quotes when he said "woo."

"I want to see why you threw away that important letter about going to college," I ad-libbed, glad I'd discovered it. "You should be proud of yourself. You have the opportunity to learn great things." Envy lingered on my tongue.

"But, with me away in college, I won't see Madeleine very much," he said, sighing. "I could just stay here and tend the farm."

I had mixed feelings about Chris leaving, too. Watching him build a relationship with Madeleine hurt my heart, but I needed him as my go-between. But I got an idea.

"You should be celebrating, my friend! You're about to

graduate from high school. That's a big deal."

"I guess."

"Well, that's why I came to you. We're going to have a significant ceremony tonight," I announced.

"We are?"

"Yes. It'll give you clarity," I said.

"Well, since you're my conscience, I guess I have no choice." His energy was the lowest I'd seen.

"You must gather special items first. Symbols for this event."

"Symbols?"

"Yes. Each item will have a deeper meaning than what it is on the surface. And it's quite a list, so you need to write it down."

"I'll type it on my phone." Chris pulled his cell phone out of his back pocket. "Okay, go ahead."

"First, you need a bandana."

"Oh, I've got one of those," he replied more enthusiastically.

"I know," I lied. "Then, get antibiotic ointment, some antibiotic pills, a whole bunch of large bandages…"

"This is a strange list," he interrupted, rubbing his forehead with his fingers.

"These items are part of the ritual. You'll have to trust me."

"A little weird, but go on."

"Do you have any soft food, like mashed potatoes?" I asked.

"My little cousin visited, and his momma left all kinds of baby food—meat, vegetables…" Chris cringed.

"Perfect. Now, two last things: a bag of dry white rice…and a red rose."

"Well, that's gotta be one of the weirdest lists for a ceremony ever."

"Go out beneath the big sycamore tree by your barn as soon as you have it all, and don't tell anyone."

"Got it, C." Chris saluted and went into his house, a bounce back in his step, fetching like a Golden Retriever.

◯ ◯ ◯

Cool wind whirled around me as I waited, planning what would happen next. Soon, Chris jogged toward me with a brown paper bag with handles dangling from his arm. I moved deeper into the foliage as he approached the tree's base.

"That was quick," I said with exuberance. "Did you bring everything I asked for?"

"Yep, but the antibiotics I found aren't for humans. They were for my dog. Is that okay?"

"They're symbolic, so they'll work." *Especially since Telber is part animal.*

"Wait a minute. I don't have to swallow one, do I?"

"No. You won't have to swallow anything."

"Good, 'cause that would be gross."

I grinned at his dramatics. "We have no time to waste," I announced, knowing Telber was getting sicker by the minute. "Let the ceremony begin!"

"I'm ready," Chris said eagerly.

"Now, lay the bag with everything you brought, except the

bandana, against the tree trunk."

He did as I asked, then returned to his spot, the red bandana hanging from his back pocket.

"I will need you to follow my direction carefully, and the first one is to hold your tongue," I said firmly.

"Lie thith?" he said, muffled.

"What?" I tilted my head to get a clearer view of him. He was grasping his tongue with his fingers. "Figuratively, not literally. "Hold your tongue" means don't talk."

He dropped his hands. "Okay, got it."

"Now, sit on the ground with your back about six feet away from the tree trunk. Then, tie the bandana around your eyes."

"Yes, sir!" He plopped on the grass, sitting with his legs like a pretzel, and tied the bandana around his head.

"Now, make sure you can't see…" I stealthily snuck down the tree trunk, snatched the bag, quite heavy from the couple dozen jars of baby food he got, and climbed back up to my branch. I set it firmly where two branches grew into a "v."

"What's going on?" Chris asked. "Am I supposed to be doing something?"

"You're doing just fine—now let the ceremony begin!"

Chris clapped his hands lightly a few times, then set his hands on his knees.

"This ceremony is in honor of Christopher Newtown," I said in my most distinguished voice. "He's a fine, young man with the whole world in front of him as he graduates from Gascony High School. Each item in this ritual represents an important phase of life."

Chris rocked on his backside.

"The bandana you wear across your eyes is a reminder that, right now, your future is unsure. By the end of this ceremony, you'll remove it and see your direction clearly."

"Yeah, I really need help deciding…"

"Silence, please," I interrupted, picturing Telber in his bed in agony.

"Right. Sorry."

"Sometimes, life is going to hurt. You may become disappointed, sad, or lonely, but those wounds will eventually heal. This antibiotic ointment symbolizes self-care. If you are feeling bad, take time to address what hurts." I took the white tube out of the bag and climbed onto the branch above Chris. Then, I carefully squeezed a glob of the thick, cloudy goo, which splattered on the back of his right hand.

"What the…?" Chris flinched, wiping it away.

"I was just anointing you."

"Oh, okay, but a little warning would be nice." Then, he wriggled his rear into the ground, waiting for the next part.

"In life, you must guard against what might hurt or make you unhappy. This bandage symbolizes the importance of shielding yourself." I took a bandage from the box, removed it from its wrapper, and unpeeled the white backing. "Here it comes…" I let it flutter downward, and the Band-Aid lightly landed on his arm.

"I was ready for that one."

"Good. Sometimes you need extra help, and it's okay to ask for it. These helpful pills have been given by another—the doctor."

"A veterinarian, really."

"Don't be afraid to seek the assistance of others when you need it."

Chris recoiled, preparing for a downpour of pills, but I didn't want to waste a single one, so I shook the bottle, and the pills rattled like rain on a tin roof.

"Cool—I didn't get pelted with anything this time."

"Shhh!"

Chris got ready again.

"Now, next steps. College is full of amazing experiences, and the chance to learn is a gift. By going to college, you'll learn skills that will help you get a job."

"Yeah, but I could stay here and farm. Then I won't have to be away from Madeleine."

"But you've got to look at the bigger picture. Do you want to get married one day?"

"Sure, I do…"

"Well, when you have a skill, you'll have a career, and when you have a career, you'll make money to use to share your life with someone. She'll be your ointment, your bandage, your pill. She'll be there when you're down, keep you safe, and assist you when needed." Then, I tore open the bag of rice and threw a handful at Chris.

He giggled. "Wedding, rice… I get it."

"Very good. We're almost done," I said, digging in the bag for a baby food jar. "Once you're married, a little Christopher Junior will be born. He'll be the living symbol of your love." I opened the baby food jar labeled 'applesauce,' and the vacuum seal popped.

Chris, still blindfolded, jumped to his feet at the sound. "Oh, no! I know what's next, and you're not splattering me with any baby food!"

"Okay, okay. Sit back down. We'll skip that step of the ceremony."

"Thank you," Chris said, plopping down where he stood.

I put the lid snugly back on the jar. "All of that happiness, love, and fulfillment begins now. You're at a fork in the road. Take the path that leads to all you dream of, including…" jealousy made me choke out her name, "Madeleine." I took the rose out of the bag and sniffed its sweet aroma, picturing the curve of her cheekbones, the swoop of her hair, the blush of her lips. Then, I pulled the petals from the stem, the fluttery red discs raining down upon Chris. "Remember, everything you do, no matter how impossible it may seem at the time, is all for the one thing that makes life worth living: love."

"You're right. Madeleine is worth it." He smiled.

At that moment, I was overwhelmed with gratitude for having Chris in my life, not only for being able to gather these things for Telber but also as a friend. "One more thing." I slipped the shell necklace Anee had given me from my neck. "Just sit still and wait for one last time, palms up." I climbed down as quietly as possible and set the shell, rainbow side up, in one of his hands.

"What…?"

I dashed back up to my branch. "You hold a symbol of hidden beauty, rough and ugly on the outside, but lustrous and lovely inside. What looks scary and overwhelming right now also has a beautiful side." I smiled at sweet, trusting Chris sitting there on the ground, blindfolded, hands out, holding the abalone shell. "I believe you can handle your concerns by yourself from now on. Just know I'm always with you, and that little voice that reminds you of things, that's me."

He nodded vigorously.

"Great! Now, after the count of three, you may take your mask off. One…two…"

I grabbed the bag of supplies and raced through the treetops back toward The Hideout. That fake ceremony rekindled my desire to talk to Madeleine again, but sadly, I'd just closed the door on that ever happening again.

In the distance, I heard Chris call, "Where's three? You never said three! Hello?"

O   O   O

I arrived at The Hideout well before the sun came up. I knocked, Anee let me in, and I handed her the bag of goodies.

Her eyes lit up with happiness. "Tah-dah!" Then, she motioned for me to follow her.

Telber lay motionless, with nightmarish threads of red still reverberating in the bedroom's darkness.

Anee spoke low. "He only woke up twice while you were gone. I think that's a good-ish sign. Sleep will heal him, so I'll give him what you brought when he wakes up next. He actually opened his eyes and smiled earlier. I think he recognized me." She grinned.

"That's excellent." I patted her back.

We walked back to the living room, yawning and bleary-eyed, too tired to talk anymore. We curled up on the rug side-by-side and slept.

PART TWO

CHAPTER TWENTY-EIGHT

Ryon - Day 11

22% Waxing Crescent

Anee and I spent the morning in the kitchen, leaning over the sink, draining blood from several freshly caught rabbits into an old milk bottle. We also lined up Chris's supplies on the countertop: baby food, fresh bandages, and antibiotics.

"Ryon, please wish Telber better, just like you wished us all to life," Anee said as she put several items on a tray.

"You think my longing to be free and human made us come to life?"

She shrugged. "Maybe."

That notion had crossed my mind as well. Could someone want something so much that it comes to fruition? But if that was true, I was also responsible for all the pain and suffering we'd endured.

"I do believe that the mind is powerful," I replied. "I hope Telber wants to get better because otherwise…"

A weak voice came from the bedroom. "A-A-Anee…"

"Telber!" We both exclaimed, rushing to his side.

"Wh-wh-where's Geid…?"

Anee interrupted, "Nowhere near us. It's just us three."

"W-w-we're…s-s-safe?" he murmured, his eyes mere slits. His threading had calmed, and the colors were lovingly light pink and a contented verdant green.

Anee and I each held one of his front hooves.

"Yes, we're safely in a remote house," Anee said gently.

"Anee has been taking great care of you, and I got some food, medicine, and bandages. Soon, you'll be as good as new," I added.

He smiled slightly, then closed his eyes.

"How about drinking something?"

Telber slowly nodded, so I retrieved the tray from the kitchen.

Anee got to work opening jars and counting pills. "Prop up Telber's head."

I lifted his triangular neck, his mane poking my skin as Anee gave Telber sips of water. Then, she used a tarnished spoon she'd found to put some beef baby food into his mouth, but more came out than went in. I levered his mouth wide open, holding onto his large square teeth, and Anee shoved an antibiotic pill into the back of his throat. I let go and stroked the outside of his throat until he swallowed several times. Anee washed it down with some sips of the rabbit blood, but he started to cough, so she stopped. But soon, he closed his eyes and settled down, back to sleep.

"Poor Telber's been through so much," Anee whispered, shaking her head. "Let's get some fresh air while he rests."

We went outside beneath our favorite tree, the branches swaying overhead as we stretched out on our sides, facing each other in the cool grass, our bodies wrapped in the warm May sun. My muscles felt less tense since Telber was awake and Madeleine was safely 1,300 miles away, so I focused on stopping

The Chimeras.

"They're taking over the theater in eleven days," I said. "I need a plan."

"Do you think Geidhuce is alive?" Anee asked.

"Well, if he is, I healed pretty quickly after the rooftop fight, and considering what Telber's been through, he's also getting better fast. The same could be for that evil monster."

"I hope not," Anee answered. Then she broke out into rhyme:

"Dreams like rubble in my head,

Flashes of our makers,

Is evil Geidhuce truly dead?

Or is he just a faker?"

I laughed. "Do you still have strange dreams of Monsieur and Ruza like I do?"

"Yep." She plucked a blade of grass and chewed on it.

"Maybe I didn't will us to life. Maybe magic is real."

Anee rolled onto her back. "You know, my memories do seem magic-ish at times."

"Some days, I can practically feel the chisel digging into my stone body, the smell of the incense Ruza burned and the flowery-scented oil she rubbed on us, and I can hear her muttering foreign words."

"And at our unveiling, the way the wind kicked up, and everyone froze like statues… everyone except Ruza, her frizzy hair blowing in the wind as she read from that ancient book."

"Do you still remember the final words she said?" I asked.

"I couldn't get them out of my head if I tried: *Postanite čudovišta kakve ste trebali biti*"

"That's it!" I grinned. "Do you remember anything else?"

"Not much." She rolled back on her side and stared into the air above me. "Wait! I remember the title of that old book she read at the ceremony: *Carolije Animacije.*" She threaded me a picture of the book cover in Ruza's hands.

"I wonder what that means."

"Carols of the Animals?" She chuckled. "Perhaps she was singing Croatian Christmas songs. Too bad we don't have a Croatian dictionary."

"Right." I snickered, but then I jumped to my feet. "You're brilliant, Anee!"

"What did I say?"

"Can you handle Telber? I need to…"

Anee sat up, squinting her giant eyes with yellow lashes like tiny fans. "You're not leaving yet, right?"

"No, I… I need to check… for Geidhuce, you know. The rooftop. The cave. To see if he's alive."

"And what else?" She flicked her thick, tufted tail vigorously against the ground.

"I'm gonna translate those Croatian words."

She sat up. "How?"

"You just need to trust me."

○　○　○

As soon as it was dark, I lit the candle I'd found in the back of a kitchen drawer so Anee would have light, and then I slipped the box of matches into a leathery fold of my neck. It was around ten when I left—I was too anxious to wait until midnight.

"Be safe," Anee said, kissing me on the cheek on her way to tend to Telber.

I walked out of The Hideout and down the hill, the darkness keeping me covered, but I knew I had to be aware. After killing Isel, The Chimeras would be looking for me, and it was earlier in the evening than when I usually left, so humans may be around. On edge, I approached the theater through the trees. Scaffolding still surrounded the outside, and the stone was chipped away in the places where we were once all mounted. Love, life, friendship, and death had different meanings than when I was a statue—and being with Madeleine in the stage curtains had electrified me, giving me aftershocks every time that memory surfaced.

I stared at the outside of the theater. Were there clues about how we came to life? But all I saw were orange road cones, ladders, and cement crumbles. Ruza… Monsieur Salles-Bris… *"Zivotinja koju si trebala biti"*… *Carololije Animacije*… these mysteries had begun to haunt me like never before.

A trashcan lid slammed in the alley behind the building, so I ducked, startled, and my nerves jangled. Then, a large skunk wobbled into view, and I realized that smelly, black-and-white guy and I had something in common—humans were terrified of us. He would have made a nice meal, but I felt sorry for him, so I gave him a nod before creeping across the street to check out our old rooftop lair.

I scaled the side of the building, senses on alert, slowly using the rough bricks to leverage each claw. I held my breath when I reached the top and peeked over the edge. Scanning the darkness, I saw nothing except a single, white paper flapping in the breeze in the center of the roof. I hoisted myself onto the rough shingles and cautiously walked over to it. There were no remnants of the gars and gros living there except for a brown, dried puddle of something. As the scent entered my beak, I knew I'd smelled it before—Geidhuce's blood.

I continued toward the paper, my name at the top catching my eye. I ripped it from the nail.

Ryon—

You think you've won, but I'll have my revenge when you least expect it.

No one is safe.

May 23rd...D-Day!

Geidhuce

I could feel blood pulsate through my veins.

Does he know I killed Isel? That Anee and Telber are with me? Is he really alive, or is this a trick?

I stuck it back on the nail and quickly scaled to the ground. I had to be extra vigilant as I traveled through the trees, along the creek, and then up the foothills to the cave. Perhaps The Chimeras knew my every move.

I moved the boulder door and kept it open to give me some light, stopping to listen for threading. I heard nothing but spotted a kerosene lantern on a nearby rock. I took the matches from my neck skin, adjusted the wick by turning the protruding knob, and lifted the base of the glass globe.

I knew these matches might come in handy.

Striking a match, it flared, and I touched the flame to the

wick.

And then there was light.

I replaced the glass chimney and searched like a blood-hound as I walked, sniffing and listening, until I reached the large meeting cavern. I touched a hanging lantern, and it was cold. Nothing was out of place. I went over to the cavern where I'd killed Isel and felt sick. I hated myself for being a murderer. Cowards killed and heroes led the living. I pushed back the boulder and stepped inside, illuminating the granite space with the lamp. The straw and blood were cleaned up—the smell of antiseptic lingered. There was also the scent of paint.

I shined the light along the walls, and through the dusky air were giant, red letters:

PAZITE!

Although I had no idea what it meant, a cold shiver jolted down my spine. I touched the dripping letters, and the paint was dry.

Exiting the tunnels was a blur—I couldn't get out of there fast enough. *The walls are squeezing in on me!* I calmed down when I saw the waxing moon and felt fresh air in my lungs. I blew out the lantern, returned it to where I found it, and slid back the boulder.

One more stop to make.

Heading toward town, I traveled through the trees to Biblio Street, where the low, white building sat in the center of the block. I'd noticed it the night I looked for Chris's house, and the sign on the front said: Gascony Public Library. I snuck around the back and peered through several windows. Silhouettes of books on shelves surrounded tables and chairs. In the center was a large desk marked "check-out." On it sat a stack of paperbacks and a large glass candle labeled "Birthday Cake."

I had to get in there.

Careful no humans were around, I checked every window and door in case one was left open. No luck. There were security stickers on a few windows, and I didn't want to set off an alarm, so I crouched behind a giant mulberry bush that grew in the back, thinking. The town clock struck eleven, and I began to grumble. Getting inside that library was a crucial part of my plan. I took big breaths to calm my inner beast, keeping it from smashing a window.

Then, an old truck lurched several yards from where I was hiding and parked. I huddled in the bush, watching. The driver's side door opened, but the car was still running.

"Now, Daddy, you go right to bed, ya here? It's late. The library looks fine," a woman's voice announced. A tall, bleached-blond woman in ripped jeans and a black t-shirt that said "Mama Bear" in metallic silver letters stepped out. She walked around to the passenger side and yanked open the door.

"Wish ya'd quit yer worryin'," a man's voice grumbled. He was frail and elderly with a long, white beard. He slid out of the other side of the truck onto the ground, holding a silver cane with a red tip and a black handle. I caught the whiff of men's cologne and buttered popcorn.

"Daddy, things can happen, like slippery puddles of water or somethin' in your path..." She stood with her hands on her hips, watching him scuffle away. "I just want ya to be safe."

He stopped for a second, twisting the top of his body toward her. The headlights caught his eyes, which were a cloudy blue and unfocused. "An' I appreciate ya carin', but goodnight!" He turned forward again and continued toward a small yellow house, kitty-corner from the library.

"Aw, Daddy, why ya gotta be so onery?" She jogged to catch up to him and kissed him on the cheek. "I'll call ya in the mornin'."

"Sleep good, sweetheart," he said gently, barely stopping.

The woman returned to her car and got in, but watched and waited until the old man reached the door of the little house. He jingled some keys, the door squeaked open, and hydraulics hissed as it closed behind him. The woman put the truck into reverse and left.

I was about to leave the bush and head home when the man emerged from his house, so I stuck to my spot. He shuffled down the path, whistling a tune, his cane leading the way in a side-to-side motion. He walked to the back door of the library, not far from where I was hiding, and pulled it hard.

"Snug as a bug in a rug," he said aloud. "The way I like it."

I approached him as he turned and started his slow journey back to his house. "Excuse me, sir," I said as gently as possible.

He wielded his cane over his head and growled, "Watch it, fella, this can be used as a weapon!" His dull eyes searched beyond me as he swung it over his head.

I jumped back to avoid being whacked. "I'm sorry. I mean no harm. I was just on my way home, and…"

"Were you at the movie too? Wasn't it a great film? I love me some John Wayne."

"John Wayne's great," I said, agreeing wholeheartedly. "I

think I see a candle burning inside the library, which could be dangerous. Who should I call?"

He grinned and whipped his cane back down. "You're lookin' at the guy. I'm the caretaker. Name's Joe Delt." He tipped an invisible hat. "Dang that Miss Sue, always burnin' those... what does she call 'em? Votives. She don't like the way books smell, calls 'em old and musty, yet she's a librarian, if that don't beat all." His unfocused eyes twinkled. "Well, I guess that means she ain't likin' the smell of me either!" He chortled.

"I guess I'm talking to the right guy."

"Yep. Been doin' it for 'bout ten years now. I'm the night watchman, which is ironic since I've been blind for fifteen. I thank you much fer lettin' me know 'bout the candle. I'll take care of that right now." He started to walk back toward the library. "One day, Miss Sue's gonna burn the whole dang place down."

"Goodnight," I said as I walked toward the road, shuffling the dirt so he'd hear me go, and then I covertly snuck back via the rooftop to a spot a few feet above him.

The man was back at the library door, and he pulled out a keychain with a blue rabbit's foot and about a dozen keys on it. I waited patiently as he rubbed each key between his pointer finger and thumb until he finally found the right one and inserted it into the lock. A steady beeping sound went off as soon as he pulled open the door. I quietly dropped to the ground and slipped inside behind him, hiding beside the large desk where I could continue watching him. I saw him push the alarm code, "1-8-8-6", and the noise stopped.

He sniffed the air and moved toward the candle, using his cane to find the desk and sliding his hand low on the counter until he touched the outside glass. I ducked.

"Well, I wonder what he saw. This here candle ain't even warm." He leaned closer to it, taking in a whiff. "But it does smell damn good." He shuffled around, sniffing the air. "I don't smell any other candle burnin' neither, and my nose never lets me down."

He shrugged and then turned, and it felt like forever for him to get to the alarm, set it, walk out, and lock the doors again.

I sat on the floor behind the checkout desk and watched the large black-and-white clock on the wall count down ten minutes to make sure Joe was back in his little house. The library smelled like a musty, old rag left out in the rain, and the candle's sweet scent of vanilla ice cream, taking me back to when I was on the side of the theater watching people eating mounded cones that dripped on their fingers.

The peacefulness of the empty library was calming, but overwhelming due to the numerous books. *Where should I start?* Then, a bank of computers along one wall caught my eye. I went over and balanced my rear on a small chair, the dark face of the screen mocking me.

I'd watched the world change from candles to electric lights, horse-drawn carriages to automobiles, and phones attached to the wall with wires to the ones that could be slipped into a pock-et. However, I'd never had any technology in front of me be-fore, but I knew it could help me find anything I needed. I just had to figure out how to turn the damn machine on. Luckily, I spotted a button with a grey circle on the side. I pushed it, and the screen filled with light, asking for a username and password. I panicked and tapped the keyboard. Letters appeared in the box on the screen beside the flashing, vertical line, but obviously, they weren't the right ones because when I hit "enter," the computer screeched at me.

I growled in frustration, jumping to my feet and slamming my tail hard against the floor, the chair tumbling. My claws plunged into the low carpeting as heat wicked up my neck. I picked up the chair and was ready to hurl it when I noticed a small sign taped behind the large checkout desk that said:

username: gplibrary

password: bookstacks24

I took a deep breath and set the chair down gently, teetering on the edge of the seat again as I hunted for each letter and typed. It took me a minute, but I figured out I could use the up and down arrow keys to move that irritating, flashing bar to the next line. I hit "return" and waited for something to happen.

Suddenly, colorful letters spelled out "Google," and there was another rectangle below that, like a mouth ready to gulp up whatever I typed inside. I tapped my clumsy, large fingers on the keys: g-a-s-c-o-n-y, then hit "return." In the blink of an eye, the picture changed to a list of articles about Gascony, France.

Then I was stuck. The arrow keys only moved the screen up and down, and I could not select an article. The heat returned to my body, but instead of letting it take over, I went back behind the desk where I had found the username and password. Surely there was something to help me… and there it was… the spine of a book said, *Computers for Dummies.*

With a quick read, I realized that I needed to use the 'mouse.' So, I typed: "Gascony, Pennsylvania," and scrolled to find an article on the city's website about The Gascony Theater, then rolled and pushed the plastic oval beside the computer.

Click! I read how Gascony had commissioned Monsieur Salles-Bris, from France, to carve seven statues to serve as protectors of the church. There was a fuzzy black and white photo of him working in the studio, and Ruza stood beside him, a young girl with distinctively wide eyes. There was a picture of the front of the theater on unveiling day, my comrades and I effigies of the real-life monsters we would one day become. Crazy to see!

Next, I searched Monsieur's name, and there was an article about him passing away at age 72 in 1913. Then, I looked up Ruza Prekrasna and an article about a professor of Antiquities and Ancient Historiography currently at U.C.L.A. named Rose Prekrasna-Smith. I knew it couldn't be her. Our building was erected in 1886, and she was 16 then. That would make her 154 years old. *Maybe they're related?*

I found another link that led me to the U.C.L.A. website. There was a row of smiling professors teaching the current spring semester on that page. Though her face looked withered, I was astonished that Rose Prekrasna-Smith looked just like Ruza. *Perhaps she's her great-granddaughter?*

I had to admit, this computer thing was exciting. I could think of anything, and Google would find it for me. So, I typed in "Croatian translator," and it took me to a screen where I could type in any word in either English or Croatian, and it would translate it. *Greatness!*

First, I typed the words that Ruza said to each grotesque and gargoyle every night, *Postanite čudovišta kakve ste trebali biti.* It meant "Become the monsters you were meant to be."

Hmmm.

I looked up *Carolije Animacije*, the book title that Anee remembered so vividly from the day of the reveal ceremony. It meant "spell of animation."

Had Ruza cast a spell to make us come to life that day?

I found some paper and a pencil at the checkout desk and quickly jotted down facts, names, and places, nervous about getting caught the whole time. Just before midnight, I grabbed my notes, cleaned up, and turned off the computer. I punched the numbers into the alarm and left quickly out the door, realizing I didn't have the key, but I couldn't worry about that.

As I reached our little abandoned house, my head spun with ideas and information. I hid my notes beneath an old, mossy terracotta pot on a windowsill, then slipped quietly through the back door to find Anee on the couch, purring in her sleep. I settled beside her on the floor, and the rhythm of her breathing lulled me.

CHAPTER TWENTY-NINE

Ryon - Day 10

31% Waxing Crescent

Anee was hovering over me, waiting for me to wake up. I stretched my wings and quickly made sure my threading was turned off.

"Well, good morning, sleepyhead! I didn't hear you come in," she said, a happy lilt in her voice. She was sitting on the couch like a cat on a fence. "And so…?" She stared at me.

"What?"

"Did you find Geidhuce?" she asked impatiently.

"No, I didn't. But he left me a note on the rooftop."

She jerked her head back slightly. "What did it say?"

"Something like…" Doing my best impression of that evil grotesque, I recited, "You think you have won, but when you least expect it, I will have my revenge. No one is safe." Then I held my hands like claws and added, "May 23rd…D-Day!"

"So, he's still alive, and he's still going through with his plan." She wrinkled her upper lip.

"I assume so. We need to be super careful right now." I stood up and stretched. "How's Telber?"

"Go see for yourself."

I went into the bedroom, and Telber was sitting up on his bed of ratty blankets, looking around.

"R-R-Ryon?" he asked with a thin voice.

"Telber! I'm so glad you're doing better." I rushed over and gave him a hug, his bones poking through his droopy pelt.

"I-I-I'm hungry," he announced.

Anee stood in the doorway, her lion's pride showing.

"Well, me too. How about I catch us some food? We can have a friendship feast."

"Hurray!" said Anee.

I went outside and brought back three birds, six mice, and a fat rat. I even found a bush of brambleberries and picked a large bowlful. Anee and I helped Telber, who was too weak to walk alone, beneath our favorite tree outside. The sun was warm as we enjoyed our meal, talking about Geidhuce, The Chimeras' plan, and the possible death of Isel. Telber shuddered as he listened, barely speaking, threads of blue fear emanating from him.

"I-I-I'm sorry I can't control my threading. I know it puts us all in danger," he said, his eyes full and dark.

"Don't worry. Soon you'll be the happy-go-lucky, donkey-dragon man you were before," I replied.

Just then, a mouse sat up and ran in a circle on Anee's dinner plate. It jumped off, and Anee set her plate down to sniff the tall grass around us, following the mouse's scent.

"Come back, little snack!" she called in a high voice. That's when the white, furry creature darted past her and hid between the protruding roots of our favorite tree.

"Y-Y-You can't be outsmarted by a little 'ole mouse," Telber said, snickering. "Y-Y-You're Queen of the Jungle."

"Well, sometimes my subjects aren't very cooperative," she replied, royalty tinting her tone.

"Your Highness, don't let it get away," I coaxed, laughing.

She crouched, her rear in the air and tail twitching. "Shhhh! It's coming out…"

We watched tiny white whiskers poke out from between the roots, and then the little mouse made a run for it. In one quick pounce, Anee landed a paw upon the poor creature's tail, and it struggled to get away.

"E-E-Eat it!" laughed Telber. "Y-Y-You've earned that food!"

"Yeah, I guess, but this one has spunk." Anee let the mouse's tail go. "Respect!" she yelled, watching it scamper across the field.

We all laughed.

"What did you find in the cave when looking for Geidhuce?" Anee asked, a stem of sour grass hanging out of her mouth. The yellow flowers at the end bobbed as she talked.

"It was empty, and the side room, where I… you know…" I hung my head. "It smelled strongly of bleach, and a word was painted on the wall: *pah-zee-tay*, spelled P-A-Z-I-T-E."

"I know that word. Pazite, pazite…" she said, her mind in a far-off place. "Ruza said it all the time." Anee sat up taller. "Yes! She said it to Geidhuce and no one else. She'd point at him and say, "This one, pazite!" And then she'd laugh. I wonder what it means."

I scratched my leathery bird head, pretending I hadn't

looked it up. It meant "danger." I didn't dare tell Anee about the library or Joe. She'd be angry I'd spoken to another human. "I thought maybe I should gather some tools from my old shed for weapons. I only saw a couple in the barn, but I want to make sure you… we are safe."

"Could I go with you?" Anee's eyes pleaded. "I need to get out for a bit."

"Would you be okay with staying on your own, Telber?" I asked. "I promise, we won't be gone long."

"S-s-sure," Telber replied. "Th-Th-Thank you for taking such good care of me, Ryon and Anee."

A lump rose in my throat.

"Really? I get to go?" Anee, giddy, pounced on me. I fell flat on the ground, her whiskers tickling my droopy condor neck as she kissed it, then she sat on her hunches. "Are you sure you'll be okay, Telber?"

"I-I-I'm good," Telber insisted.

"We know you're good," Anne said, backing off so I could stand. "In fact, you're the best they come." She bounded over to Telber, careful not to knock him over as she rubbed her whiskers on his grey donkey belly.

"Th-Th-That tickles," he chuckled.

My heart felt like it was glowing through my skin. My friend Telber had made it through the worst, and the three of us were safe and together. It was one of the best days of my life, living or while stone… well, second to the night I kissed Madeleine. I wondered how she was and if she missed Chris and me hanging around.

At midnight, Anee made sure Telber was comfortable in his little nest of old sheets and tattered quilts upon the old bed with a squeaky mattress. Next to him was a bucket of dried grass she'd collected for him to munch on, and I'd found a romance novel, *The Seeds of Change*, on the living room bookshelf, and gave it to him to read.

"I left a hoe I found in the garage beside the front door, just in case," I said. "But try not to sleep without someone here. Your threads…"

"I-I-I know. D-D-Don't worry, I'll be fine," Telber said.

I locked the house tight, and then Anee and I slinked down the hill into town.

The lighted buildings were few, like small beacons guiding us through the darkness, although I knew the way there with my eyes closed. We trekked through the bushes and into the trees until we arrived at the shed.

I paused on the roof while Anee climbed down to open the window. Madeleine's house was dark and still, except for the illuminated porchlight that attracted fluttering moths, and her car sat in the driveway, unmoved.

Then I spotted something by her front door—a white package.

I called down to Anee, "I'll be right back."

I didn't wait for her to reply. I went back up through the boughs to a tree near the porch, slid down its trunk, and landed on the grassy ground. Then, I cautiously went up the steps to the box, lying on the welcome mat. The return address was: Maddy Robin, 4444 Dusty Trail, Athens, Texas 75752. My heart overflowed with joy as I picked it up, smelling nuts, brown sugar, and butter from within. *Some sweets baked by my sweet!* I set the cardboard box back down, although it was a little soggy with drops of my saliva.

I returned to the shed the way and swung open the window. Anee had made a pile of "weapons": two rusted rakes, a shovel, some giant hedge trimmers, and another hoe.

"I think this is all we can carry through the trees," Anee said.

We carried the tools out through the window, and I closed it, thinking perhaps it was for the last time. I looked at Anee's face in the waxing moonlight, and each corner of her black lioness mouth drooped downward.

"Anee, what's wrong?"

"I know you're leaving soon, and I... never mind." She shifted her attention to the trees above. "It will be easier-ish to fly along the side of the trees with these," Anee remarked, unfurling her wings.

"Good idea," I replied, feeling tension between us.

Anee flapped and flew upward with her dragon wings, and I followed with my feathered ones, checking I had a good grip on my bundle of stuff before taking off. We traveled close to the canopy and across the meadow to The Hideout without dropping anything, and Anee gave me the silent treatment the whole way.

She got to the porch first, suddenly dropping everything she held and yelling, "Telber, Telber!" She rushed inside the house.

Then I saw it: a pool of blood beside the front door. I set my tools down and found her rushing from room to room.

"I can't find him anywhere!" she growled.

I went back to the puddle on the porch. "Look!" I pointed to a trail of red drips leading to the old barn. We followed them through the rickety door, where a bloody human torso lay next to a burlap bag on the ground. I sniffed the area and detected remnants of scales and fur. "A human-dragon-bear gar is dead, and the mystical animal parts dissolved like Isel's," I announced, my body shaking. "But where's Telber?"

Anee and I split up, searching the dark fields and bushes around the house.

We should never have left him alone. What were we think-ing?

Then, a small series of whimpers came from the creek. In the shadows of trees that lined the water, a hunched figure, highlighted by the moon, stood. Telber was crying and washing his donkey hooves.

I rushed to him. "Telber, are you okay? What happened?" I forgot to breathe while I waited for him to answer.

He slowly stepped out of the river, limping no more than usual, and plopped down in the tall grass. "I-I-I fell asleep... I-I-I know I shouldn't have... I-I-I guess he heard my thread-ing. H-H-He knocked on the door and didn't attack me... seemed kind...just wanted water... a-a-a place to stay for the night. H-H-He said he didn't want to be part of The Chime-ras anymore. H-H-He said Isel was killed and Geidhuce disap-peared...s-s-so The Chimeras disbanded."

"Are you hurt?" I sat beside him.

Telber shook his head, then continued, "H-H-He started asking me questions about what he'd heard me thread while asleep... Wh-Wh-Who were Ryon and Anee? W-W-Why were we living away from the other gars and gros? I-I-I refused to answer… Th-Th-Then, I saw his eyes fixed on the hoe by the front door…H-H-He kept looking at it as he talked… I-I-I got scared… I-I-I offered him water, and he accepted, but while in the kitchen, I-I-I grabbed the cast iron pan off the stove, and wh-wh-when I turned around, h-h-he was swinging the hoe at me! H-H-He said this was his last chance before the moratorium…I-I-I cracked his head open with the pan…h-h-he bled a lot…" Telber's eyes were distant. "I-I-I watched as he took his last breath…d-d-dragged him into the barn and cleaned the kitchen…a-a-all the mess…th-th-then I came here, to clean myself…"

"You did the right thing." I hugged him. "He was probably a spy."

Anee found us, her eyes welling up. "Telber, are you alright?"

He just nodded.

She plopped down on his other side, and we leaned into Telber as he told her the story.

"You poor thing!" Anee said, stroking his dark mane. "You both should know something else. I searched the dead gar and found a note in his satchel. It said, "Ten more days. The Chimeras cannot be stopped.""

We'd taken for granted that no one heard our sleep threads at The Hideout. Anee and I agreed to take shifts as lookouts. I was first, so I sat at the kitchen table, listening to Telber sleep-threading about cleaning the blood in the house. Anee snored like a swarm of bees, threading about me leaving them. I kept thinking about the strange gar, the note Anee had found on him and the one waiting for me on the rooftop, and the painting of "PAZITE" on the cave wall. Geidhuce had to be alive, and he was sending us messages as if he knew our every move.

With so many unknowns, we were in danger, especially if all three of us just sat and waited in one spot. Someone had to act, and as frightened as I was, it only made sense that it be me.

I did what Madeleine always did. I asked the angels. *I need a sign—something to make me sure I'm the one.*

Just as dawn's light emerged through the dirty, web-covered windows of The Hideout, it was my turn to sleep. I curled up on the rug, still warm from Anee's feline body, and distracted myself with visions of Madeleine. As graceful as the butterflies that flit in the grass, I remembered her scent as she descended her front porch steps, the day smiling upon her. My threading was turned off, but I knew Anee would hear if I accidentally dreamed about Madeleine, and it would hurt her, so I fought to stay awake.

Several hours later, I heard Anee say, "Ryon," and I opened my eyes. She looked at me intently, sitting on her haunches. "How'd you sleep?"

"Not well. Telber crying in the river reminded me of how he looked that night at the rally with Geidhuce and Isel—absolutely terrified." Heat spread across my chest, and I slammed my scaly tail hard against the old, wooden floor. "I never wanted to see that again!"

Anee swallowed hard before speaking. "I think we're safe for now..."

I jumped to my dragon feet. "We're never safe, Anee!" A bit of fire shot from my mouth.

Anee flinched. "What the heck?"

I lowered my voice. "It happens sometimes when I feel rage…" I tried to control my wayward tail.

"That's never happened to me," she replied, then she growled and breathed at the same time, trying to draw flames from her own throat. She shrugged, giving up. "While you were disposing of that horrible gar spy's body in the woods, I found something else in that intruder's bag." Her amber hackles raised. "At the very bottom, beneath clumps of berries and some rat jerky, I noticed a small tube." She bounded on silent feet into the kitchen and then quickly returned with a white cylinder in her mouth. "There's a rolled piece of paper. See for yourself."

I removed the lid and unfurled the note, holding it with both hands to keep the scroll from curling up. The page was typed and titled "The Meeting of The Chimeras." An uneasy tingling began in my extremities as I read it over. "This is a checklist of taking over the theater: hold key humans hostage, gather weapons, kill anyone who interferes…" I struggled to breathe.

"Look on the back."

I flipped it over and read it out loud:

"Mandatory orders for all gars and gros:

The element of surprise is on our side, therefore, be incognito for the next ten days. No human can see you. There's a moratorium on eating them or going outside your hiding places. I'm also in hiding, nearly fully recovered, and strategizing every detail of our takeover. On the night of the next full moon, May 23rd, we'll meet in the cavern, and each will receive their assignment. You'll be given your weapons, and we'll take over the theater. Any creature who goes against these orders will be executed. The Chimeras will prevail!

Your Commander,

Geidhuce"

A river of cold washed over my body.

"Ten days, like the other note," Anee remarked. "With the gars and gros sequestering, we're safe-ish for a bit." She studied me, her pupils thin slits in the sunbeams through the dirty windows. "You have to stop them. What's your plan?"

"Honestly, Anee, I don't know."

"It must be you, Ryon. I need to take care of Telber."

"I'm scared." I gulped. "How will I have the strength to defeat Geidhuce and an army of evil monsters? And if the beast in me takes over again, I'm afraid of what it'll do."

"I've been thinking about how you blame your past actions on your beastly side, but I don't think that's true. You're making Gascony safer. You're a hero."

"Oh, no. I'm not…"

"Go save us." She smiled. "I believe in you." She got up and headed toward where Telber slept, her rapid movement making the tattered curtains dance.

I wanted a sign and received more than that. I got the blessing of my friend.

CHAPTER THIRTY

Ryon - Day 9

40% Waxing Crescent

I used the woven satchel from our intruder to collect various items for my journey. I packed the notes I'd taken at the library and a pen and paper for writing. An old roadmap of the United States I'd discovered wedged between two books also went into the bag. I thought about bringing the dagger, but decided it was better to leave it with Telber and Anee in case they needed it while I was away. Besides, every time I looked at the thing, my stomach flipped.

I wondered if I'd ever return to the tiny, worn-down cottage. It was too heartbreaking to say goodbye to my friends since there was a good chance I'd never see them again. So, when they hunted for critters near the creek that night, I jotted a note saying I'd left on my journey and would miss them, leaving it on the kitchen table. I wanted to say more, but the blur of emotion mucked up my thoughts. With tears in my beady eyes and my heart as heavy as a river rock, I grabbed my bag and closed the door behind me.

I only had ten days to complete my quest, so I'd travel by night, hiding and sleeping by day. I'd studied the map carefully and planned to follow the blue lines representing the roads that led toward Los Angeles. From there, somehow, I'd get to U.C.L.A. and find Ruza's great-granddaughter. She was the only one who might be able to help me stop The Chimeras. And if I could, I'd stop in Texas to catch one last glimpse of my beloved Madeleine. My selfish, ignorant, lovesick heart pushed me toward her like burning coal pushes a train toward its destination.

But first, I had to find the closest thruway, 80 West. The map I'd found only had the major highways, not the roads leading to them. I thought about finding Chris and asking him to direct me, but I decided to visit my new friend, Joe Delt, instead. He was the only other human I could speak to without them running away in horror, and I knew just where to find him.

When I arrived at Joe's house, the front porch light was like a flare marking the spot. Inside one window, a round ceiling fixture glowed like a tiny moon as Joe busied himself in his kitchen. I thought about knocking on the door, but I was worried someone else might have been there. So, I decided to wait in the bushes, watching and listening.

Joe banged pots, pans, and dishes in a symphony of clanks, but I heard no other voices. *How is Joe able to do so much without hurting himself, being blind and all?* Soon, the rich smell of beef, carrots, and potatoes wafted to my beak, and drool dribbled from my mouth. And a yeasty aroma teased my nostrils like the smell from the bakery in town when I was a stone gro.

I moved closer to the house, hoping to see if he was truly alone through the window when *BANG!*, I knocked over a metal trash can.

Quick as the wind, Joe was outside with a shotgun pointed at my human chest.

"Freeze right there, or I'll letcha have it!" he announced decisively.

"Joe, it's me, Ryon." My voice shook. "Remember? From the other night."

"Ryon? I don't know no Ry-on!" He pushed the gun forward, even closer to my rapidly beating heart.

My stomach rolled as I pictured the front page of the morning newspaper: BLIND MAN KILLS MONSTER IN FRONT YARD, ONLY HUMAN TORSO AND ARMS REMAIN. "I told you... about the candle burning in the library. Remember?"

Joe's brows moved up his forehead in unison. "Oh, the candle guy. You know, it wasn't even burnin' when I went in to check." He pushed the barrel of the gun even closer to me. "Been wonderin' whatcha were up to that night ever since."

"Nothing. I swear I saw a flame. Must have been a reflection in the window or something." I lied so often to Chris that I could easily make up stuff on the spot, but guilt riddled me every time.

"Well, whatcha doin' here now besides makin' a racket?" He flicked the end of the gun up and down as if measuring my body.

"I accidentally knocked over your trash can. Sorry about that. I'm just trying to find my way to the highway. 80 West. You seem knowledgeable, and I saw your light on." I smiled as I spoke, hoping it would help make me sound kind.

"Ya went lookin' fer a blind guy to give ya directions?" he remarked sarcastically.

He's right. What was I thinking?

However, he lowered his gun. "Well, I'm quite an expert on the 'which-a-ways', although you'd never think that of an old guy with visual impairment. I've got what ya might call a sixth sense when it comes to thangs." He stood taller, his chest puffed with pride between the suspenders he wore over his short-sleeved, white button-up shirt.

"Well, that's impressive. I came to the right place."

"Ya sure did! Ya from out of town?"

"Well, the truth is, I'm from Gascony, but I had a very… sheltered life…"

"…So yer finally breakin' free. Good fer ya!" He reached out his hand, and I was grateful that part of me was human as I shook it. "Ya hungry? I got a heap of stew nearly ready for eatin'. And homemade biscuits, too."

"Directions and cooking… you're a man of many talents," I replied.

"Won't ya join me?"

I hesitated. His house was tucked behind the library, but I feared my giant and strange silhouette in the window might be suspicious to passersby. What if his daughter showed up? Or a neighbor? It was risky.

"If ya do me the favor of keepin' me company 'fore ya head out of town, I'll make sure yer belly's full and happy." He used a hand to beat on his slightly protruding belly like a drum, *thump-thump-thump*. "Hear that? It's echoin' for some vittles. Come and join me, won't ya? I made too much for one man, as usual."

It did smell delicious, and I could get the directions I needed while eating. "Okay. Thank you. Do you always eat dinner so late?"

"Yep. Don't sleep much anymore, and bein' blind makes night and day blend together," he replies, leading me up the steps and through his front door. As I stepped inside, I quickly located the light switch and flicked it off as quietly as possible. I hoped he'd be none the wiser—and it didn't faze him a bit. I watched in awe as he quickly placed his gun on a rack beside the door and scampered around the kitchen as if his eyes worked perfectly well. My condor eyesight worked fine in the dimness, and the streetlight outside, many yards away, touched objects in the room with silver brushstrokes of light. I watched as Joe passed in and out of the shadows.

"Now, sit yerself right on down at the table, and I'll fix ya up a bowl," Joe said, thrusting a large, silver ladle into a big, black pot, coming up heaped full of delicious-smelling stew.

I hung my satchel on the back of a metal chair, then pulled it away from the table, the legs scraping across the black and white checkered linoleum floor. As I sat, I tucked my tail between my dragon knees to keep it from tripping Joe as he set a large bowl of succulent vegetables and meat in front of me. The steam tickled my beak, bringing on the saliva storm again.

I was about to plunge my beak into the bowl when Joe said, "Where are my hostin' skills? Ya need somethin' to eat with." He opened a drawer, turned back to me, and held out a spoon and a white paper napkin. "Here ya go." I took them from his hand and set both to the right of my bowl. "In just a minute, I'll bring out the biscuits. Now eat while it's hot." I'd never eaten with any sort of tool before. Getting the stew onto the spoon was easy, but getting it from the bowl to my mouth beneath my giant beak without spilling everywhere took practice. Either a potato chunk would fall off on its journey to my mouth, or I would accidentally hit the tip of my beaked nose, splattering the entire spoonful everywhere. But once I got the utensil to the right place, the stew was the best food I'd ever tasted.

"Grrrow-mmm!" came out of me involuntarily, and I froze, hoping I didn't scare him.

"Good stuff, eh?" Joe asked, unalarmed. Then, he set a basket full of tan disks on the table that smelled of flour and cheese. "These are some of the best cheddar biscuits in town, if I say so myself. Butter's on the table." Joe sat in the chair across from me and put his napkin on his lap. I immediately copied him, although mine was already covered in brown splashes.

"Everything is delicious, Joe. No one's ever made me such a delicious hot meal before," I said, thinking to myself how, until then, I had only eaten old, cold human food found in dumpsters or live animals. Cooking was a remarkable thing.

"So, where ya headin' to?" Joe asked in between slurps.

"Texas," I replied. "Then on to California."

"How ya gettin' there? I didn't hear any type of motor."

"I'm walking," I replied, realizing how ridiculous that sounded when said out loud.

Again, Joe was unfazed. "I saw the whole U.S. of A. while workin' for the government. Top secret military stuff."

"What was your job title?"

Joe chuckled. "I did a different kind of service for my country. I was an electrical engineer. I built stuff fer satellites and whatnot fer NASA."

"Satellites?"

"Yes, ya know, spacecraft that floats around the earth." Joe leaned closer to me, the back of his hand along the side of his mouth as he whispered, "It was spy-craft. I built giant eyes-in-the-skies. Big Brother." He sat upright in his chair again and went back to eating his stew.

"Do you work for NASA now?"

"No, no. I'm too old fer that. Retired eighteen years ago, before my eyes got bad."

"So, you used to be able to see?"

"Yep, the blindness started about fifteen or so years ago. Macular degenerative thang. It started slow at first, but it's gotten pretty bad. I'm completely in the dark." Joe bit into a biscuit and chewed, his white beard moving up and down. I'd eaten everything he'd given me and had the impulse to lick both of our bowls clean—and I would have, had Joe not been around. "So, enough 'bout that. Ya goin' to Texas or Cali fer a lady?" He winked.

"Yes, you could say that. She's outside of Dallas. Then I'm going west to visit…family."

"So, yer leavin' family to go find other family?"

"Yes, sir." Then, I thought about leaving Telber and Anee alone in the hills and the dead gargoyle buried in nearby woods, which made my legs tingle.

Joe paused and scratched his head while electricity lit up his cloudy eyes. "I've been wantin' to get away myself." He leaned forward again, and I moved closer, expecting another whispered secret. Instead, Joe stared at me. I feared he could see more than he admitted because his eyes scanned my face. I instinctively shoved myself backward in my chair, jolting the table like an earthquake, his spoon sliding off the table.

Joe caught the spoon just before it hit the ground.

I jumped to my feet, the chair toppling over on its side. I began to shake. "So, you *can* see!" I squawked, the condor in me taking over my voice.

Joe began to laugh again. "Nope, I'm blinder than a bat."

"But you were looking at me! And you caught the spoon…"

"That's my sixth sense. Bein' blind has helped me develop what I call 'soul radar'. I can tell a man's character by focusin' on it. Don't worry—you've got a good one."

"But the spoon!"

"I also make up for what I can't see with super good listening skills. I heard its path across the table is all."

I took some deep breaths to calm the inferno inside my chest. "I need to go, but thank you for your kindness," I said as I righted the chair. "Now, how do I get to 80 West?"

Joe stood up and approached me. I took a few steps backward toward the door.

"I'm sorry, Ryon, if I frightened ya. I just had to check before I asked."

"Asked what?" My mind raced. *Does he know what I am?*

"Could I go with ya? Seems my family won't let me leave this place anymore, and I feel like I'm missin' the world. I don't have many years left, but I'm still spry for 79, just blind. I could use a friend to be my eyes. We'd have a mighty fine time."

"But we hardly know each other. How do you know I'm not a murderer?" *Or a giant man-dragon beast!*

"Like I said, I've got this sense of thangs. Now, what do ya say? I know all there is about the world outside of Gascony. I think ya could use a man like me on yer trip." Joe slipped his thumbs behind each side of his suspenders.

He'll slow me down. I can't take him with me.

"Ya know, it'll take 18 days to walk to Texas," he added.

"18 days?" I only had ten days before Geidhuce and his fiends took over.

"Stick with me. I know how to cut that to two."

I realized I needed him and would make it work somehow. "Joe, it'd be my pleasure to have you join me."

He let out a whoop like in a Western movie. "Woo-wee! Gimme a minute to pack."

Before I knew it, Joe had disappeared into the next room. I heard zippers, pills rattling in plastic bottles, and several thuds. But as I waited, the cat clock on the wall rolling its eyes to the tick-tock of time, my stomach filled with dread. *Why'd I agree to let him go? I'll be traveling by night, hiding the whole time. He'd never understand…*

I needed an excuse to renege that wouldn't give me away. I tossed so many ideas around that they became muddled like the creek after a storm.

Joe reappeared in the kitchen, an army green duffle on his back.

"Good thing I travel light," he said, grinning widely.

"Ah, Joe, I've been thinking. It's a long trip to Texas, you know, and…"

Joe burst out with laughter, his blue eyes glistening in the darkness. "I was wonderin' how long it would take ya to confess!"

"What are you talking about?" I asked, fear sparking in me again.

"Sorry, friend. Don't mean to make ya uncomfortable," he remarked, still chuckling softly in his belly. He took a red handkerchief out of his pocket and wiped each eye. "It's just that I suspected ya had some kind of… trouble yer dealin' with. I expected you'd come up with some excuse. Ya on the lam?" He put the handkerchief away.

"On the *lamb*…?"

"Ya know, are ya doin' the skedaddle, gettin' out of dodge, doin' the Irish goodbye?"

"I have no idea what you're…"

Joe stared right at me, and my skin prickled.

"Are ya runnin' away from somethin'? A crime? A bad situation? I've met a lot of fellers that needed to leave a mess behind." He set his pack on the floor next to his feet. "What ya did earlier made me a bit suspicious."

"What did I do?"

"Ya turned out the light when ya entered my kitchen. I heard the faintest click and knew. Then I checked, and the switch was down instead of up. Don't underestimate the hearing of a blind guy." He winked and then laughed again.

"Joe, I…" What could I tell him? That I was a gargoyle that had come to life? That I was a walking, talking, dragon-man-condor with a tail, wings, clawed dragon feet, and scales from the waist down? No way. "You're right. I'm running away for a little while."

"Won't ya tell me what yer runnin' from?"

"No, but I promise, it's not what you might think… I have a

…condition. My face, well, it frightens some people. I don't like to talk about it." My heart sank as I said these words. Sadly, this time, I was telling the truth.

"Well, okay, ya don't have to say another word," Joe said, feeling for a chair and then sitting. "I'm good with travelin' under the radar. Don't need no people lookin' at me neither!"

"I appreciate it."

"I feel yer kindness on my 'soul-dar,' and I ain't one to care much 'bout what anyone looks like. It's what's inside that counts. Ya need a disguise or anythin' like that?"

I hadn't thought of that. Most men didn't walk around with a bare chest like I had been doing since I came alive. "Maybe a shirt? I… tore mine on a nail on the way here," I fabricated. "But I'm pretty large…"

"I gotcha. Ya work out, eh? Well, yer in luck. My son is a muscle guy, too. Left a bunch of stuff behind when he moved out. Be right back."

Joe left the room and returned holding a huge, blue plaid flannel shirt. "Try this." He tossed it to me perfectly. "And I brought ya a pair of jeans yer welcome to." He held up a pair of pants nearly as wide as the kitchen sink was long and then set them on the table.

I'd never worn clothes before, and when I picked up the shirt, the soft fabric was like I imagined clouds to feel like. It smelled good, too, like spring flowers.

"Does the shirt fit?" Joe asked, scratching beneath his beard.

I slipped my arms into each sleeve and was able to button it. "Yes… it's great."

"How 'bout them pants? Gonna try 'em too?"

I looked back at my enormous tail and couldn't imagine how I'd get the pants to fit, even if I cut a giant hole in the back. "I'm good. Thanks, Joe. I'm happy with the shirt."

"Ya may be even more glad of what I'm about to tell ya."

"What's that?"

"I got me a truck we can drive!" Joe slapped his right thigh once in excitement.

"Truck?"

"Yep. I'll keep yer secret if ya keep mine. Ya see, I may be blind, but I can fix stuff. I got an old Ford truck in the garage. Been workin' on it by touch fer years, and I got it workin'. Got a buddy, Bruce, at the gas station, who helps me now and again, too. I haven't told a soul but him 'bout it, not even my family. My kids would have heart attacks—they'd accuse me of tryin' to drive, but even I wouldn't do that." He paused and leaned forward toward me. "Ya know how to drive, don't ya?"

"No, I never have."

Joe contorted his mouth. "Ya have lived under a rock, haven't ya?"

"More like inside of one."

"Well, that's worse." Joe smiled. "Drivin' is easy. You'll pick it up in no time."

"So, you want me to drive us to Texas? I don't have a license or anything."

"As long as ya stay on the straight and narrow, you'll be jest fine."

"I don't think I..." My skin became sticky with sweat. "How quickly will we get there in your truck?"

"About two nights of drivin'. If we leave tonight."

Two nights were way better than more than two weeks by foot, and it gave me extra time to find Madeleine and Ruza. "Are you sure I can learn to drive quickly?"

"Sure. Ya got two feet, don't ya?"

I looked down at my large, green-brown, scaly feet. "Yep."

"Ya got two arms to steer with and two eyes to see with, right?"

"Sure do."

"Then we're good to go." Joe got up and started washing the dishes in the sink. "I just gotta tidy up a bit first. Only take me a few."

"May I help?"

"I got it. Ya gather up yer stuff and get ready for our adventure," he called over the sound of the water shooting out of the faucet. He set each clean, wet dish on a wire rack on the edge of the sink and covered the entire thing with a towel from the refrigerator handle.

Then, he went toward his bag, and I jumped to help him, grabbing the handle at the same time he did. He yanked it hard enough to scrape my palm.

"Ouch," I said.

"Sorry to hurt ya but let me tell ya one thing." Joe stepped closer, enough to feel his breath on my chest. "Don't go helpin' me or treatin' me any different. I may be blind, but I can do many things," he said firmly. "About the only thing I can't do is drive. Got it? And if I need help with somethin', I'll ask fer it. There's nothin' I hate more than someone treatin' me special like, just 'cause I can't see." He held out his hand. "Deal?"

"It's a deal," I replied, shaking his hand. I picked up my satchel.

As we walked out of Joe's house, he grabbed his cane by the door and led me down the dirt driveway to an old, wooden garage. The white paint was peeling as if shedding its skin. The trim around the windows was a dingy blue and as scaly as the lower part of my body.

Joe pulled a clump of keys out of his jeans pocket, and they chimed in the wind. I was impressed by how quickly he found the right one and skillfully stuck a small key into the padlock, opening it with a *pop!* Then, he yanked open the garage door like it was as light as lifting an empty cardboard box, revealing an old Ford truck in mint condition.

"Bruce, my friend who's been helpin' me with the truck, well, he test-drove her 'bout two months ago. Said she runs real good. Ain't she a beauty?" said Joe.

Joe stood briefly as if admiring the shiny, black truck smiling at us with her silver grill.

"A 1984 F150. She's like a fine lady to me— I visit her every day, turnin' her engine on for 'bout fifteen minutes to keep her battery charged. I can tell she's dyin' to get out into the world, just like the two of us." Joe tossed his bag into the truck's open bed, and so did I. He pulled out another key, used it to open the driver's side door, and held it open for me.

"Well, go ahead. Get behind that wheel. I'll tell ya what to do."

I climbed in, tucking my tail, grateful the large vehicle gave my six-foot body enough space to fit all my parts. I was careful not to brush against him—the last thing I needed was for him to feel my scales, tail, or beak. Then, Joe walked to the back of the truck, rustled around in the garage, and threw other items in the bed. Before I knew it, Joe was in the passenger seat beside me.

"Now, all truckers need one last somethin', especially when they're on an adventure." He lifted a lever on the front of a small, hinged door in front of him, and it popped open. Inside was a black cap with a Ford logo on the front. Excitement gleamed in his murky eyes as he handed it to me.

I slipped it on top of my leathery bird head and caught the reflection of myself in the front window. The bill on the hat mimicked the one on my face and shadowed my features, making me look less like a creature and more like a man. With the shirt, I could easily be mistaken for a human from the waist up.

"Joe, I'm really glad you're going with me. Thanks."

"Ain't nothin', Ryon. I'm so excited to be gettin' out. I'm feelin' a little giddy."

"And what about your family? How will you let them know you've left but you're okay?" I didn't want the police out looking for us.

"The magic of technology," Joe said with a smile. He pulled a cell phone out of his pocket. "Siri, text Daughter Claire." Then, he leaned toward me and said, "She'll tell the other two."

"What do you want it to say?" said a female voice coming from the phone.

"I've headed out of town with a friend period no need to worry period he'll take real good care of me period I'll be back next week period talk to ya then period."

The phone repeated the message. "Ready to send it?" it asked.

"Yes," Joe replied.

"Okay, it's sent," she said matter-of-factly.

I was amazed at what a small pocket computer could do. Joe was resourceful, and I could learn a lot from him. "So, now, how do I drive?" I asked, taking a deep breath.

"Put this key in the slit to the right of the steerin' wheel and give it a right turn. Ya only use yer right foot to accelerate and stop, ya hear? Be sure yer right foot is firmly pushin' the left pedal on the floor, then pull that lever behind the wheel toward ya and down 'til the needle on the dash is on the big "D"." My dragon foot barely fit perpendicular to the floorboard, but I did my best, lurching forward and then breaking again.

Joe was nothing but patient.

And so it went, my blind friend directing me as if he could see everything. The truck lurched and revved as I practiced using the brakes, backed up, but I figured out which pedal did what. Luckily, there wasn't much traffic once we got to the vast country road. The headlights showed us the way, and so did Joe's phone.

"Where we headin'?" Joe asked.

"4444 Dusty Trail, Athens, Texas," I recited.

From then on, his phone told me exactly where to go, and I grew increasingly comfortable behind the wheel. My initial worries about traveling with Joe faded, except that his family could start looking for us. I decided to worry about that when it happened.

Driving the highway went smoothly, despite my foot getting tired from being jammed into the confined space on the floor. When a cramp erupted, I'd jerk, and the truck would slow and chug, chug, chug until I got my foot back on the tiny pedal. Road signs and green, red, yellow, and white traffic signals led the way, accented by reflective dotted lines.

I worried about Anee and Telber, but I was joyous to be moving toward Madeleine with every mile. Joe filled the darkness with stories about his life, overprotective family, and hopes for the trip. I just listened and drove.

After a few hours, an alarm went off on Joe's phone, which was plugged into the cigarette holder with an adapter and a wire. He asked, "How full is the gas tank?"

"How can I tell?"

"There's a gauge with a gas pump on it. See it?" Joe pointed his finger toward the panel behind the steering wheel.

"Yes, yes. There's a little red needle, and it's almost pointing to a white capital 'E'."

"Well, that there 'E' stands for empty, so stop at the next gas station."

Panic grabbed me by the throat, and my breathing became strained. *What if someone's there? What if they see my face, my scales, my tail?*

"I can't pump the gas. I…" I shivered.

"No worries, Ryon. I gotcha. I can pump the gas. All ya gotta do is drive on this trip, okay?"

I nodded and said, "Okay."

Joe leaned toward me and lowered his voice as if someone was listening. "After ya get to the station, pull up with the pump on the left side of the truck, then slip out around the back of the buildin'. I'll pump the gas, and when I'm ready to go, and the coast is clear, you'll hear me whistle a song, and ya can sneak on back."

My shoulders relaxed. "You've got it all figured out."

"I try." Then he paused. "Aw, darn it! Do ya have any money?"

"No." Fear rose inside of me again, like a river in storm season.

Joe burst out laughing. "Gotcha! I got plenty of money. Like I said, all ya gotta do is drive."

I let out an audible gasp. "Thank you, Joe. I'll pay you back somehow."

"No need."

Are the angels caring for me like Madeleine asked them to do for her? "I see a sign that says there's gas in five miles."

"Sounds good," he said, smiling.

Then, silence became a third passenger, and as I glanced over to see if Joe had fallen asleep, he suddenly asked, "Tell me 'bout the girl yer fixin' to see. What's her name?"

"Madeleine." I tingled, saying her name out loud. "She's just as beautiful inside as she is on the outside."

"Ya sound as lovesick as a pig is about his slop."

"Is that a good thing?"

"Yes, sir! Think how much a pig loves his dinner." Joe yanked on his seatbelt. "It's just like me and the love I got fer this here truck."

I laughed. "Joe, I'm so grateful…"

"None of that. Just look out fer that gas station."

Not a soul was around as I pulled up in the vast darkness.

I snuck out of the cab, went behind the small mini-mart, and walked to the edge of the woods beyond the building to be sure no one would spot me. I relieved myself and hunted for food, hungry again, sniffing out a sizeable grey rat. Just as I was licking my fingers clean, I heard Joe whistle a song that came to me on the warm wind. So, I carefully glided through the shadows, around the building, and into the driver's seat again.

"See? That wasn't too bad, was it?" Joe said as he rolled the top of a large paper bag. "Got us some food. Sandwiches, chips, Coca-Colas."

"How will I ever repay you for all of this?" I asked.

"Just drive, my friend. Just drive."

O   O   O

I grew nervous as sunrise neared. We'd driven over five hours since leaving Joe's.

"We need to stop and sleep. Until it's dark again," I announced. My body was sore from sitting so long and the tension of being a brand-new driver.

"Sounds good to me. I could use a little shut-eye." Joe yawned loudly.

I drove about three miles, searching for a place to stop. I chose to turn onto a dirt road that led into a giant forest of pines. The truck bumped and bounced as we traveled down the unpaved path, dust filling the headlight beams. I pulled into a clearing beneath a thick canopy of trees and put the truck into park. It felt good to open the door, stand, and stretch.

I looked up at the fading stars and quarter moon peeking at us through the spaces between branches. *Almost halfway to full*, I thought, my heart skipping a beat. *Only nine days before D-Day.*

Frogs and crickets sang to us in a strange but beautiful harmony. My heart was half full like the moon: half lighted with friendship, love, and gratitude, and half dark with worry about Telber and Anee, Geidhuce and The Chimeras.

"It's warm enough to sleep outside tonight," Joe announced. "I packed us some supplies." He flipped down the gate of the Ford to reveal an arsenal: two rolled-up sleeping bags, jugs of water, paper towel rolls, a gallon of gas, boxes of granola bars, and a large flashlight.

"You thought of everything," I said, smiling.

"And don't fergit, I got us some other bites at the gas station. We can fill our bellies before we hit the hay."

We sat on the open truck gate and ate egg salad sandwiches and barbecue potato chips, sipping the sweet brown ambrosia of Coca-Cola. Then, Joe rolled out both sleeping bags. He lay down on one, face to the sky, his eyes as if they were enjoying the celestial view. I lay beside him, careful not to get too close, watching the glowing aura of day begin to highlight the edges of the trees.

"We're off to a good start," Joe said before falling asleep seconds later, a gentle snore adding a third layer to the bug symphony.

I discreetly climbed out of the truck bed and walked to a nearby tree. Scaling its rough bark, I navigated the piney boughs until I was far up on a sturdy branch where I could see the rising sun. I watched over Joe until I drifted off to sleep.

FIRST QUARTER

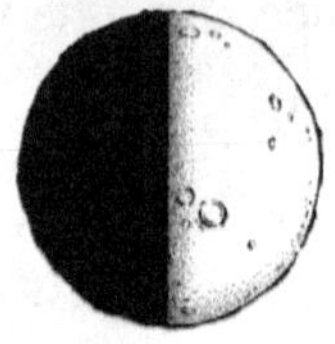

"Challenges are ahead, but if you are committed and confident, you will reach your desired outcome."

CHAPTER THIRTY-ONE

Madeleine - Day 10, 9, and 8

31% and 40% Waxing Crescent

50% First Quarter

I was sure The Arcs were trying to tell me something. I watched the Texas skies for another glittery moon the next four nights, and though its lunar body grew larger, it didn't change as it had before. And I still heard inexplicable growls in the background whenever I talked to anyone in Gascony on the phone.

"Can you hear that?" I asked my mother, father, and friends Julie and Sierra separately, and they all said no and that I probably had a bad connection on my end. But I knew in my gut something was stirring behind the scenes in Gascony, but I had no idea what. The Arcs assured me everyone there was safe for the time being.

Two days after I saw the pink sparkle moon, my grand-mother added blueberries to my oatmeal, and the intuitive voice that often spoke to me inside my head told me to count them. *Ten. So, what does that mean?* No reply, so I finished eating and then sat at the desk in my room to work remotely that day. Ten squawking mockingbirds sat outside the window in a row on the old post-and-rail fence. I didn't think about the coincidence until, at exactly 10:10 a.m., Julie Venmoed the ten bucks she owed me.

"Arcs, what's going on?" I asked out loud.

"There are no coincidences, only synchronicities," an angelic voice responded, but that was all it said.

Used to cryptic messages from beyond, I shrugged and went back to work. I'd been assigned to do fact-checking and research for the staffers who wrote the Lifestyle section online, so I Googled the rest of the morning. Then, I joined the staff meeting on Zoom right after lunch and was given a list of…you guessed it…. ten items to research. I couldn't believe it. But it didn't stop there. One staffer was writing an article on how the recent crab crisis affected Dallas restaurants.

"Ten billion have disappeared from the Bering Sea," she announced.

"Crabfest at Red Lobster is about to get expensive," remarked another staffer. "I love crab legs… by the way, how many legs does a crab have?"

"I'll Google it," I said, and was stunned. "Ten. A crab has ten legs."

Then, another staffer announced, "I have something to pitch. Jewel, the singer, has a ranch just outside of Dallas, in Mullin, and she's throwing a private concert."

Many on the Zoom call murmured accolades for the talented artist.

"She's debuting a remake of her hit song, "Ten,"" he added.

"Of course, she is," slipped out of my mouth. Everyone went silent, and my face flushed hot. "Sorry. Was talking to… ah…Grandy. Forgot to mute myself," I fibbed.

The meeting ended, and I was confused. *What the heck is*

going on?

It was time to stop working at five o'clock. I needed a change of scenery, so I entered the den and found my grandfather playing a new game on his shuffleboard table. He wore his usual khaki shorts and button-down, short-sleeved shirt, that day in baby blue.

"Whatcha doing, Grampy?"

"I got some mini wooden bowling pins. The idea is to use the puck to try and knock all ten down." His voice was deep and chesty.

Just then, Grandy burst into the room. "Why do hot dogs come in packages of ten and buns don't?"

"Good question," I said. "Are we having hot dogs for dinner?"

"No. I'm making spaghetti and meatballs," she proclaimed as she returned to the kitchen.

"Strike!" Grampy yelled, pins flying everywhere. "I did it! That deserves a high-ten." He held both palms up for me to smack.

"Don't you mean high-five?" I replied, exasperated by my grandparents' references to the number ten.

He grinned, hands still up and blue eyes twinkling. "One finger for each pin."

I sighed and slapped his hands with mine.

After dinner, I was anxious to go to bed. I hoped that sleeping would end my "day of tens." Being intuitive was sometimes tiring, but a day with constant reminders of something I didn't understand was exhausting.

◯ ◯ ◯

The next morning, the sun beamed into my room, and I awoke feeling refreshed. I got dressed and whistled a random tune as I entered the kitchen. Grandy had made mini pancakes for breakfast, and as I sat at the small white table, I was happy not to see oatmeal with ten blueberries again. There were cheery sunflowers in a white vase shaped like an old milk bottle in the center of the table, and their pretty yellow and brown faces were reassuring. Using a knife to butter those delicious discs that smelled of vanilla and cinnamon, I counted nine pancakes on my plate.

Phew! The "day of tens" is over.

I giggled as I poured maple syrup over them, and then my grandmother hummed a song.

"What's the name of that song you're humming?" I asked, then crammed my mouth with another delicious bite.

"It's an old Patti Smith song. I believe it's called "Nine,"" she answered, sitting beside me. Then she sang, "Nine a night of diamonds…" as she dunked the teabag up and down by its string to the beat into a mug of hot water. "Do you know it?"

"I don't." My enthusiasm for the day faded, and my apprehension made me lightheaded.

Grampy entered through the kitchen door from outside. He held several plastic grocery bags and clanged them on the white tile countertop. Shaking his head, he reported, "All they had was 9-Lives cat food at the store, no Fancy Feast. I hope Genevieve likes it."

I sank into my chair. I had entered a "day of nines" and braced myself for the barrage.

I went to my room and logged onto my weekly Zoom checkin with my supervisor and her assistant. They were already having a discussion:

"…and since Pluto has been classified as a dwarf planet, there are no longer nine planets," my boss, Tanya, said. "Oh, hello, Maddy. Thanks for joining us."

"Good morning," I replied, with feigned enthusiasm.

"I hope you didn't get too far on that list of research items," she continued. "You can scratch off number nine. The writer's assignment changed. So that leaves you with…"

"Nine in total," I said, my shoulders slumping, feeling worn out already, and it was only… I looked at the clock. *Nine-oh-nine in the morning. Of course it is!*

After my meeting, the day continued unremarkably as I worked on my assigned list. But eventually, I got hungry and went to the kitchen for a break. I opened the refrigerator and pulled out some bread, lunchmeat, and mayonnaise for a sandwich when I heard something crash in the family room. Quickly setting everything I'd gathered on the counter, I ran to see what had happened.

Grampy looked worried, and a large cardboard box marked "Christmas decorations" was at his feet.

"Are you okay?" I asked.

"I'm fine, but the contents of this box may not be," Grampy replied. "Grandy is gonna kill me if I break her celluloid reindeer. I was looking for my old boots so I could check out the front pasture without gettin' bitten by any copperheads. Your grandmother thinks they're too old and worn out, so she stashes them on the closet shelf out of sight." He chuckled.

"I know how much you love your boots. But what's celluloid?" I asked.

"An old-timey plastic made from camphor trees." Grampy knew a lot about antiques.

"Let me help you," I said. "I'm on lunch break."

I picked up the box and set it on the couch. Then I went to the kitchen and returned with a chair to stand on. I slid it inside the closet and stood on the seat to search the shelf.

"What do they look like?" I asked.

"Black cowboy boots with grey stitching. Size nine and a half."

Of course, nine's your size.

I pulled my cell phone out and turned on the flashlight, catching a glimpse of them smashed in the back corner. I stood on tiptoes, and they were just in reach.

"Are these the ones?" I stepped off the chair, holding two beat-up leather boots.

"Yep." There was Grampy, sitting on the couch, lining up the opaque ivory reindeer on the coffee table in some kind of pattern.

"I only found eight. Doesn't Santa have nine?" he asked.

I set the boots on the chair, walked over to the box of white wads of tissue paper, and dug around. At the bottom was one more. I unwrapped it.

"There are nine if you count Rudolph," I said, pretending to make the lightweight, plastic deer in my hand fly and land in front of his friends. "See? He's got a red nose."

Grampy smiled. "I'm glad I didn't break any. They're pretty delicate."

"Why did you set them up in a funky diamond on the table? I'd have thought you'd set them in two lines like in all the pictures."

"I just wanted to see what they'd look like as baseball play-ers." He chuckled. "Looks like you made Rudolph the catcher."

I sighed. "There are nine outfield positions?"

"Yes, there are. You're one smart cookie, Maddy dear." He looked over at his boots on the chair. "Thanks for finding them."

"Of course, Grampy." I kissed him on the cheek before re-turning to the kitchen to make my lunch.

That night, I went to bed completely spent again.

O   O   O

As I dressed the next day, I wasn't surprised to overhear my grandmother again complaining that there were only eight hot dog buns in a package, fewer than the number of hot dogs we had.

"Oh, Arcs. This is a day of eights, isn't it?" I asked, looking upwards, waiting for a reply.

I dressed in my nice grey pants and a floral blouse, making sure I looked professional, and then braced myself before en-tering the kitchen.

"Good morning, Maddy. Have a seat, dear," Grandy greet-ed, wearing the same cobalt and blue checkered apron she al-ways wore in the kitchen. "You drive to the newspaper to work today, right?"

"Yes."

"Thought so. I made you some eggs."

"Thanks, Grandy. I really appreciate all you do for me."

"Of course. You're our one and only Maddy girl," she said sweetly. Then, my kitten made herself known by letting out a loud meow and rubbing against Grandy's legs. "We love you too, Miss Genevieve." She bent over to pet her. "I'm making two recipes, each of which takes several pints of milk. Can't decide if I should get a quart or a gallon. Maybe you could look up how many pints are in a gallon on your Google thingy."

"I'm guessing eight," I said to the ethers before looking it up on my phone.

Yep, eight.

After breakfast, I drove to my internship. Once I got there, not surprisingly, the articles I was asked to research were about the octopus vulgaris (of course, it has eight legs), the only type found in the waters off the coast of Texas, and information on a new sleep clinic opening in Dallas called Siesta Ocho. I also had to write a bio on a local artist who made menorahs out of Texas Blackland clay… yes, a menorah holds eight candles.

It was crystal clear that I was living some countdown…and I began worrying about what would happen when I got to one. Were the snarls I heard in Gascony related? The Arcs had told me my friends and parents there were safe, but for how long? My shoulders ached with stress.

So, when I got home, I decided to use "the day of eights" to my advantage. After dinner, I grabbed a towel and walked down to the lake. The Texas humidity made the air soupy and hot, and I sat on the towel beneath a large pine tree on the shore, the ground covered with long brown, pokey needles. A breeze picked up, amplifying the tree's natural scent of pineapple and turpentine, shaking the needles like a gentle maraca. I waited until 8 p.m. on the dot to close my eyes, be still, and listen.

Within seconds, I heard a voice that matched the wind saying, "At 1 a.m. on day seven, someone will visit you."

"So, it *is* a countdown," I said out loud. "To what?" My gut felt something darkly ominous.

No answer.

"Who's coming? Why?" I asked repeatedly but heard nothing more.

I went back to staying still, listening, and feeling. There was an energy pulsing through the air, building turbulent and destructive momentum.

CHAPTER THIRTY-TWO

Ryon - Day 8

50% First Quarter

Joe sang, "O my darlin', o my darlin', o my darlin' Clementine!" while rolling up his sleeping bag, acting as my alarm clock that morning. The sun was high in the sky, radiating heat on all it touched, and the humidity that thickened the air seemed to settle in my stomach—hunger mixed with anxiety.

I slinked down out of the tree and acted nonchalantly as I approached. "Good morning."

"Well, there ya are. How 'bout a little lunch?" Joe asked. "I figure it's about two-thirty or so."

I looked at the clock in the center of the truck dashboard. "It's two-forty-five," I said, impressed that Joe had such keen senses. My days no longer began at midnight, and it made me feel more human.

"Well, darn—I'm usually right within ten minutes. Must be the drivin' at night and sleepin' by day that's throwing me off. Well, what do ya say? Hungry?"

"Sure am," I replied. A beast my size needed more than a bag of delicious barbecue potato chips. I planned to sneak away for hunts whenever I could.

We lingered the rest of the afternoon beneath the shade of overhead tree branches that layered the sky. We were in the middle of nowhere, and my condor senses didn't detect other creatures besides scrumptious moles, chipmunks, and squirrels.

"Joe, please excuse me," I said when a critter was nearby, hoping he'd think I was off peeing instead of dashing after my snack.

Joe didn't seem to notice, busying himself by inventorying our supplies. "Organization is key in a blind man's life," he announced as he restacked the toilet paper rolls behind the truck seat after counting the water bottles left in the pack. He even lifted the truck's hood at one point, running his hands over the rubbery belts and metal parts. "She's doin' well, yes, siree," he remarked as he lowered the wide, shiny hood and deftly clicked it shut with the palms of his hands.

Although Joe liked to narrate his actions, he also spent a couple of hours leaning against the base of a tree, thinking. After sitting for a while, he began to snore. So, I took off my shirt and left it draped on a branch, using that time to catch more rodents, gliding silently upon them with my wings and propelling myself up trees to eat. My apprehension about my future temporarily went away, and I felt wild and free to allow my beastly parts to take over.

Just as I finished a tasty squirrel, Joe's snoring stopped, so I swooped to the ground and walked to the back of the truck. "How was your quiet time?" I asked.

"Ya learn a lot about the world just by bein' still-like," he replied, his voice gravely from sleep. "I ain't got no way to see with my eyes, so I do it with my hands, ears, and mind."

"I know exactly what you mean." I'd come to understand

so much about life when I couldn't move or touch anything and had no voice, my ability to hear and see amplified.

"It feels like the sun is settin' soon," he said. "We need to get ready to leave."

"Sounds good, Joe."

Then, he walked close to me, his eyes aimed upward as he paused and took in extra air through his nose.

"You sense something?" I asked, wondering what he could perceive that I didn't. Then, something dark caught my eye— my chest was splattered with animal blood, and I'd left my shirt hanging in the tree. Anxiety returned. *I need to be way more careful.*

"Nah, it's nothin'," he replied, turning toward the truck. "Best we get movin' soon."

"I'll be right back, and then we can go," I said, grabbing a gallon jug of water on my way back to the thicker part of the woods. I rinsed myself off and put on my shirt again.

When I returned, Joe was giving the truck a loving caress as he headed to his place in the passenger seat. I climbed beside him, put the water jug behind my seat, and saw the keys were already in the ignition. I started the old girl up, and she purred like she was happy to get moving again.

Joe's phone said, "Turn right," once we got to the highway.

We drove for nearly an hour, and Joe was unusually silent.

"Any messages from your kids?" I asked.

"Siri, play my messages," he said. There were two from his daughter begging him to call her, panic in her voice. "Dagnab-bit, that girl won't leave me alone," he exclaimed.

Then, he had Siri send a message: "I'm fine and alive darlin' period will be home in less than a week period see ya then exclamation mark." Then, he turned to me and asked, "We'll be home by next Wednesday, right?"

I knew it was Wednesday night, and Geidhuce's D-day was the following Thursday, eight days away. It took one more day to get to Texas and two more to California, so we'd have to head straight back as soon as I spoke to Ruza's great-granddaughter. "Yes." *I must be back by then or else…*

"Hmph!" Joe replied, and silence resumed.

"Have you ever made this drive before?" I asked, trying to start conversation.

"Once, when my children were small. Many years ago," was all he said.

Did I do something to make him upset? Is he tired? Does he miss home more than he's letting on?

Then, after quite a while, Joe said, "Ryon, ya know I like ya. Right?"

I gulped. "Yes, Joe, we're friends."

"Well, then, somethin's been eatin' at me since we left that place in the woods."

My hands shook so much that I had trouble steering. "What?"

"I can't quite explain some things my senses were tellin' me. But, I don't want to hurt yer feelin's."

I took a deep breath. "We're friends, Joe. You can't hurt my feelings."

He adjusted his back against the seat and stroked his beard

with his thumb and pointer finger. "First of all, I heard something large in the trees."

"You probably heard birds or animals." *Oh, boy...*

"And before that, when we were talkin' before we left, well, there was a smell about ya."

"While you were sleeping, I took a walk in the woods. I probably smelled like some plant I brushed up against." I gripped the steering wheel to stop jittering, feeling my pulse inside my fingers.

"But I heard the gentle flapping of large wings. And ya smelled irony, like… animal blood."

"I… I…"

"And I didn't smell no fire, so ya didn't cook any animals."

My mind raced. I was cornered like a rat in a trap. I had to fight the impulse to immediately pull over and jump out of the truck…or drive like crazy deep into the woods and leave him there. My claws involuntarily extended—the creature inside me was close to taking over my human rationality.

Then, Joe set his hand firmly on my scaly leg. I moved away from his touch, and the truck swerved.

"I knew it!" he exclaimed, slapping his thigh and grinning from ear to ear. "I couldn't be sure, but it all makes sense now."

"What?" I asked in a roar-tinged voice, veering the truck back onto the dark highway.

"Yer one of them gargoyles. From the Gascony Theater."

Hearing him say that out loud took my breath away.

He let out a "Wahoo!" and his smile gleamed. "I've been studyin' what happened to y'all. I always ask Siri to read newspaper articles about it, and I researched the history of that building…and Monsieur Salles-Bris."

I tried to speak, but nothing came out.

"Everyone thought I was crazy—that's partly why my daughter and kinfolk are so worried," Joe continued. "They think I'm senile. But I was right!"

My words and thoughts stuck, like a clog in a garden hose.

"Don't ya worry none. Yer secret's safe with me. Now tell me all about it, from the beginnin'! I want to hear everythin'!"

I'd carried a world of secrets upon my shoulders. If I told Joe, I'd have some relief and maybe have an ally. Yet, it would take a lot of trust on my part. I looked over at his kind, anticipatory face, and my claws retracted.

If there's anyone in the world I could tell my story to, it's Joe.

So, I reminded myself to breathe again and started at the beginning. Joe listened intently, absorbing like a sponge. I explained what it was like to be a stone creature that longed to be human and free and how I'd seen Madeleine, and she'd stolen my heart. I described waking up in a dingy warehouse surrounded by my other gargoyle and grotesque comrades breaking out of wooden crates, alive. I told him about threading, Geidhuce, Vervalt, and Isel's evil plans and that they'd formed The Chimeras with other living, underground gars and gros. I shared how I'd befriended Chris and spoken to Madeleine through him and how torn I'd been to leave Anee and Telber, my best friends, behind to go on this quest. But mainly, I laid out my plan to stop Geidhuce. However, I left out the murders I'd committed. I didn't want Joe to think I might hurt him.

"I'm glad I'm here to help ya," Joe announced. "To protect my beloved town."

"And that brings us here, driving only at night, reeking like the blood of animals…" Tears filled my eyes. "There's a hideous monstrosity sitting next to you, covered in dragon scales from the waist down with large, clawed reptilian feet, topped with a man's chest and arms dressed in flannel, and a leathery head lined with black feathers, not to mention my gigantic beak nose…" I swallowed hard, like ingesting a rabbit whole. I tried to focus on the road, but my vision was blurry. I blinked quickly to clear my eyes. "I know she'll never love a monster, but what if I can't stop Geidhuce?"

I felt the *bump, bump, bump* of the yellow road reflectors beneath the tires and pulled to the side of the road, putting the truck in park. Then, I just sobbed, tears falling onto my plaid shirt.

"There, there, now. Let it out," Joe said. "We're just outside of Memphis. Only 'bout an hour further to go before the sun comes up. We can take a few." Joe rolled down his window and let in fresh air. A herd of cows grazed near a small pond shimmering with moonlight, in the field to our right. Crickets chirped assuringly, settling me down.

My voice shook as I spoke. "Maybe I should take you back to Gascony."

Joe sat up straight and stared toward the windshield. "My grandpa lived to be a ripe ol' age of 95, and he taught me all I know 'bout fixin' cars when I was a kid." Joe bowed his head. "We talked for hours as I held the light fer him while he worked on carburetors and engines. His cuticles were always black from motor oil. I absorbed all I could, watchin' his skillful hands beneath the hood, back when I could see. An' we didn't just talk about cars. We talked a lot about fishin' and huntin'… and sometimes women." Joe chuckled, turning toward me. "Grandpa also said he was 7 years old and there the day yer buildin' was revealed to the city. It was a church back then. He mentioned somethin' mighty strange the day of the unveilin'."

"What did he see?"

Joe lifted his head, eyes full of smoky fire. "'A cold wind that froze time,' is what he said. And somethin' 'bout blue electricity that zapped around the edges of the gargoyles—he swore to his dyin' day that y'all moved, growled, and clawed just before the world stopped and an eerie mist blanketed the crowd, makin' it so no one could move. He recalled checking his watch seconds before some major wind-blowin' and, afterward, four minutes had passed. Four whole unaccountable minutes." His hazy blue eyes turned steely. "Black magic. That's what Grandpa called it. He figured somethin' must have been up with the sculptor and his assistant. There was that priest at the ceremony, too, Father Marguerite, but he checked out okay."

"Checked out?"

"Yeah. Every time Grandpa stumbled upon an article about that buildin', he saved it. I knew where he put 'em, in his garage behind the gas can in one of those maniler folders. A few others admitted to rememberin' a strangeness that day, but no one believed 'em. Thought it was all urban legend. There were a few articles on the priest. Seems he was an upstandin' guy. After blessin' the buildin', he ran the church in Gascony for a few years and then took a position in Columbus, Ohio. Helped a lot of people. So, I don't think he was the one dabblin' in black magic. Me and Grandpa always thought it must have been the other two."

A prickliness came over me. The puzzle pieces of my existence were fitting together. "Well, I found out that Monsieur Salles-Bris, the sculptor, passed away over a hundred years ago," I explained. "That was one of the things I looked up the night we met at the library. I…kind of snuck in when you checked the candle."

"I knew ya were up to somethin' that night. It all makes sense now," said Joe. "The alarm wasn't armed, and the library door wasn't locked the next day. Thought I'd lost my mind."

"I've been trying to recall everything I could about Monsieur and Ruza. I don't remember the sculptor doing anything unusual besides drinking a lot of wine, but his assistant would chant, burn strong-smelling plants, and rub oil on us at night." I paused to see Joe's reaction, and he looked contemplative. "I've had numerous recurring dreams about the day we were unveiled to the town, and in them, I'm looking down at the crowd of people through a thick fog. They're frozen and cannot move, just like your grandfather described."

"Do ya remember blue electricity?"

"No. However, Anee remembers a phrase Ruza repeated: "zivotinja koju si trebala biti," and I looked that up, too. It means: "the animal you were supposed to be.""

"Hmm." Joe went back to stroking his beard. "Jist the fact that all y'all gargoyles were able to think while made a' stone suggests some kinda magic. I pretend this here truck lives and breathes, but it don't. It can't learn how to talk telepathical-like, spell, read… and it don't fall in love."

"Well, I was carved after a real farm boy and got his memories and abilities."

"Ya were always alive." Joe hit the dashboard with his hand

to accent each of his words: "Inanimate objects don't have memories."

His words opened the door to a dark space in my mind and let in sunshine. "It had to be Ruza. All those words, oils, incantations. She must have practiced black magic."

"Yes, siree!" His beard fluffed out as he grinned widely.

"That's why we're heading to California after stopping in Dallas to see Madeleine. Ruza's great-granddaughter is a professor of Antiquities and Ancient Historiography at U.C.L.A., and she may be able to help somehow. I wasn't sure how this would all go when I first met you, but now that we're a team, like Butch Cassidy and the Sundance Kid. Are you in to help me?"

Joe's smile faded. "My kids would have a conniption if they knew…" He shook his head dejectedly, then quickly added, "But what the heck, I'm in." He let out a "yahoo!".

I put the truck into drive and pulled back out onto the highway.

"I need to ask ya, since we're being honest and whatnot now, how will ya visit Madeleine when ya don't have that Chris fella helpin' ya? She won't buy a 79-year-old blind man comin' to woo 'er," Joe noted, laughing gently.

"I'll figure something out," I answered as we passed a sign that said, "Welcome to Memphis." "I just need to see her one last time, even if it's from afar, in case something happens to me."

"I understand."

"You're a great friend, Joe. Thank you," I said, impulsively patting him on the knee.

A jolt of warmth passed through me on contact, and another big, shining smile broke out on Joe's face.

O   O   O

The sunrise over Arkansas was beautiful. The light illuminated the treed hills like scalloped edges against an orange sky. Gullies dropped away, a leafy sea of ebb and flow. Joe and I were mostly silent because our conversation gave us much to ponder, so we quietly took in the beauty.

We'd gotten gas an hour before, when it was still dark, so we'd have plenty when we started up again later that night. Joe had bought all sorts of delicacies from the minimart, including a dozen foil-wrapped hot dogs that smelled delicious and a box of Red Vines, which I was dying to try. I pulled off the road in the tiny town of Taylor, feeling a sense of comfort in our routines.

A few miles later, I found a wooded spot near a creek. I parked and turned the engine off. The sound of splashing water soothed, every drop on its own journey. The frogs kicked in with a near-deafening symphony of croaks as we got out the food and ate in the truck bed. Joe encouraged me to hunt the woods if I was still hungry, and I was grateful to finish my yummy hot dog meal with a fat woodchuck.

Lying in the back of the truck next to Joe, I had difficulty sleeping. We had only six and a half hours to reach our first destination, where I hoped to see Madeleine.

WAXING GIBBOUS

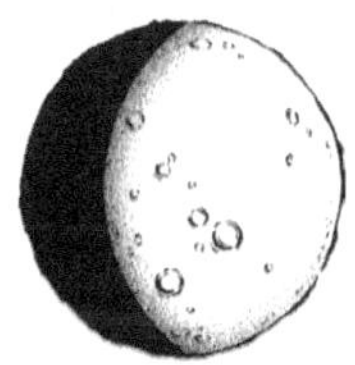

"Refine and prepare the steps to reach your goals. As you improve your plans, know you are moving closer to your true self."

CHAPTER THIRTY-THREE

Ryon - Day 7

59% Waxing Gibbous

We were getting ready to drive another day, and the sun was setting in the distance, an orange line across the western sky behind Joe. He was talking on his phone, pacing back and forth between two trees, using his cane to find the trunk of one before spinning around and walking until he thumped the other, then turning around and walking again. It made me chuckle.

"I told ya, I'm alright," he grumbled. "I just need someone willin' to come git me and my truck in a day or two." Silence. "Yep, he was gonna bring me back, but now he's got important business." Silence again. "I'll call ya with the address soon. Bye."

His words caused a tightening in my chest. I couldn't go forward alone. "Joe," I squawked, a little too condor-like. "Aren't you coming with me to Los Angeles?"

"I thought 'bout it lots, and ya should go on without me. Two days there, and then three to get back to stop ol' Geidhuce."

"But I can't…" I followed him to the back of the truck.

"Ryon, it's time ya believed in yerself. Look at all you've done to git here."

The typical shakiness came over me.

"No frettin'. We must find yer Madeleine now." He held up his phone. "Hey, Siri, how long to drive to Athens, Texas?"

Siri's voice answered, "I'm estimating five and a half hours via Highway 49 to Highway 20."

The idea of being near Madeleine again added some excitement to my jitters.

"Any word from your kids about Gascony? Do they know anything about D-Day?"

"Nothin'. I think those evil creatures are still hindin'," Joe replied, slamming the truck gate closed. "Let's hit the road."

We got into our respective seats, and I turned the key in the ignition.

"I hope The Chimeras stay missing until I'm back," I said, a flock of proverbial butterflies taking wing in my stomach. "Are you sure you won't help me?"

"I didn't say I wouldn't help. I said I wasn't goin' with ya," Joe announced.

"I don't understand."

"I'm brewin' up a plan," he said. "Just need some thinkin' time."

O   O   O

When we arrived at 4444 Dusty Trail, it was very dark out. The small house glowed in the expanding moon's light, like Mecca, and a reminder that it was getting close to full—time was ticking away. It was just before 1 a.m., which meant Madeleine was probably asleep. I swallowed hard. I wanted to see her.

I pulled up to a spot behind a large hedge where I could observe through the boughs, but our truck was mainly hidden. Aside from frogs and cicadas chattering, the night was silent, so I closed my eyes and tried to feel her presence.

"Is it a nice house?" Joe asked, jolting me out of my meditation.

"Very nice. It's a one-story, bluish-grey house with a gray roof. Lots of windows. Looks about 300 feet to a lake with a dock and a boat. And near the house, there's a tree swing tied to a giant pine branch." I pictured Madeleine swinging, hair shining in marbled sunlight that would change and move with each trip past its trunk.

"It feels good here," Joe muttered. "Peaceful and…"

"Wait! Someone's coming outside. A woman in white… It's her!"

Madeleine stepped from the shadows into the moonlight, barefoot and in a nightgown that made her look ghostlike. Her slender figure was a dark silhouette inside the fabric. She wandered into the yard alone as if she were looking for something.

"Hello?" she called gently, her voice blending with the wind. "Is someone here?" She continued to travel closer to where we sat in the concealed truck.

"Wait here, Joe," I whispered, removing the keys from the ignition, turning off any threading color, and quietly opening the truck door, leaving it ajar. The air was dense with humidity as I crept past the Ford to an enormous pine tree and scaled the bumpy trunk to a large, low branch above her.

"Ouch!" she cursed, stepping on a pile of pine needles. She scrunched up her face, and all I could think about was that the lips I kissed were only yards away.

"Oh, you've got to be here! I can feel you so strongly. The angels told me you were coming, but where are you?" And then she said, "Is that you, Chris?"

I wanted to shout, "It's me, Ryon! It's been me all along!" but I couldn't. I also couldn't tell her the truth: "It's me, a grotesque from the Gascony Theater, who was once stone and is now a living monster, and I have feelings for you! Grrowr!"

Instead, I clenched my jaw and watched her.

Madeleine stopped, face upward, right below me. I adjusted, making sure the boughs covered my body.

"I feel you right here…but you're not Chris." She closed her eyes and wrapped her arms around her body. "You care about me. I can feel it." She swayed back and forth as if drenching herself in the sensation. "I've felt you before. What are you? An angel? A spirit? A lost soul? No matter what, I'll understand. My gift—well, sometimes it feels like a curse—is hearing and seeing spiritual entities." She paused. "But you're different."

I took a deep breath and then steadied my voice. "You're right. I care deeply about you." I turned on my pink glow.

She let her head fall back for a moment, a smile on her beautiful lips, and eyes still closed—then, she opened them and dropped her arms. "You came to see me before, in Gascony, right?"

My heart thumped low in my chest. "Yes."

"What's your name?" She asked, opening her eyes and looking in my direction. I ducked deeper into the tree.

"I'd rather not say."

"I'm getting mixed messages from the angels." She bit her

lip as she thought for a second. "They say you are sweet and loving and would never harm me. But they also send me visions of animals—wolves, donkeys, large birds, horses—even dragons. I'm not sure what…"

"May I ask you something?" I interrupted.

"Sure."

"You mentioned Chris. What is he to you?" I needed to know her feelings, but braced myself for the answer.

"I'm not sure how I feel about him. I know he likes me, and he's tall, handsome, and honestly, a little dopey, but he's the sweetest. Do you know him?"

My heart dropped like a stone in a pond. "Yes, I do… I helped him."

"Helped him how?"

"The letter," I blurted. "I helped him write his letter to you. And I was there when he came to your window that night."

Her eyes lit up. "Oh, that explains a lot. That letter was beautiful and eloquent, but he could never speak to me like that." She paused. "And no wonder his voice sounded different. It was you." She crossed her arms. "I feel a little deceived."

"Someone as lovely as you would make any guy nervous." My leathery cheeks grew warm. "He meant well. Trust me."

Madeleine vigorously searched the tree. "Why can't I see you? I see most angels and spirits easily…"

"I'm neither of those things. I'm living and real. It's just not… the time to reveal myself." I felt an ache in my chest. I'd never get to show her who I really was since that was most likely the last time I'd see Madeleine. But then again, I had nothing to lose. "I can tell you this," I began. "What you feel from me is real. The words in the letter and what I said outside your bedroom window are exactly how I feel."

A small gasp came from her throat.

"And remember the spring dance?"

She nodded silently, her face serene.

"You kissed someone wrapped in the velvet curtains…"

"Yes, I kissed Chr… oh!" She gently touched her lips with her fingertips, remembering. "That kiss was…amazing."

I stopped breathing.

"I wondered why I never felt that again with Chris," she added.

Tears wet my wrinkled cheeks, and one journeyed downward, splashing on the tip of her nose. She blinked, startled. "You're crying."

"I'm in love with you."

"I can't…" She looked down. "I don't…"

"You don't have to say it back."

"Can you kiss me again?" she asked, looking up at me again, hopeful.

My heart raced faster than my breath could keep up with. I feared I'd pass out and fall out of the tree. "I'm sorry. I can't show myself to you, so that can't happen. But if we never meet again…" Heaviness took over my body. "…know that I care for you more than humanly possible."

"Why won't I meet you again?"

I gazed at her beautiful face in the dappled moonlight, longing to go to her, trying to tame the compulsive beast in me before it did something rash. "I have to go now," I lamented.

She dropped her head again and nodded. Perhaps the angels were confirming to her that I spoke the truth. I had to stifle the urge to call her back as she turned and walked away.

Once she reached the house's back door, she stopped and turned in my direction. "Thank you for caring about me."

She entered the house, and I was paralyzed with sorrow. I sat in the tree for a while, unable to move, in awe of our encounter. Then, the hoot of a nearby owl snapped me back to awareness, so I scampered to the truck and got behind the wheel, closing the door as quietly as possible.

"That was Madeleine?" Joe asked.

"Yes."

"She sounds lovely, from what I could hear."

I nodded. "She's the loveliest human ever to walk the earth."

"Well, aren't you as smitten as a kitten in catnip!"

"But this is probably the last time I'll see her." I leaned forward and rested my birdly head on the steering wheel.

"Hmmm…" came from Joe's throat, long and low. "We'll see."

"Why am I a monster?" I banged my forehead on the steering wheel. "It's bad enough to be a thinking, feeling piece of stone, but now I'm a hideous freak!" My words sputtered and convulsed, heat climbing up the back of my neck, forcing out angry tears.

"There, there, Ryon. I got a bit of advice fer you." Joe set his hands on my shoulders, bony and cool against my skin. "Find what's good. I tell myself these words every time anythin' bad happens. Whenever there's an emergency, like an accident, look fer the people who put themselves out there to care 'bout those down on their luck. True heroes." Joe removed his hands, and I sat up. "When the doctors told me I was goin' blind, I was devastated. But I was surrounded by doctors, nurses, my family… people who wanted to help me git through it."

"That must have been a tough time for you, Joe." I inhaled with a shaky breath. "But I'm far from a hero. What if I can't stop Geidhuce?"

"You'll be successful if you use what ignites you to drive ya. Hold that moment ya jist had with yer girl in yer heart. It'll fuel ya to save Gascony."

"But that's the thing. IF Ruza's great-granddaughter can help us, which is a long shot, the best thing she can do is turn us all back into stone."

Joe bit his lip and thought for a moment. "I've come to believe in the impossible. I thought my days of fixin' up cars and havin' adventures were over once I lost my sight, but look at me now!"

"I'm not as smart as you and only part human. The rest of me is beastly."

"I think you've got the makin's of a true hero, Ryon. Have ya thought about forgittin' about going to California and tryin' to beat them demons yerself?"

"I have. But let's say I figure out how to stop The Chimeras. I'll be walking the earth as a monster the rest of my life, always having to hide." The urge to cry again tickled my throat. "I'd rather sacrifice myself and return to stone to save Gascony. Madeleine lives there, and so do you. The town is full of people who should have full lives ahead of them. I'd rather secretly stop The Chimeras and keep the citizens of Gascony from ever knowing how close they were to doom."

"See there? That's the makin' of a hero," he said with verve. "Yer a good man, Ryon."

"A good monster, anyway."

"No, yer a man at the core. You've a heart of gold and a respect for life. Those evil beasts don't."

I sat taller, wiped away tears with my human hands, and then held them out. Pale skin and nails—proof I had human in me.

"Sometimes ya need to think outside the box," Joe stated sternly. "We just gotta be creative." He stroked his beard in thought. "But in doin' that, we need to think inside it."

"I'm not following you."

"There's a faster way to get ya to U.C.L.A. and right to Ruza's great-granddaughter." Joe's face glowed. "We ship ya there."

I tilted my leathery head. "How long will it take for me to get there? I only have six days before The Chimeras strike."

"I won't lie. It'd be cutting it close. I once shipped a whole car across the country in four days, from Gascony to Tucson. I'll bet we could send ya on a two-day delivery." Joe began to laugh.

"What's so funny?"

"I'm jist picturin' Ruza's great-granddaughter's face when she sees ya!" He laughed some more.

My anxious heart thumped in my ears. "Joe, are you sure this is a good idea?"

"Don't worry." Joe stopped his chuckling, his face turning serious. "If we gather supplies and git a big crate, we can have ya off by tomorrow mornin'. We'll put that professor's name on the shipping label, meaning you'll go directly to her." Joe stroked the white hairs on his chin. "And if she can't help, you'll still have a couple of days to git yerself back to Gascony. We'll create a return label so she can ship ya right back to our little ol' town."

I knew that Joe was bright, and I trusted him. And if he could get me to Ruza's daughter directly, that would save us having to find her once we got to U.C.L.A. But it was risky. "So, what's our next step?"

"First of all, let's git outta here in case Miss Madeleine decides to go on another evening stroll." I started the engine and drove as Joe continued. "We'll continue to drive west until daylight, then find a city where we can git ya a crate, cell phone, food, and stuff like that. Then, we'll book a room at a motel in a remote area nearby."

"Wow, Joe. I couldn't have done this without you."

"Ain't no time for thank yas. We got work to do."

$$\circ \quad \circ \quad \circ$$

We drove west for four hours until the sun began to rise at around six, and we were somewhere near Abilene.

"Walmart opens early, but we've got time fer ya to go huntin' if ya like," Joe said.

"I'm not hungry," I replied, my future a black abyss of the unknown.

"We're gonna need to run our errands in broad daylight, so you'll have to wait in the truck, but it'll be okay," Joe said, sniffing out my anxiety.

"Someone might catch a glimpse of my grotesque face," I replied, muscles twitching.

"Ya can slump down. No one's gonna notice. People are focused way more on themselves."

I wore the flannel shirt and Ford baseball cap Joe had given me, but I worried it wasn't enough. I tried to focus on Siri's commands, but cars were all over the road, and people were on the sidewalks we passed. Then, a silver Honda pulled up next to us at a stoplight, music blasting from inside. I quickly covered the side of my head with an outstretched hand, peeking through my fingers. The driver looked right at me and waved. I looked at the road ahead, my tail twitching between my feet. Then, he took off once the light turned green.

"I don't like this daytime errand running," I growled. "A guy just waved at me!"

"People in Texas are jest friendly, is all." Joe chuckled. "I'll git ya somethin' that covers ya more. Now, no more worryin'."

Siri guided me left and then right, and I kept the cap low over my face. After driving about a mile, the giant store appeared in the distance like an oasis, the parking lot packed with people and as busy as a squashed anthill.

"Please line my door with the entrance," Joe asked.

My palms were sopping. "Okay." I did as he asked. "You can get out now."

"Great. I'll be a bit," said Joe, grabbing his cane.

"You should get someone to help you," I said. The longer he took, the harder it would be to fight the urge to jump out of the truck and run.

"Everyone wants to help a blind man, especially in a Texas Walmart. Southern hospitality and all." Joe touched my scaly leg, and I nearly jumped out of my skin. "Yer as jumpy as a frog on butter, but it'll be alright. Anythin' worth somethin' takes a fight."

"I just don't want our plans to go sideways."

"I'll tell ya one thing." Joe reached his hand out a second time, and I took a deep breath as it landed on my leg. "Ya won't stand out much amongst the clientele at Walmart, even if ya went walkin' in right now."

I looked around, and we were surrounded by more cars, trucks, and people of all shapes and sizes pushing shopping carts—a more eclectic mix of humans than I'd ever seen.

"Joe, how am I going to keep hidden? They're everywhere!" My hands jittered on the steering wheel.

"I promise, they ain't interested in anythin' else except television mounts, barbeque sauce, and Flamin' Hot Cheetos." Joe opened his door.

"Hurry," I pleaded.

He nodded and left, and I made sure he entered the store, watching someone in a bright blue tunic greet him. Then, I drove, crouched as low as possible, and parked between two large trucks so mine would blend in, where I could see the front door. My whole body shook as I thought about what might happen if I were caught: *I'd be captured and sent to jail. No, the zoo. No, to some secret laboratory for experiments! No more Madeleine, and Geidhuce would be munching on the flesh of Gascony citizens with The Chimeras.*

I shivered.

Both Joe and Anee had referred to me as a hero, but I felt nothing like one. Heroic men in movies were always handsome and brave. I was neither of those two things. The beast in me should have given me more confidence, yet I felt inept. But movie men were ready to make sacrifices, or even die, for love, and that I understood. There was something magical about Madeleine, and though we'd never be together, she was mine in my heart. I knew I'd sacrifice my life without hesitation, like Harry Stamper in *Armageddon* or Jack in *Titanic*, just to know that Madeleine, Anee, Telber, Joe, and the citizens of Gascony were safe.

After mulling it over for a good thirty minutes, a new feeling of determination slowly bubbled inside. I saw Joe standing outside the store, so I started the engine and pulled up near him, tapping the horn. He held several white plastic bags in one hand, his cane whizzing back and forth until he found the truck, grabbed the door handle, and climbed inside.

"People are damn nice in Texas," he announced, flinging the bags between us on the bench seat and closing the door.

"Were you able to get everything?" I asked, the feeling of hunger returning to my belly.

"Yes, sirree. And I bought ya their biggest black hoodie, or so my new Walmart employee friend, Billy Bob, told me." Joe radiated excitement.

"I had an epiphany while you were inside the store, and I think I can do this," I announced confidently.

"Well, I'll be darned. Miracles do happen at Walmart. People have given birth, got married, and even claimed to have seen the Mother Mary in the cereal aisle, and here ya go havin' an epiphany in the parkin' lot." He chuckled so hard his thin shoulders bounced.

I smiled. "Well, I strive to be as resilient and clever as you." Then, I got a little choked up, adding, "I need to be the hero you see me as."

He stopped laughing and leaned sideways toward me. "Ya already are."

CHAPTER THIRTY-FOUR

Ryon - Day 6

69% Waxing Gibbous

Time moved forward, ready or not, and we made two more stops. I prayed we'd collected everything we needed as Joe bought wood and hardware at Home Depot.

"While you were inside, I used your phone and found a remote motel about fifty miles from here," I announced.

"Sounds great." Joe nodded back toward the six-by-six-foot wooden crate he'd purchased at U-Haul, strapped in the truck bed. "Is it still there?"

"Yep." I sighed, my hopes of being inconspicuous dashed.

We drove down Highway 11 with that giant thing hanging off the back for nearly an hour. I tried to remain calm, but inside, I was frantic. Then, I spotted The Triple G Motel, tucked in amongst some woods. It had seen better days, with dark green paint peeling. A string of rooms was in the back near a small, wooded creek, perfect for what would come next. I pulled up across from the front door where the word "office" had been poorly painted by hand in bright yellow letters.

"Ask for room number 12. It's the most isolated," I suggested as Joe got out of the truck and headed to the check-in desk.

I pulled my new black hoodie out of one of the plastic bags and slipped it on, feeling a lot more inconspicuous.

Joe returned quickly with a key on an orange plastic fob. "We can park in back. The desk clerk was so preoccupied with her TV show, I don't think she even noticed I was blind. Asked me to sign on the dotted line. Not sure if I even got close, but I did it."

I smiled. "Then, she probably didn't notice me or the giant box."

"Not a chance. Do ya see many other customers 'round here?"

"Only two cars are in the front lot," I said, driving around the building until we were in front of #12, painted on a shiny, gray door. "No one's parked back here by our room." I backed into the space using the large side view mirrors to see, then turned off the truck.

We both got out. I took Joe's key and used it to unlock the room. Inside, the air smelled like wet newspaper and Chlorox, with two beds, a dresser, a television, and a bathroom. I opened the window on the back wall to let in some fresh air, seeing a creek lined with bluebonnets. The sound of the water trickling reminded me of Telber and Anee. I hoped they were alright.

As I unloaded and set everything on one of the bouncy beds, except for the crate, Joe took inventory of what he'd bought, organizing all the parts and pieces on the shag-carpeted floor.

"Don't forgit the toolbox I brought from home. It's behind the seat," he said.

I retrieved it, setting the extremely long, heavy metal box, its blue paint dinged from much use, on the brown laminated dresser beside five large, plastic jars full of orange, puffy balls.

"What are these?" I asked, looking at the strange spheres.

"Something to enjoy now and use later," Joe replied. "Hope ya like 'em 'cause I got a mess of 'em. Ya can eat some now if ya like. Just save the containers."

I grabbed one and unscrewed the lid, breaking through the paper seal with three fingers and grabbing a handful. The salty taste was similar to cheese slices, but the texture was light and crunchy. "Mmmm," was all I could say as I threw more into my mouth, my fingers turning orange.

Joe smiled. "Good, right?"

"Delicious."

Then, he turned his attention back to the task at hand. "It's difficult to make that splintery crate anything but cramped, but I'm gonna do my best," Joe announced, his dull eyes scanning as if he could see the room as well as I could. "One side of the box will open from the inside by using slide locks, hinges, and a coupla handles so ya can easily git in and out, in case there's an opportunity to stretch yer legs."

Or escape, I thought, nerves rattling my knees.

"I'll bore some holes for ya to see out of on all sides," he continued, "and we'll have jars of food and water strapped on the inside so they don't roll around when they transport ya."

"Joe, what if they turn the crate upside down?" I pictured being thrown around like a stone in a jar. My mind was working overtime thinking of all the possible things that could go wrong: the crate could fall and crash open, someone could try to open my box, I could get shipped to the wrong place or person…

"That's what those are fer." Joe pointed in the direction of a stack of paper signs. "They're stickers that say: "THIS END UP" and "FRAGILE." We'll put 'em all over the outside of the crate."

I exhaled loudly.

"Stop yer worryin'," Joe admonished. "I can feel yer tension, and it's makin' me nervous too. Just think positive-like. If I worried about gittin' from one place to the other as a blind man, then I'd be sittin' in a chair all day long fer the rest of my life. When I first got the diagnosis, I admit I was afraid. Felt like my life was gonna be snuffed out along with my vision, and I didn't git outta bed fer nearly a week."

"But you're so brave now."

"I snapped out of that depression by thinkin' 'bout what I could do rather than focusin' on the things I can't. I could have become more of a statue than ya ever were." Joe laughed.

"By throwin' yerself into tasks and keepin' busy, ya won't have time to think about anythin' else."

"Joe, you're pretty amazing."

"Well, yer gonna be amazin' when ya save Gascony."

"But it's such a long shot. Ruza's great-granddaughter may know nothing about spells, or us…"

"But she's a professor of Antiquities and Ancient Historiography and teaches about ancient rituals. She may at least know how to help ya."

"I hope."

From that point on, I worked as Joe's eyes and muscles. We kept our hotel door open while we worked on the crate, which I'd strained to move off the truck and set in the parking space next to it. I kept my eyes and ears peeled for people, but it seemed the back of the hotel was vacant. While Joe directed me, I sawed, drilled, and hammered, wearing the black hoodie. We worked all night, with floodlights on extension cords so I could see.

At around four in the morning, Joe announced, "I think she's done. Go inside and practice usin' it."

I went into the crate and swung the door shut. It was pitch black, and it smelled of freshly cut wood. I felt around for the metal bars, one near the top and one near the bottom, and slid them into the silver loops to lock the door. I grabbed the two handles and tried to wiggle the door open, but it stayed firmly shut. My head grew light—I flashed back to when I'd awoken in that crate, scared and disoriented. After being alive and free, it was scary to be back in dark confinement. Dizzy, I felt around for the wooden board we'd attached on one side for sitting and plopped my backside down on it just before my knees gave out.

"How ya doin' in there?" called Joe.

I gulped. "Okay." I focused on regaining my composure.

"The camping light is to yer right."

I reached out, finding it velcroed to the wall. I found the switch, and the space filled with light. There were many peepholes for me to look out of on each wall and one plastic tub with a snap-on lid that we had screwed to the floor for my clothes and other supplies. All five of those cheese ball jars were strapped, one on top of the other, in two of the corners. One still had those delicious puffs, one was filled with beef jerky, and one with water, but the two on the opposite side were empty.

I stood and unlatched the door. "What will go into the empty jars?"

"They're for when ya gotta relieve yerself," Joe said with a wink. "Just tighten the lid afterward, so it don't give off any bad smells."

I chuckled. "You've thought of everything."

"We'll throw in some pillows and a blanket, but then you'll be on yer way. I called a local express freight company, and they're pickin' ya up at eight a.m."

"That's in four hours."

"It's time we git a little shuteye then."

○ ○ ○

The mattress creaked every time I moved to get comfortable, so I spent at least an hour lying still while Joe snored away in the other. Worry warped my thoughts. The future was a dark hole I was about to slip into. But eventually, I slept dreamlessly.

Joe's phone alarm woke us up at 7:30 a.m. "Mornin', Ryon. They'll be here fer ya soon," Joe announced before going into the bathroom and closing the door.

I stayed prone, trying to avoid fretting thoughts. Remembering Joe's words to "use what ignites you to drive you," I switched to thinking about Madeleine. Like so many leading men in the movies, I needed to be her hero.

I sat up and swung sideways to dangle my large dragon feet off the bed just as Joe emerged dressed for the day, his white hair wet and slicked back. "I'll be outside triple-checkin' everythin'. It's almost time," he said before going out the door.

I bounded into the bathroom to splash cold water on my face, my wrinkled condor neck, brown and lumpy, reflecting in the mirror. My white neck feathers, huge beak, and scaly legs were terrifying, even to myself.

Then, a beam of light came in through the tiny bathroom window, creating a golden glow around me like a euphoric aura. A tingly warmth washed over me as a voice from the ethers whispered, "It will all turn out as it should, and you will make it so."

"But how?" I asked into the air. Then, the light dimmed. "Hello?"

Nothing.

Still, I stepped out of the bathroom to the front door with my head held high. I was part of the ensuing destiny, so all I could do was my best. The giant crate loomed and made me think of the movie *The Time Machine*.

"The shipper fellers texted and will be here in ten minutes," Joe announced softly.

"And when will your daughter be here to get you?"

"Around two."

"I'm going to miss you, Joe. Besides Telber and Anee, you've been the best friend a beast could ever have." I reached out and touched his shoulder. "I don't know what I'd do without you."

I could hear the quick thumping of his heart in his chest. He sighed and dropped his head. "I know yer scared, but I think you've got everythin' ya need to succeed. Always think…"

"…positive," I interrupted.

"I got ya a few other thangs," Joe said, handing me a heavy plastic Walmart bag. Inside were a ton of batteries for the camping light, an iPhone, a hand-crank phone charger, and a very large book. "Had that crank-charger in the truck fer a couple years in case of an emergency."

"Thanks, Joe."

"By the way, they asked me yer name when I got the phone. Said ya were my nephew, Ryon Delt."

My heart warmed. I loved being part of a family, even if it was pretend. "I like that name." I took out the box and held it against my chest for a minute. I'd seen thousands of humans with phones, never expecting to get one of my own.

"And what's this book about?" I pulled it out. The title was *The Ultimate Movie Book,* and my stomach did a backflip. "Amazing."

"A little readin' to kill the downtime. It's got pictures and everythin', for ya to see more of what ya only heard over the years."

"Thank you. You really do think of everything."

"Speakin' of rememberin', don't fergit this." He handed me a roll of cash.

I nodded, quickly hugged Joe, opened the crate door, and climbed inside. Standing there, he looked small and frail. "This isn't goodbye because we'll be talking by phone, but still, I want ya to know that our time together meant a lot."

"Fer me too," he replied. "Now git before anyone sees ya."

I pulled the door shut and slid the two locks in place. I popped the lid off the tub on the floor and slid the Walmart bag and cash roll inside, snapping it closed again. Beside it were a blanket and two pillows, so I made a blanket nest next to the tub with a pillow on either side—much more comfortable than the hose in my old shack. I listened to the muffled sounds of Joe's feet pacing and his cane clicking for several minutes until deep, male voices were outside.

"What in the tarnation is in this crate, Mr. Delt?"

"Well, I got me a sculpture at a sale, and it turns out it's worth somethin', so this professor wants to pay me fer it, so I'm shippin' it to her."

"The return address is Pennsylvania. Why are ya here in Texas?"

"Well, my daughter wants me to return home, so this is the last of my stuff." Joe had his alibi all figured out, and he deserved an Academy Award. "Now, I need you to be real gentle-like with it. I want to git my money, so it needs to arrive in one piece. Then, I can finally take up my dream of racin' cars."

The men became silent. I had to stifle a laugh.

"Ha! I'm pullin' yer leg, fellas."

The men laughed, big and loud. "Where's yer daughter anyway? Don't think this run-down motel is the place for a blind man," said one of the men, concerned.

"She ran to Walmart. She'll be right back," Joe replied. "I wanted to meetcha to make sure ya take good care of my investment."

"Nothin' to worry 'bout, Mr. Delt. Russ here is the best dern driver we got. Now, let's see, Dr. Rose Prekrasna-Smith, Department of History, at the University of California, Los Angeles."

"That's it. Thank ya, gentlemen."

"Can we help ya with anythin' else?" asked a man.

"Thank ya kindly, but I'll jest go back to my room and wait fer my daughter." This time, Joe spoke the truth. His daughter was coming to take him to the airport to fly back home. He left out that she was "fit to be tied," as Joe described, especially since her husband had to come too, to drive the Ford back to Pennsylvania. But Joe figured his son-in-law would be grateful for twenty-one hours of peace.

And I suddenly realized Joe also had made sacrifices be-cause of me.

CHAPTER THIRTY-FIVE

Ryon - Day 5

77% Waxing Gibbous

The trip was bumpy and loud from the rumble of the truck engine and the rattling of boxes banging against each other. I spent hours reading the cinema book with the camping lamp on, but only when the truck was in motion. I didn't want anyone to see light coming from inside my box. The book was filled with photographs and explanations of the movies I had heard through the walls of The Gascony Theater when stone. I connected voices with faces and sounds with scenes, which made me happy. I was particularly enamored with Casablanca. Those pages with Ingrid Bergman and Humphrey Bogart were electrifying in crisp blacks and whites.

I kept my phone at 100%, and when the battery became more than 20% low, I'd crank away on the hand charger. It gave me something to do. A literal caged bird, I was a bit stir-crazy.

I always kept the blanket handy to throw over myself if someone opened my crate, and I also practiced holding still like a statue, flashing back to my days frozen in stone. I called Joe every few hours, but I had nothing to report except my anxiety.

Although I had plenty of time to sleep, it wasn't easy since doom scenarios bounced around in my head. To distract myself, I relived my favorite experiences of being alive, like the day I broke out of the crate and realized I was breathing. Or, seeing Telber and Anee for the first time with their colorful fur and hearing their voices. I also thought about how I'd lived in the shed and saw Madeleine daily, and those times I got to speak with her, write to her, and kiss her.

Then, I recalled how Telber and Anee awaited my return. The Chimeras' attack drew closer, less than five days away.

This driver needs to hurry up!

O   O   O

The truck stopped for the night at around 11 p.m., and I nodded off for a little while in my blanket and pillow nest. Then, early the next morning, my phone rang. It was Joe, and my heart nearly stopped.

"I have some good news," he said in a chipper voice. "Anee and Telber are a-okay!"

"How do you know?" I whispered, in case someone was around.

"I figured out a way to git up to that house! My friend Albert has a mighty, trusted old horse named Pickles. So, I asked Albert if I could ride 'em to a friend's house. Now, gittin' him to let a blind man ride alone wasn't easy, but I convinced him by sayin' I was gonna see a lady friend, but I'd return within a coupl'a hours."

"That's crazy, Joe. I can't believe it," I remarked, eager to hear more.

"He said he was only lettin' me do it 'cause Pickles would follow exactly as I directed and knows how to stop for traffic and go the safest way. Alls I had to do was start the navigation on my phone, yell commands, kick and steer the reins."

The idea of a blind man riding a horse through town made me laugh. "Joe, I can't believe you did this."

"Yes, sir, I did. I hopped on Pickles, and he's a right, gentle, smart horse. Took me right up to the house ya told me 'bout."

I laughed in amazement. "Tell me about Anee and Telber."

"When I got there, I called for them, and fer a long time, there was no sound at all. I knew they'd be hidin' since they don't know me from Adam. So, I stayed on Pickles and gave them a solo-type speech 'bout how I knew ya and was just there to check on 'em. Finally, they came on out."

"Is Telber better? How's Anee?"

"Well, ask 'em yerslef."

"Ryon? Is that really you?" *Anee!* I loved the purr in her voice. "I'm so glad you're okay! I've been so worried." She started to blubber.

"Anee! I've missed you…"

I was interrupted with, "R-R-Ryon!"

"Telber, it's wonderful to hear your voice! How are you?"

"B-B-Better."

"I'm so glad!" I replied. "Have you heard anything from The Chimeras or Geidhuce?"

"No. We've been staying put," Anee answered with a sniffle.

"Good, well, Joe is trustworthy. Just let him know if you need anyth…"

Just then, I heard muffled voices. I suppressed an angry growl and lowered my voice.

"I've got to go. Put Joe on, please."

"What's up, Ryon?" asked Joe.

"The drivers are coming. Am I still being delivered tonight?"

"Yep, 'bout five o'clock yer time."

"Okay, thank you. Tell Anee and Telber I miss..."

"Do you hear something?" a man announced. He was close by, and I smelled cigarettes and coffee. I pulled my phone away from my ear and could hear Joe's voice, small and far away in my hand. Then, the sound of the truck's back door clanged and wailed open.

I hung up, my hands shaking.

"Man, I must be losing my mind. I keep thinkin' I hear voices," said the driver, and another man laughed.

"Drivin' as much as we do, I'm not surprised," said the other man.

"It's a young man's voice. I've heard it ever since I picked up this load." Then the truck dipped slightly from the man climbing in.

He pushed my crate hard, shaking it. My wooden world shimmied left and right... and the movie book dropped from the bench where I had set it, hitting the floor. Blam!

"What the hell was that?" asked the other man.

"I swear that crate's got somethin' livin' in there!" argued the driver.

I swore my heart stopped.

The man continued, "Hmm... let's see."

He's about to open my crate...!

I froze like a statue, wondering how convincing I would be when my body trembled with fear. I squeezed my eyes tight, waiting for them to start prying the box open, but I heard the rustle of papers instead.

"Says here, it's a piece of art. A statue or somethin' like that."

Silence. My stomach was doing somersaults.

"It's not a haunted crate, for goodness' sake. It's probably just broken and rattling around," said the other.

"Maybe, but..."

"That's what insurance is for. I gotta git goin'. Good to see you, Russ."

The other man's footsteps faded, but I could still hear my driver breathing outside my crate.

Finally, I heard him walking away, and then his feet smacked the ground. The doors closed, the lock reengaged, and he started the truck. I realized I'd been holding my breath, so I exhaled. Soon, the engine's rumbling and the truck's motion calmed me down.

I texted Joe: "Sorry about that. The driver came back. We're moving again. I'll let you know when I'm there."

Just ten hours more. I can do this.

O   O   O

By the time the truck stopped at our destination, I was a captive animal gone mad, the dragon in me about to breathe fire and burn down the entire box. Even my movie book didn't distract me.

"Delivery," said Russ over the idling of the motor. "To the history department."

"There's a loading dock for deliveries. Let me grab a campus map," said a new voice. "Right here." Then I heard what I thought was the scraping of a pen nib on paper.

"Thanks," Russ replied.

I quickly ensured everything was battened down as the truck moved slowly, turning left, right, and right again. Then, it backed up, a *beep-beep-beep* noise sounded, and the engine turned off. The clanging of what sounded like a massive metal door sliding up caused my body to go numb. The back of the truck was unlocked and opened, and suddenly, my whole crate was being jostled. I clung onto the bench seat for dear life as my crate was dragged, lifted by a noisy machine, set down, and slid into a place where darkness came in through the knotholes.

My muscles ached from bracing myself during the jolts. The "fragile" sign on the outside did little good—the "this end up" sign did its job, though, and I was grateful.

"Please sign here," Russ asked.

"Who is it for?" a woman inquired.

"A Professor Pre-kras-na-Smith"

"It's rather large. What's inside?"

"Says here it's an art piece... a statue or something."

"Okay."

I heard the vigorous scratching of a pen on paper again, the formality of "thank yous," and Russ giving a final "Good riddance!" before his steps faded, and metallic doors rolled, rattled, and slammed.

Gentler footsteps echoed near my crate. "Dr. Smith?" the

woman asked. "This is the mail center, and an extremely large box came for you. A statue?" Then, silence for a moment. "It was shipped from Texas, but the return address is Gascony, Pennsylvania." Silence again. "We're closing now, but you can come tomorrow. We're open from eight to five."

I'm stuck here until tomorrow? I don't have time to waste! My throat tightened.

The woman's shoes tapped off into the distance, a door closed, and a lock clicked. All I could hear was my heart thumping.

I need to get OUT of here!

I carefully slid open the lock bars inside my crate and pushed on the handles, gently setting the door against the outside. The air was stagnant, but the delivery facility was large.

I scanned the room for any sign of life. The only thing moving was the second hand on a large white-faced clock telling me it was 5:10. A single, yellowish light shone above a door in the vast space. Boxes with white shipping labels were stacked near the door, and square bins, some full of letters and some empty, were lined up on a long table in the center. There was a large stack of flattened cardboard boxes. The only view outside of that room was through a small window in a door, which was dark. Another enormous, slatted, metal door took up one entire wall, which was probably how I entered.

I stepped cautiously, listening for the tiniest sound, but the gentle whirr of air through the vents was all my condor ears could gather. It felt good to stretch my legs and wings freely again. I grabbed the tub half full of cheese puff balls, sat in a corner where I was hidden, and could keep an eye on the doors, chuckling at the echo of my *crunch, crunch, crunch.*

CHAPTER THIRTY-SIX

Madeleine - Day 7, 6, 5, and 4

59%, 69%, 77%, and 84% Waxing Gibbous

I couldn't stop thinking about the mysterious being who visited me at my grandparents' house on my day of 7s, just as the angels predicted. I had set an alarm so I wouldn't miss it. I jumped when my phone alarm sounded, turned it off, and walked outside in my nightgown, disoriented. A warm affection washed over me the second I stepped into the night.

"Chris?" I asked, thinking he'd come to see me at night again. At first, I was a little disappointed it wasn't him—what a romantic grand gesture it would have been if he'd come all that way. But then, I heard that voice, different from Chris's and as familiar as family, its resonant lilt putting me at ease right away. His dark, ambiguous shape was in the tree, hidden behind the boughs, and the pink light he emanated grew brighter as he confessed, "I wrote the letter… I kissed you at the dance…" So passionate and romantic, he'd impressed me with many grand gestures.

The angels appeared beside me, whispering, "He is more than just an admirer. This entity exists beyond a man and has traveled many miles. Though timid and gentle, he must sacrifice himself to ensure that the countdown's end does not lead to disaster." Then, The Arcs reminded me of the visions I'd been getting of animals and dragons. I couldn't figure out the connection.

How can I help him?

"Express your true feelings," the angels advised. "The power that creates will ignite him while dealing with danger."

Danger?

"Yes. He must risk everything to stop the terror," they murmured. "You will not see him again in this state," they said, adding, "Do not hold back."

What state will he… will he die? Cold shot through my body.

"Just do as we say." Then, the angels disappeared.

I asked him to kiss me like he did at the dance, but he turned me down. I worried I hadn't done enough to show my feelings, so I thanked him for caring about me.

Afterward, whenever I thought about him, the warm feelings of contentment returned, followed by gut-felt worry. He'd refused to tell me his name, so I called him my "Gallant Admirer," and racked my brain to figure out what he had to do with the countdown days I'd been living, and the animals. I got through the days of 6s, 5s, and 4s easier, knowing it was all part of his crusade.

The night on the day of 4s, the humid air was 92 degrees, and I looked into the deep sapphire sky and noticed the moon was bright and nearly round. I Googled on my phone to see when it would be completely full: May 23rd, the Flower Moon, my day of 1s.

That night, my recurring visions of wild animals returned more intense and real than before: wolves with golden eyes gnashing their teeth, giant birds with sharp beaks picking apart the meat of prey, horses bucking, lions roaring, dragons breathing fire… a dozen wild animals, real and mythical, fighting. It was a horrific scene!

I woke up worrying that those visions were connected to the impending doom my Arcs warned me about. I continuously asked The Arcs to help Galliant Admirer if he had to deal with anything like that. I truly hoped that he didn't.

Just as the early morning light reached my window, Archangel Chamuel, the angel of unconditional love and inner peace, appeared at the foot of my bed. He was wearing a white robe tied with a golden rope, his feathery wings of lavender gently moving. Gold and pink rays radiated from his broad shoulders. I was rendered speechless by his magnificent presence.

"You are a driving force for this brave quest and share the burden of the vanquisher's fears and passion," Chamuel said, his voice like the gentle hum of bees in a flowering tree. "You must believe that nothing is impossible." Then, he hovered over the side of my bed and embraced me with a hug as reassuring as a fluffy blanket before disappearing.

And suddenly, I felt refreshed, like I'd slept a solid eight hours.

CHAPTER THIRTY-SEVEN

Ryon - Day 4

84% Waxing Gibbous

As a stone statue, I never had to sleep, but my body needed rest as a living creature, and sometimes, sleep snuck up on me without my knowledge. I was curled up in the corner, on the opposite side of the room from my crate, holding an empty jar of cheese puffs, when the sound of heels tapping jolted me awake.

Bright lights flashed on in the warehouse, and I could see a woman rapidly moving through the small window in the door.

Panic rooted me to my spot, frantically trying to figure out how to return to my crate. The woman approached a tall desk and sat, facing me, busily writing with a pen and shuffling clipboards. I could smell her spicy vanilla perfume.

Getting back in my box is impossible! The crate door faced away from her, but getting there was extremely risky. I waited and watched for a good ten minutes, hoping she'd get distracted or leave.

Finally, the woman smoothed her shiny black hair and knocked the pen tucked behind her ear to the ground. She bent down to pick it up.

This is my chance! I set my empty jar down and headed toward my crate, but I saw the doorknob turn. *She's coming in!* I slid across the unorderly mountain of flattened cardboard boxes and darted into my crate. But I had no time to close the door behind me.

The door hinge squeaked, and her shoes tapped closer. I could hear her breathing. Suddenly, she kicked the plastic jar, causing it to roll across the floor. "Cheese puffs? Who would leave this here?"

I shook in my crate, trying to hold still like the sculpture I was supposed to be.

Then, a doorbell went off.

"I'll be right with you!" the woman called, and soon she was walking away from me.

Still quivering, I peeked through one of the crate holes and watched the woman let a small elderly woman into her office—she looked very similar to Ruza.

"I'm Dr. Smith, here for my shipment." She even rolled her Rs the same way Ruza did.

"Well, it's a really large one. Let me get the paperwork," said the mail lady, walking to the desk and clanking clipboards together. I used that moment to pull the door back onto my crate, but I pulled too hard on the inside handles, and one came loose, plummeting and clanging on the cement floor.

"Did you hear that?" asked the mail woman, adding, under her breath, "Damn security, eating their snacks and leaving trash behind. We've probably got rats…"

I slid the locks shut quietly, then moved back to my peephole.

"Let me see how big it is, please," asked Dr. Smith, and before I knew it, they were standing right outside my box.

"That's quite large," she announced, a spitting image of her great-grandmother. Seeing her brought back the smell of the oils and incense…the touch of Ruza's hands.

"What exactly is it, Dr. Smith?"

"Aphrodite. For the sculpture garden here."

The mail lady smiled, clutching a clipboard to her chest. "Well, do you have a truck to take it in, or should I call someone?"

"Would it be okay if I get it tomorrow? I will bring a truck then. Okay with you?"

Tomorrow? I don't have another day! I clenched my teeth—I only had four days before D-Day, and if Dr. Smith couldn't help me, I needed two full days to get shipped back to Joe.

"No problem. But do you want to take a look at it now? I've got a crowbar…"

No, no, please! I pleaded.

"I'd love to."

NO!

"But I have a meeting with Dr. Brooks," Dr. Smith replied. "Tomorrow, okay?"

Phew!

"Sounds great."

And off went Dr. Smith, bent over and slow, the mail lady following her.

As other voices came and went throughout the day, I thought through my options. Leaving the warehouse was too risky, and I needed Dr. Smith to take me. So that night, I figured I'd dispose of my trash and find some tape and bubble wrap. Then,

I'd cover my body in it early the next morning and wait. If they opened my crate, I'd stand very still and hope they'd only peel back a section of the wrap and be convinced I was art. That was all I could think of doing.

The hours felt like forever, but finally, at 5:15 p.m., the mail lady turned off the lights, and silence filled the air. I waited fifteen minutes and then called Joe.

"I think yer bubble wrap plan is the best ya can do, given the circumstances," he confirmed. "Don't even twitch, no matter what. And if ya have to make a run fer it, go. Jest don't git caught."

The words "make a run for it" and "don't get caught" repeated in my head. I sighed.

"I'll work on a Plan B in case you have to come back here and fight The Chimeras yerself," Joe replied. "Check in again as soon as you can." Then he hung up.

I distracted myself by systematically removing everything I could from my crate, ensuring my essentials, like my cell phone, charger, money, and book, were in the backpack. I kept the hat, shirt, and hoodie, too—the rest I buried in the middle of several trash bins full of paper. I found a large roll of bubble wrap and a spool of packing tape and set them on the bench seat inside the crate for later.

Then, I stood in the middle of that wooden carton and practiced holding my breath and staying perfectly still. Of course, my nose tickled something terrible, or my tail twitched on its own—I began to think my plan was impossible. "Grrowr!" I tightened my fists so hard that my nails bit into my palms.

Suddenly, chains clattered against the large metal door. Is it morning already? My cell phone said it was 9:22 p.m. I secured the crate door and locked myself inside, listening and waiting.

Maybe it's security checking on things...

But the chains kept banging, and I heard the door clatter open and roll shut. Footsteps approached, so I peeked through the hole and saw a figure, all in black, creep closer to my crate. There was no time for bubble wrap, so I got into the position to pounce.

Then, there was a knocking on my crate. "Hello? Is someone in there?" The voice was muffled but familiar. "I'm sure you're scared, but I won't hurt you." There were those familiar rolled Rs!

I unlatched the crate door and slowly opened it. The small figure wore a black hooded cloak.

"Are you one of The Chimeras?" I let out a warning, "Gr-rowr!" and positioned my body to spring.

The hood was quickly lowered, and her familiar face took me aback.

"Dr. Smith?" I asked. The woman's hands flew to her chest, her mouth agape, and she did not move. She looked so much like her great-grandmother, with the same three creases across her forehead and the corners of her mouth turned up in sharp angles. Memories flooded back to me—Monsieur with his chisel, the curtains scraping the rods as they were pulled open each morning and closed every night, the smell of burning stone, and the rhythmic inflections of chanting as gentle hands caressed me.

"You look so much like Ruza," I gasped, my body relaxing.

She lowered her hands and walked toward me. "Ryonac? It is me. Ruza."

I laughed. "No, you're her great-granddaughter, Rose, right?"

"No, I am Ruza."

"How can that be? You'd be a hundred and…" My knees became wobbly.

"I am 154 years old. I used magic to slow down my aging."

Magic? Distrust and the longing for her words to be true battled inside me. Neither of us spoke, the greyness of the warehouse space floating around us as her words seeped into my cognition.

"I helped carve Cletas-Luxajo, Geidhuce, Isel, Vervalt, Anee, Telber…and you."

No one else would know our names, and she rattled them off succinctly. Relief washed over my body. "I'm thrilled it's you." I radiated green with joy. "That means you can help me."

"You have come all this way. You have so much to tell me." The lines on Ruza's forehead grew deeper with concern. "Are others alive?" She reached out a bony hand and touched my feathery neck.

"I'll tell you everything, but we need to get out of here." I pulled myself away from her, panic returning. "I don't have much time…" I growled.

"Easy, Ryonac. We shall go," Ruza said calmly, moving her frail and bent body toward the rolling door.

I yanked it open, and a swift bolt of cool evening air hit my leathered face. *Freedom again!* "I need to grab my things." I got my backpack from the crate and put on the large black hoodie. "Ready."

"Well, not so fast." Ruza pointed to a white statue in the

back of a truck. "Aphrodite… from my yard. Put this in the crate. We don't want anyone to be suspicious."

I set my bag down and lifted the clay lady from the truck bed. I set the unwieldy statue inside the crate, stuffing newspaper, bubble wrap, and shreds around her, keeping one eye on Ruza. She stood and watched me. I found a hammer and a few nails and closed the container with a few whacks.

We stepped outside, and I pulled down the metal door, then Ruza draped the door's chain through a metal eyelet. The padlock lay on the ground, the shackle in pieces.

"They will discover it was cut in the morning, so this will do for tonight," she whispered.

Then, it dawned on me. "Aren't there surveillance cameras?"

Ruza nodded upward. Pieces of black cloth were hanging from what I assumed to be cameras on each corner of the roof. She pointed at a long, clawed pole in the truck bed. "I used my fruit picker." How she rolled her Rs in "fruit picker" made me smile. "Now let's, as they say, get out of Dodge."

I followed her down the metal stairs from the loading dock and climbed into the passenger side. She got in and started the engine.

Worry set in. "Where are we going?" *Is she about to turn me over to the authorities? To a science lab?*

Ruza glanced sideways at my rigorously moving dragon tail as she drove. "I will not harm you. We will talk…even thread a little…"

"Thread?" I asked.

"Well, I created you. We are connected like you and the

other gargoyles and grotesques are."

"Why can't I hear *you?*"

"I set up the spell that way. I needed to be in control back then." She paused. "I have realized that magic can be dangerous."

"Then you understand that you must reverse this spell that brought us to life. Once we were removed for renovation of the building…"

"The Gascony Church."

"Well, now it's a theater, but I think our removal caused all of us…"

"To come alive. Yes, I know."

"So, I was right."

She nodded.

"Geidhuce has built an army of other gars and gros you created that will destroy Gascony and all the humans in it. You must help me stop them!" Beastly fury was growing in me.

She said nothing, her dark eyes focused forward and reflecting the headlights of oncoming cars. "Thread your story to me from the beginning," she said calmly.

So, I took a deep breath and mustered up as many images as possible, emphasizing the urgency of stopping The Chimeras.

"So, doomsday is in four days?" she asked, breaking the silence.

"Yes."

Ruza nodded, contemplating briefly, then said, "You care so much about humans, unlike most of the others. It's not surprising. You are mostly made in the image of a human."

"Please cast a spell to stop The Chimeras."

"Well, I don't practice dark magic anymore," she said abruptly.

Anguish burned inside me again. "You have to use your magic!" Tears dripped from my birdy eyes. "Please!" I thumped my fists hard on the dashboard.

"I can't," was all she said. "We will figure something else out."

"But there is no TIME!" I roared, punching the seat, struggling to hold back the fire from my breath. "All I ever dreamed about was being alive! You made that happen, but I'm a monster! I will always have to hide! I will never have the freedom to do things I wish for!" My claws quickly protruded, and I struggled to keep my wings from unfurling.

Ruza, unfazed, kept her eyes on the road, pulling into a small neighborhood with one-story houses. My mind raced with pleas, threading more images from my life as a beast, trying to convince her to change her mind. But her face remained expressionless.

She calmly drove into the driveway of a small, pale yellow house with stone pillars and white trim, parking in front of a matching garage, then turned the engine off.

"I can't believe you won't help me," I blubbered.

"And that beautiful-faced girl that flashes in your memories, she's your driving force to save Gascony?" Ruza asked.

"I care deeply for Madeleine, yes, but there are others to save, like Anee, Telber, Joe, and the town full of people, but she…" A flood of memories began, as simple as her smile and as monumental as our kiss. I shared how I tricked Chris, how sweetly gullible he was, and how grateful I was for that simple oaf. I also shared Joe's excitement about our adventure and how he took such good care of me. "I've given up hope of ever being with Madeleine, but she deserves to live a beautiful life. I'll gladly give up being the living creature to save everyone by being…"

"…turned back to stone," she said.

Tears were streaming down my bird face. I looked at Ruza's face, and she was also red-eyed and wet-cheeked.

She let out an uneven sigh and reached for the door handle. "Let's go inside."

I gently grabbed her arm. "I just need to know why, Ruza," I said. "Why did you cast a spell to turn stone gars and gros into living monsters?" I let go of her.

"At the time, it seemed to be my only chance." Her shoulders and head lowered as she stared at her hands, fidgeting with the car keys in her lap. "Monsieur was an evil man. He dragged me away from my family when I was just 14 years old. My father was a sculptor who taught me many of his skills the second I could hold a chisel, so Monsieur took me to America and forced me to work for him. Luckily, he had no romantic interest in me, but he beat me every time I tried to leave. I hated him."

"I didn't know…"

She lifted her head. "My grandmother had also taught me things. Magic, rituals, divination… My spell was supposed to make you all come to life soon after you were mounted to the church, and then you were to hunt down Monsieur and kill him for me. I tried it on every gargoyle and grotesque we created, but it never worked."

"That explains the oils, burning herbs, and the chanting."

"Yes, but I was only 16 at the time. Young. I didn't think beyond my situation. I never imagined it would come to this one day. I had devised a spell to turn you all back to stone the second Monsieur was dead, but nothing happened at any of the revealing ceremonies, so I figured the spell didn't work. When Monsieur finally died of alcoholism at age 72, I was 43. I had lost decades of my life. So, I created a new spell to slow my aging and regain time."

I suddenly remembered purple and green bruises on Ruza's arms and legs in those fleeting days of being carved. "I'm sorry he was so terrible to you."

Ruza leaned over and put her hand on my scaly knee. "I knew you were the kindest of the Gascony bunch. I could tell way back then."

"But you said you had a spell to turn us back to stone after coming to life. Do you still have it?"

She shook her head vigorously. "It doesn't matter if I have it or not. I don't practice magic anymore. Now, come with me inside." She opened her door and climbed out.

I wiped my moist cheeks with the sleeve of my black hoodie as I followed Ruza to her back door, my pack on my back. She opened it with a key and led me past a washer and dryer to a dark room. She reached beneath the shade of a tall lamp on a table. *Click, click.* A dim, golden light spread out over the walls of shelves covered with books, glass cases full of strange and exotic masks, carved bowls, granite statues, jars in rows filled with dried plants and mysterious objects, and candles dripping with hardened wax. Although practically every surface was covered with something, it had an orderliness. It reeked of mushrooms, sour milk, and cinnamon.

"Welcome to my apothecary," Ruza announced. "I have spent my life traveling the world collecting books on magic and lore. For years, I have searched and collected rare herbs and roots. I met medicine women and shamans in dark caves or rat-infested alleys. I backpacked mile after mile, my feet bloody and blistered, to get the rarest ingredients: Siberian henbane, Icelandic mugwort, Spanish mandrake, Indian cinquefoil." She extended her hand toward the jars. "And this is what I have to show for it."

Her face became sad, lost in distant memories. Then she shook her head and switched her focus to me. "But look at you! Standing before me, my vision, which I helped create in stone, is now flesh and blood. Astonishing!"

She cleared an oversized leather wingback chair by setting two stacks of books with shabby bindings on the floor, then gestured for me to sit. I plunked down and tucked my tail, dust rising and swirling around me.

"Dobrota! I guess my housekeeping needs some work."

"Dobrota, yes, I forgot that word. You said it a lot. What does it mean?"

"In English, 'goodness, gracious.'" She flipped a wall switch, turning on a bright overhead light that blinded me for a second. "Now, let me take a closer look at you. Remove that jacket you are wearing." She grabbed a large magnifying glass with a strap off a cluttered table and put it on her head, pivoting the lens down over her eyes.

I stood, pulled the hoodie off, and let it drop to the floor beside my backpack.

"Mmhmm," she said as she looked over every inch of my human legs, arms, and chest. "Ahha," she murmured as she studied my condor head. "Show me your wings?"

I unfurled them slowly and turned around. She touched them.

A grandfather clock struck once, reminding me that time was slipping away. "Well?" I asked, bristling with impatience.

"Magnificent, just magnificent!" she exclaimed.

"I know this must be something, to see your creation come to life, but I really need your help stopping…"

She was lost in observation.

"Ruza, please!" I growled, spinning around, folding my wings, and sitting abruptly.

"What you ask of me can't happen," she stated coldly.

"Well, sure it can. Just tell me what I can do to help. Perhaps I can gather some books and herbs? Help you find the old spell? Need a live animal to sacrifice? I smelled some rats in the ivy outside…"

"I can't," she interrupted. Then she plopped down on the edge of the coffee table across from me, her eyes distant and droopy again.

I leaned toward Ruza and re-threaded the scenario of what Geidhuce and his band of evil creatures were planning to do. I showed her the humans' terror, the bloodshed, and the town crumbling in chaos as it went up in flames.

Ruza's eyes grew wide, and then she stood up and paced amongst the cases and shelving, her mind a million miles away.

"Please, Ruza, this is urgent! Time is ticking away." I saw the oval moon outside the window across from where I sat. "It's happening on the full moon, and look." I pointed.

"I know, but I cannot make magic anymore." She continued to pace. "It's not just putting together a bunch of pepperwort and aconite… it takes strong intentions and coordination of mystical energies." She gestured wildly with her hands above her head. "That inner dynamism adds the spark that ignites the sorcery." She dropped her arms, tears returning to her eyes. "Since my husband died…my abilities died with him."

I charged to her side and got down on my scaly knees, my tail flicking up and down, hands gently grasping the frail woman's arms. I gazed into her eyes and nodded. "Let me see it," I whispered. "Thread it."

I saw a frail man lying in bed with dozens of candles, their light dancing on the walls. He was coughing up blood, and Ruza was speaking foreign words I figured to be Croatian. She mixed and boiled potions, reciting incantations from open books strewn around the room. Her desperation was like someone drowning in the undertow of a reckless sea. She had tried everything, but as her beloved husband took his last breath, Ruza's will to do magic had drowned in those wavering depths of candlelight and smoke.

I took her small, bony hands, cold and shaking, and placed them on my heart. I threaded Madeleine speaking to angels before turning out the light, nestled in bed, her kitten tucked beneath her chin, purring. Then, I showed Vervalt lurking at her window, ready to take her life. I let Ruza feel my love and anger through my hands, up into the veins of her arms until they pulsed into her heart.

"Please help," I whispered. "I stopped Vervalt, and she's still alive, but she and so many others will lose their lives without you. Together, we can make sure that doesn't happen." Ruza's eyes stayed locked with mine. "I'm sorry you couldn't stop the disease that took your beloved husband, but you can save Madeleine and others like her because those who threaten them are of your making."

"I don't know…" she murmured, her face pale. "I've never turned anything into stone before, and I didn't know I could bring something to life from stone until today."

"But now you know you have more power than you thought."

"But I…"

"Please, at least try. I can give you…" I looked at the grandfather clock ticking away in the corner of the room. It was nearly 11 p.m. "…12 hours. I know it's not much, but I need time to get back to Gascony to fight those gars and gros myself if it doesn't work. But please, see what you can do."

Ruza was silent, but I saw a light inside her eyes like the first moment of a sunrise. "Okay, I will try."

"Thank you!" I hugged her small and delicate body tightly.

"Don't thank me yet," she said, gently pushing me away. "Grab all those books on the wooden table and stack them up over there somewhere," she said, pointing. "I like to spread out when I work."

CHAPTER THIRTY-EIGHT

Ryon - Day 3

91% Waxing Gibbous

I spent the next several hours pacing the floor and watching the clock, my heart thumping loudly. Ruza worked in the kitchen, occasionally asking me to bring her something from the shelves or tabletops in the apothecary room. Smoke from candles and burning herbs lingered in the air, along with strong-smelling oils. Strange incantations were read with mystique due to Ruza's accent, and sometimes, she would shake her head and curse in Croatian. Other times, she would smile and nod, sputtering approval. I wished I could hear her thoughts.

At around 4 a.m., Ruza said, "Go, relax in the other room. I need to work on this part alone."

So, I left and reclined upon Ruza's brown, suede couch, hoping.

I called Joe to check in.

"I still can't believe it's actually Ruza," he remarked. "I jist knew in my bones yer trip was worth doin'."

"I gave her 12 hours, and she has seven left. You got Plan B figured out?"

"I'm hopin' fer the best and preparin' fer the worst. Instead of worryin' 'bout gettin' the crate back, I found a delivery truck that's takin' a load of grapes from Bakersfield to Pittsburg this afternoon. Ya can sneak in and hide the whole way. Ruza jist needs to git ya there by 3 p.m."

"How far is the truck from here?"

"About two hours. Ya can easily make it if ya leave by noon."

"That gives her an extra hour to work on her spell." I sighed. "How long will it take for me to get to Pittsburgh?"

"Several drivers tag team it, so you'll git there by Wednesday afternoon, so about two full days."

"Wednesday is D-Day." I felt lightheaded. "How will I get from Pittsburgh to Gascony?" I asked.

"I'm figurin' that out now. Got stuff in the works, but we'll get ya to Gascony before the midnight Chimeras meetin'." Joe's voice softened. "I can only imagine the heap of worry ya got rumblin' around in ya, but ya gotta keep the faith."

As I hung up the phone, I thought of Gandalf from *The Lord of the Rings: The Fellowship of the Ring*, saying, "All we have to decide is what to do with the time that is given to us."

So, my best use of the final fleeting hours was remembering Madeleine while I could.

Ruza didn't speak to me for hours, and as the sun crept in through her white wood plantation shutters, I began pacing and fretting again.

Just after the grandfather clock struck 10 a.m., Ruza entered the room. She had dark smudges of dirt and worry on her face. "You asked to not be able to think and thread when you are turned back to stone, but I can't guarantee it."

"I don't care about anything except saving Madeleine and

the townspeople," I replied. "You have two hours left," I added. "Then I'm going to need a ride to Bakersfield."

Ruza didn't seem to hear me. "Naravno!" she said to herself, deep in thought, heading quickly back to the kitchen.

I looked through my movie book for the next hour, barely comprehending what I read.

Suddenly, I was jolted by a loud cry. "Ura!!"

I bounded to my dragon feet. I reached the kitchen, where smoke billowed and black ash covered nearly every surface. "What happened?"

"Ura! Ura! Ura!" Ruza repeated, dancing around as if she were 40 years younger. "I think I got it!"

Although happiness radiated from within my scaly chest, there was a twist of pain in my gut. The end of me was near. No more Joe, Telber, or Anee in my life, and no more being near Madeleine again.

Ruza held a corked, clear glass vial filled with silver metallic liquid and wriggled it from side to side. "This, I believe, will turn all grotesques and gargoyles to stone." She smiled, her eyes crazy.

"How do you know it'll work?" I challenged.

"It worked on him, so…" She pointed to a rat, frozen in the action of running. I picked it up—sure enough, it was now a piece of granite. Sniffing it and smelling nothing but earthiness, I set it back down. "I call it my Medusa Spell."

I scratched my feathery head for a moment. "But, if I drink this potion, will all the others also be turned to stone?"

"No. At least a drop of this liquid must touch a creature's skin to turn it into stone."

Perturbation struck me like lightning. "That means I can't take it here. I must go back, in this monster form, and make sure every creature comes in contact with this potion?"

"Yes," Ruza replied, her eyes still wild with excitement.

My hero's journey was never-ending. "What if I don't make it on time? What if someone catches me before I get it there? There are over a dozen gars and…" I couldn't think clearly, so I frantically paced the kitchen.

Ruza followed behind me. "It will be okay, Ryon. Listen…"

I turned on the sink and splashed my face with water to soothe my inner furnace.

"Stop. I have more to tell you," she said, touching my back.

I shut off the spigot. "Let me call Joe. I need to tell him…"

"Listen to me!" The frail, old woman's face turned red, veins protruding from her creased forehead as she held up a second vial. This one was half the size, corked, and glowing orange like traffic cones.

"What is that?" I asked, trying to catch my breath.

"I made two potions."

"And?"

"This one will do something very different. This one will make you human."

Those words hung in the air before they got to my brain.

Human?

"Yes, human." Ruza hesitated before adding, "But…"

"But?"

"I need a grotesque that has come to life here to try it. Maybe you could do that now?" she teased, grinning.

"I'll take it!" I declared, palms open.

"I can't promise it will work." She handed me the vial. "All you need is a small amount on the tongue. This one must be ingested."

I cupped the bottom of the vial with my other hand and stared at the beautiful orange liquid.

"Remember, magic is unreliable," she reminded. "I cannot guarantee it will work, and I don't know how long it will last, but data shows…"

I didn't listen to the rest. I popped off the cork and let four bitter drops land on my tongue.

"Stop! No more is necessary," she said, standing on her tippy toes to swipe the vial from my hands.

I last remembered Ruza smiling while the walls spun around me. The room was a vortex, turning faster and faster until I plummeted downward into a black abyss, finally hitting the bottom—*bam!*

I don't know how long I was out, but Ruza was humming gibberish in my ears when I came to. The dizziness lingered, clouding my focus and making Ruza's wrinkled face appear young and smooth as if I were seeing her through layers of tulle.

"You are awake!" she said joyfully. "Ura, ura, ura!" She did her happy jig once again.

"What happened? I must have fallen…" I began.

"How are you feeling?" she asked, helping me into a sitting position.

"My head is pounding."

"You fell pretty hard."

"Why did I fall?"

"It is better if you get up and walk a little. Can you stand, Ryon?"

Feeling as wobbly as a newborn colt, I put each leg beneath myself and tried to stand while Ruza held my arm to steady me. Wooziness fuzzed my vision.

"There you go, Ryon. Can you step? Very good." She led me down a white hallway to the very end, and I was still quite disoriented.

"Now look straight ahead…I want you to meet someone," Ruza said.

A blurry figure was in front of me, standing upright in a slowly clearing fog. I squinted to make it out… a naked young man staring at me.

"What…?" I scoffed.

"Look carefully at that guy in front of you."

Then it dawned on me. "Did you find someone to go stop the gars and gros? Will he go to Gascony?"

"Yes, he will do that."

"Oh, thank you, Ruza! Thank you so much! I must have been so stressed that I passed out, but you found a guy… hello! Don't be afraid. I'm Ryon… I know I look like a scary monster, but I'm a friend," I remarked, whispering to Ruza, "Why isn't he wearing any clothes?"

"Well, when he got here, he didn't have anything to wear except a black hoodie," she explained.

"Why did he take it off?"

"Don't worry. We will find him some clothes."

"Oh, good!" I quietly replied. "Hey there, thanks for saving Gascony…" I announced loudly but then stopped. The haziness of my vision dissipated, and there, in the middle of the mist, was Ruza holding up that young man. *What?* I looked down at myself and saw only human male features: feet, legs, arms, even genitalia. "Ruza, is that…?"

"Yes, my dear Ryonac, that is a mirror… it is you!"

Tears burned my eyes, making it hard to see again. I instantly felt stronger and took several steps toward my image. I looked pretty good, my chest and arms muscular and toned, and I was happy to see hair on my head instead of droopy, leathery skin. But my face, well, it was far from the movie stars in my film book. I'd dreamed of being Clark Gable or Rock Hudson, but I was a large-nosed, beady-eyed guy with small ears. "Homely" was the word, and I was the definition of it.

"So, what do you think? Ruza did good, yah?" she remarked, holding out my black hoodie. Her corncob smile of yellowed teeth stretched wide.

I put the jacket on and zipped it up, a giant potato sack on my new body. "I can't believe it, Ruza. I'm human," I mumbled.

"You don't seem happy. This is what you want, right?"

"Yes, it is… it's just that… I wish I were a bit more handsome."

"Oh, but you see, handsome comes from within. You are a caring, devoted young man. Each feature represents the creatures you were once made of, but in a human way. They are part of your existence." She touched my smooth cheek. "If Madeleine is as good a person as you say, she will fall in love with you because of your heart." She moved her hand over my heart, and I felt a zap of electricity as if coming fully to life like in *Frankenstein*. "Besides, you look a bit like King Charles mixed with Arnold Schwarzenegger."

I returned to the mirror and smiled, my new human lips curling on each side. Magic was dancing in my eyes. I hoped it wasn't just from the potion and that Madeleine would see the spark.

I hugged Ruza and swung her around in a circle. "You did a wonderful job!" I declared, setting her back on the floor.

"Um…" Her face dropped. "Remember, I don't know how long this spell will last. It could be an hour, or it could be for the rest of your life."

"I'll appreciate my humanness while I can," I announced.

"Enough talk," Ruza continued. "I still have lots to do. I need to find clothes that fit, get you a driver's license, and immediately get you on an airplane back to Gascony. You have monsters to slay."

The dream I'd yearned for for decades had come true! No longer a monster, I was filled with miraculous awe to be walking on two flesh-covered legs, breathing air through a human's mouth and nose—even wearing the pajama bottoms Ruza had given me to sleep in made me joyous. My heart whirled with jubilation over every little detail that made me a real person.

Yet, a dark cloud of foreboding hovered overhead.

CHAPTER THIRTY-NINE

Ryon - Day 2

96% Waxing Gibbous

Ruza insisted I sleep for a few hours, and though I thought I was too wired to succumb to it, slumber took me to the land of nod. Awakening to the nutty smell of coffee, I ran to the bathroom to look in the mirror.

Phew! I'm still human!

As I leaned forward, studying my smooth skin and dark brown irises surrounded by white, my breath fogged a small circle on the glass. I was instantly taken back to my peephole in the shed, realizing how wonderful it was to no longer see the world through a three-inch hole. However, my heart skipped a beat in a fit of trepidation. As a human, I'd become more vulnerable, and I was the only one who could stop those evil Chimeras—if I could get close enough to turn them back to stone.

Ruza stood in the doorway, radiating so much happiness that she looked decades younger. "Good morning!"

I swallowed hard. "Can you still hear my thoughts?"

"No, threading no longer exists for you." She frowned. "But I can see your worry. A little breakfast will help you feel better," she said, beckoning me with her hand.

I followed her into the kitchen. The potion-making mess was all cleaned up, and the white walls and appliances shone. A small wooden table was pushed against a wide window with white lace curtains. It was dark outside, and the clock on the oven said it was 3:33 a.m.

"So many amazing smells! Better than when this was your laboratory," I joked.

Ruza grinned. "I made you coffee and freshly baked cinnamon rolls."

My senses and hunger were just as acute as when I was a grotesque, only the cravings for birds and rats had gone away, thank goodness.

"Eat before they get cold." Ruza sat and pointed to a chair across the table from her. A giant swirl of crusty pastry covered in creamy frosting and aromatic spices was on a green plate.

As I sat, I reached behind and swooped my hand across my rear.

Ruza burst into laughter. "You forgot you don't have a tail."

I nodded, my face hot.

"Being human takes getting used to… even for us who are human all our lives," she said.

Next to the cinnamon roll was a cup of coffee and a small, clear glass of amber liquid. "What's this? Another potion?" I asked, changing the subject.

Ruza laughed again. "You could call it that, but it's the breakfast drink of my country: rakija!"

I picked up the tiny glass and sniffed it. "Ah! It burns my nose!"

"It is made from fermented fruits like plum and pear, and how do you say it?" She thought for a second. "Apricot. It is fruit salad in a glass. Drink it slowly." She picked hers up and gently slurped its contents. "This is my favorite: *sadna rajika medica.*"

"Medica? So, it's a type of medicine?"

"I suppose some think brandy heals, but in Croatian, "medica" means "honey.""

I timidly sipped. It felt thick on my tongue and warm as it trickled down my throat. "Tastes a lot better than what you gave me last night."

Ruza smiled widely, then held up her glass. "We must toast to what has happened and what is to come. *Zivjeli!* which means 'long live.'"

"Zivjeli!" We clinked glasses, and I took a gulp, wincing as the liquor went down, hot and strong.

"Here." Ruza slid a card with the word "Pennsylvania" across the top.

"Who is that?" I asked. Inside a small rectangle, the card showed a picture of a dark-haired stranger apparently named John Court.

"A student left his driver's license in my classroom on Monday, so I figured we would borrow it. The same name is on the plane ticket."

"I don't look exactly like him." I held it up to take a better look.

"Well, it's close enough. You'll have to express mail it back to me when you get to Gascony." She smiled. "It was a happy accident that he left it behind."

My eyes prickled. "Ruza, I'm so grateful. I couldn't have made it to this point without you."

She became emotional as well. "… You are a miracle! I created you, you needed me, and I was able to help. My heart will be happy for as long as I live." She squeezed my hands hard, then quickly let go to wipe the wetness from her cheeks. "We must leave for LAX in thirty minutes."

"Won't you come with me, Ruza? You can meet Joe and help me make sure the potion works and…"

"I am too old." She looked off into the distance. "When my husband died, I wondered why God kept me around. For decades, I suffered that loss as well as the pain of my failure to help him. But now, I see the purpose for me to carry on." She shifted her gaze to me. "Perhaps my magic didn't fail after all. Maybe it was just my husband's time to be with the angels." Ruza threw back the last of her brandy.

The talk of angels brought Madeleine to mind. "You believe in angels?" I asked.

"Absolutely. I saw them above my husband when he passed." She sighed. "Enough of that. I believe you will slay those monsters. So should you."

"I'll try hard to make you proud." I half-smiled, unsure about what was ahead of me.

Ruza raised her brows. "I want to ask you…May I call you Cudo instead of Ryon?"

"Cudo?"

"It means 'miracle' in Croatian."

"Sure." Then, I chuckled a little.

"Why do you laugh?"

"I'm just glad you didn't give me 'Cujo' as a nickname."

Her face looked puzzled.

"It's a movie by Stephen King about a rabid dog named Cujo."

"You and your movies," she said, shaking her head.

But I couldn't help but feel that "miracle" was a lofty word for such a homely, fearful human like me.

O   O   O

After breakfast, I dressed in Ruza's husband's old clothes and sneakers, my hair wet and combed into place, and my backpack slung over one shoulder, I looked like your average 16-year-old boy.

"Off to face Geidhuce and his posse," I said to my reflection in the bathroom mirror.

"Ryon, we need to go!" called Ruza from the front of the house.

I got to the door just as she went outside and followed her to a small silver Prius parked in the driveway. The sky was dark grey, and the moon was a great glowing ball hovering over us— D-Day was a day away. Nausea struck my midsection.

"Where'd the truck go?" I asked.

The doors unlock with a click. "I borrowed the truck from my neighbor. Told him I was taking my Aphrodite statue to get repaired. He even loaded it for me. So nice." She climbed behind the wheel.

I got in and flung my backpack in the backseat. Without warning, Ruza accelerated, and we were down the street.

"Put on your seatbelt," she remarked.

"You didn't give me a chance," I teased, pulling the strap across my chest and clicking the metal piece into the receptacle.

She just smiled, her eyes on the road.

Soon, we were zipping down the freeways of Los Angeles. Cars whizzed around us, but the city was quieter than when I arrived. Palm trees were everywhere, and the road was lined with shrubby brush.

"It smells like the sage from last night," I asked, trying to ignore my nerves.

"All that arid planting is called 'chaparral.' We get wildfires often because of it." She laughed again. "I guess that's when the whole city gets smudged. Now, let's go through the checklist again…. Do you have the ID? The money? My VISA card?"

"Yes." I tapped the bulging pocket in my pants where I'd slipped her late husband's black leather, fold-over wallet she'd also given me. "You're sure it doesn't matter that it's your name on the credit card?"

"No one even checks anymore. And if they do, call me."

I put my hand into the other pant pocket to make sure my cell phone was still there. "I think I have everything. The vials are in my backpack and all wrapped up. Joe's friend parked the truck at the Cleveland airport, so it's ready and waiting for me. I think I'm good."

Soon, signs with the silhouette of an airplane popped up along the road, which Ruza followed, leading us to pass beneath one that said "departures." I marveled at the giant airplanes that flew overhead, lights flashing in the dark morning sky. Airplanes had zoomed past me for many years while I was on the theater, from military jets to commercial ones, but I'd never been so close. We pulled up and parked against a curb as people bustled about with suitcases, hugging goodbye and hello.

Ruza grinned from ear to ear as if she were a proud parent. "You, Cudo, are going to be great. I feel it."

"I'll make sure Joe keeps you updated." I gulped.

She leaned close to me and took my hands in hers. "Cudo, sometimes what you wish for isn't always best. Trust that what is meant to be will happen." She squeezed my hands before letting them go and getting out of the car. I couldn't move. She opened the passenger door. "Come on now."

I grabbed my backpack, heaving it between the two front seats, then forced myself to stand.

"Do you have your printed ticket?" she asked.

I held up the folded paper. "Yes. Thank you for…" The words clogged in my throat.

The tiny woman pulled me to her with a surprising amount of strength, her head pressed against my belly. "Say no more."

She released me just as an enormous, bird-shaped machine passed overhead. My heart did acrobatics in my chest.

"Metal winged dinosaurs— pterodactyls of the 21st century!" Ruza announced, pointing to the sky.

"I can't believe I'm going to ride in one of THOSE!"

"People do it all the time. Besides, it is the quickest way to get back to Gascony." She reached into her coat pocket. "One more thing." She held up a silver wristwatch with a metal band. "This, too, was my husband's. I give this to you with the advice of the great Albert Einstein: "The only reason for time is so that everything doesn't happen at once."" She took my left hand

and slipped the watch on my wrist, closing the shiny clasp. "The tiny second hand must go all around the face before the big hand can move one small spot, and the shortest hand must wait for the big hand to do the same before it can move. A watch takes one small step at a time to make bigger things happen. As you embark on this journey, remember this."

"I will."

"I'm grateful you found me." Then, she looked far off, into the sky, as if speaking to an angel. "I can finally let go."

"Maybe you can make a potion to help you live forever," I suggested.

"Oh, no. I have found the treasure at the end of my rainbow," she said, briefly pressing a finger to my chest. I blushed. "Now go. Don't be late!" She closed the car door, walked quickly to the other side, got in, and drove away before I could say "goodbye."

I had added another person to the list of those I couldn't fail, and I shook a little more inside.

Following the people around me, I entered the building and got through security by showing my borrowed ID, trying to act calm, although I was a wreck. I got through the metal detectors Ruza warned me about without a problem and found my gate. The place smelled of pretzels, hamburgers, coffee, and sweat. I was in a hazy world of light and sound, forgetting I was no longer a monster and could be around people, expecting them to scream and run any minute. I repeated, "I am human. I am human," inside my head.

People were already lining up to get on the plane, so I did, too. When the worker scanned my ticket and wished me a pleasant flight, he had no clue he had just let a former monster pass.

I crossed my fingers that the spell wouldn't wear off. I had no good plan if I became a monster again while in the air, except that I'd brought my giant black hoodie with me.

"If you don't want it to rain, bring an umbrella," Ruza had said to explain why I should take it.

I needed that to be true.

I found my seat number, wedged myself by the window, and prayed no one would sit in my row, but then a young woman, who smelled of peppermint, plunged a purse with rhinestone skulls onto the middle seat. I used my peripheral vision to look at her. She had light blond hair with black roots that spiked around the pink headphones she wore over her ears. She lifted a small suitcase into the overhead compartment, wearing cut-off jean shorts and a white t-shirt with an illustration of a kneeling fairy with black wings and the words "Pixie Dust Magic." Her arms were covered with tattoos of toadstools and butterflies inked with color. She plopped into the aisle seat, avoiding eye contact with everyone, including me.

Sitting so close to a stranger caused me to sweat, and the thought of another person sitting in the middle seat made me claustrophobic. I tried to slow my breathing and relax the tightness in my chest. Every passenger that passed by on the aisle could potentially sit in the middle seat, and relief came when each one kept moving.

Soon, though, the people stopped coming, and a voice announced through the speakers, "Prepare for takeoff."

I exhaled, and a tiny bit of tension released.

The girl stowed her purse beneath the middle seat, her hair practically tickling my arm as she bent down. Then, she settled back into her chair and closed her eyes, nonplused about the plane taking to the air, rattling and groaning as if it would fall to pieces any second.

I liked using my own wings to fly a lot better. I grasped the armrests and held my breath.

The giant metal bird bounced in the air, rumbled, and shuddered, but we both calmed down a bit after a while. No one seemed worried, playing games on their phones or sleeping like babies.

I watched from the corner of my eye as my seat partner pulled up a list of films on her phone. I hadn't watched a single movie since coming alive, and Ruza had told me I could watch them on the plane, but I didn't know how. I took a deep breath and tapped my seat partner on the shoulder. "Can you help me get there?" I pointed at her screen.

She smiled only halfway, looking me up and down. Then, she held out her hand, so I handed her my phone. She quickly tapped away on its surface and gave it back. The same list of movie graphics was on the screen. Lightness washed over me.

"You got headphones?" she asked.

I shook my head, happy to watch without hearing anything. She leaned over and grabbed her bag from the floor, digging through its contents until she pulled out a wire with two ear-buds. She handed it to me. "You can keep them. Plug the metal end into the hole on the top."

"Thanks."

She closed her eyes and settled back into her seat, the tinny sound of rock music coming from her large headphones.

I turned to the list of movies and recognized half of them. I knew some of the dialogue by heart because I'd heard it echoing through the theater walls many times. I scrolled through the list a few times, making sure I didn't miss the movie I had dreamed of seeing most, *Casablanca*, but had no luck. I could have chosen a romance like *The Notebook* or a musical like *West Side Story*, but I decided on the original *Resident Evil.* I hoped it would inspire me to be brave since the movie was about a military team that must stop hungry zombies. I could get some tips.

As the opening music began, goosebumps formed on every inch of my new human skin. Then, I was enraptured for the entire hour and forty minutes. I only paused it once to order a Coke like my seatmate. Flying in an airplane was growing on me.

As the final credits rolled, I lingered, marveling at the greatness of cinema. I wished I could have stayed in the ethers forever, watching movies on my phone. But I knew that couldn't happen—I was getting inevitably closer to my quest.

As the plane approached landing, it lurched and dipped, and I held so tightly to the armrests that my knuckles turned white. The cell phone in my lap lit up with messages, but I didn't dare move until the plane was on the ground, rolling to its gate. Ruza wanted to see if I had arrived in Cleveland safely, and Joe had sent pictures of where the truck was. It was in the green Smart Parking lot, level 2, section B.

"The key is on the front left wheel. Call me when you're about to leave the airport," his text said.

Warmth radiated through me. I was lucky to have people helping—people who cared. The other humans around me were texting or chatting on their phones with colleagues or loved ones, and I was just like them. It gave me chills.

While we taxied, I spoke to the angels as my sweet Madeleine often did. *Please help me make everyone proud. Whatever happens, make sure those I love are safe!* I shut my eyes and focused on trying to see an angel. *Are you real? Are you listening to me?*

A light glowed in my periphery, and my soul felt at ease. I opened my eyes when a tingling sensation began, and I swore something ethereal was beside me to my left, but I saw nothing. The girl in the aisle seat bobbed her head to the beat of the music in her ears until the ding that told us we were free to go.

As the people congregated in the aisle to exit the plane, my seat partner gave me a quick smile, said, "Good luck," and then took off into the queue. During that calm before the storm, I was grateful for so many things, including the kind stranger who helped me experience the miracle of cinema. I was sure about one thing: I was hooked on being human and hoped Ruza's spell would last forever.

○　○　○

Harsh daylight slammed my eyes as I stepped out of the airport, but once my eyes adjusted, I saw the sign for the green Smart Parking lot across the street. The day was pleasantly warm as I climbed up the stairs, and right in front of me was my old truck friend waiting for our next adventure. I got the key off the wheel and climbed inside, thinking I fit much better without a tail and giant dragon feet. First, I texted Joe to let him know I had landed and was ready to go. Then, I texted Ruza and told her the same.

Using the charging wire, I plugged my phone into the cigarette lighter with a gadget Ruza gave me to use in the older truck—the time: 1:44 p.m. I put Gascony, PA, as my destination, and it was a two-hour drive. It dawned on me that I could go anywhere I wanted in the U.S. Liberty was intoxicating. So, I cleared it and punched in 4444 Dusty Road, Athens, Texas—a 19-hour drive. In my mind was Madeleine in the moonlight, asking for a kiss…*I could drive that way and be with her.*

But then, I pictured Geidhuce and The Chimeras marching down Main Street, death and destruction all around them. I shivered at that image. I knew what I had to do, so I reset the navigation and turned the key to start the engine.

Using Ruza's credit card, I got out of the lot, and my phone told me to go left to the highway. The city of Cleveland was crowded with people on the streets and wild drivers that came up from behind, darting around and causing me to slam the brakes.

A bunch of killer gargoyles will probably be a piece of cake compared to this.

At around 3:50 p.m., the truck bumped like crazy going up that final hill, the grasshoppers and butterflies dodging the tires, dust floating up all around. The old white house, paint peeling in strips like a bad sunburn, waited silently in that familiar meadow beside the tree where I hung out with my friends. The place still looked abandoned, and I couldn't help but picture it with shutters rehung and a fresh coat of paint.

I pulled up and tried the front door, but it was locked. I knocked, but of course, no one answered. So, I walked around to the back door and banged hard on one of the glass panes, using the rhythm we'd agreed on.

"Hello! It's me, Ryon!" I hollered.

Nothing but silence.

It was frustrating that I could no longer thread.

"Anee! Telber! I know I don't look like myself, but I've been to see Ruza, and she made me human! It's not what I expected, but trust me, I'm Ryon!"

Still, nothing.

"Okay, let me prove it to you. We used to live attached to the Gascony Theater together, Geidhuce is planning to take it over tomorrow at midnight with The Chimeras, and I went all the way to California to find Professor Prekrasna-Smith, who turned out to be Ruza..."

A golden paw pulled back the curtains on the door, revealing a familiar furry face. The latch turned from the inside, and the door opened a crack. "Ryon, is that really you?"

"In human flesh." I smiled. "Let me in?"

"Sure." Anee barely opened the door, forcing me to turn sideways to fit through. Once I was inside, she locked it behind us and bared her teeth. She circled once, sniffing my essence in the air.

Scared she might pounce on me, I pleaded, "Anee, really, it's me. Ryonac."

Suddenly, she grabbed me roughly with her large, furry arms. Overwhelmed by her strength and a little frightened, I realized she was just hugging me.

"Gotcha!" she proclaimed.

"I thought you were going to eat me," I admitted.

Telber galloped from behind a door in the hall and tackled us both to the floor, nuzzling his mule face beneath my chin. "B-B-Buddy! Heehaw!" Then he stood up and offered each of us a hoof to pull ourselves up.

"We were worried you'd never come back," Anee said, studying me closely. "It's funny, but you look a lot-ish like you used to, just humanized. Want to sit down?" She pointed toward the kitchen.

"Could we sit beneath the maple tree outside?" I pleaded.

"Sure!" Anee twittered.

"W-W-Well, we don't … g-g-go out much… d-d-during the day…" Telber disclosed, blinking rapidly. His speech was slower and choppier than usual.

"We always used to…" I began, flashing a worried look at Anee.

She rolled her big eyes, but only I saw. "Telber, it'll be alright. We'll sit behind the trunk, deep in the grass," Anee suggested, a sweetness in her voice that I'd missed.

Telber crossed his hooved arms and shook his head from side to side.

"Please, Telber, just for a little bit. It's such a lovely spring afternoon," I coaxed.

He pressed his lips together in a tight grimace but dropped his arms to his side. "F-F-For a short… t-t-time… o-o-only."

"Great!" I exclaimed, heading to the tree with Anee bounding closely behind and Telber merely shuffling.

I plopped down in that familiar place, Anee diving next to me. The sweet smell of the blue-eyed Mary flowers surrounding us made me elated to return to that place again. It felt like I'd been away a lot longer than a week—I'd already lived two different lifetimes, and I had just begun my third. Near the river, squirrel-corn flowers had bloomed, white and heart-shaped, scrolling throughout the grass and symbolic of the love of friends.

"Tell us everything!" Anee declared, tapping the grass next to her to get Telber to sit. He slowly crouched down on all fours, his eyes darting left and right the whole time. Anee watched him with worried eyes.

So, I started with Joe and my road trip and told them about the crate he shipped me in. Then, I described getting delivered to Ruza, not her great-granddaughter, as I had thought, and how she turned me human.

"So, we could drink the potion too and become human?" Anee asked, her furry ears twitching excitedly.

"Yes!" I announced. "But Ruza said she wasn't sure how long being human would last. It could wear off at any moment—or never."

"B-B-But you've. . . l-l-lost your. . . a-a-ability to thread," Telber said weakly. "H-H-How will you. . . kn-kn-know when the others. . . a-a-are around?"

"I don't." I looked at his donkey face and saw fear. "Soon, none of that will matter, though, once the potion is given to The Chimeras. Ruza thinks that one drop on their bodies is all it will take to turn them to stone, but, again, she said there are no guarantees since magic is practiced and not precise."

"Can we become human now?" asked Anee excitedly.

"Sorry, but not yet." It broke my heart to disappoint her. "Joe and I worked out a plan, and we need you and Telber to stay gargoyles until after the others are turned back to stone."

"Okay," she murmured, clearly disappointed.

Telber let out a prolonged, apprehensive "Heeeee-haaaaw!" and added, "Y-Y-Your plan sounds…v-v-very dangerous." His whole body began to shake.

"I know it sounds scary, but I need your help. You'll need to attend The Chimeras' meeting and blend in. But after they're defeated, you can both take the potion immediately," I explained, then laid my hand on Telber's knee. "Trust me, if I had thought it out, I would have stayed a gro myself. So now, if I were to show up as a human, I'd be in greater danger."

Anee lifted her beautiful, amber head and half-grinned. "You're right. It's better this way." Then, she rolled around in the tall green grass. "But I cannot wait to see what Telber and I are like as humans! Will I have long-ish hair? How tall will I be?" She giggled. "Will Telber still bray?"

Telber froze, his eyes dark and round. "I-I-I don't want to… t-t-turn human," he announced. "Th-th-this is what… I-I-I am…wh-wh-what I was…m-m-m-meant to be."

Anee rolled over to face Telber. "But staying a gar means you'll have to hide all the time," she said gently. "As humans, we can live freely together."

"B-B-But not…f-f-forever," replied Telber. "H-H-Humans die."

"You're right, buddy, but since you're a living creature, your lifespan isn't as long as when you were a statue either. Don't you think freedom as a human is better?" I scooted closer to Telber. "Remember how it felt to be trapped in stone, thinking and feeling? Pure torture. Being human will be so much better. We can travel, see the world, fall in love…" The last part fell from my lips without thinking. Out of the corner of my eye, I saw Anee's head drop.

Telber faked a smile and nodded but kept silent.

"I'm going to share every detail of the plan with you, and then we'll prepare," I said, glad they couldn't see the knot inside my belly. "We're going to be victorious, and then we'll be free."

Anee sat up and pulled Telber and me against each side of her warm, soft body. We all embraced, and I hoped Telber would come around and become excited to be human with me and Anee. We could be a real family.

○ ○ ○

Unlike when Ruza mixed the potions, the minutes ticked away like seconds. It was nearly seven o'clock.

Joe had taught me the importance of planning, quoting a Chinese philosopher's words: "A man who does not plan long ahead will find trouble at his door." So, I sat at the kitchen table with a pen and paper, writing down every step and making a list of supplies, but my mind wandered. I was distracted by what Madeleine would think of me in my new form. I looked better than a monster, but knew I wasn't nearly as handsome as Chris. She deserved a movie star type, assuming I'd get to see her again.

As I refocused for the twentieth time, Anee appeared in the doorway holding.

"The day after you left, these posters were taped up outside the cave where The Chimeras meet," she said, laying it on the table in front of me:

"May Full Moon

@ Midnight—

Preuzeti!"

"The same message has been in the personal ads the last few days," Anee added. "I've been hiding outside the cave every night, listening for threading and anything suspicious, but these posters are the only thing I've noticed."

"Let me Google 'preuzeti,'" I said, tapping on the screen of my phone. "It means 'takeover' in Croatian." I shook my head. "Mind going up to the cave again tonight? Maybe some gars and gros will come early."

Anee put her paw above her eye and saluted me. "You got it!"

"Where's Telber?" I asked.

"He's sleeping. He does that a lot." She sighed and shook her head.

"What happened to him while I was gone?"

"Honestly, I'm not sure." Her furry forehead crumpled. "Between Geidhuce beating him up, him killing that intruder, and the stress of what we're about to do, I think he's become neurotic-ish."

"Poor Telber's been through a lot." I slammed my pen down. "Maybe he shouldn't help us. He could stay here and wait instead."

"Sometimes waiting around is worse-ish. I don't know."

"We have until midnight tomorrow to decide. In the meantime, I'm heading to a thrift shop before it closes to find glassware worthy of a gargoyle rumpus." I stood and pushed in my chair.

"Good luck," Anee said. "I'm gonna make sure our black cloaks are ready. I'll need your sewing skills later." Then, she skittered off.

I went outside and got in the truck. My phone directed me to a large Goodwill Store about ten miles away that closed late. I took the route by Madeleine's house, and it was just as I remembered, and so was my shed. Not a soul was around.

The opposite was true about The Goodwill Store. Groups of people entered with anticipatory smiles and left with treasures in their hands. I never had possessions as a gro, so I was thrilled to be shopping for the first time. I walked down rows of clothing and through a section of toys and books toward the sign hanging from the ceiling that said "housewares." I loved seeing all the human gadgets, from toasters to rain boots to furniture. I had to find what I needed quickly that day, but I swore I'd return if I survived D-Day and play with everything. In the houseware section were glasses with oranges printed on the outside and lots of clear cups, but nothing worthy of an evil gargoyle party…then, I tripped over a box on the floor. Inside was a set of dark red, thick-walled glasses. The sticker said: red crystal wine goblets, box of 20= $20. Beside them was a matching giant bowl with a rather large, bent spoon taped to it. I got that, too. It was $15.

I gathered the items, then walked to the counter to set them down, jittery about interacting with the man who would check me out.

"I'll take these, thank you," I said, trying to act nonchalant.

"One punchbowl, with a ladle and twenty glasses." Then, the man behind the counter typed numbers into a small machine with a strip of paper coming out of the top. He was barely over five feet tall, with grey hair and large sideburns but bald on top, and he wore a white button-down shirt with a red bowtie. "$37.89, please," he said.

I dug two twenties out of my wallet. "Here you go."

"You havin' a party?" The man leaned in close and looked me right in the eyes. "No liquor, young man. I can tell ya ain't even close to 21."

"Yes, sir, I promise. There won't be a drop of liquor served out of this bowl," I answered, amused that it would be full of animal blood tinged with a magic potion, which he would have considered by far worse.

"Good boy," he said as he stood upright again. Then, he whistled a song as he wrapped the cups, setting each one inside the punchbowl. I recognized the tune, but I couldn't remember the words. "Think you can carry this alright?"

"Yes, sir. Thank you." I picked up the heavy bowl and headed to the door, and the man quickly jogged past me and held it open. I stopped just before the threshold. "What's the name of the song you were just whistling?"

"Ah, it's an oldie from 1954. It's called "Earth Angel.""

I got in the truck and set my purchase on the passenger side floor, then found that song on iTunes and played it: "Earth angel, Earth angel, will you be mine? My darling dear, love you all the time. I'm just a fool, a fool in love with you…" Madeleine was definitely my Earth Angel.

I arrived at The Hideout a few minutes after 9:00 p.m., and Anee had left a note on the kitchen table: "Telber and I went to catch ourselves dinner on the way to spy." So, I unwrapped and set each piece I bought on the counter and called Joe to discuss the plan.

"I think we got it all figured out, Ryon, as long as all them monsters show up and ain't suspicious or nothin'," Joe confirmed. "Do ya trust Anee and Telber to do it?"

"Anee, for sure. Telber's a bit wigged out. We'll see how he's feeling tomorrow." My muscles tensed. Our plan needed to go perfectly, and Telber wasn't well. "I wish I could help them."

"Ya know a human can't show up. They'll sniff ya out. Promise you'll stay away."

"I promise."

"Yer helpin' by gittin' all the pieces of the plan in place," he added and then chuckled, low and throaty. "Still can't believe we actually gotcha to Ruza in a crate!"

"I owe you so much…"

"Nah—jist knowin' ya and bein' a part of this here secret mission has been a highlight of my 79 years."

"You're the best, Joe. I'm so glad I went to the library."

Melancholy lingered in the air. We were happy at the moment, but knew something unexpected could blow up our plans.

"Hey, when y'all are humans livin' yer best lives, please keep my truck. You'll be needin' 'er."

"You don't have to…"

"Now, what does an old blind man need with a truck, fer goodness' sake? Besides, it'll make my children happier not to have 'er 'round no more. They think I might could git the notion to drive 'er myself."

"I wouldn't put it past you either," I joked. "Thank you." My phone vibrated. "Ruza's calling. I'll be in touch."

"Ya got this, Ryon," he said before hanging up.

"Hey, Ruza," I greeted, then told her about the punchbowl and glasses.

"The punchbowl will be good for mixing the potion with

blood. Just be sure that you, Anee, and Telber don't even get a drop on yourselves. It only needs to touch the skin to work. And don't dilute the punch with any water. It will neutralize the magic."

"Good to know. I'll make sure we're protected." I made a mental note to buy rubber gloves and something to cover our bodies. "Thank you for all you've done for me."

"Because of me, you must risk your lives to defeat the horrible monsters I made. I thank you for fixing my mess," Ruza said.

"Well, if things don't go as planned, I want you to know how much I appreciate…"

"Hush, now. You taught me a valuable lesson. Doing our best in the moment is all we can do."

Her words instantly became my mantra: "Doing your best is all you can do."

"Now, get ready for tomorrow night," she said before leaving our call.

I paced the floor. There was no way I would sleep. I was worried about Anee and Telber being near the cave so close to D-Day. I reviewed the plan repeatedly, looking for holes and devising solutions to worst-case scenarios.

CHAPTER FORTY

Madeleine - Day 3 and 2

91% and 96% Waxing Gibbous

I barely slept the night before my Day of Threes, and I could feel sickness creeping into me like ivy pushing through the cracks of a windowsill. Achy, tired, with the threat of a headache about to pounce, I grew more irritated as everything I encountered came in trios: three squirrels were chattering loudly in the tree outside my bedroom window, then my grandmother served me three pieces of French toast on a plate with three syrup choices: blueberry, maple, and raspberry, and once I sat at my desk to work, I had thirty-three emails to answer which was difficult because my boss called me three times. Then, at 3:33 p.m. on the nose, a clap of thunder announced a storm outside, and an oven-like fever enveloped my body. I stopped working and had to crawl to my bed and lie down, dark clouds and lightning bolts hovered outside my window.

My grandmother knocked on my door sometime later. "Maddy, it's time for dinner."

All I could do was moan, "I'm not well."

She came in and touched my forehead. "You're burning up." Shaking her head, she added, "Poor, poor, poor dear," the trifecta making me even more nauseous, and then she left to get me a cold cloth, some Tylenol, and a glass of water.

That night, the weather and I got worse. The growling an-imals in my head were so loud and menacing that I couldn't think, and I had this overwhelming feeling that something was extremely wrong back home. Tree branches smacked the side of the house as thunder rattled through the dark skies. Torn between resting my weary body and staying awake to avoid the nightmares, I finally fell asleep after seeing the clock say 2 a.m., beginning my Day of Twos. Monstrous animals in pairs, made up of mixed animal parts, taunted me with snarls and groans, swiping at me with elongated claws. I slept on and off, sweaty and exhausted.

Sometime the next day, my grandfather knocked on my door. "Time for some nutrition."

Struggling between being awake and asleep, I managed to prop myself up with several pillows, but just holding my head upright was a throbbing chore. The storm rumbled on, rain dumping in gallons upon the roof as Grampy carried a lap tray with two bowls of soup over to my bed and set it over my out-stretched legs.

"Why two?" I asked wearily.

"I wasn't sure if chicken noodle or vegetable beef sounded better, so I brought you both." He beamed.

"Please. No matter what, don't bring me two of anything today," I pleaded, the room spinning as my intuitive worry es-calated.

He gave me a funny look and then said, "Okay. Well, at least drink water, please. I don't want you to get dehydrated..."

I grabbed his arm, entering delirium. "Call Gascony. Make

sure everyone is alright," I pleaded, starting to cry. "I think they're in danger!"

"Honey, you have a fever." He patted my shoulder, his eyebrows raised. "It's messing with your mind. We called your mom about your illness, and everyone there is fine," he reassured in his low, soothing voice.

"But the roars and animals…" and then I stopped myself. If no one would understand about angels talking to me, there was no way they'd get the monsters plaguing my mind. "Okay," I whispered, slumping lower on the pillows. I picked up a spoon and pretended to eat.

"That's my girl," he said, turning to go. "I'll come back in a bit. Ring the bell on the tray if you need anything."

As soon as he left, I set the tray on the floor and tried to get some sleep, tossing and turning, fearing that my imagination might tear me into pieces. Genevieve slept near my head so she wouldn't be disturbed by my constant movement.

Eventually, I drifted into a light sleep until visions of Gascony on fire, the sound of panicked human screams, and the smell of flesh burning jolted me awake. I shakily got out of bed, barely able to move. Overwhelmed with impending doom, I scrambled for my cell phone that sat charging on my desk.

"You have to get out of there!" I told my mom the second she answered. "The monsters are coming. They're starved for human flesh and will destroy the town!"

"Maddy, get your grandparents and put them on the phone now, please," she said calmly. "You're hallucinating and need rest."

"But I see it when I'm sleeping!" I wailed, standing in the

center of a room that was beginning to spin, the wind and rain outside sounding like a freight train. "The cave, the monsters, the guy, black cloaks…" Then, the floor fell away, and all I saw was darkness.

The Arcs came to me, standing close, beacons of light inside the smoke, saying, "You must be strong. The young man you see can defeat the demons if you believe in him."

So, I followed him in my dreams, whispering encouragement as the angels had always done for me. But I wondered if I had died and become a spirit like my little brother.

FULL MOON

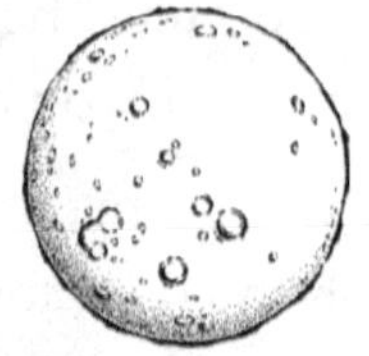

"Your life has reached a turning point, but emotions run high, so keep your cool as you honor what has come to fruition."

CHAPTER FORTY-ONE

Ryon - D-Day

100% Full

It was just before dawn, and Anee and Telber hadn't returned. I hoped they were alright. My mind raced with terrible things that could have happened to them, and my impulse was to look for them, but I knew my human state would jeopardize their spy mission. It took all I had to wait.

When I was sure I'd worn a hole in the old hardwood floors, Anee and Telber arrived at the house. Relief washed through me. They both plopped on the tattered, dingy area rug in the front room where I'd been pacing.

"They'll gather just before midnight," Anee announced. "As the clock strikes twelve, they plan to grab some hostages and kill those who get in the way of them taking over the theater."

My heart rose to my throat, making it difficult to breathe.

"Geidhuce wasn't there, but a few of his thugs were getting the cave meeting space ready," Anee continued. "We watched them carry in a bunch of stuff. They're hanging a lot of propaganda about tonight. And get this, they're turning the Gascony Theater into a real-life escape room, where humans will be challenged in mazes and clues, racing against the living gargoyles and grotesques to see who will be victorious. I think we know who will be victorious."

I shook my head. "How many of them are there? Could you tell?"

"One of the gars read a job assignment sheet, so we heard it in his thread. Twelve positions from guard to soldier, the five from the Charleston building that was torn down, and the five from the one in New Orleans, so eleven including Geidhuce."

"That means I did kill Isel." I didn't know whether to cheer or cry.

A sudden growl made me jump—but it was only Telber, already curled up and snoring.

"How did Telber do when he was with you?" I asked, lowering my voice.

"He was nervous, even shaking, and a bit lethargic." She nodded toward the door. We quietly left and sat at the small kitchen table. "Once we were on our way home and out of the mile-ish range of the caves, he asked me why I wanted to become human."

"What did you tell him?"

"I want to live life freely and see the world." She half-smiled, affection for me in her eyes. "Then I asked him why he was hesitant-ish, and he said it was bad enough being a live monster made of flesh. Humans are even more vulnerable."

"Do you think he'll be okay to help carry out the plan?" I asked.

Her great golden eyes rolled upward in thought. "I think his lingering trauma causes his brain to process things slower-ish, so it makes sense that his acceptance of change is slow, too. He'll come around, but maybe not by tonight."

"And you, Anee? Will you be okay?" I took a deep breath. "You know, if this all works out…" I gulped. "I'll pursue Madeleine."

Anee grinned sideways before speaking. "Honestly, that was the first thing I thought of when you came to the door as a human yesterday. Even though we can't thread anymore, I knew she was on your mind."

"I'm sorry. I know that's not what you want to hear." I sighed. "But it probably won't be a problem. I didn't turn out very…handsome." My body involuntarily slumped as I pointed to my giant nose.

Her furry paws went immediately to her hips. "Well, then, she's an idiot. Not only are you uniquely handsome, but I know how pure your heart is." She chuffed. "One day, I want someone to adore me like you adore her." She walked over to me, wrapping her tufted tail around my waist, speaking as gently as a drifting feather. "I think your nose is wonderful—no '-ish' on that word. And I was thinking that in this light, you look a bit like the movie posters of Humphrey Bogart."

My face flushed.

"And who knows what I will look like. I may put Madeleine to shame," Anee added as she yanked her tail off me and slinked confidently away to check on Telber.

O O O

The air cooled after the sun set, and the constant chirp of crickets was like a metronome, reminding me that our plan was simple, as Ruza said, if broken into small, steady steps. We could systematically destroy those thirteen evil gars and gros. However, I still worried. *Have I omitted a detail I hadn't considered? Will Telber's trauma affect him during our siege? Was Geidhuce tricking us somehow?*

Around nine o'clock, Anee and Telber returned with a potato sack full of dead rabbits, rats, and squirrels, ready to be made into a bloody cocktail fit for evil beasts. I could no longer track and catch animals like when I was a monster, but my sense of smell was still quite potent. As a human, the metallic smell of blood turned my stomach, and I no longer craved it.

Everything Telber and Anee needed to take to the meeting was carefully packed into two cardboard boxes, checked, and re-checked. We used extra precautions to ensure that not even a drop of the potion would touch their bodies, such as using black, extra-strong, gallon-size plastic garbage bags to create impenetrable suits. I used scissors to cut holes, adding sleeves, pants with room for tails to be tucked inside, hoods, and big plastic booties, attached with lots of duct tape, one of the best human inventions ever. I helped them slip their cloth cloaks over the plastic suits, adding the clear face shields I'd bought before the hoods were pulled over the plastic ones. The final touch was black rubber gloves with the fingers inverted and taped on the inside, to cover paws and hooves.

I had to laugh. "You two look like space aliens!"

"It's hot in these suits. Hope no one passes out," she remarked, nodding toward Telber, who was in the bedroom resting.

"Well, let's make sure, again, we're ready to go. We have the potion, the red glasses, the ladle, the punchbowl, and the blood in gallon-sized jugs. I'll mix it when we get there." Anee sounded calm. "Before you know it, Telber and I will be back here taking the human-potion and becoming shiny and new-ish."

Telber entered the room, stretching his arms.

"How are you feeling, buddy?" I asked him, still unsure if he should go.

"I-I-I'm good…a-a-a little hot," Telber said.

"Are you sure you're up to doing this?"

He laid a rubber-covered hoof gently on my shoulder. "F-F-For you and Anee…I-I-I would… d-d-do anything." He stood tall as he spoke, his upper lip revealing his long donkey teeth.

I hugged him, feeling a small amount of relief. "Remember, I'll come at 1:30 a.m. to help clean up. Those supplies are already in the truck."

"Don't you dare come sooner." Anee glared at me through her plastic visor. "It's our turn to be the heroes." She hugged me, handed Telber a box, then picked up the other box.

I watched them walk away, side by side. The moon was full, so there was plenty of light to see their silhouettes travel farther and farther into the distance. I stayed on the front step, and as they disappeared into the darkness, I prayed to the angels they'd be protected. My stomach growled, so I went back inside—I'd forgotten to eat.

I made a sandwich stacked with lunch meat, cheese slices, lettuce, tomato, and mustard, which I bought at the grocery store that day. I gobbled down the first two bites, more like a beast than a human, but I quickly lost my appetite as uneasiness began to build inside me. According to my watch from Ruza, it was 11:30 p.m., and my two friends would be setting up the giant punchbowl of blood mixed with the potent magic potion just inside the cave.

I reviewed the plan for the millionth time: *Anee will stand inside the entrance. As she hands out a goblet to each monster, she'll thread that the bloody brew was for a toast in Geidhuce's honor, emphasizing it would be disrespectful to have even a drop early and even more impolite not to take at least a tiny sip during the toast. Telber's only job would be to set a glass of the concoction on Geidhuce's podium. Then, just as Geidhuce took the stage, Anee would yell, "Here's to the great Geidhuce!" and they would all ingest the lethal brew together, turning to stone shortly after. Easy!*

However, I knew there were risks, and I reviewed the back-up plan to reassure myself: *Surely, Geidhuce's ego would make him drink during cheers to himself, but in case he didn't, Telber would be hiding on stage, ready to jump out and throw the potion-punch from the podium on him. Also, we were counting on those greedy imbeciles not to sneak an early sip, but if they did, most likely, no one would notice since they were all wearing cloaks in the dark, torchlit cavern. But Anee would be watching in case she needed to drag any newly formed statues away into the shadows.*

But all this thinking, supposing, and waiting tore me up inside. *How could I allow my dearest friends to risk their lives tonight?*

But I was way smaller than those beasts, and they were tuned into the scent of humans, so I agreed to stay until it was all over. But what if something goes wrong?

I compulsively made myself a 'garbage bag' suit, and panic overcame me as I struggled to slip the new black sweats over the plastic ones. *I bet these garbage bags will hide my human scent...*I ran to find my new black shoes, socks, and old, giant black hoodie.

I looked at myself in the bathroom mirror, and my face, especially my large nose, was a glaring contrast to my black outfit. So, I went to the living room fireplace and rubbed my face with soot, grabbing a face shield and a pair of gloves. Then, before I knew it, I was driving the Ford toward the cave.

I parked as close as possible without being in plain sight. The truck clock said it was five minutes after midnight, so I quickly put on my face shield and gloves and went on foot to the opening in the hill. Stepping inside the cavern, I kept to the shadows as I moved inward through the stone tunnel. The growls and squeaks of those terrible amalgamations of beasts were just ahead. I listened for threads of thought out of old habits, frustrated that I no longer had that gift.

I continued through the corridor and peeked around the corner at the dark-draped shapes waiting for their leader to appear, and the sanguine glasses were held in paws, claws, and tails. Golden light bounced around the stage and podium from torches mounted on the walls and lanterns hanging from the ceiling. Large speakers were in each corner of the space, and two giant, hand-painted posters hung on either side of the stage, advertising "Gargroteny: The First Live Gargoyle Escape Room in the United States." Behind the podium was another enormous poster with a bird's eye view of the town, showing the old, abandoned underground railroad tunnels and where each one led. One connected the cave to a passageway beneath the theater—an easy way to take it over. Another poster to the right assigned a townsperson to a gar or gro to kidnap and bring to the theater via their underground route: the mayor, the police chief, the head councilwoman, and the librarian. Each human's address was listed by their name.

Across the bottom, in bold, red letters, was:

In the words of our creator: "Bagujte mesom!"

I took a picture with my phone and texted it to Ruza to ask what those words meant. She quickly texted back:

"Feast on flesh!" I used to say that to you all because I wanted you to kill Monsieur…But why are you there?!"

I clicked off the phone, slipped it back into my pocket, and slid into a crevice between two boulders to hide while viewing the rumpus. I spotted Anee standing to the left of the stage, her eyes vigorously scanning the horrific, growling audience. I saw no sign of Telber and hoped that was a good thing.

Suddenly, music poured from the speakers, a trumpeting that announced medieval kings' entry in movies. Geidhuce entered, looking as strong and confident as ever. He wore a black cloak with a red cape like a superhero, wolf teeth bared and white as bone, his pointy ears poking through his hood and casting a giant Devil-shaped shadow behind him.

The group cheered, gnashed their teeth, and scratched the ground with hooves and claws, as manic as the music blasting. The bloody potion swirled and sloshed as the beasts moved, and I held my breath, hoping no one would spill on themselves or their neighbor.

"Please, please," Geidhuce roared over the din, this time without a microphone, walking behind the podium. The audience quieted, and the music faded. "Let me speak, friends."

I watched Anee hover near the stage. *Now, Anee! Toast him!*

"Welcome, my good citizens and the future founders of Gargroteny!" barked Geidhuce.

The crowd went wild again.

"Tonight is the end of our seclusion and the beginning of our freedom. We will take back The Gascony Theater, turning it into the home base of Gargroteny, where we can live as we choose."

Howls and chittering rose, my human heart pounding in fear. Anee continued to scan the crowd, and then she saw me. Her eyes grew wide and angry. I gestured for her to go up and speak, but she crossed her arms and turned away.

"We honor our makers, Ruza Prekrasna and Monsieur Salles-Bris, by creating this sanctuary. They planned for this day, making it possible for us to come to life. We will honor their opus by showing humans how superior we are!" Cheers broke out, then died down. "We have collected weapons, handcuffs, ropes, and chains, but these are minor tools since we are naturally powerful. Four prominent citizens will be taken as hostages, and no one can stop us unless, of course, they want to be devoured on the spot. "Blagujte mesom" is what we are meant to do. We will dominate, and we will prevail!" More roars of approval resonated throughout the cave. Then he spoke in a hushed tone: "I know I've been away, injured by a lowly rogue gro who turned against us, but I discovered that not only are we extremely strong, but we have supernatural healing abilities." He flexed his human chest muscles. "So, it goes without saying, if you see any of the three traitor gar and gro murderers, Ryonac, Aneeguaru, or Telber, kill them immediately." In a tone to gain sympathy, he added, "Ryonac tried to kill me…" Then he yelled, "But take a look at me now!" The earth shook as the audience pounded their tails and feet upon the stone floor, angrily rumbling and sputtering.

Anee moved closer to the stage as Geidhuce waited for the group to quiet again. Then, he sniffed the air and turned toward her.

He smells her, even through the plastic! Sweat dripped down my forehead as she bounded onto the stage. *No, Anee!* It took everything I had to stay in my hiding spot.

She raised her glass, growling loud and low to disguise her voice. "Let us drink to the great Geidhuce!"

The Chimeras rumbled carnal versions of "cheers," drinking from their red goblets as Geidhuce swiftly grabbed Anee from behind, pinning her lioness paws and dragon wings behind her. He let out a horrific howl, and the cave was quiet, except for the shattering glass that echoed. Anee's golden face flashed terror through her plastic shield as she struggled against Geidhuce's grip—then Telber leaped from backstage onto Geidhuce's back, catching the monstrous wolf-beast off-guard, allowing Anee to free herself.

Then, Geidhuce flung Telber to the ground, picking him up by his wings and putting him in a Nelson hold. A blinding rage took hold of me, and I dashed to the stage, bolted up the stairs, and grabbed the drink from the podium. Poised to throw its contents on Geidhuce, I had to be sure the liquid would only get on him.

"Let Telber go!" I yelled.

"Who the hell are you to command me to do anything, human?" he roared, yanking Telber and making him cough.

"I'm Ryonac! Ruza turned me human," I replied, puffing

out my chest to try and look bigger.

Geidhuce looked puzzled momentarily but then bellowed, "Get them!" The cave was silent. "Gar and gros! These are the traitors!" He looked around. None of the cloaked black shapes in the audience moved.

"Yell all you want," I announced. "We turned your perverse posse back into stone." I held the potion in my hand higher. "You're next!" Geidhuce's eyes filled with rage, and Telber's body went limp, so I moved closer. "Let go of him!"

Geidhuce dropped our sweet donkey friend, his unconscious body landing on the stage with a thud! Then the horrid wolf-monster stepped on Telber's chest, pinning him down with one great dragon foot, talons extracted. "Good luck not splashing your friend," he baited, sweeping my feet from under me with his long, scaly tail.

Everything was in slow motion as I fell to the ground. I glanced over at Anee, and she was ready to pounce. I slung that goblet, globe first, like an arrow straight at Geidhuce's head just before I hit the ground. I wished I could thread to Anee, but something in me trusted she'd do what I needed. The rim hit his protruding wolf nose, splashing the contents onto his face. Luckily, Anee yanked Telber by the underarms from beneath Geidhuce's foot before the goblet hit. I quickly rolled off the stage, away from the spill. The glowing splatter was nowhere near Telber—Anee had successfully pulled him away to the side of the stage. Then, we watched in awe as Geidhuce's extremities turned to stone before our eyes, his rigid body moving into the same position as when he was a stone grotesque on the theater. In less than a minute, the evil gro was completely still.

A great sense of relief overcame me, but my stomach roiled,

and I tore my shield off to throw up on the dirt floor.

"Telber's breathing," Anee announced, touching his moving chest. "I think he's okay."

I wiped my mouth on my sleeve. "You were great, Anee! You saved Telber," I praised.

"We did it together!" she celebrated, gently letting go of our donkey friend. Then, she walked to the edge of the stage, studying the audience of stone gars and gros. "I can't hear them anymore. The threading has stopped."

But what I was looking at took my breath away. I shook my head vigorously, unable to speak.

Anee looked at me, her brow furrowed. "What's wrong, Ryon?"

"NO!" I finally cried out, pointing.

Anee turned back around, the terrible sight before her. Telber had turned to stone and was up on his hind legs, mouth open as if in the middle of a bray— the same pose as on the building.

Shocked, Anee threw off her shield and ran toward him.

"Stay back!" I yelled. "He must have gotten potion on him."

Anee stopped and searched the floor, tears pouring from her large eyes. "How could this be? The potion is only on Geidhuce. I was so careful to get Telber away." She walked around the spill and the two in stone. "It's nowhere near Telber," she sputtered, her bottom lip twitching.

"I don't understand it," I replied.

She started to bawl, and I immediately pulled the cell phone from my pocket and called Ruza. "Telber has turned to stone!"

I cried.

"Tell me what happened," she demanded.

I told her everything, then asked, "Do you think it splattered on him?"

"Maybe." Ruza was quiet for a moment. "You said Geidhuce's foot was on top of Telber just before Anee pulled him away?"

"Yes!" I felt as if I'd throw up again.

"Did Geidhuce scratch Telber as Anee pulled him away?"

"I don't think so but let me check." I approached our sweet friend and studied his cloaked, stone figure. "There are claw marks on the front of his cloak."

"Probably the magic hit Geidhuce while his claws were embedded in Telber's body. It works very quickly through the blood." She sighed. "I'm sorry."

I lowered the phone, still in disbelief. Anee embraced me, sobbing softly, then grabbed the phone from my hand. "Ruza, can we still give Telber the human potion?"

"I wish, but it has to be swallowed to work."

"I can't believe he's gone," she cried, handing me the phone. "And I can't hear him, not even a bray."

I lifted the phone to my ear again. "Ruza, are these stone gars and gros threading? And maybe Anee can't hear them because she's living?" I asked, Anee still gripping me tightly.

"I tried to remove the thinking and feeling from these statues," she said. "I think it worked, if Anee can't hear them."

My cheeks were wet as I hung up the phone. The torches on the walls crackled, their light shimmying across the faces of the hideous stone creatures scattered around the room. Black cloaks were still draped over them, and red shards of glass covered the floor, mixed with the thick, brown blood potion.

Anee let go of me, tears glistening on her fuzzy cheeks like diamonds. I should have felt relieved, but the loss of Telber was hard to take.

We still had a lot to do and needed to work quickly. So, I ran down the dark tunnel into the bluish light of outdoors and across the field, the full moon painting silver on everything. In a thick fog of sorrow, I reached the truck and drove it back to the mouth of the cave where Anee was waiting in her hooded cloak, the stony version of our donkey friend beside her. I backed the truck up, parked, and jumped out.

"I doused him with the water we brought before I removed his cloak," she said, pain in her voice. "I just don't know how we'll live without him."

"I don't either," I moaned, grabbing Telber around his midsection with my gloved hands. I bent my knees and heaved but could barely budge him.

Anee let out a small, sad laugh. "Guess you've lost your gargoyle strength. I got this." She hoisted Telber onto the open bed, set him on his donkey legs, and lay him down on his back.

"This wasn't supposed to happen…" She sobbed again as she covered him with the extra blanket I had in the truck.

I could only say, "I know." She jumped and landed next to me. "Now, let's clean up so we can go home."

We each took two twenty-gallon water bottles and the mop, broom, dustpan, and extra garbage bags from inside the truck cab and carried them into the cave. Making sure every inch of us was covered first, we started with the twelve statues on the floor. We dumped the water jugs on each one, and the water puddled around them, every drop of potion vanishing.

"Whoa!" I said, trying to lighten the mood. "Just like Ruza said. This is going to be easier than I thought. Only a little water does the trick, but let's get the other bottles."

We emptied the truck of the other fifteen jugs, lining them up by the cavern entrance so they were easier to get.

"We're gonna be out of here in no time," I said, entering the meeting cavern again, getting back to work.

"Ah, Ryon..." Anne froze, staring at the stage. "Geidhuce is gone!"

"That's impossible." I looked, and there was the pool of potion and broken glass, but Geidhuce's grisly stone body was no longer there.

"Stay here, Anee!" I exclaimed.

I searched the nooks behind the stage and ran down each granite tunnel, searching for evidence of someone else being there, but I saw nothing. I went back to the stage and studied it. "There aren't even any marks to show that he'd been dragged."

"Well, we'd better hurry up in case whoever grabbed Geidhuce comes back," said Anee, swiftly pouring water on the red puddles and statues.

After we were sure all the potion was dissolved, I swept up the glass and disposed of it while Anee removed and crammed all the black cloaks into large garbage bags. We kept a constant eye out for anything suspicious.

Then, Anee lined up the stone statues in two neat rows of five, their hideous faces and demonic expressions making a terrifying montage. Each was part dragon and part human, with a unique third species added to make them extra frightful, from bat to hyena to gothic unicorn. Over half had wide, open mouths where water would pour out—those were the gargoyles. I took pictures of each one with my phone, front and back, to send to Ruza for her catalog.

We hauled the garbage bags and supplies outside, double-bagged everything to ensure nothing was contaminated, and piled them into the back of the truck next to the large, covered figure that was our friend.

Fighting the weight of regret, I tried to stay focused on our tasks. "Now, all we need to do is take the trash to the dump," I announced, carefully peeling off the clothing and plastic protection I was wearing, turning everything inside out like a surgeon, and disposing of them in one last garbage bag.

Anee did the same, tossing the empty potion vial in the bag before removing her gloves. "Don't want to take the chance if even an iota of magic is left in that thing." Then, she glanced over, seeing me in my underwear. She turned away.

"I hope you remembered to bring a change of clothes," she teased.

"I did." I pulled out a bag from the back seat, slipping on shorts and a T-shirt while she tossed the last bag of trash into the back of the truck and scampered to the passenger side.

I slid into the driver's seat. "Soon, we can go home, and then you…" Considering the ache in my heart, I smiled as big as possible.

"…get to be human." She smiled back, but it was lackluster. I knew what she was thinking without even being able to thread: Telber was supposed to join her in the transformation.

I drove across the field toward town but stopped before getting onto the dirt road leading to Main Street. Anee scrunched her large, furry body as low as she could so no one would see her silhouette through the windows. I made sure we weren't being followed, but no car or person crossed our path as we traveled down the main highway, turning onto a twisty, dirt road leading to the local dump.

There was a large sign that said "closed" when we got there, but I drove around the back, parked as close to the tall chain link fences as I could, and then Anee jumped out, quickly chucking all the garbage bags into the abyss of trash. Anee seemed to get some of her anger out, growls bellowing from her throat as she tossed each one, including all the cleaning supplies we'd planned to save, until it was only Telber, still covered up, in the back.

"What in the world could have happened to Geidhuce?" I asked, still in disbelief, once she got back into the truck.

"He always does something we don't expect, " she sighed. We drove home silently, trying to get our heads around everything that had happened.

CHAPTER FORTY-TWO

Madeleine - The Day After D-Day

I rejoined the real world, relieved that the one full of monsters and destruction I'd been trapped in had only been in my mind. The pungent smell of bleach was my first clue that I was in a hospital room, and then I noticed the IV bag attached to a tube in my arm. The back of my head was sore. I touched it and felt a lump.

What happened?

Bright light shone through the slats of the window blinds. I spied my cell phone charging on the bedside stand and picked it up. It was 3:30 a.m., the morning after my Day of Ones. I set my phone back down and climbed out of bed, pulling the IV stand with me and turning the clear, plastic rod to level open the blinds. The night was still through the glass, and the gloriously round lunar body smiled in the black sky.

"You're up!" said a young nurse who had quietly entered. She had bleached blond hair with dark roots that was up in a twist, and she was wearing sky blue scrubs and a plastic name tag on a lanyard around her neck. "You had us worried, young lady."

"What happened?"

She hustled over and grabbed my arm. "You should be in

bed in case you black out again."

"I blacked…?" Then, I remembered being on the phone, my wobbling legs, and the dark abyss that had swallowed me. "That explains the bump on my head."

She helped me return to the bed, and I sat on the edge. "You had quite a fever, and you passed out. You're lucky you didn't get a bad concussion." The nurse pulled back the covers and lifted my feet as I pivoted on my derrière to lie down again, and then she covered my legs with the sheet and blanket. "I'm Nurse Celèste. Would you like me to raise your bed so you can sit upright?"

"Yes, please."

She pushed a button, and I heard a humming sound as the top half of my bed moved upward. "There you go. Now, let me check your vitals." Nurse Celèste busied herself for several minutes while hazy, dark images of dragon-like creatures popped back into my memory. "So, I must ask you," she said nonchalantly. "What is Gascony?"

"My hometown. Why?"

"You kept repeating it over and over." She picked up a clipboard, took a bejeweled silver pen out of her front pocket, and jotted down some notes. "I think you were the most restless and vocal of any unconscious patient I've seen."

"A fever can cause a person to say crazy things, right?" I worried just how much I'd confessed.

Nodding and studying the chart, she said, "Everything looks normal." After hooking the clipboard back on the bottom of my bed, she stared into my eyes. "But I promise, everything that troubled you is behind you now." She set the sparkly pen on the bedstand beside my phone and winked at me. "I'll go get your parents. They're very worried."

Her wink felt like we had an inside joke I wasn't aware of. Then, I flushed, realizing she had probably heard all kinds of crazy things come out of my mouth about monsters, fire, angels, numbered days…

"They're here?" I asked, changing the subject.

She nodded and walked to the door. "I'm sure they'll be relieved to know you're okay." Then, she left.

A few minutes later, my parents rushed in. With tears in their eyes, they took turns giving big hugs.

"Our Maddy girl is back!" announced Dad, sitting in a chair beside my bed.

My mother walked to the other side of the bed and sat on the edge but was so verklempt that she could only nod and grin.

"I'll go tell the night nurse she's awake," my dad said, leaving quickly.

"A nurse was just here and said I'm doing fine." Concerned that my parents knew about my delirious talk, I nervously added, "Nurse Celèste also said that I was so out of it that I was saying all sorts of crazy things."

My mother grabbed my hand, finding her voice. "I'm sure that's normal, honey, but who is Nurse Celèste?"

"The nurse who was just in here. The one that let you know I was awake."

"Nobody told us, sweetie. We had stepped out for coffee and just came back." Concern returned to her face as she pointed to a whiteboard on the far wall with dry-erase markers in a cup mounted beside it. "See? Your nurse is Marc."

I tilted my head, wondering what was going on.

Then, Nurse Marc whisked in, a tall, lanky man in green scrubs. "Welcome back, young lady," he said, taking the clipboard from the end of the bed.

"Nurse Celèste just updated my chart," I told him. "She gave me a clean bill of health."

Nurse Marc looked up. "No one by that name works here," he said, looking confused. "You were probably still groggy when you first woke up."

I slumped back into my pillow, worried I wasn't as well as I thought.

Then, my phone vibrated on the side table, and I looked over at it—beside it was the jeweled pen. I grabbed the twinkling stylus, clutching it to my heart.

CHAPTER FORTY-THREE

Ryon - Day After D-Day

When we pulled up to the old house, it was 4 a.m. and eerily quiet. Anee got Telber out of the truck and dragged his granite body into the old barn. I didn't even try to help since my human strength wasn't like hers. I did help cover him with an old blue tarp and secure it with bungees.

Then, we entered the dark house. "I hope he can't think in his state—he didn't like that musty barn, but it's the best-ish place to hide him right now," Anee remarked.

I lit a candle and paced the kitchen while Anee checked the house to make sure no one was there. Worry had taken permanent residence inside of me. *If someone stole Geidhuce away, they'd know Anee and I are still alive and will try to find us.*

Anee returned. "The coast is clear." Then, she held out her two fuzzy front paws. "I'm ready now. Hand me the potion." Genuine excitement twinkled in her golden eyes for the first time that evening.

"Are you sure you want to be a human? You're pretty handy to have around as a gargoyle. You can lift giant statues, sniff out intruders, pounce on rabbits…" I teased.

"Although I like being appreciated, I want to be human, like you!" She grinned, her canines glinting in the candlelight.

"But you won't be able to fly through the treetops any-more…"

"We'll work through our human shortcomings together. Now go get the vial!" She jumped up and down on her scaly dragon feet.

I walked over to a framed picture of a basket of flowers covering a hole in the living room wall. I unhooked it from its nail, revealing an orange glow. I reached in and took the vial from its hiding place, the potion oscillating and churning like I'd imagine lava to be. I returned to the kitchen, and it illuminated the room even more than the candlelight. I held it out.

"What do I do?" she asked, staring at the luminescent liquid.

"You only need to ingest a drop. But you should do it in the bathroom, alone, where I can't see you."

She tipped her head to the right. "Why?"

"Once you turn human, you won't have any clothes on."

"I've never had any clothes on." She smirked.

"But it's different when…" I fumbled, feeling my face turn red.

"I'm just teasing. You can wait outside in the hall."

I followed as she bounded to the bathroom, the potion in my hand a bright beacon. "Wait here," I said, walking to the bedroom closet and grabbing the dress I had bought for her while getting supplies. It was still on the hanger. "For you, my dear." I held up the yellow sundress with pink daisies and purple butterflies.

"It's beautiful, Ryon. You thought of everything!" She grabbed the hanger and drew back the moldy, red, checkered curtains that covered the small side window, letting in a burst of bright moonlight. She held the dress in front of her furry chest, studying her orange-tinted reflection in the dingy mirror over the sink.

"There are undergarments in that drawer—a few sizes to choose from."

Anee clapped her hands. "Thank you, Ryon. I think I'm ready."

"Lie on the floor and say 'ah!'"

She did as I asked, her giant, flat, pink tongue rolling out her mouth. "Ahhh…"

I pulled the dropper from the bottle, and as if in slow motion, one glimmering, marigold-colored drop fell onto her tongue.

She swallowed and looked at me as I recorked it. "Bitter! But I don't think anything is happening…" Then her body went limp, and the fur from her arms was already turning to beautiful brown, fleshy skin.

I stepped outside the room, closing the door and listening with my ear pressed against it to make sure she was okay. It was hard to tell. The potion in the vial in my hand bubbled and churned, and I decided to return it to its hiding place but immediately went back to my place outside the bathroom door.

After ten minutes of silence, I started to worry. "Anee? Anee? Are you alright?" I knocked, hearing nothing. My throat started to constrict. "Anee?" I waited again, my hand on the knob. Nothing. So, I turned it and opened the door a crack, keeping my eyes averted. "Are you okay?"

"Ryon?" she finally cooed. "I think it worked."

I pulled the door shut and let out a sigh of relief. "Hurry up.

I can't wait to see you," I called.

"Give me a minute to get dressed," she hollered back.

I heard her rattling around, drawers opening and closing, then the knob began to turn. The door swung open, and there she was! With moonlight dancing upon her new form, the scales on her dragon feet had melted into chocolatey, brown skin. Her golden mane was replaced with billowy, black hair that was long and kinky, and her face was smooth like coffee with cream. Her eyes were still amber, like when she was a lioness, with dark lashes and full pink lips.

She took my breath away.

"How do I look?" she asked, spinning on one foot, her dress billowing, and nearly falling because her legs were still wobbly.

"You're beautiful!" I pulled her new body into me and held her close for a second, then let go so I could look at her again.

"I know, right?" she said, returning to the bathroom to see her reflection and posing with both hands on her hips. Then, she studied herself from all angles, moving and turning. "And you know what's even more amazing? Even though I don't look like myself, I still feel like myself. Weird, right?"

"I know what you mean." I laughed. My Anee was truly the human version of herself, which warmed me. "The model for your carving was 20 years old, according to Ruza, but if you want, you could say you're 16, like me. Ruza told me I could pick any reasonable age I wanted."

Anee stopped and looked at me. "So, you could have been older, but you chose to attend high school?"

I swallowed hard and nodded.

Anee's face fell for a moment, but it was fleeting.

"Let's FaceTime Ruza," I suggested, changing the topic. We went outside, where the full moon illuminated us like a night sun, and I dialed.

"Tah-dah!" Anee sang, the phone held up to her glowing face. "Guess who this is!"

"Anee, is that you?" Ruza gasped. "You're lovely!" She briefly put her hand to her mouth. "And you look so much like Gertie Davis, the model I used to sculpt your human parts. She was one of Harriett Tubman's adopted daughters, and the lady who created the Underground Railroad, you know."

Anee grinned and nodded. "That's so cool."

"I am so relieved the potion worked and turned those beasts back into…" Ruza got choked up. "But I'm sorry about Telber."

"Somehow, even with all our planning, we still messed it up." Tears sprang to Anee's eyes. "He was supposed to turn human with us."

Ruza was silent for a minute. "But you turned those monsters into stone and stopped their horrible plans."

"Yes, but we still don't know what happened to Geidhuce."

"The good thing is you saw him turn to stone with your own eyes, so he's probably not a threat anymore," she assured. "And look at you now."

Anee's smile was infectious. "Thank you, Ruza, for making this possible."

Ruza humbly nodded. "Is Ryon there? I want to give him some good news."

Anee blew Ruza a kiss and handed me the phone.

"Well, Cudo, I researched The Hideout property, and the

bank owns it, so…" She paused.

"Coo-dough?" mouthed Anee, scrunching up her pretty, new face.

"…I purchased it. It will be yours and Anee's at the end of the month."

Anee cheered and danced around. "Thank you, Ruza! That's amazing, no -ish!"

"Yes, Ruza, you've done so much!" My throat was thick with emotion as I spoke. "How will we ever thank you?"

"You've brought my life so much sunshine. You two are my best creations."

I tapped my hand on my heart. "Did you call the police anonymously, as we planned?"

"Yes. I told them my friend and I were hiking in the hills directly above the old Miller farm and stumbled upon some caves, so we looked inside and discovered ten statues. I said they look like medieval beasts." Ruza chuckled. "Hideous ones."

Anee and I burst into laughter.

"Now, isn't that the truth?" Anee remarked. "And isn't it wonderful that's not us anymore, Ryon?" Her eyes glinted.

"Absolutely," I said, enfolded in that bittersweet moment.

CHAPTER FORTY-FOUR

The First Day of School - Ryon

August 28, 2024

My cell phone buzzed on the bedside table. It took me a second to realize I was in The Hideaway—nearly every night since D-Day, I'm back in the cave fighting those evil monsters in my dreams. Although I'm always victorious, Geidhuce remains alive, slinking into the darkness with a dark, human-like figure by his side. I always wake up unnerved.

"Hello?" I said, answering the phone just in time to keep it from going to voicemail.

"Howdy!" It was Joe's belting voice. "I hope I didn't call ya too early, but today's a big'un fer ya. I wanted to wish ya the best of luck, Ryon."

Lying in bed, I stretched, checking that my body was still human, an everyday event. My pink toes poked out from under the covers as I yawned. "I was about to get up. Thanks for the kind wishes."

"There's finally somethin' in the mornin' news. The police got an anonymous tip 'bout them missin' gargoyle statues in Miller's Cave." Joe couldn't contain his excitement. "They think Stéphane Breitwieser, a notorious art thief, collected 'em and hid 'em in our lil' ol' hills. Apparently, Monsieur had a son who was Breitwieser's friend."

"Well, that's a coincidence we didn't count on," I said, a bit of worry lifting from my shoulders. I pushed back the covers and slid out of bed. "It took more than two months for them to print anything about it. I thought they thought Ruza's call was a prank and never looked for the stone Chimeras."

"I was fixin' to call 'em myself, but I couldn't figure out how to explain why a blind man was hikin' in caves, let alone able to see those onery thangs." He chuckled.

"I feel bad for that Breitwieser guy. We both know he didn't do it."

"They'll have to sort it out, but the police wouldn't believe the actual truth anyway."

"How many of the statues did they find?"

"The ten. Mr. Big-and-Ugly is still gone."

Joe's nickname for Geidhuce made me laugh.

"Besides him, all the statues Ruza created are accounted fer, including the ones still affixed to their original buildings," he added.

"Well, thanks for the update, Joe. You still good for visitors tonight?"

"Absolutely! Grab Anee and come on over. I'm makin' my famous chicken and dumplin's. We gotta celebrate today, bein' your first day at school an' all."

"We sure do."

Joe, Anee, and I had become our own kind of family over the summer, having dinner together at least once a week, for- ever sharing a bond no one else would understand. We got the utilities up and running, then fixed up the house together by cleaning, painting, and buying new furniture. We even built a mausoleum for Telber beside our favorite tree out back, with a cement floor and gleaming white wooden sides, with doors that could be unlocked and opened. We couldn't bear to leave him in the dirty old barn he despised so much, and we were able to visit him all the time.

"My kids stopped watchin' me like a hawk. Guess they don't see me as a flight risk anymore." Joe chuckled. "I think me givin' ya the ol' truck helped."

"Still, you're always tinkering with something. How's the hydroponic garden?"

"Never imagined I'd git into all that hocusy-pocusy stuff, but here I am workin' with a mage."

"Ruza appreciates you growing rare herbs and plants for her spells."

"We're teachin' each other all kinds of thangs…but I don't mean ta keep ya. Good luck today, son."

My stomach did a backflip. I was more nervous than I expected. "Thanks for the call, Joe."

"Go make some good learnin'," Joe said, then hung up.

I heard the distant clanking of dishes and smelled smoky bacon from the kitchen. I quickly showered, dressed, and combed through my wet hair, avoiding the mirror. I wanted to focus on just being me without worrying about my appearance.

"Ryon, breakfast is ready!" Anee called.

It was strange how the desire for delicious human food like cake, ice cream, cheese, and hamburgers quickly replaced cravings for the raw blood of animals. And bacon—I understood why many humans talked about it so much. It's salty and crunchy, melts in the mouth, and better yet, there's no fur to clog the throat. Delicious!

I dashed into the kitchen where Anee busily worked, perching with my feet on the seat and elbows resting on my knees just like when I was a living monster grotesque. "I'm here!"

Anee, dressed in jeans and a white t-shirt, spun around with a plate piled with appetizing breakfast food and set it on the table before me. Then, she noticed I was roosting and giggled. "You can change the grotesque to human, but you can't take the grotesque ways out of the human… or something like that."

"Ha! It's actually pretty comfortable. I think I'll sit at my desk in school like this today," I teased.

"That'll make a good-ish first impression." She winked.

"Maybe I'll even bring a live rat in my backpack for lunch, too." I sat like a human should, smacking my bottom hard on the chair.

"A good conversation starter," she said sarcastically. "What do you like on your rat? I prefer ketchup." She laughed. "That will surely impress…"

Then, tension rolled into the room like fog. I watched Anee move about, filling her plate.

"I wish you were going with me today. I'd be much less nervous," I said, trying to keep things light.

She sat in the other chair. "You don't seem nervous."

Then, we both ate in silence for a while.

"This is delicious, Anee. Thank you." I shoveled a large

forkful of cheesy scrambled eggs into my mouth. "My appetite is still as big as when I was a condor-dragon beast."

She nodded, focused on her plate.

I set my fork down and took a deep breath. "You know, Anee, I'm thrilled we're both human. We still have things to figure out about our new lives, and it won't always be easy, but I'm so glad to be here with you." She continued eating. "Are you sad that I might make new friends today?"

She set her fork down and bowed her head. "I'm not upset about that. I just…miss him."

Suddenly, I wasn't hungry anymore and pushed my plate away. "I can't help but think I could have done something to make sure Telber was alive with us, too."

Anee picked her fork back up and poked at the fluffy yellow eggs on her plate. Then, in a steady voice, her beautiful, human caramel eyes looking into mine, she said, "Ryon, I've been thinking about all this a lot, and first of all, no one should apologize for loving who they love. Our time on this earth is no longer infinite. You wanted to be human for centuries, knowing the risks, and now that you are human, all that matters is that you be a kind one. Never be self-righteous or a bully like Geidhuce. *He* is the reason why Telber isn't here, not you." She smiled, her eyes shining. "There are many types of love, and I love you, but as a close friend. I want others to know how wonderful you are, and I want you to follow your heart. Trust me, I'll follow mine."

I got up and hugged Anee hard, burying my nose in her billowy, black hair that smelled like gardenias. Then, I let go and reached to clear my plate.

"I got that. You get yourself to school," Anee said, shooing me away by waving her hands.

I blew her a kiss and went to the bathroom to brush my teeth—something else I never did as a monster. I focused on the sink as I brushed, but as I spit, I inadvertently caught a glimpse of my reflection…and there I was, still a stranger staring back at me. What first impression would I make? A homely teenager with eyes too far apart and an enormous nose?

There's no way Madeleine will fall for me at first sight, like I did for her.

I'd heard people say, "It's what's inside that counts," a million times.

Is my heart good enough to override this face?

〇　〇　〇

As I walked to school, the sun warm and bright, my pulse thumped vigorously in my temples. I spotted a newspaper on someone's lawn as if it were purposely put there for me to see. The front page had a photo of those unfortunately familiar stone monsters with the headline: "A Dozen Stone Gargoyles Found in Miller's Cave." I sighed loudly and thought of Telber, glad he was safe beneath our tree.

I looked up at the blue sky lined with white clouds. "Please, angels, help Ruza come up with a spell to make him alive again," I whispered. Although she doubted she could do it, Ruza's self-awarded clemency after turning Anee and me human, and the others to stone, gave her the confidence to try.

I trembled as I approached Gascony High. The hubbub of students passing and talking, with many looking at their phones like their lives depended on what was on the screen, made me feel invisible. I figured that was a good thing.

Still, as Joe would say, my hands were as sweaty as a cowboy in the Texas summer while I contemplated my new life: *Maybe I should have stayed home. What business do I have starting a junior year without ever being at school before?* But Ruza and Joe thought I was smart enough, and it was my chance to get to know Madeleine. And with Chris off at college, we wouldn't compete for her attention. Undoubtedly, though, other guys were probably pursuing her.

Judging by how the students looked as I walked, with their hair styled just right and wearing the latest cool styles, I had my work cut out. From the neck down, I retained the muscular, lean body of the farm boy who modeled for my physique, but I was no Paul Newman from the neck up. My heart raced as I opened the main office's glass door.

The plump, blond woman standing behind a long counter greeted me with, "Welcome. How may I help you?"

"I'm new here. My name is Ryon Delt."

She rifled through an accordion folder that sat to her right. "Ryon with an 'o.' That's unusual," she remarked as she fished out a white paper.

I nodded.

"Well, here you go." She handed me a printout of my classes, slapping a yellow Post-it note on top of it. "That's your locker number and combination. Your Peer Buddy will be here to show you around in a minute, so have a seat." She nodded to the row of chairs along one wall.

"Thank you," I replied, removing my backpack before sitting.

I looked over my schedule. Ruza and Joe, my legal guardians, had signed me up for shop, but I was most excited about the cinematic appreciation class. I also had English, math, science, history, and P.E. The idea of learning was exhilarating.

"Here's your Peer Buddy now." The woman said, looking past me. I heard the glass door open and shut. "Maddy, meet Ryon with an 'o.'"

Maddy? I stared straight ahead and couldn't move to see who stood beside me. *There's no way it's…*

I flung my backpack onto my shoulder, got up, and forced myself to look at the person beside me. There, a few feet away, was her radiant smile, glowing hair, and sky-blue eyes. I'd gone through hell to be in that very heavenly place at that very minute. Her presence pulled me in, and I felt lightheaded. This could only be the handiwork of those celestial beings.

Thank you, angels.

"Hi, Ryon, nice to meet you." She stared at me for a second. "You seem… familiar. Have we met?"

I just shook my head, my heart bounding in my chest like a deer in tall grass.

"Well, let's get started," she said sweetly, yet I could tell she was racking her brain to figure out how she knew me.

We left the office without another word. My mind had gone blank, and my tongue was tied.

Don't be like Chris. Think of something to say.

"Is Maddy short for something?" I finally asked. Following my dream girl through a set of doors and into a long hall, I felt like I floated above the shiny floor.

She chatted happily, her gaze forward. "Madeleine, but only my grandmother calls me that. Anyway, welcome to Gascony High," she continued. "I moved here two years ago, so

I know what it's like to be new, but don't worry—I'm here to help. Where did you move here from?" she asked.

"Ah, Los Angeles," I lied. "But I was born in Gascony." Less of a lie.

She turned and studied my face. I wanted to recoil but just smiled, feeling heat spread up my neck. "Well, you have similar vibes to this guy I know, Chris Newtown. Do you know him?"

I shrugged. I couldn't lie to her again, so I chose to be vague.

She pointed to the schedule in my hand. I handed it to her, and she studied it. "So, you have Mr. Paradis for math first. I think you'll like him. Let's find your locker, and then I'll walk you there."

"Sounds great."

We walked past more students, and they were whispering to one another, probably about me, the new kid.

"I'm a junior too, so we can help each other, but I have a tough schedule. Lots of AP classes… my goodness, I don't know what's come over me. I'm usually not this talkative."

"No worries. I'm a good listener."

She looked at me and smiled, then nodded toward the bank of lockers on the left. "What number are you?"

"444," I replied.

"What? You're kidding," she said with astonishment.

"Is that good…?"

"Incredible!" she said, lighting up like a jar full of fireflies. "But why?"

She blushed and looked at her feet. "It's an angel number… but never mind. Why don't you practice opening it?"

Right to 11, left to 33, right to 22. "Voila!" I announced, pulling up on the metal lever and opening the door.

"Nice job. You have the knack—these lockers usually stick and take three or four tries."

"Must be my lucky day," I said, slamming it shut.

Her cheeks turned pink.

"Well, let's get you to class. This way," she said, so I continued beside Madeleine, still feeling like I was walking on the moon. She led me to a door with a sign that said, "Mr. Ed Paradis, Math."

I didn't move. I just looked at her, not wanting to leave her side. She studied me just as much, and I could tell she was thinking.

"Are you sure we haven't met before?" she asked, cocking her head to one side.

"I don't think so," I lied again, wishing I didn't have to. Wishing I could tell her everything then and there.

Then, she looked up toward the ceiling like she was listening to a voice.

Feeling awkward about waiting there, I opened the classroom door. "Thanks for the tour," I said, walking inside.

"Wait!" She grabbed me by the shoulder and nodded toward the hall. I followed her, and then she spun around, saying, "This may be a strange question, but do you believe in angels?"

"Sure. I guess," I answered, going the nonchalant route.

She leaned toward my right ear, softening her voice. "Well, 444, your locker number, is considered an angel message. It means you're being divinely guided and protected." She stepped back, worry on her face. "I'm sorry. That was weird of me to say."

I smiled. "It's not weird. I believe that."

She lit up again, her smile turning my knees to rubber, happiness filling me nearly to bursting.

Thank you, angels! I cheered in my head.

CHAPTER FORTY-FIVE

Madeleine

The summer had flown by once I returned home from the hospital. My grandparents told me to rest for another week, but I was fine, especially since the monsters in my head had disappeared. I had one more week at the internship, although I'd missed nearly eight days. The angels assured me it was necessary, and my febrile energy had served others well, though they wouldn't tell me how or why.

Then, a few days after arriving back home in Gascony, it was the first day of my junior year.

"Mom, I'm leaving," I announced before walking out the front door.

"Why so early?"

"Peer Buddy, remember?"

"Well, sit down for a quick bite. You can spare five minutes," she called.

I dropped my backpack on the floor and rushed to the kitchen, where my dad was reading the paper. He bent back one side of it to peer at me. "You need a little protein, Maddy girl. Listen to your mother." Then he flipped the page back up.

I groaned and plunked down in a chair as my mother set a soft-boiled egg in front of me in a ceramic cup, the shell cut off at the top. Then, she handed me a tiny spoon and set a saltshaker on the table.

As I quickly ate the gooey, sunflower-yellow yolk, scraping the inside of the shell with the spoon to get all the white parts too, I noticed the newspaper headline in Dad's hands: "A Dozen Stone Gargoyles Found in Miller's Cave."

For just a second, the same sickening feeling came over me as when I had my fever. Then, I saw the photo of the twelve statues, and those beastly faces and grotesque bodies had an overwhelming familiarity. I couldn't eat another bite and just stared at that photo.

"Maddy? Are you alright?" Mom asked, breaking my trance.

I looked at the Apple Watch on my wrist. "I need to go, " I said, standing. "Dad, will you save that section of the paper for me? I want to read it when I get home."

"Sure, honey. But why?"

"My internship made me more interested in current events," I said, which was partly true, but I needed to study the picture more. "Just leave it on my bed. Bye!"

Gascony High was only five blocks away, and I was excited to meet my assigned buddy. Since we lived in such a small town, there weren't many new kids, but I'd received an email a week before that someone named Ryon Delt would need my help. I wasn't sure if Ryon was a girl or a boy.

I pulled open the office door at 7:48 a.m. Miss Francis, the office lady, smiled when she saw me enter. "Maddy, meet Ryon with an 'o.'"

A boy about a foot taller than me stood up, wearing jeans and a solid red T-shirt. His arms were muscular, and he had a distinctive nose, but it was his deep brown eyes that drew me in, giving me the same warm feeling as when I saw the pink light.

"Hi, Ryon. Nice to meet you," I said, trying not to stare. You seem… familiar. Have we met?"

He shook his head, but I swore I knew him.

We started with small talk, and I tried to listen, but the feelings I got from being near him distracted me. He said he moved from Los Angeles but was born in Gascony, which puzzled me even more.

I tried to consult The Arcs, but they told me nothing about this mysterious boy. Even his voice seemed recognizable, its cadence profoundly comforting, and he radiated kindness.

We walked down the hall silently for a minute, allowing me to check in with my angels. *At least give me a sign that I'm not wrong about this guy. I have a connection to him somehow, don't I?*

Nothing.

I sighed, then suggested, "Let's go find your locker."

As we walked further, I chattered away, embarrassing myself. That always happens when I'm nervous or with a guy I like, and he emitted a sweetness I found attractive.

And then, I got a sign.

"What locker number are you?" I asked.

"444," he replied.

Incredible! 444 is an angel number signifying guidance and support. That's when his four guardian angels appeared, protecting him on his new path, assisting him in finding success, and helping his desires come to fruition. I wondered if he believed, but I held back at first.

He opened his locker easily, which was astonishing on its own. "Nice job. You have the knack—these lockers usually stick and take three or four tries to open."

"Must be my lucky day," he said, possibly inferring a double meaning.

I felt my cheeks flush.

I swore a cushion of air held me up above the walkway all the way to his first class, math with Mr. Paradis. I wondered if he could also feel the comforting familiarity that enveloped me.

Before he went inside the classroom, I saw his aura—bright pink! The Arcs rallied, encouraging me to ask him, "Do you believe in angels?"

"Sure. I guess," he answered.

So, I risked a little more. "Well, 444, your locker number, is considered an angel message. It means you're being divinely guided and protected." My heart raced. Would he be wary of the crazy angel girl he'd just met?

Luckily, he smiled and said, "It's not weird. I believe that."

At that moment, I fully understood the expression of being on Cloud Nine.

EPILOGUE

So, that is how that boy and that girl came to stand in the cacophony of Gascony High's bustling hallway, students blurred into a backdrop of backpacks, books, and clanging lockers, noticing only each other.

The first day of their junior year fades into insignificance.

Everything that had transpired those thirty harrowing days—death, magic, and hardships—has etched their souls with secrets that each carried alone.

Yet, because of that and the help of divine intervention, they were brought to this very spot, eye-to-eye, the air charged between them, locked in magical kismet.

About the author

Author Jill K. Sayre is an elementary and middle school teacher with a rich understanding of storytelling for teens. Jill resides in Dallas, Texas, where she cultivates enchanted fairy gardens and watches the skies for gargoyles. Discover more about her literary adventures at www.jillksayre.com.

www.ingramcontent.com/pod-product-compliance
Lightning Source LLC
Chambersburg PA
CBHW021334310726

48971CB00001B/129